# 10/10

a novel by
GORDON MOTT

# 10/10

a novel by
## GORDON MOTT

VAL DE GRÂCE
BOOKS

Val de Grâce Books, Inc.
Napa, California
707-259-5350
www.valdegracebooks.com

ISBN 9780997640571
Library of Congress Control Number: 2018911888

Printed and Bound in China

1  2  3  4  5  6  7  8  9  10

*For the Doc*

## CHAPTER 1

CALEB DRAKE STOOD IN HIS usual place. He was waiting for his morning train on the southbound platform at the Metro-North Railroad stop in Ossining, from where he had commuted into Manhattan for as long as he could remember. Across the expanse of the Hudson River, the steep, rocky cliffs of the Palisades gleamed with the first rays of the morning sun.

For Caleb, this day had started like so many others: a hurried shave and shower, a muffin and coffee, a goodbye hug to Brenda and the kids, and then the quick drive to the station. But on the platform something unusual caught his eye: two small planes flying low up the Hudson, heading north, the sun glinting silver off their wings and clashing with the red, orange, and yellow hues on the cliffs beyond. Caleb glanced to each side, wondering if anyone else on the platform was struck by the sight of those two small planes flying so low over the water.

No one else seemed to notice. Even though they shared the same view across the water, with the twin towers of the Tappan Zee Bridge and the Palisades framing the river, everyone else was wrapped in their usual early morning fog, their heads down in the morning paper or staring blankly ahead. Caleb scanned the river back to the north, looking for the red lights on the domes of the Indian Point nuclear power plant, the aging—some thought decrepit and dangerous—power station less than 10 miles away. But he saw no sign of them. Then a voice came to his ear.

"Excuse me, is this train usually on time?"

The voice was a deep baritone, and on the usually quiet platform it struck Caleb as unnaturally loud and out of place.

"Uhhh, yeah, I guess so," Caleb said without turning toward the man. "Most days, it comes when it comes. But it's usually on time. Why, is it late?"

"Yeah, by a minute or two, at least by my watch," the man said. "But I'm not used to this shit. My limo broke down."

Caleb turned and fully took him in. The man was big and burly and dressed in a dark pinstriped suit, set off by a gaudy yellow tie. Wall Street. Caleb had never seen him on the platform before. "Oh, here it comes," the man said. Just then the train's horn let out a low, sonorous howl, alerting riders to step back from the edge. Caleb smiled at the man and said, "Have a good day."

The train, slowing, passed in front of him and glided to a stop, cutting off his view of the river. After the doors slid open, he turned briskly toward the front of the train, heading for his usual double seat on the river side. In the aisle, he passed the familiar woman with the perfectly-coiffed strawberry blond hair. He nodded and smiled as he slipped past her. He had noticed her for years on the platform, but they had never spoken, though Caleb wasn't sure why, since she usually stood right next to him each morning.

Caleb found an open aisle seat facing toward New York City, and when he sat down, he looked back and saw no further sign of the planes. In his mind, he began checking off the possibilities. Were those a pair of military Citation Xs, the fastest small jets in the air? Maybe. Were they headed north for some ceremonial fly-by up at West Point? Maybe. But they were certainly not in any typical landing pattern for Westchester County Airport. So was this some sort of training run? Maybe. But Caleb had never before seen jets flying that low over the Hudson. No, this was no training run. Caleb felt the hair on the back of his neck begin to tingle.

Something wasn't right.

The train's signal buzzer sounded, the lights above the exits flashed, the doors closed, and Caleb tried to put the planes out of his mind. Just another day, just another commute.

## CHAPTER 2

**A** FEW MINUTES LATER, THE TRAIN lurched to a stop. Caleb was buried in The New York Times, but he looked up abruptly. What was this? He knew they were now well beyond the next station after Ossining, because the chatty, rapid-fire conductor—"good to go, there," "yup," "you got it, sport," "good, good, good," "good to go"—had already checked his ticket. But why the stop now, and in the middle of nowhere?

Caleb glanced at his watch. It was 7:46. He had been on the train for eight minutes. Out the window, the Hudson River lapped at the rocky embankment just below the tracks. As he waited for an announcement, Caleb could feel his anxiety rising. Those planes. The unexpected stop. His own instincts.

The driver's disembodied voice then came over the intercom: "Ladies and gentleman, we're waiting for instructions. We should be moving soon. The signals have gone out. Nothing serious…" In the ensuing pause, Caleb and the other passengers could hear the crackle of the on-board radio and the dispatcher telling the train's motorman to hold in place. Then several cell phones start ringing, and within seconds a cacophony of ring tones, ranging from La Cucaracha to Beethoven's Fifth to weird 1990s Muzak-like elevator music, echoed up and down the aisles.

Then, from a few rows behind him, Caleb heard a chilling "Oh, my god!" It came from the strawberry blonde he had so often stood beside on the platform. Other people too, their phones at their ear, were now talking and looking anxiously back up river. Then Caleb felt his own phone start to vibrate.

He grabbed it from the inside pocket of his jacket and saw the number was his own at home; it was Brenda.

"Honey, what's going on?"

"Caleb, Caleb, I don't know. Something's wrong. Sirens are going off everywhere," Brenda said, a distinct note of panic in her voice. "The kids are already at school but they had a field trip scheduled today so I'm not at all sure where they are."

"Sirens? You sure it isn't a drill?"

"I'm sure. They always announce those beforehand. And they never hold drills before 8 o'clock in the morning. And Caleb..."

"What, honey?"

"I can see smoke rising, up in Peekskill. A lot of smoke. I'm calling the police. I'll call you right back!"

Before Caleb could say a word, the line went dead. He glanced at his new iPhone and flipped the ringer off mute. Then he went to "Favorites," found his home phone and hit the call button. After two rings, a digitized voice came on: "All circuits are busy; please try your call later." He tried again but got only "Call failed." Close to him, only one passenger seemed to have a working line: the strawberry blonde, and what he heard was anything but reassuring: "No!" she said. "No! Are you sure?"

"You getting anything on your phone?" a deep baritone voice asked Caleb. It was the man he had spoken with on the platform. He seemed bigger, and more broad-shouldered, than he had before.

"Nothing. All the circuits seem to be busy."

"Goddamn fucking cell phones," the man said, plopping back into his seat. A second later, though, he jumped back to his feet and strode past Caleb to the blond woman. "What's going on, dammit?"

His voice was so rude, so loud, so aggressive, that suddenly everyone in the car stopped talking and looked at the man. But the woman just waved her hand at him as if to say, Don't interrupt me!

But that only made him angrier. "Damn it, lady, you're the only one here with a working line. What the fuck is going on?"

"Just a minute," she said to him. "Please…"

No one spoke. A palpable tension filled the car. A man across the aisle from Caleb kept stabbing furiously at his cell phone. Another man, directly behind Caleb, sat frozen, his lip trembling. And a couple who sat together every day were holding hands now, and Caleb could see the uncertainty in their faces.

Now the man started yelling again: "Lady, tell us what the fuck you're hearing!" When she didn't respond, he lunged at her and tried to grab her phone. "Get away from me!" she screamed, clutching the phone to her chest. "Get away!" But the man grabbed the back of her jacket, trying to pull her up and get at her phone.

For a moment, Caleb sat frozen, hoping someone else would intervene. But no one else moved. And as the woman continued to fight the man off, Caleb suddenly rushed down the aisle and grabbed the man by the arm. "Hey, leave her alone! I'm sure she'll tell us as soon as she knows something!"

"Back off, asshole," the man hissed at Caleb. "She's got the only working phone! And I need to know what's going on!"

For an instant, Caleb hesitated. The guy was 50 pounds heavier and at least six inches taller, but then Caleb got right in his face. "Look, mister, you gotta calm down. Please!"

Out of the corner of his eye, Caleb saw the fist coming and he deftly ducked it. Then he threw himself into the man, knocking him into the man sitting across the aisle and then to the floor. Caleb jumped on top of him, while the man across the aisle stepped on the big guy's arm and pinned it to the floor. Caleb let his weight fully settle on the man: "Okay, now take it easy," Caleb said. The man's eyes were bulging and his face was red with fury, but he didn't move.

Caleb's action drew murmurs of support from a half dozen people around him. "What's wrong with that guy?" someone said. Then another added, "Yes, but what the heck is happening?"

The blond woman at the center of it all was crying now. Caleb pushed up off the man on the floor, fairly certain he was subdued, and then he watched him slink back to his seat. Caleb leaned over the frightened woman. "It's okay. You're going to be all right," he quietly reassured her. "Don't worry. It's under control."

"No, it's not under control!" she sobbed. "I called my daughter's school to get a message to her, but the school operator said something had happened and they're now evacuating all the kids. She said the police are on the way to help, and I could hear sirens blaring in the background. Then she put me on hold!"

Caleb put his hand on her shoulder: "Evacuating?"

"Yes, evacuating! And Indian Point is right there, not three miles away! I just want to know if everyone's safe…"

Caleb froze. Sirens. Indian Point. Evacuation. Oh shit…

"Move over," he said. "Let me sit with you."

As Caleb edged in beside her, Rachel Silver's heart was pounding. Her phone was pressed to her ear as she listened to the high school switchboard operator talking in the background. "Yes, ma'am," she heard. "The school is locked down. The kids are safe. We're bringing the buses back now. Ma'am, one minute, please…" After a long moment, the operator came back on the line to Rachel:

"Ma'am, are you still there?"

"Yes, yes. Did I hear you say the kids are safe?"

"Yes, ma'am."

"Thank god for that. But please don't hang up on me. I'm on a Metro- North train into the city, and no one else can get a call out. What more can you tell us?"

"I'm sorry, ma'am, but I don't know anything more. The sirens went off about five minutes ago, and it's been chaos ever since. Please, I have to take another call…"

For a moment the line went quiet, then came that insipid Muzak. Rachel's fears were now right in her throat: her kids. Their friends. Evacuation. Police were on the way. And where was her husband Daniel? She had no idea. Damn! What's happening?

"I'm sorry," she said to Caleb. "I'm back on hold."

"Don't worry. She said the kids are safe, right? Who were you talking to?"

"The high school switchboard. She said the police are on the way, and they're waiting for the school buses to get back there, too. My kids were supposed to have a field trip today," she said, her voice trembling, "to Indian Point."

Indian Point. So that's it, Caleb thought. But he decided not to share his fears and upset the woman further. "Tell me, which high school do they go to?"

"Cro…ton," Rachel said, barely able to get the word out. "We live on the edge of Ossining, just beyond Crotonville, but our kids go to school in Croton."

"You get on the train in Ossining, don't you?" Caleb said.

"Yes," Rachel replied.

"I've seen you on the platform for years. My name's Caleb, Caleb Drake."

"Hi, I'm Rachel, Rachel Silver."

"Nice to meet you, I guess," Caleb said. "I mean, well, you know, I wish the circumstances were different."

"What do you think happened?"

"I have no idea," he said, masking his concern, "and I don't want to venture a guess. I'm sure we'll find out soon enough." In a gesture of comfort, he patted her leg, then quickly pulled it away.

Rachel looked him right in the eye: "I'm a wreck, Caleb. Thanks for protecting me. Thanks so much."

"I'm worried, too," Caleb said. "My kids go to school at Hackley, so they're not too close to Croton. But I suppose they are being sent home, too." Then Caleb paused. "And if they are sent home, I have no idea how they will get there. It's possible the police will block the roads."

Blocking the roads? Rachel gave him a strange look, and then the train's loudspeaker crackled to life:

"Ladies and gentlemen, we are still awaiting instructions. Dispatch tells us there is now some sort of power problem, and they're working on it. We've been ordered to stay right where we are, and to keep everyone on the train. As I know more, I will let you know. So please stay seated. And please stay calm."

Caleb gave an inward groan. The damned motorman seemed to have no clue what was going on—or at least that was what he was pretending. But what if those two mysterious planes he had seen racing up the Hudson were actually flying missiles of terror, aimed straight at Indian Point? And what if they had struck their target and damaged the plant's aging containment domes? Yes, and what if waves of deadly radiation were right now beginning to spill out across the whole of the Hudson Valley? What then?

"Calm down," Caleb told himself. "Get a grip."

## CHAPTER 3

9/11. 9/11. 9/11. IT'S ONLY *a matter of time until terrorists strike again.*

He tried to stop it, but that terror epigram was now pounding inside Caleb's head as he sat on the stalled Metro-North train. Every day, or maybe it only seemed like every day since 9/11, his mind kept circling back to his painful memories of that fateful September morning: the sight of those two Boeing 767s slamming into the twin towers; the resulting fear; the floods of adrenaline; the brief paralysis that then morphed into the most primitive survival instinct: Escape. Get as far away from the escalating damage as humanly possible.

Yes, those memories were always with him. And whenever Caleb reflected back, with those terrifying visions running in his head, he was consumed by the guilt-laden idea that he alone, and no one else, had managed to come through alive. And now, he found himself trapped and unable to get out, just as so many of his friends had been trapped in the World Trade Center on that agonizing September day. A day that had begun just like today.

Many of his friends who had been close to ground zero on that day suffered similar episodes of fear and guilt. Few of them talked about it openly, with Caleb or even with their spouses, but everyone knew what to call it: PTSD. And some of his friends had been in therapy for years, trying to escape the memories and the pain.

For Caleb, though, there was a whole other dimension to these episodes: Vietnam. What he had seen in those jungles, what he and his platoon members had done—there was no escaping that pain either. And when those memories surged up, he stuffed them right back down, with alcohol or work. For long periods he had been able to keep those memories at bay. But not after 9/11. Vietnam, 9/11, in Caleb's mind, those two national traumas often lost their edges and fused together. And right here, on this bright October morning, it was happening again, triggered by the sight of those two planes flying low over the Hudson, headed god knows where. As he sat there, Caleb tried to tamp it all down, tried to slow the pounding of his heart, tried to calm the awful twitching in his neck.

Around him, there was an uneasy quiet in the car, as people sat stoned-faced, whispered among themselves, or jabbed nervously at their cell phones. From his years in Vietnam, he knew the natural human tendency was, first, to deny the reality of the situation and tamp down the surge of gut-wrenching fear, to keep on believing that nothing bad was happening. Many of his fellow passengers appeared to be trying to do just that: ignore the unexpected stop, ignore the fist fight, ignore the palpable tension inside the car. Caleb's mind, though, just kept on spinning.

Would today be a repeat of 9/11—and everything he had felt for months and years afterward? Like the victim of a home invasion, Caleb had never been able to recapture the serenity that comes with believing, or at least hoping, that you live in a safe place. For years after the al Qaeda attack, he never crossed the main hall at Grand Central Station during rush hour, and even at off hours he kept to the side passages. He figured that Grand Central, as one of New York's primary hubs and links to its suburban communities, would be a likely target, and any terrorist bent on mass destruction would set his bomb off right at the kiosk under the Grand Central clock.

In his mind, Caleb even envisioned a swarthy version of Cary Grant standing under the clock in a gray suit and with a heavy bag at his feet, looking the picture of innocence as he calmly awaited his call to martyrdom. The extra gym bag he kept at work not only contained tennis shoes now, but two bottles of water, several power bars, an LED flashlight and a small hunting knife; he stopped short of including a gas mask, though many of his colleagues at work had bought one in the days following the al Qaeda attack.

Ever since 9/11, avoiding risk, or at least controlling risk, defined Caleb and conditioned his actions, just as it had during his time as a platoon leader in Vietnam. Whatever risk-taking fantasies he harbored following his time in Vietnam he had been able to vent harmlessly through watching James Bond movies or the Jason Bourne series. Caleb imagined that he would always survive those "kill first, think later" situations; trained as he had been, he figured he was smart enough and skilled enough to always see the risks and plot his way past them. Still, at Grand Central, or now on the train, whether he liked it or not, Caleb knew he always had to be ready, ready for anything.

"Nothing yet?" he asked his new seatmate.

"No, just recorded music," Rachel replied. "She put me on hold last time so I can't hear what's going on in the background."

The extended wait wasn't calming her down, but at least amid the tension in the car, the numbing calm of the Muzak was a welcome refuge, though Rachel was sure that everyone in the car had their eyes on her back, waiting to see when she got more news.

"Mrs. Silver?" the school operator broke in.

Rachel held up her hand to Caleb.

"Yes, yes, I'm here."

"Ma'am, I don't have anything solid to tell you. There are some reports of an explosion in the area, but nothing has been confirmed. We do know, though, that local and state officials are right now setting up a series of emergency evacuation points."

Explosion? Evacuation points?

Rachel felt a chill run up her spine. "But I'm stuck on a damn train! My kids are there! Where are these evacuation points?"

"Ma'am, we don't know yet. We have told our students to stay calm, follow orders, and to phone their parents as soon as they can."

"Listen, the phones aren't working! And once I hang up with you, I won't be able to talk to anybody! Don't you understand?"

"Ma'am, I'm sorry. But I've got 10 lights flashing in front of me. You're not the only one who's freaked out. We all are. Oh my god, I've got to go!" the operator suddenly said. "There's a fireman here! With a gas mask. Oh, no! What's happening?"

Now, in the background, Rachel could hear a male voice telling the operator: "Yes, ma'am, that's the report: two planes have crashed into Indian Point. Emergency teams are on the way..." Now the school operator came back on the line:

"I'm sorry, Mrs. Silver. I have to hang up. The police are ordering us all to leave. Please hang up and get yourself to safety."

"But you can't..." Rachel shouted into the phone, then the line went dead. "Damn you," she screamed. "Damn you!"

Now she turned to Caleb, in the faintest whisper: "I overheard a man. He said there was a report that two planes had crashed into Indian Point. Then the stupid line went dead!"

An instant later a shout went up behind her. "The lady says two planes have crashed into Indian Point!"

Caleb's entire being began to reel. He was trapped. Again. With no way out. Just as in his worst post-9/11 nightmares. But this was no nightmare. Caleb knew it was real: terrorists had struck again. And they had struck right at the heart and soul of America itself. Again.

## CHAPTER 4

**A** WAVE OF PANIC NOW REVERBERATED throughout the train. "Planes have hit Indian Point!"—the news Rachel had heard was now being passed from passenger to passenger. Soon most everyone was on their feet, grabbing their jackets and briefcases or purses, and many were still stabbing at their phones.

Charlie Murray, the chief conductor with the rapid fire voice, moved quickly up the aisle, edging his way between row after row of teal blue and sea green leather seats. "Scuse me, scuse me, madame," he kept saying as he pushed forward. Word of the attack had not yet reached him, but he knew something terrible was afoot.

Up near the front of the car, Charlie grabbed the arm of a man he often saw on this same 7:38 out of Ossining. "Tell me," Charlie whispered to him. "What the heck is goin' on?"

"You know nothing?" the man said, incredulous. "That lady up there, the blonde, she says two planes have crashed into Indian Point. So, get busy! You gotta get us the hell out of here!"

Charlie kept moving, too shocked to respond and not knowing what to say in any case. Indian Point! The aging nuclear plant. And with that, Charlie felt a rush of fear buckle his knees. He lived with his parents up in Peekskill, not three miles from the reactors. His mom was getting discharged from Phelps Hospital today, so they weren't home right now and they probably weren't aware of what was going on. Was his dad okay?

"Hey, train man," another passenger snarled at him. "Can't you tell us something? Anything? We're all freaking out here!"

Charlie reached Rachel, the source of the news. She was dressed elegantly, as usual, and with a quick glance Charlie took it all in: the blond mane, the tight skirt, the sleek business jacket, the bulge of her breasts inside. He longed to stop and ask her what she had heard. But he didn't dare. Everyone was panicky now, and all he wanted to do was get up and see Bobby in the motorman's compartment and lock the door safely behind him.

When he reached the motorman's door, Charlie pulled out his steel key and shoved it in the lock. Then he ducked inside and slammed the door behind him. "Bobby, we've got a problem!"

"No kidding," the motorman said drily. "What do you hear?"

"People are saying it's a terrorist attack. And that blonde—you know the one—people heard her say that two planes have slammed into Indian Point. Bobby, what are we supposed to do?"

The motorman just shook his head. "Charlie, they're not telling me anything. All I get from Dispatch is 'Stay calm. Stay calm.' And the last time I talked to them, they didn't know shit."

There was a crowd gathered now outside the motorman's compartment, and one passenger was banging on the door: "Get us the hell out of here! Open the damn doors!"

"This is bad, Bobby. We gotta do something!"

"I understand that, Charlie," the motorman said. Then he punched a button on his console: "Dispatch, this is 48. What can you tell us?"

"48, I told you we'd let you know as soon as…"

"Listen, I need something to tell these people! People are going nuts in here! And it's just me and Charlie, and Estelle is way in the back. People are screaming and demanding we open the doors! They can see smoke rising back up north! We all can!"

Now the dispatcher lowered his voice. "Okay, 48, listen to me. Homeland Security has us on lockdown. The whole metropolitan area is now on lockdown. Nothing is moving. Airports, buses, trains—nothing. But we have been told to tell people as little as possible."

"Copy that," the motorman said.

"Holy shit," Bobby said, leaning against the wall for support.

"Okay, Dispatch," the motorman said. "What do we do?"

"Stay as calm as possible, 48. Remember your training. Follow the protocols. Make an announcement. If you need to, tell them Homeland Security is in control of the situation and that we are awaiting further instructions. And no matter what, do not open the doors! We cannot have people running up and down the tracks!"

"Copy that. How much longer before we can move?"

"No idea, 48. Just sit tight."

Then the dispatcher abruptly clicked off.

Charlie was a total wreck. He knew he had to go back and try to reassure the frightened passengers. But he also knew he was destined to fail. "They won't listen to me, Bobby," he said, almost on the verge of tears. "They think I'm some sort of retard."

The motorman took a deep breath and opened the train-wide intercom. "Ladies and gentlemen," he started, and then with more force: "Ladies and gentlemen! Please take your seats! I know you are concerned, but you must stay calm. We have just received an update and I will tell you what we know…"

"We have an emergency. Of unknown origin. The Department of Homeland Security is in control of the situation. They have imposed a lockdown on all trains, planes, and buses throughout the tri-state area. Federal regulations are now in effect. You must stay on the train. That's an order. And I remind you that it is a federal offense to disobey our orders. As soon as we receive clearance, we will move the train on to the next station, Philipse Manor."

A lockdown! Totally trapped! And as soon as he heard that, Caleb took Rachel's hand and their fingers immediately intertwined. Then Caleb felt someone looming over both of them. It was him.

"Listen, buddy," he said, in that deep baritone.

Caleb flinched, half-expecting to glimpse another shot coming at his head. But not now. The man in the Wall Street suit and yellow tie was a ghostly white and trembling.

"Listen, I am so sorry about what happened before. I just lost it," he said. "I am so sorry, ma'am… My name is James. Please, please forgive me, but I'm in a terrible bind and I have to get off this train. It's a matter of life and death. And I'm hoping you will help me. To make up for banging me to the floor. Please…"

Caleb bristled. "Are you out of your mind? Look, there's no way these Metro-North guys are going to open the doors for you or anyone else. Federal rules. And I'm not about to go to jail for you!"

James' phone beeped. He grabbed it out of his pocket like someone reaching for a lifeline. Then he read the text: "Wass going on? R u going to make this meeting or not? You damn well better!" It was his wife, Sheri. That was the way she texted.

Fingers flying, James shot back: "WTF am I supposed to do!!! Trapped on the g.d. train! Not moving!"

Sheri: "Get off the damn train and get in there! We are leaving now. Irv will go ape shit. Do what u have to do. Or else!"

James thrust his phone back in his pocket. "My wife," he said apologetically to Caleb and Rachel. "I have to get off this train!"

Caleb was beginning to think the same thing. A terrorist attack. On a nuclear power plant. Reports of evacuations. His wife and kids. And he was stuck on a damn train. Still, he had no desire to help this shmuck from Wall Street. Caleb stared at him coldly:

"Look, uh, James… I don't know what you have in mind. And frankly I don't give a damn. Please leave us alone!"

But there was no stopping him. "Look, I said I was sorry. And these Metro-North guys are a bunch of idiots. All they say is stay calm, stay put. But if this is an attack, we have to get off this train! We all do! And I have to get into the city… fast!"

"And how are you going to do that?" Caleb said. "In this stretch of rail, it's a steep climb down. The tracks are dangerous. There's barely room to walk. And then what? You haven't got a car. So how in the hell are you going to get into the city?"

"I'll find a way," the man said. "I'll call a cab, or a town car, or Uber. Or, damn it, I'll hitchhike! But I have got to get into the city!"

Caleb just hissed at him: "You idiot! Don't you realize what's going on here? Where were you on 9/11?"

The man rocked back, as if he had been smacked in the jaw. For some reason, in his personal frenzy, he had failed to put the pieces together. 9/11. All over again. But that only hardened his resolve: "Okay! Then all the more reason we have to get the hell off this damn train! Now are you going to help me or not?"

Caleb looked down. Rachel now had both her hands in his, and she was squeezing them with all her might. And in an instant he knew: It was time to act.

"Okay," Caleb said, standing up, and helping Rachel up beside him. "Anything would be better than just sitting here. Let's do it!"

With James leading the way, the three of them pushed back down the aisle, trying to seem calm and natural as they headed for the exit in the rear of the car. There was a crowd gathered in front of the door, but James used his bulk to push on through.

"Clear the way, clear the way, please!"

James tried to pull open the doors. When that failed, he wrapped one hand in a monogrammed handkerchief and smashed the glass covering the red emergency lever beside the doors. James pulled the lever, but the doors still refused to open. Then he jammed his fingers into the rubber crease and managed to yank them open.

"Geez," he said, looking down. There was a five-foot drop to the narrow sleeve alongside the track, and then another three-foot drop to the rough gravel surface below. And the rail bed itself was covered with debris and garbage, everything from coffee cups and soda cans to broken bottles, and even an old ruptured tire.

James jumped down. And when he hit the ground, instead of waiting to help Rachel and Caleb down, he took off running along a long stone wall, toward a clearing about 200 yards to the south.

"You son of a bitch!" Caleb shouted. "Come back here! Help us down! Who the fuck do you think you are!" But James kept right on running, the profanities soon fading behind him.

Caleb felt foolish for having been duped. He looked down at the rail bed, then gingerly made his way down, trying to find se-cure footing. But he slipped and dropped the last three feet to the gravel, almost tumbling onto his back. He looked back up and saw Rachel standing in the doorway, her eyes wide with fright and tears pouring down her cheeks. "I can't do this!" she pleaded.

"Yes, you can," Caleb said, holding up his arms. "Sit down on the edge, and jump into my arms. I'll catch you!"

But Rachel just stood there frozen, clutching her phone and her purse to her chest. And now a crowd of passengers was right behind her, all of them desperate to get off the train.

"Come on, Rachel, you can do it!"

"No, wait!" she said, and disappeared back into the train.

Charlie by now was a hopeless mess. He saw the crowd of passengers pressed together in the doorway, ignoring his orders, but he had no idea what to do about it. A part of him wanted to jump off the train, too. Then he saw the familiar blond woman pushing back toward her seat and he hurried back down the aisle to help her.

"Madame," Charlie called, "Are you okay? I saw that guy grab at your phone. You wanna file a complaint?"

"No, that's okay, really. He was just scared, like everybody else." Then she paused. "On second thought, maybe I should file a complaint. If I decide to, how do I get ahold of you?"

"Why don't I give you my phone number?" Charlie said.

"Good," Rachel said, readying her phone.

"Okay, my number is 914-667-4366. And my name is Charlie Murray. Now, can I have yours?"

Rachel hesitated. Then she thought, what the hell? I'll give him my work number. "Okay, mine is 646-712-7777. It's an easy one for my clients to remember."

Charlie scribbled it down, a bit unnerved by her beauty and her womanly presence. Rachel was now bent over, putting on the tennis shoes she had grabbed from her day bag, and her skirt had slid way up her thighs. Now she could feel Charlie's eyes traveling up the length of her legs, and she shuddered with disgust.

"Then, thanks, ma'am," Charlie stammered, as he put away his pad. Outside the window he could see passengers scrambling down to the tracks and then rushing away in both directions but most headed south toward the hospital above the tracks. "You'd better go, ma'am. No one really knows what's happening."

"Thanks," Rachel said. "What are you going to do?"

"Oh, I guess we're just stuck here," he said. "Like the captain and his ship—we can't leave."

Rachel nodded and rushed back to the exit. Caleb was still there, helping the last people off the train. "Go south," she heard him tell one elderly couple. "The Phelps Memorial Hospital is there. They'll know what to do." As Rachel could see, he was now calm, helpful, and comfortably in command. Rachel was impressed.

When she appeared in the doorway, Caleb reached up his arms. "It's okay now. Just take it slow…"

For a moment, she looked back into the car. The only people left were a few elderly men and women who were apparently hesitant about the climb down, plus the remaining Metro-North employees, all of them dressed in their sky blue shirts and matching blue pants. Poor folks, Rachel thought. Attack or no attack, they were stuck right there.

"Come ahead, Rachel," Caleb called. "There are some sharp edges to watch for, but just jump down into my arms. I'm right here, and I've caught everyone… so far," he laughed.

Rachel slid down and Caleb caught her around her waist, letting his hands glide gently along her ribs as he eased her to the ground. For a long moment, they were almost in a full embrace. Caleb released her slowly, savoring how good she smelled and how strangely familiar she felt in his arms. Rachel was trembling now, and her face suddenly felt warm and flushed.

"Whew, that was easy," she said. "Thanks to you."

## CHAPTER 5

RACHEL AND CALEB TRACKED ALONG the muddy footsteps of the other passengers, climbing up the slippery slope from the railroad tracks, toward Phelps Memorial Hospital and the Kendal on Hudson assisted living complex adjacent to the hospital. At the top of the slope, most of the passengers were milling around without really knowing what to do next, or where to go. Some talked to the elderly residents leaning over the edges of their balconies as they looked up river to the pillars of smoke billowing high into the sky.

"Let's keep going," Caleb said. "The emergency room is right up there, and they may have more news."

"I'm following you," Rachel said.

As they passed the first row of cars in the parking lot, Caleb spied an elderly man, dressed in the casual uniform of local retirees—khakis, loafers, a button down plaid shirt and a tan nylon jacket—leaning precariously against the trunk of a car. The man suddenly slumped, slid off the car, and collapsed face down on the ground.

"Go get a nurse!" Caleb shouted to Rachel as he ran to the man.

Within seconds, he was at the man's side, gently rolling him over. Blood trickled from his forehead, and he was mumbling, "My car. My wife. My car. My wife."

Caleb felt for a pulse on his neck. There was a faint, rapid throb, almost obscured by his shallow, quick breathing. Rivulets of sweat ran down his forehead. Caleb loosened his shirt at the collar. He heard the wheels of a gurney rolling across the parking lot toward them, then he turned and called out to the nurse, "Over here!" Rachel was right behind her.

The nurse quickly bent over the man, pulled up his eyelids, and then with her hand on his chest she checked his heartbeat. "Do you know him?"

"No, I was on a Metro-North that's stalled just down below. I was coming to check to see if there's any news. I saw him fall."

"Help me get him onto the gurney. Everyone is inside watching the news."

The nurse positioned herself on one leg, and said to Caleb, "Put your arms under his armpits. Hold him steady. Ma'am, help me with his other leg," she said to Rachel. "Ready, 1, 2, 3," and the three of them lifted the man up and onto the gurney.

Caleb and Rachel helped the nurse push the gurney while she guided it down the row of cars in the parking lot.

"Do you know what happened? Is it Indian Point?" Caleb asked, knowing he only had seconds to get any info out of the nurse.

"There are not many details. Apparently one or two planes crashed into the reactor domes. We got a call from Westchester County emergency services about 10 minutes ago, advising us to get ready for patients with critical injuries and burns."

"Nothing more?"

"No," she said as they entered the hospital, then she began shouting, "Get me a doctor!"

Caleb grabbed her arm before she rushed away. "Hey, I know this is crazy. May I borrow your car? I promise I'll bring it back."

The nurse was taken aback. "Now why would I do that?" she asked, as she did a quick head-to-toe scan of this handsome man, covered in mud from the climb up the hill from the train tracks.

"How do I know you won't just take it and never come back?"

"Listen, I need to get to my house. My family is there. And scared stiff. We live less than three miles away from Indian Point. Please, I swear I will bring your car back. You can copy my driver's license, anything you want…"

"Okay, okay," the nurse said, abandoning her doubts. "Follow me. I'll get you my keys. I'm going to be here all day anyway, and I've got to get this guy treated. But please, please, bring it back."

"On my life, I will."

When the nurse handed Caleb the keys, she simply turned and walked briskly back into the treatment area in the emergency room.

"I can't believe you asked her for her car," Rachel said, obviously impressed. "I would have never thought of that."

"I can't believe it either! Come on, let's go. She said it's in the back parking lot."

+++

THEY FOUND THE car and moments later Caleb was speeding out of the parking lot. "Would you slow down?" Rachel said. "Please! I know we're in a hurry, but if we're going to die, I'd rather not do it slammed against a tree in Sleepy Hollow!"

Caleb eased off the gas pedal. "Damn it," he thought. "We've got to hurry!" But he kept the thought to himself. "Look," he said, "I'm a little rattled, and I'm not that familiar with the roads back here. But we have to get home to our kids. Fast!"

"I get it," Rachel said. "Just please be careful."

Soon they came to a major intersection. "Turn right here," Rachel said. "I ride bikes here, and this will take us into Briarcliff on 448 and eventually to Route 9."

"No," Caleb said. "We might get stopped. The nurse said all

roads are closed going towards Peekskill, and I bet the cops will be focusing on main roads like this one. Do you know another way?"

"Okay," Rachel said. "Just follow this road. It will get us into the village the back way."

Caleb looked at Rachel out of the corner of his eye. The woman was not only beautiful, she had regained her composure and now seemed cool under pressure. "So you ride bikes here?" he said. "I'm surprised I've never seen you. I ride here, too."

"Oh, I saw you once," Rachel said, "but you were riding like a bat out of hell, and we just passed each other by."

"You recognized me?"

"Oh yeah. On a bike or a train platform, you're hard to miss."

"And so are you. Very hard to miss!"

Their banter, light and flirtatious, was a welcome respite from the tension they both were feeling.

"So, Rachel, are you married?"

"Kids in high school, a house in the suburbs, married? Me? No," she said with a teasing irony in her voice. "I'm just footloose and fancy free!"

"I'm sorry," Caleb said. "But these days you never know…"

"And you?" she said. "Married, I presume?"

"Guilty as charged," Caleb said. "Twenty five years and counting."

"So, twenty five to life," Rachel teased. "You're not going to start telling me all your marital secrets, are you? That happened to me on a plane last week. Guy sitting next to me got hammered and told me everything, right down to his wife's favorite cries and whispers."

Suddenly, strangely, Caleb was back in Vietnam, getting ready to go out on patrol. He was cleaning his rifle, checking his gear, doing what he could to joke with his pals and put the war aside. Combat was like that. Before a patrol, and often right after, he and his pals would talk about the craziest things, make up the wildest stories, swap tales about this woman or that—whatever it took to calm their nerves and erase the horrors they had seen or committed. Caleb quickly cut that memory short.

"No, I won't tell you all my marital secrets," Caleb said. "Why don't you try to call your house again? Maybe you can get a line through now."

Rachel sensed his discomfort and began looking for her phone. But she wanted more of their easy banter. It was fun. It was exciting. It was intimate. Her husband was so different. Daniel was a good man, but a workaholic. A lawyer in the office—and at home. He was always guarded, needing to be in control, so he kept his feelings to himself, as if his wife were opposing counsel. Caleb was so different. When she needed him, back on the train, he was there for her. No questions asked. His openness, his readiness to help, conveyed to her an inner strength and power, and deep inside it made her tremble.

To her surprise, she now had a dial tone, but as she punched in her number, she suddenly looked up and screamed, "Watch out!"

Caleb slammed on the brakes. "What the…???"

In front of them, small clusters of pedestrians were trudging along the narrow street. The trees and bushes, where there should have been sidewalks, had forced them out onto the roadway. It was a rag-tag group—men, women, and small children—all lining up under an eight-foot-high blue pole. On the pole was a blue and white sign marked "Evacuation Route," and under those words were numbers identifying the precise gathering point. People were coming from the other direction, too. Caleb immediately assumed they had been ordered there, for imminent evacuation by bus.

"Who-ee," Caleb murmured. The scene was downright surreal: forty-five minutes into an emergency and here was this stream of people, looking totally out of place and time in an otherwise serene and undamaged neighborhood. Their fright was etched on their faces, and by the things they carried, they clearly feared they wouldn't be returning any time soon.

Caleb rolled down his window, and the raw howl of an emergency siren blasted into the car and into his ear. He had heard those sirens dozens of times over the years, as tests, but this was clearly different. This was no test.

"Excuse me," he called out to a young mother clutching a photo album and pushing a stroller. In the stroller, Caleb could see a small child holding a teddy bear tightly to her chest, and she had a stack of framed photos shoved in next to her. "Excuse me, ma'am. What are they telling you?"

"Why are you driving?" the young mother said, her voice angry and indignant. "They told us we'd be arrested if we drove!"

"It's okay. I'm a doctor, and my friend here is a nurse. We're headed up to Brandywine to help out there," he said, somehow remembering the name of a nearby nursing home. "Our radio's not working. What are they telling you?"

"No one is telling us a damn thing," she answered, barely breaking stride and talking over her shoulder.

Caleb couldn't blame her. Clearly, she didn't want to get any further back in the line at the emergency gathering point.

"The radio issued instructions to evacuate," she said, "and then police cars with loudspeakers cruised up and down our street ordering us to leave as quickly as possible."

"Anything else," Caleb called after her.

"Yeah," she said, shouting to be heard over the siren as she walked away. "I talked to a friend up in Peekskill, and she said there's radiation everywhere. A lot of people are already dead up there."

"Dead?"

"That's what my friend said."

## CHAPTER 6

J AMES STRAIGHTENED HIS NEON-GREEN TIE in the mirror of his private bathroom next to his office, the glass all steamed up from his quick shower. His favorite dark-blue, pinstripe Brioni suit was balled up in a laundry bag, a casualty of his escape from the train and the slippery scramble up the muddy slope from the tracks.

He looked into the mirror and admired himself, quietly talking under his breath, even though he'd left the door ajar. "Less than two hours after being trapped on that bloody train, here I am in my office, in the fresh clothes that I always keep in my closet. That's me: ready for anything, any curveball. Clem is polishing my shoes, I'm getting a cup of coffee, and I'm going to turn on CNN and figure out what the hell is going on…" Then he winked at himself in the mirror and said, "Damn! I'm a king of the universe!"

"So, you talking to yourself again?" Don Williams said, popping in unexpectedly. Don was one of the firm's traders, but they had come up together through a series of jobs, and James had brought him along for the move to Goldfarb & Case, his father-in-law's M&A firm. They were pals and colleagues, but they were also competitors, so friendly jabs and barbs were just a normal part of their daily back and forth, and had been for years.

"What the fuck are you doing in my private bathroom?" James teased.

"Just admiring you, as always," Don laughed.

James gave him a playful sneer, then he pushed by Don and out the door and crossed his expansive office to his mahogany desk. From there, a great sweep of lower Manhattan was spread before him, with the Hudson River gleaming beyond the Freedom Tower, and his floor-to-ceiling windows framing a magnificent panorama reaching from the George Washington Bridge to the Verrazano Narrows.

Don Williams followed James to his desk. "Sorry to barge in, old boy, but Diane told me you looked like a mud wrestler when you arrived."

"Well, a better looking mud wrestler than you'll ever be," James retorted.

"Well, I thought you might like to know I covered your position on that Japan Railway bond issue. There was a margin call this morning because it dropped big time overnight, and you were getting dinged for $10 million, but I knew you wanted to hold onto it, so I covered the firm," Williams said. "Oh, and where the fuck were you?"

"Where was I? Why should I tell you? Well, the truth is my goddamn limo broke down on the way to my house. Then I was fucking stranded on a train on the biggest day of my career. In case you haven't noticed, the world has gone to hell. I was on a goddamn train about 10 miles from Indian Point because I was trying to get here. And, asshole, what got into you, covering the firm's position? Get in early for once?"

"Yeah right. Fuck you. I covered your contractual obligation. I tried to get ahold of you, but you were incommunicado. I managed to fool myself into thinking you'd do the same for me. Nice shoes, by the way," Williams said, pointing out that Roth was still in his stocking feet.

They both started laughing.

"You're shitting me. You were near the attack?" Williams said, in a more personal, less aggressive tone.

"Are they sure it was an attack?" James asked, relieved to drop their usual locker room banter.

"Looks like it," Williams said. "Last report I heard, but hey, you never know these days with the bloggers and Twitter. There's still a lot of confusion. I've read everything from a flotilla of boats and a squadron of jets attacking the nuke plant to an asteroid strike. In any case, it doesn't look like an accident. CNN says there's a big fire at the nuclear plant and they are trying to confirm details. So far, no one is saying there's any danger down this way."

"Nothing was clear up there either," James said. "Everything was at a dead standstill, and nobody seemed to know anything. Some lady on the train was told two planes hit Indian Point. Then I managed to get a ride and made it here. In any case, I got bigger problems right now. By the way, you did the right thing with the Japanese bond. I figured I would be at my desk before the margin call hit, but that didn't work out. So thanks. But now let's get cracking on this deal."

"What? Are you trying to figure out how to take advantage of this mess?" Williams said, with a mocking, incredulous look on his face. "We should probably be trying to figure out how to get the hell out of here! Oh, right, you've got the Secor/Brightline deal today, don't you? I almost forgot."

"Yeah right, you forgot. Uh-huh. $5 billion and it slipped your mind," James laughed.

"Hah, good luck, buddy," Williams said. "Those guys are probably halfway back to Texas and California by now."

"Yeah, lucky for me they've shut every airport on the East Coast," James said. Then he called his secretary: "Diane!"

"Yes, sir," she said, instantly appearing at his door. "Well, sir, you look nice. Much better than 15 minutes ago."

"Very funny. Have you heard from the principals this morning?"

"Not yet."

"Call them. They're not going anywhere. The airports are all shut down. Tell them we are convening as planned, if for no other reason than to watch the news together. If I have to speak with them I will. I want London market pricing for both companies. Secor will be on the big board there. Brightline may need an over-the-counter quote, but it's been trading ever since word got out they were in play. Get it. I'm going to need it. There's no way I'm letting a $5 billion deal crater today, right, Donny boy? Plenty of cards up my sleeve. Diane, get moving, get those people in here. Send cars if you have to. Move!"

This is what he loved, what he was made for, James thought to himself. He was in his wheelhouse, operating in that sweet spot where all his natural abilities were being used to maximum advantage. He was made for a crisis. Decisive. Determined. From the outside, overwhelmingly confident. He knew how to get things done, and get them done quickly. His firm didn't understand what they had, or maybe they did, if money counted as the yardstick.

Since he was a teenager, and that fateful night when he had stopped his dad from beating up his mother, James had been at the center of the action, although not necessarily at the center of power. That night was a dividing line, when he stopped craving his dad's approval and began pushing for himself. He was captain of his high school lacrosse team, named by the coaches, but he didn't get elected class president. He was in charge of entertainment at his college frat house, but no one even nominated him to be fraternity president his senior year. He could do things, but when the position required the consensus of a group of people, he never made it; he was too overbearing, too arrogant, never well-liked, but envied and respected for his ability to get things done. As for what other people thought of him, he really didn't care. The material rewards had always been enough for him.

As Diane and Don headed out, James heard them both say, in a deferential tone, "Good morning, sir."

Then Irv Goldfarb, his father-in-law, stuck his head in, filling the doorway with his authoritative presence. "You crazy son of a bitch, what makes you think you can still pull this off, in the middle of some blasted terror attack?"

James laughed. "You know I can, Irv. That's why you keep me here!"

Irv just gave him a thin smile. "Anyway, Sheri told me not to worry, that you'd be here. I guess she was right, as usual. Too bad, though: I was ready to meet your guys, show my stuff, and let the whole damn world know I still got it. But never mind. Want to tell me how you managed to get here, in this mess? No, I don't want to know…"

"The important thing, Irv, is that I am here."

"Yes, I agree with that. Now let's see if you can bring it home in glory. Good luck, James. FYI, the desk is betting against you!"

"Fools."

Irv chuckled as he left the room. This was James' moment, this was his deal. He had been trying to impress his father-in-law ever since he was brought into the firm. Maybe it had something to do with his own father but he wasn't one to reflect too much on those deeper psychological motivations. Sheri had come out of left field and into his life, the woman who finally had been able to bring him under control. She had even gotten him to sign a pre-nup that gave her nearly everything if he ever walked out on her; she had heard the story—everyone had—about how he had moved one long-term girlfriend's possessions out of his apartment, changed the locks, and left on a two-week business trip after attaching a note to the door saying, "We're done." Sheri reminded him of that story when she handed him the pre-nup.

But Sheri left the firm in a panic-stricken rush to the suburbs after 9/11. Overnight, James became the heir apparent. If Irv had any remaining doubts—and a guy like him always had doubts about everything and everyone—today James would lay them to rest, and that would pave the way for his big secret move to go out on this own.

Yes, ensconced now in his spacious office, James felt good, he was ready to crow. The biggest payday of his life was at hand, a masterstroke of innovation and networking, bringing together Secor, an old-line petroleum producer from the Texas oil fields, with Brightline, a new alternative energy firm built from scratch with Silicon Valley venture capital and already with a dominant market share in both solar and wind technologies. This was it: the perfect 21st century match. Even better, he had brought the two sides together. And this deal was his and his alone, and it was sheer genius to have brought cowboy-boot-wearing Texas oil executives together with a bunch of New Age visionaries who thought they could save the world. No one else could have created this deal and no one was going to stop him now, not even some crazy terrorists.

"Mr. Roth," his secretary Diane said, breaking his reverie.

"Yeah? Are they here?"

"Yes, sir."

"Give me two minutes, then show them in. Is Irv with them?"

"Yes, he was speaking with Mr. Watkins from Secor."

"Good," James said.

He surveyed the conference room, the broad expanse of windows, the long wooden table with leather chairs, the original Jean Basquiats hanging against the silvery sheen of the metallic walls. The big flat screen TV on the far wall, at the head of the 20-person table, was dark, flanked by the trading screens from London with not only Secor and Brightline prices displayed, but a handful of other major energy company prices, all showing green this morning. He also punched in the symbol for Westinghouse, which made nuclear reactors and was down 10 percent in offshore trading. Might as well give them a dose of reality about what this attack was going to do to the energy markets. Then he turned on the TV, but kept it muted. Better to leave the impression that he wasn't worried about the events of the day.

CNN's Breaking News banner flashed onto the screen, then came an image of a billow of black smoke rising from Indian Point, clouding the colorful fall trees lining the hills of the Hudson Valley.

Roth took a deep breath. He was ready. For anything.

## CHAPTER 7

CHARLIE JOINED THE MOTORMAN in the driver's compartment at the front of the train after the last of the passengers who were going to leave had climbed down to the ground. On the tracks ahead, there was nothing but red signal lights as far as they could see.

"Bobby, we could be here all day," Charlie said, "and I'm worried. My dad was supposed to pick up my mom at the hospital. Now his phone isn't answering. I was planning to take the afternoon off and go home to help her get settled. You know, she's been in the hospital for two weeks."

"Yeah, you've told me that a hundred times, Charlie," Bobby said. "Call the hospital."

"I tried. No lines, or no answer." Charlie said. Then his phone rang, and when he answered he heard his sister's voice, filled with anguish.

"Charlie, Charlie, where are you? I thought you were going to go help Dad today!"

"I am, Sis, after this run. But you've heard what's going on up here, right?"

"Yes, but I just got a call from the hospital saying Mom is ready to be released, but Dad's not there," she said, her voice loud enough that even Bobby could hear it. "You've got to get there to find out what's going on!"

"Susan, I can't just leave my post. It's an…"

"You've got to," his sister pleaded.

Charlie then felt Bobby's arm on his. "Go, guy," Bobby said softly. "The hospital's just up the hill. We aren't going to move for quite a while. Get back when you can. If I have to move, I'll tell them something about you helping the passengers get to safety."

Charlie gave a warm salute to his friend, then turned back to his sister on the phone: "Okay, Sis. Okay, I'm goin', I'm goin'."

A few moments later, Charlie was climbing the muddy slope leading up to the hospital, then he made his way across the hospital parking lot, kicking and scraping the mud from his shoes as he ran. When he reached the entrance to the ER, he could see that his black work shoes, the sturdy, round-toed kind that cops and conductors wear, were still caked with mud. For a moment, he worried about tracking dirt in, but he quickly put that aside. There was no one in the entryway, so he walked straight into the interior of the ER and approached the nurses' station. A woman in a pink uniform looked up, obviously startled to see him.

"Sir, you are not supposed to be in here," she said.

"I'm sorry," Charlie said. "But my dad, my dad's supposed to be here, to pick up my mother, and and and he's not. At least that's what my sister just told me…"

"Sir," the nurse said patiently, "I'm afraid I don't understand."

"My mother's getting out today and my dad's supposed to pick her up and my sister called and said he hasn't shown up and that's not like him and we're afraid something's happened to him. I'm a conductor on Metro-North but we're stuck down on the tracks and I couldn't just sit there waitin'. I have to find out, what's happened to my dad?"

"Okay, okay," the nurse said. "What's your dad's name?"

"Sean. Sean Murray."

"And yours?"

"Charlie Murray, he's my dad."

"I need to see some ID," she said.

Charlie pulled out his Metro-North ID badge and showed it to her: "Charles Murray, see right there."

"Okay, wait here."

Charlie shifted nervously from foot to foot in front of the nurses' station, looking at the clipboards on the desk and the small cabinets nearby filled with bandages and small vials. The ER was eerily quiet, and Charlie wondered why it wasn't filled with patients streaming in from whatever had happened up in Peekskill.

Then the nurse returned. "Mr. Murray, please follow me," she said, and then headed down an adjoining hallway.

In a small treatment area, she pulled back the curtain and led Charlie in. On the left was a big cabinet filled with boxes of gauze pads, rubber gloves, and small plastic tubes. A little further inside, a doctor in a white lab coat was staring at a monitor on the back wall, and there on the bed in front of him was Charlie's dad.

Charlie's heart sank. His dad's face, deathly white, was covered with an oxygen mask, and one arm was hooked up to an IV and a drip bag. The doctor was holding his other arm, tracing a vein down to the wrist and apparently feeling for a pulse.

"Who's this, nurse?" the doctor said without looking up.

"It's his son," she said.

"I'm Charlie. That's my dad."

The doctor gently laid down his patient's arm and turned directly to Charlie. "My name is Dr. Jones, and I am sorry to tell you this, but your father has had a massive heart attack. We do not know the full extent of the damage, but the blood flow to his extremities is very limited. We were able to get his heart re-started after he was brought in, but he seems to have suffered serious brain damage. He was out, well, no one knows for how long."

"What?" Charlie said, having difficulty taking it all in. "I don't understand. Brought in from where?"

"He was found on the ground out in our parking lot."

"But, but he just had a physical! He was fine a week ago! He was fine yesterday!"

"I am sorry, sir. You never know about these things. Maybe it was the stress of this morning. Now, you'd better step outside."

For Charlie, there seemed to be a strain of coldness in Dr. Jones' voice, and Charlie didn't like it at all. "Listen, he was fine this morning! He just came here to pick up my mom. And now you say his heart is barely workin'? What's goin' on here?"

The nurse took Charlie's arm and drew him aside. "Mr. Murray, we are as confused as you are. Your dad was found out in the parking lot, collapsed on the ground. Do you know how he got here?"

"What do you mean?" Charlie said, now totally confused.

"Just that. He was alone, on the ground, in the parking lot."

"I don't understand. He drove here this morning. In his car. He and I went over the directions and the routine last night."

Over the doctor's shoulder, Charlie could see his father's ashen face, and his eyelids seemed to be fluttering. Then, as he watched, the green line on the monitor began to bounce erratically, and right away Charlie knew his dad's heart was failing.

"Get him out of here!" the doctor barked. "Nurse, we have a code blue. Get a crash cart in here. Now!"

The nurse led Charlie out, but over his shoulder he could see the doctor pushing a machine to the bed, then another nurse arrived and quickly drew the curtain closed. Now Charlie had only one thought: find his mother. She must be in a total panic, waiting for her husband and having no idea where he might be.

"Please," Charlie said to the nurse, "you have to help me find my mom! My poor mom, she's all alone and not knowin'…"

"I have to help the doctor. We're trying to save your dad," the nurse said. "Look, head down that corridor. There's an elevator to the first floor. That's where reception is. Maybe they can help you. I have to go."

Charlie wandered through the maze of corridors in the basement level of Phelps Hospital. The emergency room was at the rear of the hospital, one floor down from the main entrance where visitors or day surgery patients or the day's discharges came and left the building. He finally found a bank of elevators on the other side of the cafeteria, and waited impatiently for the doors to open. Once inside, he punched the 1st floor button, and as he exited the elevator, a candy striper was standing there.

"Miss, can you help me, please?" Charlie said.

"Of course, what do you need?"

"You can help, help me find my mother," Charlie said.

"Okay. Do you know what room she is in?"

"No, I mean, well, I did. But she was discharged this morning, and my dad was supposed to be here, but he had a heart attack or something and he's downstairs in the ER, and I don't know what happened to my mother. Her name is Rose."

"Sir, she's probably up in the visitor waiting room by the front door. Let's go see," With that, she took his arm and began leading him down the hall.

"Call me Charlie. And I really appreciate this."

Near the reception desk Charlie spotted her. His mother was

sitting in a wheelchair in a small waiting area, and she had her small night bag in her lap and Charlie could see the worry on her face.

"Mom!" he called out.

Now the elderly woman looked up at her son, bewildered.

"Charlie? Why are you here? Where's your father?"

"It's a long story, Mom," Charlie said. "Are you okay?'

She was wheezing a little, and started wringing her hands. "I guess so. I'm just worried about your father. He was supposed to be here an hour ago. I've just been sitting here waiting."

"Mom, I'm going to get you home. I have to find Dad's car first."

"Where's your father? Where is his car? He was supposed to be here hours ago!"

Charlie kneeled down next to his mom and took one of her hands in his.

"Come on, Mom. Come with me. Dad's downstairs with the doctors. You need to see him. Now." With that, he thanked the very kind candy striper and told her he'd take it from there.

She touched his shoulder as Charlie began wheeling his mother to the elevators. When they got to the ER, the same duty nurse told them to sit right there in the waiting room. Charlie stroked his mother's hand. He remembered her doing the same thing to him when he was a little boy, reassuring him with a quiet whisper that everything was going to be okay.

"Don't worry, Mom," he said, "Everything's goin' to be fine."

She mumbled something that he couldn't hear.

"What, Mom?" he asked.

"No, it's not, Charlie. No, it's not," she whispered.

"Mom, wait here a minute. I'm goin' to find Dad's car in the parking lot."

Charlie walked outside, searching up and down the rows for

his dad's black Lincoln Town Car. It was nowhere to be seen. He circled the lot again, confused why his dad's car wasn't there.

As he re-entered the building, Dr. Jones appeared at the door of the ER waiting room and said loudly, "Rose Murray?"

"Yes, this is Rose Murray. I'm her son," Charlie said. "She's a little disoriented. My dad was supposed to pick her up this morning. She's been here nearly two weeks and it's been hard on her."

"I understand. Would you come with me a minute, sir," the doctor said. Charlie walked through the swinging door and stood in front of the doctor.

"I'm sorry, I forgot your name," the doctor said.

"Charlie. Charlie Murray."

"Mr. Murray, I've got some bad news. Your dad didn't make it. He had a massive heart attack, and even though he was right here, we couldn't save him. There was just too much damage. I don't think we could have made any difference."

Charlie just kept shaking his head, "I just don't understand, I just don't understand."

"Would you like me to tell your mother, or will you?" the doctor said.

Charlie hesitated. "I don't know. I guess, I guess I'd better tell her. I don't know what she's going to do. And I don't where the car is. It seems to have disappeared."

"Maybe it's out there somewhere. Shall I get you someone to help look for it?" the doctor asked.

"Where could it be?"

"Mr. Murray, I don't know, I'm sorry," the doctor said. "Look, I have to get back to the emergency room. The nurse will give you the details about how to arrange to pick up your father's body. Her name is Nurse Woods."

Charlie didn't want the doctor to leave. "Please, please, can I just ask…"

"Mr. Murray, I understand how you feel. All I know is he was brought into the ER. He was unconscious by the time I got to him. Maybe Nurse Woods heard something. You can ask her. But I have to go."

The doctor turned on his heel and left Charlie standing in the hallway. He was frozen, not wanting to go back to his mother and not knowing what he was going to say to her. He walked back into the waiting room, but the wheelchair was empty and at first he couldn't see her. "Mom?" he called out. Then he saw her standing outside the glass doors, staring out into the parking lot.

He walked out, took her by the elbow and quietly said, "Mom, come back inside, we're going to have to wait for a cab."

As he led her back inside, memories of his parents together flooded his head. For 50 years, they had been inseparable, high school sweethearts who had spent their lives together. She took care of Charlie and his sister, working hard to keep a home together and in these later years, just taking care of him, cooking his dinners and keeping his room clean, just like she did when he was still in high school. And he remembered her pouring his dad a glass of Scotch every night before dinner. As he thought about his dad sitting every night in his chair with the Scotch, Charlie started crying.

"Charlie, Charlie, why are you crying?" his mom asked, coming out of her daze and speaking directly to him.

"Mom, Mom," Charlie said, barely able to get the words out. "Mom, I've got bad news. You'd better sit down."

"What are you talking about? Where's Sean? I want to see him now."

"Please, Mom, sit down."

"Why?"

"Mom, Dad's dead. He's dead. He had a heart attack in the parking lot this morning and he died. He died. Just like that."

The slightly dazed look on Rose's face slowly twisted into torment, the pain tightening her eyes and lips. "No. No. I don't believe it. He was fine yesterday."

"Mom, that's what the doctor just told me."

"I want to see him. Now! I want to see him," she said. "Please, Charlie," taking his hand in hers and again, without a hint of her earlier disorientation. "I need to see him one more time before they take him. Please, Charlie, ask them for me, please."

"Okay. Wait here. No, come with me. We'll find the nurse."

Nurse Woods was still in the hallway when she saw Charlie come through the swinging door with a woman in a wheelchair. Right away she knew it was his mother, the dead man's wife. She approached them and said, "You really shouldn't be back here. Let me show you out."

"Nurse," Charlie said, his voice beseeching her. "She just wants to see my dad one more time before they take him away. Please."

The nurse paused and looked over her shoulder. "Well, I'm not supposed to do this, but come," she said, taking control of Rose's wheel-chair and pushing her to her husband.

In that same examining room, Charlie could see his dad, his eyes pulled shut, and a blue pallor already setting in. Charlie hung back as Rose was wheeled up to the gurney. She took a deep breath and laid her hand on his chest, "I love you, Sean. I always have."

Then she stood up, wobbling a bit, and leaned over and kissed her husband on the cheek. Charlie came up behind and steadied her, "Come on, Mom, let's go. They'll take care of him."

Rose took another deep breath and then exhaled. Her shoulders slumped. She patted her husband on his hand, and quietly said, "I know they will, Charlie. I know they will."

## CHAPTER 8

CALEB GRIPPED THE STEERING WHEEL tightly. Still ringing in his head were the words from that woman rushing with her baby to the evacuation point: "a lot of people are already dead."

The nuclear reactor up in Peekskill, was it destroyed? Was a rush of deadly radiation right now headed their way? And where in the heck were Brenda and the kids? Were they safe? With all this anguish rushing through him, it was taking all his resolve to not speed up on the narrow back roads around Ossining to race home as quickly as he could.

Rachel put her hand on his arm. "Caleb, what are we going to do? Do you think that woman was right? That a lot of people are already dead?"

"I don't know," Caleb said, keeping his eyes on the narrow, twisting country road, hoping to avoid running into another crowd of evacuees. "There's no reason not to believe her. But I can't, well, I'm trying not to think about it. I just want to get us home as fast as I can."

Rachel fell back into the uneasy silence inside the car. The mention of dead people, and the specter of radiation flooding the area made it too frightening to think about anything else. And it certainly overwhelmed any connection they had made earlier.

"Turn here," she said suddenly, causing Caleb to brake hard.

"Why?" he said.

"There won't be any roadblocks or cops on that road."

Caleb spun the wheel to make the turn without stopping. "I'm sure you're right, but geez, Rachel, don't do that. You scared me."

"Caleb, I can't help but think, why are we doing this?" she said.

"Rachel, you could be right. But I have to be sure my family's safe. The phones are down, I don't know where they are. And I told them to stay there. It was my fucking plan that they stay put until I could get to them if something, anything happened."

"Okay, I get it," Rachel said, a little stunned by Caleb's brusqueness. "But I'm in the same boat you are. I don't know where my kids are. I guess my only hope is they've left a message on the machine at home and I can find them. I mean, you won't just leave me at my house, right? You'll help me find my family, too, right?"

"Of course I'll help you. But we have to get there first. Can we just focus on that for now?"

Caleb drove past a couple of other lines of people waiting to be evacuated. But there was no sign of any buses yet that could get them out of the danger zone.

Then, as they began a climb up the hill, now in Croton-on-Harmon, the car suddenly began sputtering and then the engine just quit. With a glance Caleb saw the gas gauge was on empty.

"Shit," he said.

"What's wrong?" Rachel said.

"We're out of gas."

"That's okay," Rachel said. "We're really close to my house, and we can't be that far from yours. Just do me a favor, help me check that everything's okay in my house before you leave me. I've got my keys here," she said, pointing to a small elegant sling purse on her back.

"Okay, but let's hurry."

"You don't have to tell me!"

They began walking briskly up the hill. Rachel led the way, her dress hiked up a little so she could take long strides. Caleb was pushing to keep up, but he also couldn't ignore Rachel's tight buttocks and long legs in front of him. In a minute or two she turned into a driveway that led to a big Normandy-style house.

"You live here?" Caleb said, "I always wondered whose house this was."

She unlocked the door and walked in, the faint aroma of her morning coffee still lingering in the air. Caleb was startled by the familiarity of a wall lined with family photos: two smiling kids in Martha's Vineyard, and in London, Paris, the Grand Canyon, Disney World, and another with their grandparents in front of an old Victorian house. There were a couple of pictures of Rachel, usually with the kids, and there was one of her standing in front of the Paris Opera, looking stunning in a long lavender gown and with a huge jeweled necklace running down into her cleavage. Behind her an elegantly dressed crowd was walking up the steps. Nowhere did he see a picture of her husband or of them together.

"Guess your husband is the photographer in the family," Caleb said quietly, almost to himself.

"What's that?" Rachel said from the kitchen, where she was checking her family's phone messages.

"Oh, nothing. Well, I mean the pictures. They are all of you or of you and the kids. No sign of your husband. So I figured he was the photographer."

"No, he almost never goes anywhere with us. You might say he's a workaholic. Aren't all lawyers?"

"I wouldn't know. The ones I know I never see."

"Exactly."

Caleb came into the kitchen and drew near to Rachel. She had the phone pressed to her ear as she dialed a number.

"Who are you calling?" he asked.

"The school."

He stood quietly near her as she listened to the voice on the phone. Her hair, appearing more auburn than blond in the soft indoor light, fell down the back her neck. For the first time that morning, he noticed her perfume.

"Damn," she said.

"What?"

"There's a recording that says the school is closed and that the kids have been transported out of the evacuation zone by bus. There's a number to call. Would you hold the phone to my ear, please? I've got to listen again to write the number down. I'm having trouble juggling the pen and phone." Then she punched the button on the phone to repeat the message. He stepped closer to her and took the phone, pressing it lightly against her ear while she waited to hear the number again. She brushed her hair back with her hand from the phone, and he felt it caress his arm.

"Caleb, Caleb," she said, her voice coming from some faraway place. "Caleb…"

"Oh, yes, sorry," he said, handing the phone back to Rachel.

She stared at him with a quizzical look. "Are you okay?"

He took a deep breath. "Sorry, I was lost in thought."

"Lost someplace far away," she said. "Your eyes were a million miles away."

'Yes, I was remembering a night a long time ago," he said. "In a whole other life."

"What was her name?"

Caleb recoiled a bit, and Rachel felt it right away. "It's okay," she said. "Do you want to try calling your wife?"

"Yeah, that's a good idea," he said, picking up the phone again. He dialed, waited as it started to ring, and then it switched over to that annoying "all circuits are busy" message.

Rachel studied him carefully. He was a handsome man, even up close. There was a certain kind of urban cragginess to his face, with its high cheekbones, angular nose, and full lips. She had to admit, however, that his tightly clipped, blond hair made him look serious and almost, well, dangerous, a Daniel Craig likeness that translated for her into a visceral magnetism.

Caleb walked over to the television and turned it on.

"You have a generator, right?" he asked, having noticed that the refrigerator was running, and the clock radio in the kitchen was close to the correct time.

"Yes, it comes on automatically," Rachel said.

He flipped the channel to CNN, and there it was: their corner of the Hudson River Valley, with a reporter standing in front of a dark, billowing cloud of smoke. "…the reactor will be fully shut down within the hour," the reporter said. "A Power Corporation spokesman has just confirmed that despite the damage and smoke, there has been no, I repeat, no leak of any radiation. Folks, if you had been ordered to evacuate, the Westchester County authorities now say it's safe to go back home. And if you are home, stay there. Power is expected to be restored by noon, and cell phone service as well. That's the latest word from here, Wolf."

"Oh my god," Rachel said. "Did I just hear what I thought I heard? We're out of danger?"

"Shhh," Caleb said.

"Thanks, Bradley," the CNN anchor said. "It's been a very difficult morning, with two planes making an apparent suicide run at the Peekskill nuclear power plant north of New York City. We do not have a full report yet on potential damage to the plant, but it appears that a major catastrophe has been averted. We are told that the emergency evacuation plan has been halted. Evacuation buses are being re-routed. Federal and state transportation authorities are saying the commuter rail system is still on lockdown, and all the airports in New York, New Jersey, and Connecticut are still closed to all air traffic. Homeland Security officials are telling us that those restrictions are going to remain in place for now. As you remember, we all thought 9/11 was over after the New York attack on the World Trade Center, and that proved to be wrong. One official said off-the-record that they hoped the lockdowns and the suspension of operations will be lifted later today. But they are being extremely cautious until they are certain the danger has passed."

"Wow," Caleb said. "Can you believe it?"

"And we were right in the middle of it," Rachel said. "Do you think it's over?"

For an instant all Caleb wanted to do was go home and hug his kids. And as soon as he thought of doing that, Caleb could feel some of the tension in his neck and shoulders begin to melt away. But another part of him remained wired for danger; was there a second wave of attack now headed their way? Back on 9/11 two planes had hit the World Trade Center, but another was still headed for the White House; on this crisp October morning could anyone be sure the danger was really over? Rachel read his mind exactly:

"Now what, Caleb?" she said, slipping her arm in his. "Do you think it's really over? You didn't answer me."

"I don't really know," Caleb said. "I've been trying to ignore for years that we might live something like 9/11 again. And, here we are. So no, I don't really know."

Caleb turned to Rachel and felt a rush of conflicting emotions. He was still on edge, not ready to stand down, and anticipating more trouble. But he also craved the relief that he sensed, that he knew, could come from Rachel's waiting arms.

Rachel stared wide-eyed at Caleb, again reading his mind with precision. Their eyes locked, and Caleb felt his stomach flutter, passion surging from deep inside him.

"Rachel, Rachel," he murmured, his knees suddenly feeling weak. "What a morning it's been…"

Rachel stopped him. "Please hold me, Caleb. I feel like I'm going to faint."

Caleb took one step and wrapped Rachel in his arms. They embraced tightly, the tension and fear of the morning starting to drain out of them.

When he pulled back from her, just a little, her face was inches away from him. She pulled him to her and kissed him hard on the lips, their tongues quickly finding each other's and their hands starting to caress their bodies. Neither of them wanted the moment to end.

Rachel finally stopped kissing him and whispered in his ear, "Now what, Caleb?" she said, pressing her body into his. "What are we going to do?"

He eased her away a bit, but kept his hands on her shoulders, looking straight into her eyes again.

"I don't know. I wish I knew, Rachel. All I know is that I was fighting the urge to do that all morning."

"Really? That?" she said, brushing his lips with hers.

"Yes, hug you. Kiss you. Feel you," Caleb said. "And right now I'm imagining pulling you upstairs to your bedroom and…"

"What's stopping you, Caleb? Can't you tell I'm fighting those very same urges? You're making me feel things my husband hasn't made me feel in years."

"Rachel, that's exactly what I'm feeling too, and it's scaring the hell out of me. My wife hasn't turned me on like this…"

"Of course, she hasn't," she thought to herself, but instead of talking, she kissed him again. They embraced tightly, the urgency of their kiss even more intense.

Rachel finally pulled away, just far enough to break off the kiss. "See, that's what I want. To feel like that…"

"No, NO," he said, abruptly pulling away. "You're okay now, right? You're safe? All is well?"

"Well, yes I am," Rachel said, her voice puzzled.

"Good!"

With that, Caleb turned on his heel and walked out the door.

## CHAPTER 9

THE BOARDROOM AT GOLDFARB & CASE was classic corporate design. A long, rectangular maple wood table occupied the center of the room, and paintings from some of New York's hottest talent over the last 50 years hung on the wall: a Basquiat, a Pollock, a Warhol, among others. Every seat at the table was taken, but there was little small talk, as everyone tried to absorb the shock of the morning's terror attack. Given the potential dangers outside, why were they even in the room? The answer, of course, was money.

"Gentlemen, thank you all for coming, especially in such trying circumstances," James said, as he took his place at the head of the table. Down one side sat the senior management team of Secor, the oil drilling and production company from Texas. On the other sat the young executives of Brightline, the Silicon Valley-based wind and solar energy company.

"Okay, let's get right to it," James said. "We'd like to get this deal closed quickly, especially given what's going on around us. You wouldn't be here if you didn't believe what I've been saying all along. This is a deal that works for both sides here in the room today."

"Mr. Watkins," James said, speaking directly to the Secor CEO and chairman, "I think everyone knows you. But would the rest of your team kindly introduce themselves, please?"

As the Secor representatives and their investment banker gave their names, James studied their faces, looking for clues as to how they were reacting to the stunning events unfolding just up the Hudson River Valley. The mostly older Secor executives appeared stoic, and he knew from his background checks that there were Vietnam vets among them, and at least one senior exec had served in the Korean War. They had that subtle swagger of men who had lived danger before, and felt no need or desire to show it.

A distinguished older man in a crisp, navy blue pinstripe suit stood up after the others had finished. "I'm Shelley O'Bannon," the man began in a slow Texas drawl. James knew he was one of the most venerable M&A lawyers in Dallas, not anyone you would want to fuck with but renowned as one of the straightest shooters in the legal profession. "I speak for Secor and Mr. Watkins today. And, I have to add, they are here against my advice."

James held up his hand. "We'll get to your objections soon enough, Shelley." Then, pointing to the other side of the table, James said, "Cameron, will you introduce your team, please."

At a glance, James could see that the young team from Silicon Valley was rattled. Earlier that morning they had the sweet smell of $5 billion in their nostrils—until news came of those two jets that had stormed up the Hudson bent on murder and mayhem. Now the young dynamos from Silicon Valley looked a little ashen, and many kept sneaking glances at their cell phones. What James saw in their eyes was not quite a "deer in the headlights" look, but damned near.

"Morning everyone," said Cameron Ballack, the CEO of Brightline. "James, it's quite a welcome you organized for us here in New York City!"

His quip was met with welcome nods from everyone at the table.

"Seriously, we had our doubts about coming here this morning, given the news. But James here convinced us it's the right thing to do. And we are grateful he did." From there, pointing to each man, Ballack introduced his team: "Dylan Simpkins, our VP of Production; Bowie Mattson, our Chief Financial Officer; Luis Suarez, our Chief Information Officer, and last, but surely not least, our lawyer, Daniel Silver."

Daniel Silver stood up, his black suit rumpled and ill-fitting, and his shirt looking like it had never, ever been ironed. Silver conveyed the air of someone who wasn't sure why he was here—and wished he wasn't.

James almost laughed out loud. He knew that un-lawyerly appearance was a carefully constructed act designed to put people at ease and have them underestimate his skill and savvy. But James knew all about Daniel Silver; most people around Wall Street did. Brightline's attorney was considered the most astute guardian of intellectual property in the whole of the United States.

In a soft, modest voice, Silver then started in. "Shelley, not to step on what you were going to say, but I have advised my clients that if Goldfarb & Case wants us here, we need to hear them out. But we make no promises up front. The situation is very fluid."

"That's fair enough, Mr. Silver," James said, fidgeting a bit in his seat at the head of the table. "Before we dig in, gentlemen, are there any questions? No? Okay then, Shelley, you're up."

With that, Shelley O'Bannon cleared his throat theatrically, clasped his hands and leaned forward on the blond wood conference table. Right away James knew that it wasn't going to be good news.

"Thank you, gentlemen," the Texan started. "And Daniel, nice to see you again, too. But to be straight to the point, Secor Energy has some serious reservations this morning about closing this deal, given what's gone on at that nuclear power station in Buchanan up the river. For that matter, we almost didn't show up today, but then they shut down Teterboro so we didn't have anywhere else to go."

"For the benefit of our out-of-towners," James interrupted, "Buchanan is where the Indian Point power station is located."

"Thanks, James. I should remember that not everyone knows about Indian Point. But here we are, getting ready to put $5 billion dollars into an alternative energy company. That's more than 10 times their earnings. And given what just happened, we have no clue what's going to happen to the price of oil today. Or tomorrow."

"As a result," O'Bannon continued, "we want an extension for, say, 10 days. By then the situation should be a little clearer. We don't think that's too much to ask."

While Bannon spoke, James quietly used the TV remote control to find and put on the screen a graph of the spot crude price from London. The graph traced the price, in 5-minute intervals, since trading began that morning. The result was clear: there had been a spike in price at 8:05 a.m., just about the time news of the attack at Indian Point hit the wires. After that, the price of crude had trended back almost to pre-attack levels.

"Shelley, let me break in here, please," James said, standing up and walking toward the screen for emphasis. "As you can see, the market took the hit and is recovering nicely—just as our research predicted. We have studied past episodes, in depth; you will find our conclusions set forth on page 25 of your folder." Everyone at the table hurried to find the page. Then James went on:

"One scenario we studied was based on the sort of incident that occurred at the nuclear reactor at Three Mile Island, back on March 28th of 1979. That was not a terrorist attack, as today's attack appears to be, but the possible consequence was the same: a major disruption in energy prices, with nuclear power essentially off the table as an alternative energy source for another 10 to 15 years."

James was now warming to his task. He and his team had done their homework, and it was all right there in the folders.

"We at Goldfarb & Case," he went on, "believe this kind of incident, with its potential impact on existing energy sources and prices, only enhances the potential value of the opportunity now before you. Indeed, for our friends here from Brightline this makes your campaign to improve solar and wind technology and expand your distribution capabilities all the more valuable. If anyone should be having second thoughts today, it should be Brightline looking for a better deal."

"Oh shit," James immediately thought to himself, "why the hell did I say that?" Was he handing his young entrepreneurs a ready excuse to bolt out the door? DAMN! But instead of acknowledging the slip—and appearing weak—James deftly turned his mistake to his advantage. Or so he hoped:

"Gentlemen, let me sum up: we at Goldfarb & Case are of the firm belief that whatever the price of oil today—and no matter what happens to the wider energy market going forward—this deal, this alliance, is pure gold for both of you. It brings together one of the most esteemed companies and brands in Big Oil with one of the most esteemed young firms and brands in the rapidly evolving world of alternative energy. Imagine the intellectual, scientific, and research assets you will bring to each other. And, as we've laid out in the offering sheet, Secor diversifies its core portfolio, and Brightline gets the capital to make its technology even more broadly available."

James paused, reaching for the glass of water in front of him and taking a short sip. Then he issued what amounted to an ultimatum. "Gentlemen, the time to do this is now. Shelley, I'm afraid that with the 10-day extension you ask for, neither Goldfarb & Case nor Brightline will be able to make that an exclusive period. As you know, there are other interested parties, and I will re-open the offer window if you insist on that extension."

With that, James sat down, clasped his fingers, and waited for a reaction to his hardline stance. Now the seasoned executives from Secor moved into an informal huddle, and so did the young hotshots from Brightline. James could feel the tension on both sides. The stakes for both sides were huge: that price tag of $5 billion was just the most visible part of the iceberg.

On the Secor side of the table, James could see a lot of furrowed brows and anxious glances. Then their lawyer, Shelley Bannon, leaned in to whisper something to Bob Watkins, the CEO and chairman. Watkins just shook his head slowly. Then he leaned forward and scanned the faces of his team down the table. No one flinched, but at least one man gave an affirmative little nod.

The young Brightline executives sat stone-faced, obviously uncomfortable. But James knew they were smart enough to keep their mouths shut, given the $5 billion payday in play, and he knew that the four young men at the table would see their combined net worth go up between $500 million and $1 billion.

As the huddles continued, James carefully watched the men and tried to gauge their reactions, but he wasn't getting any sort of conclusive feel. His heart was now in his mouth; the fate of his prized deal seemed to be hanging precariously in the balance. Then, up on the screen, James saw CNN break into their newscast with a bulletin announcement. Immediately CNN cut to an alarming shot: a picturesque shot of the Hudson River Valley, in all its autumn splendor, but with a tall column of dark, ugly smoke rising behind.

"Gentlemen," James said, "CNN appears to have an update. Shall we listen in?"

At once, the teams from Secor and Brightline fell quiet, and all eyes went to the big screen. With his remote—and a gambler's instinct—James hiked up the volume and suddenly the entire room was filled with the familiar voice of Wolf Blitzer:

"As we have been reporting, there was some sort of attack this morning at the Indian Point power plant north of New York City. Initial reports said that two small planes, probably corporate jets, slammed into the big containment domes protecting the two nuclear reactors at the Indian Point facility. Details have been sketchy. And no group has claimed responsibility. But for a live report from the scene, we now turn to Steve Wallace.

"Steve, what's the latest?"

"Wolf, police and emergency personnel have cordoned off all access roads to the Indian Point facility. I'm two miles south of there, at a staging area for the emergency response teams. I'm with Brian Lynnen, the spokesperson for the Power Corporation that owns and operates the facility. Brian, what can you tell us?"

The spokesman, in a company vest and hard hat, responded in a calm, reassuring voice: "First of all, Steve, let me say that we have been extremely lucky this morning. Yes, there was an attack on the Indian Point facility this morning. Two planes were involved in the attack. One damaged—but did not breach—the containment dome on the No. 1 reactor at Indian Point. That reactor has actually been shut down for the past six weeks, as part of its federally mandated 15-year inspection and renovation. That smoke you see behind us is the fire caused by the crash and the plane's fuel. There has been no release—I repeat—no release of radiation.

"The second plane, apparently headed for the No. 2 reactor at Indian Point, missed its target completely. Instead it crashed into the transmission station east of the reactors and exploded on contact."

"Brian, have there been casualties?"

"At this point, we have not accounted for all the workers who were on site at the time of the attack. At this hour, though, we think that casualties have been minimal. As I say, we were very lucky."

"Brian, we heard that at the time of the attack the Indian Point facility was not operating at 100 percent capacity. Is that correct?"

"That's correct, Steve. Reactor No. 2 was operating at its usual overnight capacity of 75 percent, but was getting ready to go to 100 percent to meet daily energy requirements."

"The plants were not operating at 100 percent this morning?" the reporter asked.

"That's correct, Steve," the spokesman repeated. "And thanks to quick thinking by the operator on duty, plus the strength of our safety controls and our backup power system, we have been able to start the power-down of the reactor, in total safety. Within the next 12 hours we should have a full shutdown of the reactor without any threat to the public. As long as the power transmission station is out of commission, we'll have to keep the reactor off-line until we can find another way to deliver that electricity."

Now Wolf Blitzer jumped in: "Mr. Lynnen, we're hearing reports that the two planes were loaded with explosives, essentially turning them into flying bombs. Can you confirm that?"

"I can't confirm anything about the planes, Wolf. You'll have to ask Homeland Security."

"Okay, but let me be sure we're totally clear here," Blitzer said. "Are you telling the public that the crisis is over?"

"Not exactly, Wolf. In terms of possible radiation, yes, the crisis is over. But there are a number of customers without power in Westchester County. We have implemented emergency plans to bring in electricity from other suppliers around the Northeast, and that process should be complete by the end of the day. For now, our priorities are providing power to crucial public facilities, such as hospitals and evacuation centers throughout the area. We hope to get Metro-North up and running soon, so that commuters who were already in the city can get back home to check on their homes and their families."

"Okay," James said, as he flicked off the sound on the TV. "Gentlemen, may I presume this allays your concerns today?"

Shelley O'Bannon made a quick check of his clients, and James could see them all nod in agreement. The Brightline folks also nodded in agreement. They were ready to go. Indeed, in their heads they were already making plans for spending that $5 billion.

"Good!" James said. "But, to be sure, we do need to address one last point: the final pricing. Thanks to the off-market listing of Brightline in London, we do have a current market price, and it still falls within the range, including the premium, that is set forth in your documents. Are there any remaining issues regarding price?"

"No, we're fine," said Bob Watkins, the CEO of Secor. "You've answered everything in here," he said, patting the deal folder. "And very professionally, too."

With that, James buzzed in his assistant and gave him his instructions: "Dennis, please make sure that everyone signs in the proper place. Dennis is also a notary, so he will add his signature and seal at the bottom of your copies. Then the lawyers can go over the documents to be sure they are in order and properly executed. There are engraved pens on the table, yours for the keeping, and your commemorative tombstones, saluting this historic deal, will arrive in the coming days. Gentlemen, this is truly an historic moment—a transformative deal for all of you and for the American energy industry as a whole—and I want to congratulate each of you for bringing it together. Now, my friends, champagne!"

With that, everyone at the table rose en masse and began applauding. "Hear, hear, James! Fine job!" O'Bannon said. "Yes, hear, hear," everyone chimed in.

James let out a silent sigh. Shee-it, he thought. Just a few hours before, he was trapped on that goddamned train, surrounded by idiots, and with no way to get into Manhattan for the biggest damn deal of his life. And now here he was, king of the hill, happy and triumphant. Man, what a morning!

Shelley O'Bannon came up to him, all Texas smiles. "Well, James, you did it," he said. "I must say I was a little dubious this morning, when all hell seemed to be breaking loose, but you not only got lucky, you had the right answers. Very impressive, sir!"

Then Daniel Silver joined them. "May I echo what I just heard Shelley say? A fine job, Mr. Roth. Just as Shelley said, you had all the right answers today. And a little luck, too."

"Thank you, gentlemen," Roth said. Luck? He thought to himself. You guys have no idea what I had to do just to get off that frigging train and get in here today! But he said not a word about it. And with any luck, he would never have to tell anyone what he had to do to get his ass in here. "Now, how about some champagne?"

With one arm around each man, Roth led O'Bannon and Daniel Silver to the credenza where his staff had set out a tray with glasses and three bottles of Dom Perignon, 2004. With rising joy,

Roth deftly stripped off the black lead foil cap, untied the wire basket, and pushed out the cork quickly enough to produce that wonderful celebratory "Pop!" Then he began pouring.

"Gentlemen, enjoy!" he said. "You've earned it!"

And so have I, he thought with a silent chuckle. So have I!

## CHAPTER 10

RACHEL GLANCED AT THE CLOCK on the kitchen wall, just next to the refrigerator. She was standing with her hands pressed against the granite top of the kitchen island, feeling a little shaky, and trying to absorb what had happened, what was still happening. At least 30 minutes had passed since Caleb had left her, and nearly three hours since they had rushed off the train. It seemed like a full day had gone by, and yet it was still only morning. The TV announcer was still talking rapidly, and the sharpness of his voice gave her a jolt.

"...order has been ended. People are advised to stay in their homes for now," the announcer said. "The evacuation has been halted, and those who are already in the shelters, including children from schools in the Croton/Peekskill area, will be transported home during the day. We will have a live report from the Indian Point power generating facility shortly."

Rachel walked over to the window. In the distance she could see the Hudson swarming with police boats, and at least one fire-fighting tugboat, too. In the foreground off to the right, twin columns of smoke rose dramatically over the treetops into the sky, but to her eye they weren't as black, or as high, as they had been earlier. In her ear, she heard the news anchor speaking to a reporter, who apparently was somewhere below her, near the entrance to Indian Point. She suddenly realized their golden retriever was barking in his fenced-in enclosure; she went out and let him out, and then brought him inside.

'Roger, they are telling us there has been no radiation leak and very few injuries. Twenty minutes later, and there might have been several hundred more people working on the site. The day shift was just starting to arrive. That's the rescue workers' main focus now: searching the lot where one of the planes crashed and exploded. There is a huge crater there, and we can see cars on fire there, along with debris from the plane. But Roger, let's be clear about one thing. No Power Corporation or Westchester County emergency official has admitted this yet, but it is going to be a long time before Indian Point starts generating power to the New York area. If you have power, you are lucky this morning."

"Andy, is anyone warning of further attacks?"

"No, Roger. The people here aren't saying much of anything beyond what they can see."

"Okay, Andy, we're going to cut to the federal building in New York City. The FBI and the Department of Homeland Security are about to start a briefing there. We'll be back to you soon."

How odd it all was, Rachel thought. Less than an hour ago she had been imagining outcomes that obliterated even the simplest outlines of her daily life. She had been ready to pull a stranger to her and seduce him, fulfilling a train platform fantasy she had had for many years. At that moment, being wrapped in a strong man's arms seemed so right, so very right. And she had basically told him that to his face. And even now she could feel the back of his hand against her neck, and the way his touch had pulsed down through her entire body.

Adultery was not an alien thought to her. In her real estate rounds, she couldn't count the number of times male clients had come on to her in apartments where they were alone together. But she had never given in to those temptations. From the time she was old enough to know her beauty unsettled men, and what sex was, she had learned a Tai Chi-like behavior that absorbed their sexual energy and turned it into something else, something less explosive. And, frankly, by the time she was out of college, she had been propositioned, hit on, flirted with, and seduced so many times that she believed she had seen it all. By the time she was in her mid-20s, she knew instinctively, down deep, that she could have any man she wanted. That conviction freed her, it gave her license to be friendly and open to a degree that most women never dared to even dream about. Of course, for some men, her open-ness and self-confidence made her even more alluring—but she had learned how to handle that kind of attention as well.

She shivered, a head to toe tremble that left her shaking. Was it fear? Guilt? Was it relief after a couple of hours of constant adrena-line rush? Or had the adrenaline stripped away her filters so com-pletely that her desire for Caleb had overwhelmed her? Maybe it was just that it had been years since she felt anything that strongly with Daniel.

But after Caleb abruptly walked out, she had nothing but ques-tions. Who was that man who attacked her on the train? Who was Caleb Drake? Was she really ready to risk everything for him? Her kids would never understand. They would blame her; after all, she'd be the one leaving, and they would be right in asking, "Why did you make it seem like everything was all right all those years?" She knew she would not have an answer.

Now what? Rachel didn't know where to turn next. Calling Daniel seemed out of the question; she knew he was headed for the closing of a major deal, so there was no reason to try to call him even though it seemed impossible that any business might get done today. She realized she needed to stay where she was, to be there for her kids. But she couldn't move. She felt empty.

Without any idea how to reach Caleb, or what else to do, she decided to call her office. There was nowhere else to turn. Her car was at the station. Daniel's car was in the garage, but she didn't know where the keys were. The office seemed like a good idea. She dialed her private line, and immediately Yvonne picked up.

"Ms. Silver's line. May I help you?

"Yvonne, it's Rachel."

"Oh my gawd, are you all right? The TV makes it look like the bombing was right in your frigging backyard. Oh, I'm sorry, ma'am. Where are you?"

"I'm home."

"No! Isn't that dangerous? You should get out of there!"

"There's a bus stop down the street, and I can see people still standing there. But CNN says the evacuation order is lifted. So, I'm just going to stay put."

"You must be scared to death! I'm scared to death for you!"

"Not really. Not anymore, anyway. It's been a long day, but I'm sure everything will be okay. Just tell anyone who calls that I'll be in touch to reschedule or whatever. Is anyone there?"

"Yes, William and Steve came in, and Barbara is already out on a call. A couple of out-of-towners called, apparently after the TV said everything was okay. They said they'd come all this way, and wanted to see something today."

"That can't be all bad. Oh well, I'll be in tomorrow."

"Can I transfer calls to your cell, ma'am?"

"Cells aren't working out here yet, Yvonne, at least they weren't 15 minutes ago, but sure, you can try."

Rachel hung up. Hearing Yvonne's voice had been calming, a welcome reminder that some semblance of ordinary life was going on just a few miles away. She was still feeling shaky, and a bit disoriented too, but now she knew her life was not about to end, no matter what had happened up the road at Indian Point.

## CHAPTER 11

T HE CHAMPAGNE WAS ALL GONE now, but James was still staring out the windows of the company's top floor boardroom, the taste of victory still fresh in his mouth.

The building was located at the corner of Pearl and Broad streets, in the Financial District of Lower Manhattan, and from high up Roth could look west toward the Hudson and the Staten Island ferry terminal, and if he craned his neck a little and looked north, he could see the sleek sides of New York's fabled Freedom Tower. It was an exhilarating place to be, there in the nexus of Wall Street power, and Roth was savoring the moment, feeling the rush of success from closing his historic deal between Brightline and Secor.

"That was some performance," Daniel Silver said, suddenly intruding on the moment.

"Sorry to disturb you," Silver added, hoping the ruse to get back inside the boardroom wasn't too obvious. "I forgot a folder. Too much champagne! There it is, on the table. I need it to complete our documentation."

"Sure, sure, go ahead," Roth said, his voice a little icy.

"Congratulations again," Silver said. "That wasn't the easiest sell in the world for those white shoe guys from Texas. And to be honest, I had some early doubts. But you answered all of them, and quite masterfully, too."

"Well, thanks. But it didn't take all that much. Everyone in the room knew it was the right deal at the right time. We got a little lucky too, not being affected by that damned terror attack."

"Very true," Daniel Silver said. "Now I have to figure out if my family was just as lucky. I've been worried sick all morning."

Now Roth turned and looked at him more carefully. "Why, Daniel? Do you live up that way?"

"Yes, only three miles from Indian Point, in Crotonville."

"Wow, me too. We're in Briarcliff, a bit further away. Still, this damn well could have been Chernobyl all over again."

"My fear exactly," Daniel Silver said. Then he approached Roth and put his hand on his shoulder. "James, you know I would appreciate the opportunity to get to know you better. Maybe we can have dinner sometime at my house. Nothing fancy, just a casual weekend dinner…"

Before he could reply, James felt his cell phone buzzing in his pocket. "Excuse me, must be my wife. Sure, Daniel, leave your info with my secretary. I'll get back to you once all this settles down."

Daniel, looking even more rumpled now, nodded his assent, picked up his folder, and left the boardroom. Then James put the phone to his ear, knowing that his wife would be chomping at the bit, eager to hear what happened with the deal.

"So?" she said.

James, still on his high, decided to be a little playful. "So what, darling? How's your morning going?"

"Funny, Roth. I'm fine. Everybody up here is fine, as if you didn't know. So what the hell happened with your precious deal?"

"Deal? What deal, darling?" He was intent on making her squirm a little. "What, you haven't talked to your father?"

"Stop screwing with me, Roth. What the hell happened?"

"Done, of course. Signed, sealed, delivered, and toasted with some very fine champagne." Now he paused for effect: "Both sides said I was a fucking genius, not that you would ever agree."

"Damn," Sheri said, her voice trembling with emotion. "You actually pulled it off. Well, bravo! You are a fucking genius!"

"Sorry, Sheri, I didn't hear that. What did you say?"

"Kiss off, Roth. So how did you convince them? Did you have to make any changes to sweeten the deal for either side?"

"Nope. I got really fucking lucky. I'll give you the blow-by-blow when I get home. But let's just say I called O'Bannon's bluff by saying we'd open the offer window again if they wanted a delay."

"Whoa, ballsy, Roth. Could have backfired."

"Could have. Didn't," he said, smirking even though no one could see him.

"You didn't tell me how you got there. Dad said he didn't know."

"So, you did talk to him, you sneaky bitch."

"Hah, I wanted to hear it out of your mouth, genius."

"Never mind. It doesn't matter how I got here," he said. "It's ancient history now."

"Well, you made history today. They'll be talking about this deal until the day you die," Sheri said. "When are you coming home?"

"I don't know. Too much still to do. But keep the champagne cold; we'll be celebrating tonight," Roth said. Then he hung up, now feeling even more like a master of the universe.

## CHAPTER 12

CHARLIE WAS STILL AT THE hospital. He had signed a few documents to release his dad's body to a funeral home in Peekskill, and then explained to the nursing staff that he had to get back to the Metro-North train stopped on the tracks below the hospital. The nurses quickly arranged for the same social worker who had helped him find his mom to take Rose back home, and she promised Charlie she would stay with her until he got home later in the day.

As Charlie watched the two women drive off, his cell phone started to vibrate. He hit the answer button.

"Charlie! Charlie!" Bobby the motorman was calling from the train, and he was almost shouting.

"Yeah, Bobby. Bobby, I'm comin'."

"You'd better hurry. I'm sitting here talking to dispatch, and I'm pretty sure we're about to get a green signal to move. I'll have to start rolling if I get it. You know that. And I'm keeping Estelle in the dark. Can't do that if you're not here on the train."

Charlie just ran out the emergency room door, and began running across the parking lot. A big black man in a dark leather coat with a cop's badge hanging from his outside pocket was walking toward him.

"Hey, buddy, you okay? What are you running from? Slow down and talk to me," the cop said.

"I'm sorry, officer. I have to get back down to the tracks to my Metro-North train."

"Why were you up here at the hospital? Was someone hurt on the train?" the detective asked.

"No, nothing like that. But why are you stoppin' me?" Charlie said, starting to get agitated. "Can't you see I'm in a hurry?"

"Look, I'm Arnette Williams of White Plains police. I'm check-ing on everything out of the usual today, and you running across a parking lot like a scared deer makes me wonder what the heck you're doing. So tell me: what's going on?"

"Officer, nothing. Really. Well, my dad, my dad. He had a heart attack and I can't find his… That's why I left the train to come find him, and now, I have to, I have to…" Charlie said, again speak-ing rapidly and starting to stutter. "Really, really, officer. I gotta get back to, get to the train, or it will leave without me."

Williams did a quick up and down survey of the conductor and decided that either he just wasn't very bright or he was just hy-per-anxious.

"You were about to say something," Williams said.

"Oh, nothing," Charlie said, starting to walk backward and ready to turn and break into a run.

"Wait! Here's my card," Williams said. "If you want to tell me something, just give me a call."

Williams watched Charlie jog across the parking lot, and dis-appear around the back of the building. The cop turned around, walked through the glass doors of the ER and headed inside. It was quiet, almost deathly so, and totally out of sync with what he'd been hearing all morning on the news.

Detective Williams stood for a second at the nurses' station, then a nurse in a blue V-neck cotton pullover, light blue drawstring pants and white nurse's shoes, approached him.

"You look ready for business," he smiled.

"Yeah, so do you," she said, nodding at the badge.

"Oh, I guess I could put that away. Seems we've all been expecting something that didn't happen. You got anything I need to know?"

"No, some old guy died of a heart attack out in the parking lot. Here to pick up his wife who was being discharged. You must have seen his son who just ran out of here."

"Couldn't miss him."

"Well, that's it. We were expecting a lot more, but it's been pretty quiet here. Peekskill police called and said the evacuation order is on hold. Any injuries are headed to Northern Westchester Hospital. Not here. We're standing down."

"Okay, but I may check back in a few days just to be sure. Chief wants to know about anyone or anything unusual that might be related to the attack."

"Sure, come back anytime."

+++

As CHARLIE REACHED the ridge looking down over the tracks, he saw Bobby leaning out of the motorman's window, waving frantically at him. Charlie slipped and fell twice going down the steep embankment, finally finding a route with enough bushes and branches to hold on to. Then he climbed into the open passenger door on the front car of the train. He had barely got his feet inside when the door lights flashed, the buzzer sounded, and the train started to move.

"Boy, are you lucky. I couldn't have waited another five seconds," Bobby said as Charlie entered the motorman's cabin.

"Bobby, I'm sorry I left," Charlie said.

"No problems, Charlie, nobody knows."

"Well, Estelle will figure it out, and she's never liked me."

"I'll talk to her, Charlie. I mean we have to be in this together. You know we're all going to get reprimanded for letting the passengers off the train, and if they find out you left your post, you could get suspended or maybe even lose your job."

"I know, Bobby. I know," he said. "You know I can't get another hit on my record. You gotta help me. And, Bobby, my dad died up there in the hospital."

"Charlie, Charlie. I'm so sorry. Jesus. Don't worry, I'll make sure you stay right with the railroad. I know you got screwed last time. This is different. And we're in it together."

A few minutes later, the train rolled into the next station in Philipse Manor, and the red lights came on again down the tracks. Bobby started talking to Dispatch. The dispatcher wanted a status report on the train's passengers, and Bobby had to tell him that only a handful remained on the train. He explained how one passenger had led a revolt and broken open the doors, and those who could leave, did. He said the only people left were some older men and women who didn't want to climb off the train, or climb the steep banks around the tracks. The dispatcher told the motorman to put everything in his report when they got to Grand Central.

"Just sit tight, you'll be moving in five minutes," the dispatcher said.

"So Charlie, your dad died? How?" Bobby asked.

"Gee, Bobby, it's terrible, just terrible. He had a heart attack in the parking lot. Someone found him out there just lyin' there on the ground. I don't know what happened. No one does. His car is gone, too. It's like somebody stole it. But who knows? He, he…"

Charlie started sobbing again at the thought of his dad dying there outside the hospital. "I tried to tell the cop, but I didn't have time. Had to get back here."

"The cop?"

"Yeah, some officer was at the hospital. I'll call him sometime. But I don't know what to do. I, I, I, I don't know what to do."

"That's okay, man, I understand."

"Oh, no you don't. My whole life," Charlie could barely get out the words. "He and my mom, that was just about my whole life. There's this job. But that's it. Now he's gone. And my mom, who knows, she's not well. And I could lose this job, too. Then I'd have nothing."

"No sweat, Charlie. No one's gonna make a big deal about this. Let's just get our stories straight. We tried to stop the passengers from getting off the train, but some guy broke the glass and got off the train. Once he was gone, people just followed him."

"That's the way it was. Hey, I know who broke the glass, too. It was that same guy in the suit who got in the fight over that woman's phone."

"Put that in your report, Charlie. You may need that information. And it might just help. He was a big guy, right? And, maybe that woman will vouch for you."

"Oh, right! And I couldn't have stopped him if I wanted to. She'd know. She was pretty, too. I did get her phone number."

"Hope he got where he needed to go."

"Yeah, he probably did."

## CHAPTER 13

C ALEB UNLOCKED THE FRONT DOOR of his house. Silence. It was never quiet when he stepped over the threshold; two kids in their late teens and a couple of friends running around the den, a dog that barked in delight at his arrival, Brenda's light-hearted banter followed by a hug and kiss, plus a TV turned on somewhere, all filling the house with a low-level din. But none of that greeted him now.

He walked into the kitchen where the clock on the stove was still dark. Brenda clearly had not had time to clean up after break-fast: his coffee mug and the kids' dishes were still on the table by the window. He sat down, and his eyes wandered around the room, everything at once so familiar, but now suddenly so alien as well.

The eerie quiet laid bare the outline of his life: the loss of in-timacy in his marriage, his lack of connection with his kids, the emotional emptiness inside the four walls, leaving not much more for him than a bedroom and a place to hang out on weekends. For awhile now, his suburban life had seemed more and more of a trap, and this morning, in the wake of the attack, instead of feeling protected sitting there in his own kitchen, he felt exposed. But he knew where that feeling of vulnerability came from; it was like a familiar touch on his arm, his nagging PTSD coming out of hiding, just like had happened on 9/11.

Suddenly, the electricity came back on. Caleb heard the hum

of the refrigerator starting up, and soon the house was ablaze with light, and it was filled, too, with the distant echoes of a life that had been in full-swing but had abruptly stopped. The TV, though, was blaring. Brenda must have been so freaked out by the sirens that she dashed out without thinking or turning off anything.

The TV filled in the silence. "Let me recap what we've been reporting this morning, Wolf. It's been nearly four hours since the attack, and we know two jets crashed into the facility. One missed, or bounced off one of the domes. One apparently partially damaged the containment structure on Dome 1, but that isn't supposed to be possible. The police here are speculating that the plane was loaded with explosives, like a guided missile. It may be some time before we know the facts."

Caleb left the TV turned on, and started checking out the house, room to room, the drone of the talking heads masking any other noise. He paused at the bar in the living room. Did he want a drink? God, he wanted one badly, but not yet. He went upstairs and stood for a moment at the door to his son Caleb Jr.'s bedroom, looking at the posters of the now retired Derek Jeter and Mariano Rivera, but drawing a blank on the last time they'd been to a game together. Abby's door was closed, but he opened it anyway, just to be sure the lights were out; they were, but he was a bit taken aback by the nearly life-size posters of Rihanna and Beyoncé and the clothes scattered all over the floor. Where had his little girl gone?

As Caleb walked into the master bedroom he was startled by the strong aroma of Brenda's perfume, like she had just been there. He'd been leaving earlier and earlier to work and for what seemed like years now he hadn't been with her as she was getting ready for her day. Brushing her long brunette hair, putting on a touch of makeup, slipping a dress over her shapely, athletic body. Where had those intimate moments gone? Now, though, her perfume and their rumpled bed became cherished reminders of their life together and it jarred him, partly because it reminded him of what was now missing in their lives together, partly because suddenly he was desperate to find out where she was, and because he felt guilty about what had just happened with Rachel.

Caleb pulled his cell phone out, and immediately saw there was service again. He dialed Brenda's number, and the first four times it switched to the overwhelmingly annoying, "All lines are busy; please try your call later" message. But on his fifth try, the call finally went through and Brenda picked right up.

"Caleb, Caleb, is that you? Oh my god, are you okay? Where are you?" Caleb could hear and feel the panic in her voice.

"Brenda, calm down. Yes, I'm fine. I'm back home."

"You're home. When I called you, you were on the train. Did you come back home looking for me?" she said.

"Yes, that was our plan, remember?" Then he quickly added, "But you did the right thing by getting out quickly."

Brenda was deeply upset and Caleb could feel it through the phone line. "It's okay, sweetie," he said. "I came back because I wanted to be sure everything was okay. I knew you'd left in a hurry and just wanted to check it out, in case we were going to be gone for a long time. Now I'm here."

"Thank you for doing that, Caleb. And did you hear?"

"What?"

"The radio said the evacuation order has been lifted."

"Yes, I just heard that on the TV, too. The electricity just came on here at home. So I'm just going to sit tight. Where are you?"

"Well, I remember you said head north, so I'm coming up to Poughkeepsie. I'm about an hour from the house. I guess I'll turn around and come home."

"I think that would be a good idea. I won't be going in today. I'll just wait for you here. We can try to get my car later. And I need to return a car back to Phelps... It's a long story."

"I can't wait to see you, Caleb."

"Same, Brenda. Come home."

The line went dead. He sat down on the edge of their king-size bed. He looked straight into the mirror on Brenda's dresser, where a family photo was stuck in the frame. Despite the unacknowledged atrophy in their relationship, Caleb couldn't imagine a life without her. But at the same time, he could still feel Rachel's embrace and their kiss, and the longing that he felt just thinking about what happened not more than two hours ago. He tried to sort out the two possible futures staring him in the face: his old, familiar marriage or a dangerous affair with a woman he barely knew.

He knew the answer: decisions made during a crisis or in the heat of the moment are almost never good. And whatever change they caused, those changes were rarely permanent. Time to calm down, he said to himself. Time to keep Rachel at arm's length. Give himself some time and space. If he could.

Caleb stared at the keyboard of his cell phone, the home phone of the Silvers already punched in and ready to be dialed. He hesitated. What was he going to say?

He was taken aback at the attraction he was feeling toward this woman, this stranger, someone he had not even known half a day. If anything, the strength of those feelings scared him even more, made him feel like he needed to put some distance between them, at least for a while. He hit the call button.

"Rachel?"

Silence.

"Rachel?"

"How did you get my number?"

"You remember phone books? Well, I still have one. Silver. Crotonville. Orchard Ridge. Seemed a safe bet that this might be your home phone. I was just there, remember?" Caleb chided.

She laughed. "Oh yeah, right. You were. Was that you with your lips on mine?"

"Rachel, stop."

Silence again. She was remembering the kiss. That was the easy part.

"I had to talk with you," Caleb said. "I kinda walked out on you."

"Yeah, you kinda did. It's a wonder my knees didn't buckle."

"Well, I just wanted to say I'm sorry. Well, not entirely, but I wanted to explain."

"I'm listening."

He paused. He did want to explain. But was this the right time or place? He had just reached out to his wife, and the impulse to call Rachel had been, as much as anything, a desire to immediately stop anything between them, and maybe help quiet some of his ambivalence about Brenda.

"Remember in the car, you asked if I was going to reveal my deepest, darkest secrets, like the guy on the plane?"

"Well, his weren't exactly deep, dark secrets," Rachel replied. "Are yours?"

"No, that's not what I mean." He stopped again. He knew he had to explain now. So he took a long, deep breath.

"Listen, Rachel, I can't really explain it, at least so it might make sense to you. It goes back to the morning I got on the plane to Vietnam, and as I began to walk up that metal stairway, everything suddenly turned white. The world around me just faded into a fog, and the air was shimmering, and it was impossible to breathe. My knees got weak, and I started hyperventilating."

"You must have been terrified," Rachel said.

"Well, I guess the gunnery sergeant had seen it before, because he said, without any rancor, 'Move along, solider. You'll be okay.' Walking through that door, I sensed that nothing would ever be the same again, that I was headed to a different place, a different time, and that if I came back from there, nothing would be as it had been. And you know what? I was right."

"And you felt that way about kissing me?"

"Yes, Rachel. I did."

"Well, we didn't do anything more," Rachel said. "So we were just two people helping each other through a crisis…"

"I guess," Caleb said.

"Still," Rachel said, "this much I know: I want to know more about you, Caleb Drake."

Caleb spent a long moment collecting himself and then said, "Listen, Rachel, all my life I've followed a certain set of rules. One of them is pretty simple: don't make rash decisions when the world is collapsing around you. I know it hasn't today—thank heaven!—but at times like these there is an instinct to grab the closest living thing and hold it close. But too often you end up embarrassed, or out of control, or totally misinterpreting what's happening. That's why I'm calling. I don't want any confusion about the future."

"What do you feel now, Caleb?"

"Oh, not fair. Are you still trying to make me feel foolish?"

"No, not at all. I know what I'm feeling."

"Rachel, what do you want?" There was silence on the line.

"I don't know. But what's to stop us from finding out, from exploring that a little bit?"

"What's stopping me, Rachel, is exactly what I said. I don't trust those feelings right now. I'm scared."

"Scared? So where does that leave us?"

"That's it. For now. Maybe forever. That's why I tracked you down and made the call. I wanted you to know you wouldn't be hearing from me for a while. At least until things settle down. I am 100 percent convinced that this morning is not the time or place to do anything other than what we've done…help each other get through this. Let's let it be."

"Caleb, I know you're right. Of course, I do. But…"

"But?"

"Oh, this isn't the time. Promise me one thing, Caleb."

"What?"

"That there will be a time. A time when we can talk about this morning. Just you and me. Maybe over a glass of wine somewhere, in the city. Away from this, away from our regular lives. Maybe not this week, or next. But soon."

He breathed a silent sigh of relief. Good, push it off into the future. Delay. Avoid. That was comfortable. And a relief.

"Okay. But no promises. I'll be back in touch. I've got to sort out the things going on in my head."

# PART II

## CHAPTER 14

JAMES PICKED UP THE FRONT section of the suburban Journal News newspaper. He had been lounging all morning in the back sunroom off the kitchen and the den, checking his weekend sports bets, and looking for ways to make up his losses. The fire in the den had warmed the room, holding off the chill from the snowy winter landscape in his back yard. And then he saw it.

"Oh my god," he said.

In a picture above the fold, the conductor from that Metro-North train the morning of the terror attack on Indian Point was standing next to an elderly woman, identified as his mother in the caption. The first paragraph wove a story about how they too had been victims on 10/10 when Sean Murray had died at Phelps Memorial Hospital from a heart attack, and mysteriously, his car had disappeared.

"What's wrong?" said Sheri, who had just walked into the sunroom.

"Nothing."

The words "fatal heart attack" jumped off the page as he scanned the rest of the story. James' pulse quickened. He searched for clues about whether or not the car had ever been found and whether or not there were any leads about exactly what had happened to the older man. The story said the conductor had been suspended from his job for three months because he had left his post during an emergency. James reached for his coffee mug, his hand shaking.

A hundred times, maybe a thousand, he had been tempted to call the hospital, or search the local newspapers for death notices, looking for anything that might have told him what had happened after he had left that parking lot, with the sight in the rearview mirror of the man slumping to the ground. But he never had, deciding that knowing would be far worse than not knowing, and better to put the entire morning's bad moments behind him. And he had.

His only consolation now was that the story made it clear that the car had never been found. All he had to do was stick to his story—he got a ride from a stranger and was at his desk by 9 a.m. There was no way to trace anything back to him. No need to imagine the worst. He didn't have to panic.

"James?"

James felt the hand on his shoulder. He nearly jumped out of his chair.

"Damn, Sheri, you scared the shit out of me!"

"I told you to watch your language, James. The kids are in the den watching cartoons," Sheri said. "What's wrong? You look stricken."

She looked over his shoulder at the Journal News story. "Oh that poor man. Channel 12 did a story a couple days ago, as a follow up to 10/10, you know, people who were affected by it. He seems a little slow, or something. He's a Metro-North conductor, but I'd never seen him."

"I remember him. He was on my train on 10/10."

"Really?"

"Yeah."

"You've never told me much about that morning, you know."

"You never asked."

"That's not true," she said. "I asked, and you basically told me to mind my own business, or something along those lines, so I never brought it up again."

"It's nothing. Nothing. It was just a disturbing morning."

"I always wondered how you made it to work."

"I told you: I got a ride."

"Uhhh, you told me you borrowed a car."

"No, you must have misheard me. I got a ride from some guy who I ran into in the parking lot, then he took me to the Upper East Side where I took a cab to work. That's all."

"Well, that's more than you told me before."

"Like I said, never mind. I don't want to talk about it."

"Okaaaaay. Touchy touchy!"

"Look, there's nothing to say. Let's leave it at that."

"Fine, whatever. Remember we're heading into the city to have lunch with Dad, today."

"How could I forget? We go nearly every Sunday," James said, a touch of resignation in his voice.

He was dreading the lunch, more so than usual. He was reaching the final stages of putting together investors for his own hedge fund, and leaving Goldfarb & Case. Sheri deeply disapproved of the move, but up to now she hadn't interfered. But he knew after nearly a month of soliciting funds for the company to add to his own war chest, there was a strong likelihood that Irv Goldfarb had caught wind of his plans.

"Do I need to be ready for you to tell Dad your news today?" Sheri asked. "I want to be prepared for that scene. If you hadn't sworn me to secrecy, I would have told him already."

"Whose side are you on? I need to have the whole plan in place before I tell him."

"I get that, James. But you won't listen to me. I told you I'm sure he would have been happy to put money behind your plans, but only if you'd told him about them up front."

"I don't want his money."

"You still haven't heard me. You're in for a hard ride out there. He has a lot of friends. But like you said, I am not about to interfere in your business."

James jumped out of the chair and put his face six inches away from Sheri's.

"That's enough. Don't ever fuck with me! This is for us! For me. I've worked my whole life to make other people rich. I'm fucking done with that, do you understand? DO YOU UNDERSTAND?"

At first, Sheri cowered, but then she braced her shoulders and stood ramrod straight, her face still within an open palm of her husband's face. Her voice was a flat monotone. "Don't threaten me, James. Don't ever threaten me. I have told you: I am in this with you. But don't ignore my counsel. I know my father better than you do. And if you think he's going to smile, shake your hand and wish you good luck, you are out of your fucking mind. To him, it will be war. First, you take his daughter, and now you're going after his business."

"It's not his business. He's stuck in a 1970s mindset about doing stupid deals with a bunch of old farts from Yale and Harvard. And I'm SICK of it!"

"Honey, honey, you don't understand," she said, holding her ground. "You were taken into the fold—against my advice again, I might add—when you went to work there. He made you a partner, in everything but a name on the door. When I left to raise your kids, and his grandkids, you became the heir apparent. You're not doing some prodigal son thing by leaving; there will be no going back. He will take it as the ultimate betrayal, a blood thing. Hell, I'll be lucky if he doesn't disown me."

James lurched back from her. He felt like striking out at anything or everything within his reach, even Sheri. He clenched his fists, the blood throbbing in his neck, and his teeth clamped tight.

They both heard the kids, Jimmy Jr. and Elizabeth, at the same time, a chorus of "Hey, you guys, what are you doing?"

James took a deep breath, trying to figure out why he had flown off the handle. He knew all too well; the fear had been bottled up inside him since he had seen that elderly gentleman—now he knew his name, Sean Murray—slumping to the ground in the rear view mirror. The certainty of what had happened was rapidly eroding his inner serenity, that place where he managed to almost always remain calm and in control. Was it fear or guilt, or both? He had not been able to put his finger on what had been eating at him for months. Now he knew what it was.

Sheri recoiled at the stranger now standing in front of her. She had seen James angry before, but not like this. The panic in his eyes startled her and put her on edge. She saw the fear but there was something else, too, something that she didn't recognize, and it scared her.

"Kids, kids. It's okay. Daddy just flew off the handle. He's already better. Go back to your TV show," she said, then turned to him with a lower voice. "James, James. What's going on? I, I..."

He waved her off, trying to compose himself.

"Don't worry about me, Sheri. I've been keeping things pretty bottled up these last few months—it's been a whirlwind. The new fund. The spotlight on me after the Secor/Brightline deal. And, I guess, the aftermath of 10/10. That picture of the conductor in the paper brought it all up. Somewhere in all that, you touched a nerve by bringing up Irv and my plans.

"And I do hear you about your father. He and I will have a man-to-man talk; going out on my own is something I have to do, something I've wanted my entire life. You know that about me."

Sheri didn't respond immediately. She was watching him intently, every gesture of his hands, every inflection in his voice, and she knew he was back in control.

"Aren't you going to say something?" James asked.

"I don't know. You scared me, James. For the first time. Ever. I don't know what to say."

"Tell me you love me," he said.

"That, you know," Sheri said. "Let's just leave it there for now. I've told you what I think about your plans, both the good and the bad possibilities. So don't be surprised at my father's reaction."

Then Sheri turned and walked out of the room.

"Shit," he muttered under his breath.

## CHAPTER 15

C ALEB DROVE DOWN THE RAMP at the Croton-Harmon train station. He had left home early to get his favorite parking space,
near the end of the commuter parking lot but still a quick walk to
the stairs at the far end of the train platform. As he pulled into his
spot, he looked out over the tall grasses in the river marsh on the
edge of the parking lot.

A light rapping on the rolled-up window of his Audi startled
him. Rachel stood by the car door. She smiled, a thin, nervous, almost apologetic smile. She seemed different, her hair pulled back
in a ponytail, less make-up on her face, and despite the cold, her
open fur jacket exposing a pearl white V and an emerald pendant
necklace that hung down to her cleavage. Suddenly, Caleb's heart
started pounding.

Rachel motioned to roll down the window. He fumbled for the
button, then the window slid down with a soft scrape.

"Sorry, sorry, I wasn't thinking. I mean, I was," he said.

"Caleb, relax. My heart's pounding, too. But I decided I couldn't
wait for you to call. I had to see you. Are you going to invite me in?"

"Is that a good idea?" he said.

"Me standing here isn't a good idea."

"Of course. Of course," he said. "Come around; the door's open."

Rachel walked around the front of the car, never taking her
eyes off him. She opened the door and sat down, swinging her legs

in, and flashing her knees and thighs at him as she did.

"Thanks," she said. "I was getting cold out there. I've been here for almost an hour."

"You were waiting for me?"

"Yes. About a week ago, I saw you leave home, and when you didn't show up in Ossining, I figured you had to be here. So I came early, parked near the entrance, and *voilà*, here I am."

"I can see why you're cold," Caleb said.

"I wondered if you'd notice."

"Jesus, Rachel. What do you think? That I've forgotten?"

"Well, Mister Drake, most women would have thought that not only had you forgotten, but you didn't care." She reached out and touched his cheek. "But I can see that's not true. You're blushing."

"Yes, I'm blushing. For a lot of reasons. I've been trying to avoid this moment for the last four months," he said. "I guess that's pretty funny, isn't it? One kiss, and I start acting like a 12-year-old. Why didn't you just call?"

"Well, maybe a 15-year-old," she laughed. "Caleb, you said you would call, and I was tempted to call you. But maybe I'm just old-fashioned. Or maybe I didn't want your wife picking up the phone. I just wanted to see you. Maybe just for a cup of coffee."

"How long do you think that would last?" he asked.

Rachel laughed again. "Well," she said, "at least I know now we're on the same page about what might happen. Or what I want to happen."

"And this conversation is heading right where I imagined it would all these months," he said, "I guess that's what stopped me from calling."

"Caleb, why not call me? Nothing happened that we have to be embarrassed about, at least nothing big. You kissed me. Then you walked out. What's the big deal?"

"Is that all that happens in your fantasies? A kiss?" Caleb asked.

She tilted her head to look at him, and then turned to gaze out into the parking lot, looking out into the distance.

"Well, I'd be lying if I said all I wanted to do was go to bed with you," Rachel said. "During that morning four months ago, I watched you. The way you dealt with the situation excited me. Today, listening to you struggle with your feelings, I know that I want more. To know more. But so what? Isn't that what people do? They meet. They get to know each other. They make love."

"In that order usually," Caleb said. "Get those out of order, and everything gets out of whack. I mean, here we are, having spent what, 45 minutes, at most a couple of hours together, and we're talking about having an affair. Doesn't that give you any second thoughts?"

"Of course," Rachel said. "But I can't get you out of my head. And, honestly, I don't know what your problem is. We're adults. No, I haven't had affairs, not since I got married, but I'm tired of my life at home, tired of my husband. I need something new. Don't you?"

"Jesus, Rachel, you're not making this any easier, are you?"

"No, I'm not," she said, "And I don't really care. I just realized something: I don't believe you."

She leaned across the console, and kissed him hard on the mouth, running her hands across his chest and arm, and grabbing his hand tightly. For a second he thought about pulling away, but in an instant his hand was running up her thigh and around her bottom, as he returned her kiss. Hard. In another instant his hand was sliding between her legs, fondling her and feeling her warmth. With that, Rachel reached down and found his erection.

She pulled away from him just enough to stop the kiss and let out a moan, "Caleb, Caleb, please…"

But he stopped. Caleb gently removed his hand and softly removed hers. "That's just what I imagined would happen, and what I was afraid would happen. And, yes, maybe what I wanted to happen. But not here, Rachel."

"Oh god, why not?"

"In a car, like two teenagers? In a commuter parking lot?"

"I'm not thinking like a teenager, Caleb. I want you. And as a woman, I know what that feels like."

"Rachel, stop. Just for a second. Think. Look where we are."

"Daniel already left for work. The kids' bus comes in 10 minutes. We could wait and then go to my house. You remember being there, don't you?"

Caleb nodded. "I have thought about it a thousand times."

"Only a thousand?" she smiled again, letting her breathing slow down.

But then she turned again and looked Caleb in the eye. "Stop fooling yourself. You've been hiding from me for months. What have you been doing? Thinking about running away. I bet you've been thinking about divorcing your wife, selling your business, and moving. Haven't you?"

He didn't reply immediately. He could feel the bemused look, the little curl of his upper lip, crossing his face, but what he was really thinking amounted to "How do you know what I've been thinking?" Worse, he knew she was right, and even if she were only half-right, that he wasn't just running from her but from the essential emptiness in his life, it was disconcerting to have someone so clearly read his thoughts.

"You guessed it, but it's not all about you," Caleb said. "I wanted to make real changes in my life after 9/11, and I didn't. And that morning in October on the train was another wakeup call for me. So, yeah, I'm struggling. Because here it is four months later and I'm still doing the same old shit."

"We could take care of that right now," she said.

"Damn it, Rachel!"

"Okay, okay," she said. "But look, I've thought about what I was going to say to you for months now. There's no going back. I can't forget what I felt. And what I'm feeling has nothing to do with that morning, other than that's when we met."

"Look, okay. Okay," Caleb said. "Let's make a pact. Let's have dinner in the city next week. Today's Monday," he said, pulling out his iPhone calendar. "No, let's do it this Thursday."

"I can't this Thursday. Daniel has set up some dinner at the house with a business acquaintance from the city on Saturday night," Sheri said. "Have you heard of a man named James Roth?"

"Yeah, I have. He's a big M&A guy on Wall Street. Lots of stories about how he closed a deal on 10/10. Guess he's becoming a legend," Caleb said.

"That's him. Daniel represented one of the firms in that deal. One of the reasons I couldn't reach him that day," she said. "And his wife is Sheri Goldfarb. Her dad owns Goldfarb & Case where Roth works. She is New York society."

"I've heard she's a stunner," Caleb said.

"That's what everyone says. I think I've worked with some of her friends. I know she'll be looking fabulous. So, I have to take extra care for it. Daniel, who never invites anyone to dinner, says it's really important to him. Didn't really tell me why. But I have to get ready for it. So I can't do it this week."

"Okay, how about next Tuesday?" he said.

"Fine. You pick."

"I'll pick. And, I'm going to say that I'm having dinner with a real estate agent who is presenting some ideas about a new office for my firm."

"Whatever," Rachel said, leaning over and literally thrusting her tongue into Caleb's mouth. "I guess you'll pick a place where I can't do that. I gotta go. I can't stand this. If I stay here another 10 seconds, it won't matter where we meet next week." She smiled, opened the door, and then stopped.

"I almost forgot to tell you something. You remember that twerpy little train conductor? He's been calling me, at least three or four times that I know of, asking if I can help him out. I guess he got suspended for a few months. Did you read about it yesterday in the paper? You should check it out. He has a story. I've been ignoring his messages, but they are starting to get creepy. I've had some hang-up calls too, often about the same time he had called on other nights. I can't believe I gave him my phone number. Somehow he found my home number, too. Thank god, I haven't seen him on the train."

Then, with a glance over her shoulder, and as quickly as she'd been there, she was gone.

Caleb sat for a long time in silence. He had missed his usual train, but in truth he didn't give a damn. He couldn't articulate it, but someplace in his gut he knew he had reached a crossroads, some crucial new moment in his life. So he just sat there, drinking in the rich smells of Rachel's perfume. Maybe she was right. Maybe she could shake him out of his apathy, this feeling that he was sleepwalking through his life. If only he knew what he really wanted, what was missing.

## CHAPTER 16

CHARLIE'S MOTHER SAT COMFORTABLY IN his dad's old dark green Barcalounger, her feet up on the fold-out foot stool, staring, maybe without hearing, at Oprah and her guests, some sprightly young women with Teach America t-shirts talking about their jobs in inner city schools. Since it was one of his mid-week days off, Charlie was working down a list of chores, mostly small household repairs—changing light bulbs, tightening a couple of screws on some door hinges, cleaning out behind the refrigerator and testing the fire alarms in the house.

The Murray home was on a steep street lined with two-story, clapboard houses, an old white working class neighborhood in Peekskill that now was half African-American families. Many of the Murrays' old friends had retired and moved to Florida or somewhere in upstate New York, leaving the row of porches, some with hanging plants, some now looking abandoned, virtually empty most nights, even in the summer. During his suspension, Charlie had caught up with most of the big things needed in an old house like this, but there were always little chores that kept popping up. They were all things that his dad used to do, never letting anything that he noticed go for more than a day or two, and always reminding Charlie that a chore left undone was the same as not mending a broken button on your shirt.

'Mom, you okay?" he asked between two minor tasks.

She turned her head toward him, and smiled, a small, not very convincing smile.

"Charlie," she said, "you have asked me that question every 15 minutes all day long. Are you bored?"

"No, Ma," Charlie said. "I guess I'm just worried about you. You haven't been out in a few days. Aren't your friends getting together for bridge today?"

"Oh, Charlie. I haven't been goin' for a while. Just don't feel like it. You know how it is. Not much to look forward to these days."

"But those ladies love you. They always have."

"Charlie, you wouldn't understand. They kinda stopped calling awhile back. I know why. They got tired of me talking about Sean all the time, and wondering what had happened to him. No one wants to hear me patter on and on about that. I can't help it though."

"Mom, you gotta let it go. I know it's hard. We did all we could. It's been four days since that article in the newspaper. Bobby's the one who talked me into it. He's real smart and he said if anyone reads it, and saw or knew anything, they might call. But we haven't heard anything. It was kinda our last shot."

"Charlie, I know that. I knew that before you ever talked with the reporter. But I just know something bad happened to Sean. I know it. You know it."

'Mom, we're never gonna know. Just like we're never gonna know who those guys were that flew the planes into the nuclear power plant." Charlie pronounced it "nukular."

"Mom, I've had to let some things go, too. After that mess at work, the hearings, the counseling, and then the suspension. I thought I was going to lose one of the other things that I love. You know I do. It was my dream growing up to work on the railroad,"

Charlie said.

"I know, dear," Rose said. "And I felt terrible for you. By helping me, you nearly lost your job."

"Sure, Mom. I know," Charlie said. "I'm not sure they ever would have fired me for what I did that day. But there are rules, and I broke the rules."

"Well, I'm glad it's over. And you're right. I know that I need to move on. But I just don't know how," Rose said.

Charlie couldn't help but remember the way his mom and dad used to be, eating dinner every night together, with him too, when he didn't have a night shift. And he remembered arguing with his dad over the Yankees and the Mets, which his father loved, probably as a substitute for the old Brooklyn Dodgers and his hate for the Yankees. But that was all just a memory now.

Then the doorbell rang. A large black man, dressed in a brown leather jacket, jeans and running shoes, stood waiting on the porch. Charlie's suspension for leaving his post had ended three weeks before, so he doubted it was a Metro-North representative. But seeing a strange man on his porch set off his alarms.

"Can I help you?"

"Are you Charles Murray?"

"Yeah, but who are you?" He held tightly on the door handle.

"My name's Arnette Williams. I'm a detective from the West-chester County Police," he said, holding up his badge and ID. "I read about your father this weekend in the Journal News, and I just wanted to ask you a few questions about that morning. It's my day off, but I have been thinking about that morning ever since it happened."

"Gee, Mr. Williams. Wait a minute. Wait a minute. I ran into you at the hospital that day. Remember? I had to get to my train,"

Charlie said, releasing his hold on the door handle.

"Call me Arnie. Yeah, I do remember. And since reading that story on Sunday, I've been kicking myself that I didn't follow up with you. But your story puzzled me. I had to find you."

"Ok, Arnie. Well, I'm glad you feel that you needed to find me. But my mom and I are just tryin' to, uh, you know, put that morning behind us."

As usual in such moments, Charlie started stuttering and tripping over his words. "It's been rough these last four months, you know, but we're about to put it behind us, put it behind us. You know what I mean?"

"I can only imagine. And the truth? I've been trying to forget about that morning, too. But then I saw the article, and it made me think it might help if I tracked you down. Close some of the gaps in my investigation of the attacks. There really hasn't been much to do. A couple of home break-ins while people were away from home that day. Some people who swear they saw the two terrorists casing Indian Point. Stuff like that."

Arnette was trying to make the conductor feel at ease. And he just had a feeling about his story, something in his 20 years as a detective told him to dig deeper.

"Well, I'm telling you, the Westchester County police have done their best in the investigation, but your dad slipped through the net. I guess no one asked how he came to have a heart attack."

"Maybe they would have found the guy who stole my dad's car. Gee, you think the thief could have been another terrorist?"

"You sure it was stolen?"

"You know, my mom and I are. She's been saying nothing would stop my dad from picking her up. Something happened to him that morning. But nobody saw anything. If they had, don't ya think they would have found us by now?"

"What kind of car was it?"

"A Lincoln Town Car. Black. He loved that car. He bought it from a limo service. It had like 200,000 miles on it. But he took care of that old car like a baby. It still looked brand new. Shiny leather. He polished it like every weekend."

Arnette pulled out a notebook and started scribbling something. The February sun was still weak, but out of the wind on the porch it wasn't too cold.

"What are you writin'?"

"You've already told me some stuff that I want to remember. If you don't mind, I'm going to investigate. Sometimes you can find an abandoned car. If that's what happened to it. And who knows, maybe whoever took it was involved in the attack somehow."

"You're kidding?"

"Charlie. What's wrong, Charlie?"

He had a sad, distraught grimace on his face. "For the last four months, I've been tryin' to forget that morning. I lost my dad. I almost lost my job because I left my post. I was startin' to forget about hopin' we'd find his car, find something out about that morning. I was tryin' to get my mom to do the same thing, help her get on with her life. Now you show up."

"Charlie, I don't hold out much hope that I can help you. But I guess it's the cop in me. I can't help but wonder what went on that morning."

Charlie took a deep breath. "Look, I don't want to bring my mom into this, okay? She's still pretty upset. Probably always will be. But I can tell you this: when I heard they found him lying in the parking lot, I knew someone did something bad to him. He was old, not a lot of fight left in him, but he woulda never just let that car go."

"That makes sense to me, Charlie. Is there anything else you can remember about that morning, anything that might help me?" Williams asked.

"Well, there was this pretty woman on the train that morning. I've been calling her because two guys got in a fight over her, well, over her phone. I've been calling her, too, hoping she would call me. She's real pretty. She and the guy who protected her left the train together and headed to the hospital. At least that's where everybody went. Maybe she saw my dad in the parking lot. Maybe she knows if something happened to him. I mean, he just wouldn't let his car go. But she never called back. Told me to stop bothering her."

"Well, Charlie, maybe he offered his car to someone, and then just had a heart attack."

"You don't understand. Yeah, maybe he would have let the car go. It was just a car. But not when my mom was waiting to go home after two weeks in the hospital after she'd almost died. She was all he had left, except for me. He loved my mom. He wouldn't have let anything get in the way of gettin' her, nothing in the way, absolutely not nothing."

Charlie had started his rapid-fire chatter again, running words and sentences together so fast it was hard to understand.

"Charlie, Charlie," Arnette said, raising his hand. "Slow down. I think I get it. Back up. Let's just go over what you know. Do you have papers for the car? I need a VIN number, and maybe the plate numbers, too. And maybe the phone number of that lady, too."

"Yeah, yeah, sure. I'll get them."

"Did you ever file a stolen car report?"

"Uh, no," Charlie paused at the door with his back to the door, and then turned slowly to face the detective. "I don't know. There was so much goin' on, and the cops were so busy around here, and I was being investigated by Metro-North, and Mom wasn't doin' very well so I had to cover all the funeral stuff for my dad, and…"

"I understand," Arnette said, interrupting the barrage. "But I think we should do one now. That's why I want those numbers."

"Sure, sure, good to go. I'll get them right away."

## CHAPTER 17

R ACHEL STOOD NEXT TO THE dining room table, mentally seating her guests. She re-arranged several pieces of her Christofle silverware, and moved a couple of the crystal wine glasses closer to the plates. She was feeling stressed about the preparations and how the house looked, and still annoyed with Daniel for announcing that he had invited guests without asking her first, or without much explanation other than their names.

She decided to put Daniel directly across from James Roth. With nothing more than Daniel telling her the man's name, she had found a Wall Street Journal article saying that he was the current big thing in financial circles, largely because of the deal Daniel had worked on with him on 10/10. That was all the research she had time for. She put herself next to him, with Roth's wife, Sheri, across from her. That way the men's inevitable business talk wouldn't stop her from talking to his New York society wife, a woman who was well-known in Rachel's real estate world as a possible buyer before she got married.

While tussling with the seating, she was suddenly flooded with memories: her Metro-North train coming to an unexpected stop, the loss of phone service, the rising panic—all those jumbled memories from the morning of 10/10. And then there was Caleb. Coming to her rescue. Helping her off the train. Holding her in his arms. Caleb. She ached to see him again, and now she couldn't help but feel that this dinner had interfered with their planned date. She leaned on the table, remembering surprising him in the train station parking lot, then she was in his arms again, feeling flushed and happy now, and wishing she was back in his arms right now—and not getting ready for this damned dinner with a bunch of strangers.

Rachel went back into the kitchen and picked up the glass of Chardonnay, the second one she had poured since beginning the final preparations for dinner over an hour ago. She wasn't just angry at Daniel. There was some social anxiety in the mix, too, brought on by having to entertain a couple that was well-connected in New York society. It had also been more than four months since they had dinner guests, and she was feeling the strain of getting ready while still working in the city every day, and on top of that, today her hired maid had canceled at the last minute.

Daniel walked into the kitchen. "I like the table. It looks really nice. You have a knack for these kinds of dinners."

But Rachel, feeling the flush of the wine, said, "Thanks, but really, no thanks to you. You pretty much left me hanging out there all week, trying to figure out who these people are. I left half a dozen messages for you, and you didn't even respond. Getting home at midnight doesn't exactly leave much time to talk, and you're out the door at 6 a.m. before I even wake up."

"Rachel, geez, you know I've got some big cases on my desk right now."

"Damn, that's what you always say. But really, I don't understand what's going on. For that matter, I don't understand you anymore. When I asked why you were insisting on this dinner party last week, all you told me, as you rushed out the door, was the guy's name, and that it was important to you. But you haven't suggested a dinner party in years, so why is it such a big deal? And, by the way, I've worked my butt off getting ready for it."

"First of all, he's a neighbor," Daniel said, adjusting his blue and red rep tie, and smoothing out his grey cardigan sweater, as he watched Rachel with her wine in hand across the island in the kitchen. "And, knowing you, you've read all about James Roth by now."

"After you mentioned his name, I found a Journal article, so yeah, I guess he was impressive that day," Rachel said. "At least I was able to connect with his wife. I've sold apartments and rented Hamptons houses to her friends for years. But I never met her. And since she married James Roth, neither were in the real estate market anymore."

"He was a total professional, and a really cool customer," Daniel said. "To pull off that merger between that solar panel company, my client, and that big oil firm, I was impressed. And I made sure to let him know that's how I felt. Thought I was pretty clever, too: I purposefully left behind a folder, and I was able to get him alone for a quick chat. He is definitely worth the trouble to get to know."

"It's clear you feel that way. But there must be something else other than he's a neighbor. You haven't filled me in on the details," Rachel said, smoothing out her black Donna Karan dress and making sure her pearl necklace was in place. She had carefully chosen her outfit to impress Roth's wife, another reason she felt nervous about the evening going into it, but she knew she had nailed her look for the night.

"I figured this was a good way to get to know him. And…" Daniel paused for effect, "there is a rumor on Wall Street that he's getting ready to start his own firm. Maybe he needs a lawyer."

"Aha! So the real story comes out!" Rachel said. "But isn't that a conflict of interest?"

"No, the Secor deal is done. And the solar company doesn't want to retain us."

"From what I read, Roth's firm, Goldfarb & Case, is becoming one of the biggest on Wall Street," Rachel said. "So that would be quite a coup for you. Does his wife still go by Goldfarb, or Roth?"

"I'm not sure," Daniel said. "But she used to work there before she married James. I heard that when she retired, everyone was surprised. Actually, when she married him half the Street went into mourning. Every red-blooded guy there had either lusted after her or tried to date her. I'm sure you remember that she and Roth were the society story of the year four or five years ago."

"Well, I remember her. Not him. I don't think I've seen a picture of him. But it was longer ago than that. More like 2002. Right after 9/11. Maybe even a couple of years before that. She used to be a target for every real estate broker in Manhattan. But once she met that guy, she was off the market," Rachel repeated herself.

"Could be."

"They must be one of those couples that couldn't take the anxiety of living in the City after 9/11. What did they know? They ended up with a disaster in their backyard," Rachel said. "Goes to show, there's no place that's really safe today."

"True, there isn't," Daniel said. "Rachel, I want to be sure you know that I'm grateful for this tonight. Thank you. I know you've worked hard getting ready. I've smelled some of the stuff you've been making every night for the last two nights. What are we having?"

"Nothing special. My beef bourguignon. That garlicky scalloped potato dish you like and asparagus. And, of course, your favorite cake."

"Sounds like you did more than what was necessary."

"Like I've said, I like doing these things, and since you never ask, I thought I'd make you realize what you've been missing."

"Oh, don't think I am totally oblivious to that," Daniel said. "I just don't have anything socially out here in the suburbs, so there's never much chance. From what you've said, you don't have much of a social life here, either."

"That's true. I don't," Rachel said. "And part of the reason I don't is because you're never available for anything. Damn, it, can't you see, it's starting to get to me? I'm bored silly out here most of the time. Daniel, would you consider moving back into the city?"

She impulsively threw out the question, knowing the answer but also knowing that she had been wanting to talk about their future. For several years, the boredom of essentially living alone during the week, and often on weekends, had left her ready to try something different, anything. Was that part of the reason Caleb had become so attractive to her? But the shock of 10/10, and the abject terror she had felt for those first couple of hours, had also wormed its way into her daily life. Since then, she hadn't felt the same about her otherwise comfortable life in the suburbs.

Daniel ignored her question, arranging some of the bottles on the bar on the other side of the den, which was open to the kitchen. "Do we have another bottle of gin somewhere?"

"Yes, it should be under the bar. I asked you a question."

"Oh, here it is," he said and then paused to look at her. "I heard you. I don't know. Maybe when the kids grow up and leave."

"That's not that long. Four years, more or less. You think the kids would be upset if we sold the house?" Rachel asked.

"Who knows. You know them better than I do. I hardly see them anymore, not even on weekends," Daniel said.

"Doesn't that bother you?"

"I guess. But my dad was the same, maybe worse," Daniel said. "At least I'm here every weekend."

"Sort of," Rachel said. "Daniel, we used to talk a lot. But now, now, it seems like we don't have anything to talk about or even discuss. I mean, thank god, the kids aren't problems, but we have a life together, or at least we've been together now for 20 years. And yet, we don't share much day- to-day anymore"

"Rachel, we've talked about that before. I'm a work addict. I know that, but the firm demands a lot, too. There's no free ride anymore in law firms, no matter how long you've been a partner. Just last week, the managing partner called a meeting and served notice to one of the senior guys. Said he hadn't been pulling his weight. Did it in front of nearly the entire partnership."

"Gee, that's pretty harsh," Rachel said. "Who was it?"

"Oh, you don't know him. He's only been there 10 years. But it put everyone on notice."

"Well, like I've said many times, I don't know anything about your work life, and here's a partner with 10 years, and he's in trouble, and I've never met him," Rachel said.

She paused for a second and then pressed on. "You know I'm bored, Daniel. You know because I've told you that I want us to do more things together, vacations, social stuff, just days with the kids," she said. "But you never have time, and you make excuses when I think you might be able to do something."

"Rachel, stop. That's not going to change any time soon. I've told you: I'm buried in the cases I do have, and now I'm having to go out and hustle for more work, which is what tonight is about."

"I get it, Daniel. I get it. But you have to hear me. I'm bored out here, and bored with our lives right now. If something doesn't change…"

The doorbell rang. Daniel nearly leapt toward the front door, with a saved-by-the-bell sigh of relief.

## CHAPTER 18

J AMES AND SHERI HAD NOT said a word during the short drive from Briarcliff Manor to the Silvers' house in Croton. Their now five-day-old argument, which had erupted over James' refusal to talk about the events of 10/10, had lingered all week long. Sheri had not forgotten his menacing physical and verbal threats and the tense stand-off in their kitchen.

When James stopped their black BMW 7-series in the driveway of the Silvers' pretentious looking French Normandy-style house, he wanted to break the ice, and get her talking before they went inside. When he turned to her, Sheri's high cheekbones were highlighted in the glow from the dashboard. It was like she was someone else's stunning wife, her whole look screaming, "I am beautiful and I know it."

But before he could open his mouth, she had opened the car door and was walking up the driveway. He hurried after her and managed to get to the front door just as she rang the doorbell.

"You look," his words came out slowly, "absolutely fabulous tonight."

With a sideways glance she whispered, "Don't try to flatter me, Roth!" Of course, his comment was exactly what she'd been looking for while she took even more time than usual to get ready: a little more make-up, a low-cut but not provocative dress and careful dabs of Chanel No. 5, her favorite. But she wasn't going to make it easy for him. It was clear he needed to be reminded of her place—and be put back in his.

"I mean it," he muttered, frustrated and annoyed by her unremitting aloofness. As the week had worn on, and her coolness hadn't faded, he had been puzzled, not unlike how he had felt around her during their early months together. She had never shied away from him. Something had changed. Maybe he had changed.

Then the door swung open. Daniel Silver stood there, a caricature of Mr. Rogers in his gray cardigan sweater and rep tie, white shirt, gray pants and loafers.

"James, welcome!" Daniel said. "Nice to see you again. This must be your wife," he said. "I've heard a lot about you."

"I'm sure all of it bad," Sheri said.

"On the contrary, the only bad things I ever heard were about your husband, and he managed to dispel all of those a few months ago," Daniel said. "I mean no offense, James, but you know…"

James chuckled. "Mr. Silver, you're like most men. You hardly know what to say to me when my wife is around."

James put his arm around Sheri. Daniel noticed that while she didn't flinch or move away from her husband, neither did she relax and lean into him. The unnatural way they stood there together made Daniel think that there was some tension between the couple, but he wasn't sure.

"Now, James, don't assume everyone is like you," Sheri said.

"Come in, come in," Daniel said. "Let me take your coats." He helped Sheri off with her black, slim-cut cashmere coat, and then took James' sleek brown leather duster.

"The living room's right this way," he said, leading them into a large, high-ceilinged room, with graceful wooden beams and a roaring fire in the fireplace along the far wall.

Sheri surveyed the room. It was suburban chic, a touch of Laura Ashley with an old colonial feel around the edges, very unlike their own modern minimalism, which they had worked to carry off in their Frank Lloyd Wright copycat house.

"Nice room, Daniel. Very traditional," James said.

"I leave all that up to Rachel. But yes, you're right," Daniel said. "Have a seat, please."

James knew his wife was having a conniption, wondering "How did my husband get me into this?" He was thinking the same thing, and had been ever since the man in that dull grey, buttoned sweater greeted him. All that was missing was the pipe and martini glass with an olive. He remembered how Silver's rumpled appearance had put him off at the Secor/Brightline closing, but his management of his client was impeccable. And James' agenda was clear: Silver's intellectual property law credentials were a perfect fit for the kind of deals James wanted to do in his new fund.

"So, are the boys out in California still happy with their deal?" James asked.

"Haven't heard from them since the new year," Daniel replied. "Our engagement with Brightline ended with the deal's closing. You know what I think? Those young Turks were never very comfortable with a New York law firm. What can I get you two to drink?"

James laughed. "You're probably right. But the way you handled Brightline, and how you kept your cool that morning, was impressive. I may have some work that I will want to talk to you about in the near future."

"I've heard rumors on the street that you may…" Daniel said.

Sheri interrupted them. "Gentlemen, we haven't even been here three minutes, and you are already talking business. As long as you keep that up, I won't be getting my glass of wine."

"She's right, you know," Daniel said. "White or red, Sheri? And what can I get for you, James?"

"Bourbon, rocks would be great."

"Coming right up. And you? Chardonnay or Pinot Noir?"

"Chardonnay," she said, wondering if it was going to be a Kendall Jackson or something more drinkable.

"James, Jack Daniels or Bookers?"

"Bookers, please. So, I take it your firm is free now?"

"Yes, that's right."

"Gentlemen, I can see I won't be changing this conversation any time soon. Mr. Silver..."

"Please call me Daniel."

"Okay, Daniel. Is the kitchen through that door? I'll go help your wife. What's her name?"

"I apologize. I thought the white wine was here, but it must be in the kitchen. Her name is Rachel. She'll get it for you."

"Now then, James," he said, rattling the ice into the bottom of the glass.

Rachel had heard the murmur of voices out in the living room. And when she heard that man's voice, his tone and inflection carrying into the kitchen over the soft clatter of her preparations, something set her on edge. She couldn't put her finger on it, but she was certain she knew the man.

Sheri came into the kitchen: "Hi! May I help?"

"Sure, thanks for coming in. I'm Rachel."

"Hi, I'm Sheri, Sheri Roth."

"I bet you're looking for the white wine, right?" Rachel said. "I brought it in here earlier. Needed a glass. No need to help. Relax. Everything is almost ready. I thought you still used your maiden name, Goldfarb? Or I guess I had heard that."

"I do sometimes, but more and more in social get-togethers, I use Roth. James does like it when I do."

Sheri was surprised: at first glance, Mrs. Silver was nothing like her Mr. Rogers husband. This woman was Upper East Side chic: if not Barney's, then every designer boutique store on Madison Avenue had sold this woman clothes, shoes and jewelry.

Rachel quickly wiped her hands on a towel and reached out to shake the woman's hand. Rachel too was impressed: Sheri was tall and blond, with a kind of Sharon Stone-like charisma and sass, highlighted by the straightforward look in her hazel green eyes. Not a wisp of hair was out of place. Not a discordant note in her make-up and jewelry, and she had the confidence to hide nothing about her figure; the clingy green silk dress—Rachel guessed Versace—fell gracefully over her hips.

Sheri radiated what Rachel expected from a former denizen of Wall Street and the heir to a powerful firm, a woman skilled at navigating the serpentine maze of Park Avenue and the Hamptons. Yes, Sheri Roth lived up to her reputation—all the way up.

"You look fabulous," Rachel said.

"As do you," Sheri said. "From what I've heard, you are the best realtor in New York City."

Rachel laughed. "Well, that's flattering. I'm surprised we haven't met."

"Well, I haven't been in the market for a new apartment in a long time. My husband's was more than sufficient, and when the kids first arrived, we just bought the apartment next door and expanded. And then, after 9/11, I... I just had to get out of the city. Get away from that horrible day."

"I know the feeling, even though we moved to Westchester

years before that day. I'm from Queens, a real native New Yorker, but I had no desire for my kids to grow up in Manhattan. Since Daniel is a workaholic, it didn't much matter where we lived. It makes my job a little harder, but I love getting away from the city. That day, I couldn't express how glad I was we weren't living in the city. Still, I'm pretty sure I know some of your friends."

"You do," Sheri said, quickly rattling off the names of three close friends who had used Rachel in finding their new homes in the city. She had called them during the week to ask about Rachel Silver. She had remembered them talking about their purchases, and they all confirmed the same thing: that Rachel Silver was a top-notch realtor, as well as beautiful. All true, Sheri concluded.

"Oh yeah, I remember them. Nice ladies." Rachel wondered exactly what Sheri had asked them about, but the confirmation told her all she needed to know: that Sheri Roth was not someone to be taken lightly. Anything less would have been a mistake.

"Now, could I get that glass of white wine?"

"Of course, it's right here in the wine fridge," Rachel said. She pulled out the Corton Charlemagne she had bought at Dodd's over in Millwood. "We've been drinking this Jadot Corton for years. I love it."

"My, my. I've had this a few times. James loves good wine. He'll be impressed."

"Good!" Rachel said. "I figured him, like Daniel, for red wine; I have a California Cab for dinner to go with the beef. Let's go join the men. I don't want them getting into any trouble out there."

"Don't worry. They are dancing around the idea that my husband is going to open his own firm and needs a lawyer," Sheri said. "But James really doesn't know what he's getting into. That's confidential, by the way."

Rachel laughed, putting the finishing touches on a tray of appetizers. "Oh, I know enough about Wall Streeters to know that they pretty much live in a world of secrets, especially when it comes to their deals. New York lawyers like Daniel are only a half-step behind. They never want to talk about what they're working on."

Now Sheri laughed. "You're so right! But enough of that. Let's talk about plans for the summer. Do you go to the Hamptons?"

"I do sometimes, with the kids. Daniel almost never joins us," Rachel said, picking up the tray of appetizers and heading for the living room.

The two men were seated and still rapt in conversation. James Roth's back was to Rachel, and when he turned toward her, and she saw his hulk and then his face, Rachel almost dropped her tray.

It was him!

For a moment, Rachel trembled, but then she forced herself to regain her composure. She could feel the color draining from her face, as she struggled not to reveal her shock.

Then James stood up and faced her. "Hello! Nice to meet you! It's Rachel, right? My wife told me she had done some asking around about you."

Rachel could only nod in agreement. "Would you like some hors d'oeuvres?"

James picked up a shrimp and dipped it in the small bowl of cocktail sauce. Damn, the woman looked familiar, Roth thought, but he couldn't place where he had seen her before. He let the thought pass. Because he was so focused on soliciting Daniel Silver, without being too obvious, he didn't want to lose the thread.

Out of the corner of her eye, Rachel caught a glimpse of Sheri. She was watching her husband, studying his face. Rachel sensed it: Sheri's radar was up. Did she have any idea what had happened on that train? Did she have any idea what her damned husband had done?

"Daniel," he went on, "tell me, if you can, how did the boys from Brightline react after the deal was signed, sealed, and delivered?"

"Well, I can't really reveal too much, but let's just say they were all very happy with the increase in their personal wealth."

"Yeah, I bet," James said. "I thought I was getting rich that day, but they made out like bandits."

Daniel just laughed. "Well, that is open to interpretation. Let's just say they had a good product that the men from Secor were happy to pay a lot of money for."

"Very diplomatic, sir! Those old boys hardly know what they got. But they'll figure it out."

Their words reached Rachel as if through a muffler. All she wanted to do was dump her entire tray of hors d'oeuvres in James' lap and then disappear. This man, this pig had attacked her. If it hadn't been for Caleb, he might actually have hurt her. She kept her eyes away from that face and focused on taking slow, deep breaths. Suddenly she felt completely alone in this room full of people. Her one thought was this: Keep it together. He doesn't even seem to remember me. Sheri was perplexed. A moment before, Rachel had been warm and convivial; now she was avoiding eye contact. What had changed? Sheri figured Rachel must have had an encounter with James in another life, maybe before she was married even, and she was having an attack of nerves. Sheri waited, and when Rachel finally looked up, Sheri caught her eye and mouthed silently, "Are you okay?" But she got no reaction from Rachel.

As James kept probing Daniel with questions about the deal, Rachel suddenly interrupted them: "Excuse me for a minute. I'm, I'm not...I'll be right back." With that, she quickly stood up and left the room, not heading for the kitchen but the hallway on the opposite side of the front door. There was a bathroom there, and she knew she could lock the door and regain her composure.

Inside the bathroom, the murmurs from the living room were still audible, and all Rachel could do was put her hands over her ears, trying to shut out the voices. That voice! That day! Images of Caleb, and how he had protected her that day and how much she had been wanting him, now flooded her being. Rachel could feel her control fading, and she was fighting the overwhelming urge to cry. A clear image of Caleb, his handsome face, his strong hands, his embrace swept over her, and she could feel her knees getting weak. But she refused to lose it. She had to go back out there and… and what? Be gracious. Yes, that was the only option.

Rachel checked her face in the mirror to be sure she hadn't shed any tears or smeared her mascara. Then she took one deep breath, and then another, and finally she opened the door.

As she walked into the living room, she said, "Sorry about that…everything is fine. And I think dinner is about ready. I'll let you know in a few minutes. Daniel, you'll show them in? And, Sheri, please stay with the men. Maybe you can get them talking about something other than ancient history!"

Rachel hoped that Sheri would listen, and give her a few more minutes to regain her composure. She was already adjusting the seating plan in her mind; James and Sheri would have to sit next to each other on the same side of the table, and she would put herself as far away from James Roth as possible.

A few minutes later, dinner was ready, and she called out to Daniel, "Dinner's ready. You can bring everyone in."

"Is there anything I can do to help?" Sheri said, walking into the kitchen.

"No, I'm fine. The waitress I had hired for tonight canceled at 5 p.m., so I'm a bit disorganized. But I'll be in in a minute. Please sit on the far side of the table next to James. I'll need to stay close to the kitchen."

Sheri left the kitchen, and Rachel could hear that the men were already in the dining room. She took another couple of deep breaths. So far, so good. Now she could concentrate on dinner and try to suppress the memories of that horrible morning on the train.

Dinner seemed interminable. The conversation did venture beyond the business interests of the two men at the table, but every time Sheri posed a question to Rachel, all she got were short, curt responses. Sheri decided to try talking about real estate.

"Rachel, do you have any listings for rentals in the Hamptons this summer? James and I will definitely be looking for something in Southampton this year, or maybe Water Mill."

Finally, Rachel thought, something she can talk about without having to look at that face. That man James.

"Actually, I do. With all the action last summer, I spent a lot of time this fall contacting owners, and I have about a dozen listings in Southhampton. They are all in the range of $10,000 to $20,000 a week."

"That's no problem," Sheri said. "We don't want waterfront. Too noisy and no privacy. Something within walking distance of the beach. We have a membership to the beach club, so somewhere close."

Of course you have a beach club membership, Rachel thought; it's the most difficult membership on the island, but given her family's background, she had probably been going there her whole life. But Rachel remained gracious: "I'll be glad to send you a couple of listings next week, Sheri. They are pretty competitive so you'll have to move quickly."

"James," Sheri said to her husband, "you are interested in Southampton again this year, right?"

"Yes," he said, smiling at Rachel, and again, sensed he had seen this woman before. But he still couldn't place her. He started to ask, but thought better of it.

Rachel brought out the dessert and asked for coffee orders. When James ordered his black, she went back to the kitchen to turn on the coffeemaker. Sheri got up from the table and followed her.

"Rachel," Sheri said.

Rachel flinched. She had not expected to be followed.

"Is everything okay?" Sheri asked.

"Yes, yes, why do you ask?"

"I don't know. You just seem… upset," Sheri said.

"Oh, it's just the dinner. Without the waitress, I was worried that something would go wrong. Seriously, I'm fine, but thanks for asking." Rachel wanted the conversation to end right then and there. "I'll be right out with the coffee. Thanks again, Sheri."

"Okay, whatever. I do look forward to getting those listings next week. We'll be thrilled if you can help us, Rachel." Then she left the kitchen. She seems awfully nice, Rachel thought. How could she be married to that creep?

Alone in the kitchen, Rachel sat down on a stool, while the coffee brewed. Her thoughts ranged from "What the hell am I doing here," to "I shouldn't have to put up with this kind of crap from my husband!" to "The only time he thinks about me is when I can do something for him, like tonight, setting up a lure to score a big new client." She knew Caleb wouldn't be like that, but rather, he'd be a lover, a true partner. He was still doing that with his wife, even though he wasn't in love with her anymore, or at least Rachel imagined him not being in love with her. Why had she been so silent with Daniel for so long, not even giving him a hint about her frustrations? Seeing this man Roth triggered a whole new wave of resolve inside her. Her life as she knew it had to change.

Rachel picked up the coffee tray, and once again took a deep breath and headed back into the dining room. From there, the rest of the evening went quickly. Rachel didn't offer any after-dinner drinks, and she gave all the signs of a hostess ready for the night to be over, picking up dishes from the living room and clearing the dining room table, even though her guests were still there.

Sheri finally said, "James, I think it's time to go. It's getting a little late." It wasn't much after 10 o'clock, but Rachel's discomfort, or at least what Sheri perceived to be discomfort, was making her uncomfortable, too. It was all very strange, Sheri thought, and she had every intention of finding out why.

James stood up and headed for the door. Daniel headed that way too, but Rachel stayed behind. Then, to be polite, James walked back toward her, and suddenly he saw her, felt her, recoil.

"Rachel, thank you for a lovely evening. The wines were outstanding and the food was delicious," he said. But when he reached out his hand to say goodnight, he saw her hesitate.

With her hand at her side, she said, "You're welcome, James."

Then, suddenly, he remembered where he had seen her. On the train. On 10/10. Instantly, James felt his face flush. Oh my god, it's her, the woman from the train! Why had she kept from outing him? Fuck. He turned quickly away from her, and headed toward the front door, his mind racing, waiting for her to say something to him, to call him out for that morning on the train. But there was only silence behind him. He looked over his shoulder as he left the room and her face was blank and impossible to read.

The goodbyes were said quickly, and Rachel could hear the Roths' voices fade and disappear outside. Soon she was in the kitchen, her back pressed against the refrigerator door and her arms wrapped tightly around her chest. She was staring blankly across the island piled with dirty dishes when Daniel came in.

"Hey, are you okay? What happened tonight? You got very quiet right before dinner and you were so silent during dinner. I've never seen you miss a chance to line up a big summer rental in the Hamptons. Wow. Why not?"

Rachel cut him short. And then she turned on her husband: "No, I am definitely not okay. I want to throw up. That man!"

"What? Rachel, what in god's name are you talking about?"

"That man! That bastard! He attacked me on 10/10, right there on the train! As soon as I saw him inside our house, I felt sick. And I didn't want to be anywhere near him! All I could think about was him grabbing at me, trying to rip my cell phone out of my hand."

"Rachel, you never said anything about being attacked that morning! All you ever said was it was a rough morning. What the hell happened?"

"You never asked." Her voice was now sharp and angry.

"You never suggested there was anything to ask about."

"Well, that creep violently tried to grab my phone, to call his damned office, and then a nice man tackled him and protected me."

"What? They had a fight? Over your phone?"

"Yes."

"Rachel, I'm stunned. This is the first I've heard about a fight on the train. Are you kidding? James Roth? How am I supposed to react to something that sounds so absurd? What's going on?"

"Why did I never mention it? Because, Daniel, you never fucking care what's happening in my life, or in the kids' lives. You have your head so buried in your work you never even bothered to ask what it was like being trapped on that train. Then, you set me up for some goddamn business meeting, not a social dinner, here in my own house, as if I were your little stay-at-home housewife doing everything for her sweet, adoring husband. Make me throw up!"

"Whoa, Rachel. Where's this coming from? You never even hinted that this dinner was anything more than some inconvenience. Damn it, I'm not a mind reader! And now I'm a bad husband on top of it all and a bad father, too. Jeeee-sus…"

"Bad, bad?" Rachel said. "No, just absent. Never here. Never for me. Never giving a shit about me or the kids. Hell, that morning, you didn't call me to see if I was okay. For all you knew, I could have been dying in our living room from radiation poisoning. But no, not a fucking word out of you! After 20 years of marriage!"

"Rachel, calm down. Jesus. I probably knew before you that things were going to be okay. But don't change the subject. Roth attacked you? I find that hard to believe. He was perfectly calm during the meeting that morning."

"Oh, he had to be, didn't he? All that money on the line. His reputation. Well, he grabbed me on the train. He yelled at me. I was petrified he was going to hurt me. And, you, you still don't care. Thank god, Caleb was there."

"Caleb? James Roth? Not once in four months have you ever mentioned either one. Who in the hell is Caleb? Does…"

"Oh, forget it. Just forget it," Rachel interrupted. "Just get out of here. I have to clean up."

"But…"

"Get out. Now! Please!"

## CHAPTER 19

"CALEB?"

Brenda's voice jarred him.

"Are you okay? You've barely touched your dinner, and you've got that look on your face, and, well, I'm not sure what…"

"I'm fine," he said. "I'm just preoccupied." He stared at her across the table. They were sitting in a small alcove in the kitchen, at a breakfast room table that looked out over the dark backyard through a pair of casement windows. Through the filigree of the winter's naked trees, he could see the lights in other kitchens, living rooms and upstairs bedrooms, a simple, quiet suburban scene.

"About what?"

"Nothing. Everything."

"Caleb, I'm worried about you. I thought you were finally putting the Indian Point thing behind you. But you suddenly, well, got really moody again. What happened?"

"I don't want to talk about it."

Brenda's face turned rigid. She abruptly pushed her chair back from the table, stood up and glared at him. She brushed her long, brunette hair off her face.

"That's all you've got to say? You don't want to talk about it? You never want to talk about anything. You haven't been here, I mean really here, connected to this family, in months, hell, maybe years for all I can figure out. What the hell are you up to?" she said, her voice rising with each word.

A pained look crossed his face. For most of the last 25 years, he had loved his wife in a way that blurred any distinction between them; they were so intertwined that there was no "you and me," just "us." But now what? He knew he had spiraled down into some dark place. Again.

He knew this blackness. Each time the feelings washed over him, as they had many times in the last 45 years, he was surprised that this insidious worm still lurked inside him. The years of therapy, and the years that had passed without recurrence, gave him hope that those memories of Vietnam, of war, of the horrors he had seen, and the feelings they generated, were in his past. And then, one day, one minute, he would get bitch-slapped by some trigger—a face, a sound, a certain way a car moved through an intersection, the furtive glance of a stranger in a public place, a nightmare—and he knew that beneath the surface nothing had really changed, and that nothing ever would, and that he would always live with not just the memory of the horrors from Vietnam, but the stomach-churning, throat-gripping, anxiety-causing residue they had left behind.

This time the trigger was Rachel's perfume, or at least the memory of it as he held her. As the months had passed since 10/10, he had calmed down and the searing anxiety and guilt of that morning had almost disappeared. He was slipping back to his normal, his status quo. Even though he desperately wanted change, he couldn't resist the comfort of settling into the easy boundaries of his life: an alarm every morning, a quick cup of coffee with Brenda in a bathrobe, a short jaunt to the train station, a commuter train into the city and a 15-minute walk to his office. The routine was comforting, and it deflated the desire to make changes. When Rachel reappeared at his car window, it was that familiar slap, the sharp reminder that he had promised himself that his life would not remain the same, that this time he wouldn't revert to the same old pattern, the same old routine, the same old mistakes. Maybe he would dust off that old manuscript that he had put away when his PR career got started. Or talk to Brenda about his dream of moving to the mountains with the kids.

Right now, he was paralyzed, just like he had been since the Rachel moment earlier in the week. But four months after 10/10, he was still waking up in the night, the image of Rachel's raised skirt and her lips fresh in his dreams. Sometimes he was sweating. Sometimes his night erection was almost painful, like it had been there for a while. And it didn't take long for his waking fantasy to cycle around to him thrusting into her in a passionate mutual climax. The frequency of that dream had finally faded. And then, suddenly, she had appeared at his car, setting off all those dreams again, every night, the same vivid image of her under him, around him, over him. The easy choice going forward was simply to confront Rachel, to tell her there was no chance they would ever be together and to go home.

"What do you want me to say, Brenda? That I'm depressed? That I'm back in my dark place? Can't you see that?" he asked, drawing the words from some inexplicable place, trying to forget the images of Rachel.

Brenda's face softened for a second, then it hardened again. "Not good enough, Caleb Drake. I've known you for a lifetime. Yeah, I see the similarities. This, this," she paused for a long second, "…is different. Something else. I don't know what it is. But you know I'm right."

There was another pause. Neither spoke. There was a combustive air in the room, a recognition that in another second their neatly packaged, safe little corner of the world could shatter in a violent outpouring of emotion, never to be put back together again. Caleb knew what could lead them down that path. Brenda didn't, but she feared whatever was lurking behind his mask.

"Is it another woman, Caleb?"

He recoiled at a question that was as unexpected as it was razor-sharp. He laughed. "Brenda, that really ups the ante, doesn't it? After all these years, you think that's the answer to my behavior over the last four months? When would I have the time?"

"You're not answering my question. And what kind of answer is that? You leave here at 6 in the morning. You come home at 7:30, sometimes 8:30 at night; in fact, it's gotten later and later. You could be flying to Chicago every day for all I know about what happens during your day. You rarely call me. You don't talk to me about work. What am I supposed to think? You could have another family, for all I know."

"I come home every night. I am here every weekend. You're fantasizing."

"Oh, right. I'm fantasizing. You come home. Eat in silence. You sit around on weekends watching your goddamn baseball, or football or basketball, and if you're not doing that, you're off with Junior at his baseball, or football, or soccer games. We never do anything together. Just you and me. Ever. Do you hear me? It doesn't matter whether I'm here or not."

Her voice was rising again. And there was a fire in her eyes as she kept slowly backing into a corner of the kitchen, like a feral cat, cornered, trying to find safe angles to protect herself. She started shaking, and suddenly she grabbed a glass from the counter, threw it across the kitchen, smashing it against the stove's back-splash and shattering it into tiny pieces.

"Jesus, Brenda…"

"Don't just sit there. Answer me!" she shouted.

"No. No. It's not another woman. Not…" he stopped.

"Not what. Not exactly? What the fuck does that mean? Is that what you were going to say? Not exactly what?"

"Never mind."

"Noooo. There are no 'never minds' here. Not now. You tell me, Caleb! I have a right to know!"

"I said no. I said it's not another woman. It never has been. Never will be. I would leave you before I ever did that."

Brenda stared at him, her breathing rapid and her eyes still wide with anger. A minute passed without a word, and she didn't once take her eyes off him.

Then she began speaking, in low measured tones: "You are lying. Don't ask me how I know. I just do. I can feel it. You are simply not being honest with me, and who knows, maybe not even with yourself. Whichever it is, I can't live with you like this. Yeah," she said, ignoring his surprised look. "I can't live with you like this. You need to go. Get out! Come back when you're ready to talk."

Caleb stood there, unable to make a decision, at a crossroads where the choices were painfully clear: Change? Or continue the stultifying status quo? One path, heart-pounding, thrilling and unknown. The other, safe, dull, predictable. And deadening.

The second hand on the kitchen clock moved slowly around the dial, just at the edge of his peripheral vision.

"Fine, I'm out of here," he said, standing up, grabbing an old leather coat from the rack and storming out the back door. Running felt good and different and smart. Normally, he would have stayed stone-faced and silent, waiting out the uproar. Not this time.

Before he even knew where he was, he was behind the wheel of his car, backing out of his garage and heading down the street in the direction of Rachel's house. As he neared her driveway, he saw the blink of lights from a car door being unlocked by remote, and as he drove past, he recognized the guy getting behind the wheel: It was him! The guy who had attacked Rachel, the guy he had tackled on the train back on 10/10.

What the fuck was going on?

## CHAPTER 20

**D**ANIEL WAITED IN THE DEN, listening to the rattle of pots and pans and the clinking of silverware and plates that Rachel was putting into the dishwasher. He felt numb. Rachel's accusations about his lack of involvement in their home life were painful truths. But he couldn't help but ask, why now? What had pushed her to blindside him like that, why unfurl now, after all these years, that cruel litany of all his shortcomings?

No one, her included, had ever doubted the core reason for his devotion, his addiction, to his work. She had worked hard too, and together they had built a safe, secure life, with all the rewards of financial success: the big house, the fancy cars, the kids' private tutors, and the ability to buy almost anything they wanted, and whenever they wanted. But Rachel now seemed ready to dismiss all that; was she having an affair with this mystery man from the train? He couldn't just sit here and let her turn their life upside down in one night—and not without talking about it.

So Daniel got up and walked back into the kitchen. Rachel was staring out the back window, but she turned as he entered.

"What do you want?" she said. "I told you to leave me alone."

"The noise in here stopped. I thought you were done cleaning up," Daniel said. "And no, you don't get to shut me out without some explanation. Rachel, nothing here makes any sense, at least not to me. You're not telling me the whole story, that I know."

"The whole story? You want to know the whole story? Now? Four months later? Well, it's about time!"

"Rachel, stop it. Talk to me."

"What do you want to know that I haven't already told you? It was a terrible morning. You have no idea how horrible it was."

"If you had told me about it, I'd be a bit more understanding, but maybe it's the lawyer in me. I'm wondering what else there is that I don't know. You're telling me things I find hard to believe about James Roth."

"Oh, so you're still taking his side? After what I told you? I can't believe it. He wasn't just rude. He was threatening, and he tried to steal my phone while I was trying to find out what was happening to our kids—your kids and mine."

"Maybe he was just trying to find out what was going on," Daniel said. "I can understand how he might have been a bit berserk. The craziness of that morning, him having to be in the city for a huge meeting. But you said all along nothing big happened that morning. How does all this add up?"

"Look, I wanted to forget that morning. Put it behind me. My little scrape didn't seem like a big deal at the time, especially given everything else that happened that day... or could have happened."

"See, Rachel, now you're saying it wasn't that big a deal. You say that's why you didn't tell me. But now you want him thrown in jail because he did such a terrible thing. Which is it? What the hell is going on, Rachel? Damn it, I want to know!"

Rachel was shocked. Daniel had never raised his voice to her, had never showed much emotion toward her at all. Maybe he was sensing the real reason she hadn't told him much: Caleb. Was her quiet, controlled husband headed into a jealous rage?

"Daniel, if you showed half as much emotion about us as you are showing right now, maybe there wouldn't be anything to talk about! So let me remind you again: You never even asked me about that morning. Yes, it was a bad morning. Yes, Caleb helped me get home safely to our kids. And yes, I have wanted to see him again, every day for four months, but I haven't. There. That's it!"

"Caleb? Who the hell is Caleb? Are you telling me you're having an affair with this guy?" Instead of allowing his rising anger to show, Daniel now instinctively slipped back into his lawyerly mode, his face stern, his eyes unwavering. Caleb. With that mysterious man's name suddenly dropped in his lap, he didn't want Rachel to see him so angry—or insecure.

"I did not say I was having an affair. Just that for a moment I wanted to. But let me tell you something else, Daniel Silver: there is something wrong with that man. Seriously wrong."

"Which man?"

"James Roth. There's something about his story that just doesn't add up. You say he made it into the city for your meeting, less than two hours after he got off the train? How did he do that?"

"I don't know. He must have gotten a ride. How else do you get from one place to another these days?"

"Well, listen to me, Daniel. When I got up to the parking lot, there was a man lying on the ground, an old man. And he was mumbling something about, 'He just took it. He just took it.' That man died, Daniel, from a heart attack. What if…"

Daniel cut her off. "What if what? Don't even go there. That's ridiculous. Totally circumstantial. Did you see him take a car? How do you know the old man was talking about a car? It could have been anything…"

"See," Rachel said, "you're defending this asshole. You don't even want to hear what I think? Ever since that morning, after I helped get the old man into the hospital, I've wondered what happened, and how he ended up on the ground all alone like that. And I didn't accuse Roth of taking the car; you jumped to that conclusion."

Daniel took a step around the island, and moved closer to Rachel. To her, he seemed bigger, not exactly threatening, but getting ready to assert his authority, to make a statement.

"Rachel, didn't you see the story in the Journal earlier this week? His son and wife, they talked about how he was just an old man. And, they did say his car was missing. If James Roth took the car for some reason, don't you think he would have returned it?"

"And what if he stole it? Risk his reputation? His career? His big dream that he talked about with you tonight, his dream of starting his own hedge fund? How could he do that… from jail?"

"He's not going to jail," Daniel said. "Trust me on that one. If for some reason, he is guilty of your wild suspicions, he'd pay a fine, do some community service. What? Why are you looking at me that way?"

Rachel couldn't believe what she was hearing.

"Look, Rachel, at worst, it would be manslaughter. Roth didn't know the guy was going to die, if he was even involved in it at all. Sounds like you're having some weird fantasy…"

"Damn you, Daniel Silver! Where's your head? Where's your conscience? Wouldn't you like to know if this guy you're thinking of representing is a killer? Or at the minimum a thief? Forget the fact that he attacked me, your wife. Obviously, that makes no difference to you…"

"Wait! From what I heard, he didn't attack you. He just tried to grab your phone, and he got his ass kicked. Hard to believe, guy his size. Must have been taken by surprise…" Daniel said.

"Taken by surprise? No! The truth is, a very brave man jumped in to protect me. More than it seems you would have been willing to do."

"What's with this brave man? This Caleb? How well do you know him? Have you seen him again?"

"No. No. NO! I haven't seen him again. I already told you that, two minutes ago and you've already forgotten. Too bad. I'd like to, though. Yes, that's the truth, Daniel. I would love to. I'm tired, you hear me, tired of this fucking empty life you and I have out here. Didn't you hear me, earlier? See, you never, ever pay real attention to me. I could be a damn statue for…"

With that, the phone rang. She walked over to the handset and looked down at the number. She was pretty sure it was that guy, Charlie Murray, the conductor from the train. She recognized the number; he had called at least a dozen times over the past four months. Rachel had finally stopped answering his calls, after she told him that she couldn't help him, and that she did not want to be involved in anything related to that awful morning on the train. "So please stop calling," she told him, as firmly as she could. Now, though, and even though it was late, she decided to answer, if only to break away from her painful conversation with Daniel.

"Mr. Murray, I told you to stop calling me."

Charlie started stammering. "I, I, I, didn't know, didn't know, you were, you were going to answer. Please listen. All I need is a letter from you telling my bosses I helped everybody that morning. That way, they might clear my record. Please, just have coffee…"

"I told you, no! And I'll tell you again: no! And why would I have coffee with you anyway? Now stop harassing me, please!"

"Bitch," he said, and hung up.

She stared at the phone. "Well, of all the…"

"Who was that?" Daniel asked.

"Oh, something else I never told you about: Charlie Murray. You know, the son in the Journal article about the dead man? He was the conductor on the train that morning, and he says he got suspended because he left his post. He's been calling me for months, asking for a letter of commendation from me about how much he had helped all the passengers. He's a creep. I'm sorry, but I don't want to get near him. So I have constantly refused to see him or even talk to him. And he just called me a bitch."

"Well, it sounds like helping him might be the civil thing to do," Daniel said. "Why not help him? Or what else did you do on that morning? All the men on the train seem to remember you…"

"Oh my god, Daniel, what's wrong with you? That's a horrible thing to say. Is everyone else entitled to your defense, but not me? I can't fucking believe you."

She turned around and left the room. She was done.

Daniel couldn't move. Everything that he considered a constant in his life was now dissolving in front of his eyes. Was his wife really threatening to leave him? Was she really tired of their life? Did she really have the nerve to walk out?

He figured he'd just better let her calm down. Tomorrow was another day.

## CHAPTER 21

"JAMES, WE NEED TO TALK," Sheri said.

They were driving home to Briarcliff from what had turned into a nightmare dinner at the Silvers'. James could feel the two Bourbons and the wine, and he was trying not to swerve over the white lines.

"Talk about what? There's nothing to talk about."

"You mean there's nothing you *want* to talk about with me."

"That's not what I said."

"You might as well have a neon sign on your head that's flashing: 'I'm hiding something.'"

"What do you mean?"

"Back at the house. The second that woman saw you, she freaked out. She wasn't the same after that, all night long."

"That woman means nothing to me."

"Oh, I'm sure of that. For a second, though, I enjoyed watching you squirm because I figured she was some old flame that you hadn't recognized."

"You're sick."

"Hardly. But then something dawned on you, right before we left. When you walked out of the dining room from saying goodbye to that woman, you were almost white. I've never seen you look like that. What's going on, James? I know you. You're not telling me something."

James' pulse quickened. He thought about pulling over, but his first thought was, "What if a cop stops us and asks what's going on?" And his very next thought was, "Am I really going to have to live like this for the rest of my life?" Sheri's radar was indeed spot-on: Seeing that woman tonight had ignited every fear James had been harboring for the past four months, namely the fear of the truth coming out.

"Ohhhhh, I, I, I..." he sputtered.

"James, what IS the matter? You've got to talk to me. I can, no, I will help you."

James hesitated for a long time, then he could no longer hold it in: "Sheri, I'm in deep shit."

"What the hell are you talking about?"

James couldn't keep driving. He turned off the highway into a residential neighborhood lined by small, one-story houses and neatly manicured front lawns. He stopped the black BMW 750 and turned off the ignition. The inside of the car was dark but from a streetlight outside there was a pall of dim light coming through the tinted glass.

"Damn it, all I want to do is forget that, that goddamn fucked up morning on the train. But you're right about her. I didn't recognize her right off. She looked familiar, but I... Then, right before we left, when she refused to shake my hand, I remembered."

Sheri reached across the console and laid her hand on top of his. "Don't worry, darling. Let it out. Tell me now. We'll figure it out... together. Whatever it is."

James took a deep breath, then, silence.

Sheri waited. And she began to wonder if she wanted to hear it or not, and at the same time she felt her anger beginning to build.

"Come on, honey," she said, still trying to sound sweet.

"No, I can't. I just can't."

"Goddamn it, James! Either you tell me, or I am out of here! Let me be clear about something: She recognized you immediately. I knew it the second she couldn't talk straight. And you know what? They're back there right now, talking about it, she and her milquetoast lawyer husband, who for some reason you think is a legal genius."

He slammed the palm of his hand so hard into the steering wheel that she thought he might break it. "Why are you so goddamned stubborn? Can't you see? I don't want to talk about it!"

For the second time in a week, she thought he was going to lose control and start hitting her, not the steering wheel. And suddenly an unpleasant, rancid odor flooded the car. She had never smelled fear, but she had read about it in books, and here it was: unmistakable, petrifying fear.

James' shoulders slumped, his hands fell into his lap, and he began letting it all stream out, like a court stenographer rereading testimony from a transcript. The words and sentences did not have a rehearsed quality, but as he rambled along Sheri sensed that for months James had been repeating them over and over in his head.

In about two minutes, he recounted every moment on the train—his frantic search for a working phone, the fight, getting knocked to the floor, and then hatching the plan with Rachel Silver and the stranger who had attacked him to get off the stalled train and into the city.

"Well, okay," Sheri said, in a matter-of-fact way, "that's a bad story, yes, but that won't take much more than a direct, maybe face-to-face, apology to calm her down. It's actually not criminal, or at least no one is going to charge you with anything, given what was happening around you. 10/10, and all that. You should be able to charm your way right through that."

"That's not all."

He paused and turned toward her, an anguished look on his face. Then he dropped back into the same monotone, and quickly described how he got off the train, climbed the hill to the hospital parking lot and tried to offer the old man a lot of money for his car. But the man refused, so James had to struggle with him for his keys. Then he took the car and sped off like a madman even though he saw the man slump to the ground in the rearview mirror. He drove to the Upper East Side of Manhattan, where he dumped the car and took a cab to his office.

Sheri gasped, "Oh, my god. No!"

"Yeah, it's all true. I really didn't know what had happened to that man until this week. I thought a million times about trying to find out. Now I know. And I don't know what to do."

James' account ran through Sheri's mind like a grainy news-reel. And as she watched it, she saw her own life vanishing in an avalanche of newspaper reporters and TV cameras. And in her mind she also saw her father's firm, Goldfarb & Case, collapsing with the news that one of its top executives looked to be a callous murderer, too busy chasing a deal to help an old man collapsed in a parking lot.

Now what?

Could these disaster scenarios possibly be averted?

Okay, she thought. If some or all of this were to come out, couldn't a top-quality lawyer defend James' actions and get him off? After all, it would be a dead man's word against her husband's, and James could be coached into contriteness and a sympathetic pose, couldn't he? Hah! Sheri quickly dismissed the very idea. A hulking Wall Street banker with slick hair and a pinstriped suit? James would be about as sympathetic as Rasputin at the height of his power.

No, there had to be a better way, a more effective strategy. She wasn't sure where her reaction was coming from, but she knew instinctively what had to be done right then. Turning to her husband, Sheri regained her composure and laid out her plan: "Listen to me, Roth: here's what you're going to do. First, you will never, ever repeat that story to anyone else. It's over. I don't want to hear one more word about it. Are we clear?"

With Sheri's steely voice reverberating inside the car, James nodded his agreement. "Second, what you are going to do, for me, and for my father, is you are going to shelve all your plans to go out and create your own firm. A move like that would draw far too much public scrutiny, at a time when you need to lay low. Besides, you are not in any shape right now to head out on your own. And if you did, there is no way I could protect you from the wrath of my father.

"Look at me, Roth: Are we clear?"

Again, Roth nodded in agreement. Back in her Wall Street days, the toughness and the decisiveness of Sheri Goldfarb had been the stuff of legend, and now here she was, back in control, as she had always been on the trading floor. With every word and syllable that came out of her mouth, Sheri knew she was right; their lives and her father's firm now hung precariously in the balance, and she was not about to let some bleeping sob story about an old man in a parking lot rise up from the ashes and destroy everything they had built.

"But that woman from the train," James said, "as we left their house tonight I could have sworn I saw the guy who attacked me from the train driving by, just as we left. Sooner or later…"

"Shut up, Roth!" Sheri said. "I don't want to hear it. Like I said, you do nothing, you say nothing. Ever! Now, drive," she snapped. "I need to think."

Almost mechanically, he started the car, did a three-point turn and headed back to the highway. The cocktails, the wine, all the turmoil raging inside him—Roth knew he shouldn't be driving. But somehow Sheri's strength steadied him, and he managed to get them home and into their garage without knocking off a mirror or scraping the side of the car. A moment later, he was sitting at their breakfast table, chugging a large glass of ice water and trying to get a grip. For four months, he had avoided the worst. Then, thanks to one damned dinner party—*BAM!*—his perfect life was now teetering toward ruin.

Sheri wanted no part of him now. But before she headed up to bed, she issued another warning: "No second thoughts, Roth. From now on, this is strictly between you and me. Nobody else. Got it?"

"I got it," James said. "I got it. Don't worry."

James heard her footsteps as she headed upstairs. He put his elbows on the table and pressed his hands into his face. He wanted to scream again. His dream of starting his own firm was gone, just when he had felt it within his grasp.

Still, he had been here before. Indeed, nothing had ever been simple or easy for him. He had struggled throughout his life to win his dad's approval. But the parental pat on the back never came. More often, he never measured up, and was harshly criticized for whatever he did. Now he had created his own catastrophe that threatened what should have been his moment of victory.

But something else was happening, too. For the first time since

10/10, he couldn't ignore the guilt and shame of what he'd done. He didn't have to fantasize too long or hard; he could hear the judge's words describing his depraved indifference. And the vengeful mob, his peers and competitors who envied his success, would smell blood. They wouldn't give a shit about what he had done for them in the past. They would all walk away from doing business with him, with smug looks on their faces, turning him into a pariah.

Throughout his life, whenever problems were hammering him, James could always bottle it up and overcome it. This shouldn't be any different. But it was. In the face of Sheri's demands, and his own guilt, his control over his future was vanishing and his fate was in other people's hands.

He had known for months that he was failing to keep a lid on that morning's events. As random and fragmented memories of his actions repeatedly popped into his head, he had become more and more unsettled, and less and less able to ignore or rationalize them. Now, after tonight, the import of those actions was crystal clear, and he knew they were going to haunt him forever.

He finally pushed himself up from the table, and climbed the stairs to the master bedroom, each step an effort.

"Are you okay, James?" Sheri said as he entered their room.

"I'm not sure. But I'm going to take two aspirin and go to bed. I'm exhausted."

"Well, that's probably a wise decision. I can't sleep. I'm going back downstairs."

In the kitchen, Sheri poured a glass of wine, and went into the den where she had a desk that served as her home office. There, between staring at the backyard and the ceiling, she tried to figure out the next step. There were plenty of good lawyers who could minimize the damage to James—if anyone ever connected the dots. And there weren't more than a handful of people who could make the connections. One was the conductor whose father had collapsed in the parking lot. The second was the bitch she met tonight. And then there was that so-called mystery man, the gallant creep who had attacked her husband. She saw the fear and suspicion that came into Rachel's eyes tonight; had Rachel put two and two together and decided that James had something to do with the old man's death? Is that why she acted so strangely?

Maybe more importantly, and certainly for the worse, Sheri worried that her father would somehow blame her, and accuse her of being derelict in her duty to the family by marrying this rogue. She could easily see her dad just disowning her, leaving her without the safety net that had always been there, especially if he discovered James had been secretly plotting to leave the firm. She could try to argue that it was too harsh to condemn James for an incredibly rash decision, taken, one might say, in good faith because something important was at stake for the firm and for the family. But she knew that wouldn't fly with her dad. There was simply no way to argue that James' actions were justified. And she knew her father was a hard, ruthless man.

There at her desk, in the quiet of her den, something was welling up inside Sheri that she hadn't felt since she left Wall Street. She had been the master on the trading floor, possessed of a cold, hard, laser-like ability to make quick, reflexive decisions, like a major league hitter connecting with a hard, inside fastball. Now she could feel that surge of adrenaline again, like used to happen almost daily. She had an opportunity that would require a precisely executed plan to throw off anyone snooping around, and to cast doubt on any accusations against James. But she couldn't hesitate, and any second-guessing would lead to failure. She needed to think it through, figure it out. James needed to completely buy into whatever plan she devised. She would talk to James about it in the morning.

She couldn't move. She thought she heard a sound from upstairs, but then she didn't hear it again. She was watching the darkness and waiting. Waiting for something.

## CHAPTER 22

CALEB'S CELL PHONE RANG, ECHOING over the car's speakers. He hit the answer button on the steering wheel.

"Caleb, it's Rachel. Are you alone? I need to see you."

Caleb's heart skipped a beat. He was half expecting a call from Brenda, but not Rachel.

"Caleb, are you there? Can you talk?"

"Yes."

Silence.

"Caleb?"

"Yeah, yeah. I'm here."

"Did you hear me?"

"Yes."

"Well?"

For a moment, he tried to come up with a logical reason to turn her down, to once again sidestep the ache in his heart and his desire for her. Maybe if he had been in his den, with Brenda right next to him, he could have found the right excuse, but not sitting in his car alone at 10:30 at night, within a stone's throw of Rachel's backyard.

"Well, guess what, Rachel. I'm parked on the first street to the right after your house."

"What? What are you talking about?"

"I'm in my car. Parked. Just down the street from your house, on a little side street lined with houses. I don't know the street name. I drove past your house and turned right."

"Coming from your house?"

"Yes."

"What's going on, Caleb?"

"That's my question. You just called me in the middle of the night."

Rachel was silent awhile, then she said, "Okay, let me figure this out. I'll be there soon. It may take me a while. Wait for me."

Rachel hit the red hang-up button on her phone and laid it carefully on the bedside table. She scanned around the room, her eyes searching for something to focus on. The master bedroom seemed small, almost claustrophobic. She had retreated there for privacy, but suddenly it was just confining. Rachel was beside herself, trying to muster up the courage to walk out the door in the middle of the night, all the while feeling her desire for Caleb getting stronger and stronger.

She changed out of her dinner clothes, and put on a pair of sleek black workout pants, and a Scottish cashmere sweater that zipped up the front, and a pair of slip-on boots. She left her fancy black lingerie on. She quickly gave herself a once-over in the mirror, and then headed downstairs, not quite sure how she was going to get out of the house. She checked the dining room, then the living room, and then walked back into the kitchen to be sure everything was clean and in order.

Seeing Daniel sitting at the kitchen counter, seemingly oblivious as usual, she suddenly knew what she had to do. She walked right past him without a word, pulled a dark leather coat from the rack by the back door, and started outside. Daniel was still reading the newspaper and pretending to ignore her, but he watched every move she was making.

"Where are you going?" he said finally.

"Out. I need some fresh air."

"Rachel, just a min…"

But she slammed the door and kept right on going. As she walked around the back of the house and passed the living room window, Daniel was standing there watching her stride across the lawn and out toward the street. The corner was far enough away that she knew Daniel could not see where she was headed. Still, she worried that he might follow her.

As she turned the corner, she saw a car parked about 50 yards ahead. The parking lights were on, and there was a small light over the license plate and a dull red glow inside the car. She recognized the car and her step immediately quickened.

Rachel walked up to the passenger side and pulled on the door handle, but it was locked. Caleb was startled, but he quickly unlatched the door. Instead of climbing in the front seat, Rachel got in the back seat, leaned back against the door, opened her coat, unzipped her sweater and said, "Damn it, Caleb Drake, what are you waiting for?"

By the time Caleb had gotten out of the car and into the back seat, Rachel had pulled off her sweatpants and was reclining in the back seat, her lacy black bra exposed beneath her sweater and her thighs open to her black panties. Immediately she pulled him to her, and started kissing him with her tongue darting in and out of his mouth, and her hands fumbling for his belt and zipper.

"Oh, my god, Caleb," she moaned. "I couldn't stop thinking about this since I called you. Please, please."

There was no stopping now. Caleb, his pants down around his knees, pulled her panties completely off, running his hands up behind her buttocks and then up her back, unsnapping her bra and lifting it off her breasts. He pressed his mouth down on her rising nipples, and then his mouth found hers. Again. Their passion quickly overwhelmed both of them, and soon Caleb was lying on her breast, spent and panting as he felt her spasms rise and subside beneath him.

"Oh, my. Jesus," Caleb started, but Rachel put her fingers to his lips and drew him toward her, kissing him slowly, almost languidly, letting her tongue dance around his lips and mouth. They lingered like that, touching and feeling, for what seemed like an hour, until finally Caleb gently pushed away.

"We stay like this much longer, and I'm going to need help unfolding myself out of here," Caleb said, kissing her neck. "Geez, and look at the windows. This is like parking with my girlfriend back when I was 15."

Rachel started laughing. "You were screwing your girlfriend at 15? God, I barely knew what sex was!"

"Come on, I'm going to get back up front. Just in case some nosy cop comes by," Caleb said.

They both struggled to get their clothes back on, jostling around awkwardly as they did so, but finally they were back up in the front seats, both happy and slightly dazed by what they had just done. They sat silently together for a few minutes, holding hands and listening to each other's breathing. Then they both started talking at once.

"Caleb…"

"Rachel…"

"You first, Caleb. Why are you here? What changed?"

Caleb hesitated. "Well, Brenda and I had a fight. And it wasn't a normal one. She accused me of having an affair," he said, looking

Rachel in the eye. "Which I denied, but she didn't believe me, almost like she sensed my feelings more clearly than I did."

"Well, you weren't lying. Then."

"Hah, good point," Caleb said, running his fingers through Rachel's long, soft hair. "Running out the door, without saying a word, probably hasn't helped anything. But I needed to see you."

Rachel responded to his words and caresses by running her fingernails lightly up and down his arm, causing him to shiver.

"What else can I say, Rachel? I'm here because I've thought about almost nothing else since you surprised me in the parking lot this week. I've dreamed about it, about you, and every time I got in the car, I could smell your perfume."

Rachel smiled and kept right on stroking his arm. There was a wonderful, tender feeling flowing between them.

"Darling," he said, "I have to tell you: this moment, right here, is just what I've been longing for. And I've been longing for it since 10/10, hell, since 9/11. I've hinted to you about it: I knew I needed to change to my life, to jump into something new. But I hadn't budged an inch, not until you came storming into my life."

Rachel ran her fingertips along his forehead and down along his nose and around his lips. "I understand," she said finally. "But don't be too hard on yourself. The kind of life change you are talking about is hard, even impossible for most people. Some of us dream and plan and struggle and we still never succeed at making the kinds of changes we really need to make."

Caleb felt a strange sensation in his chest: it was his heart opening wide to this woman he knew so little about. But he welcomed the feeling: "Bless you, Rachel Silver," Caleb said. "But now it's your turn: Why are you here?"

Rachel leaned her head back against the leather seat, while

nestling her hand into his. "Just like you, Caleb. Daniel and I had a nasty fight, and I really lost it. We talked and got nowhere and then I found myself alone in our bedroom, and I could think of only one thing: calling you. Hearing your voice. Wanting you in my arms."

Now Caleb reached across the console and pulled Rachel to him, kissing her deeply and slowly. "I'm flattered," he said finally. "You're not disappointed, are you?"

By way of answer, Rachel pulled on one of his ear lobes and sunk her teeth into the other, as gently as she could. "When I heard your voice, when you said you were just down the street, all I wanted to do was rush to you, to wind up just like this…"

They kept cuddling and petting, but then Rachel pulled back and said, "Oh, there's something else I have to tell you."

"Remember I told you that Daniel had invited some business prospect to dinner? You won't believe it. It was him, the guy who attacked me on the train. His name is James Roth. And as soon as I saw him, I was beside myself, furious that that asshole was in MY house. After he and his prissy, perfect wife left, the floodgates opened. I screamed at Daniel and I told him about you, how I wished I was having an affair with you."

Caleb was stunned. "What? I thought I saw that guy leaving your house when I drove by the first time, but I couldn't believe it," Caleb said, seeing the fury in Rachel's eyes.

"It's okay, Rachel, he's gone. Just calm down," Caleb said, rubbing her shoulder. "I suppose your husband was a bit shaken up by all this…"

Rachel relaxed under his touch. "Daniel just got all lawyerly on me, as usual. I tell him about wanting another man and what's his biggest worry? That I might blow up his big deal with Roth."

Caleb kept rubbing her shoulder, and then reached up to turn her face to him.

"Rachel, that's probably a little harsh. But geez, I have to ask, what was Roth doing at your house? Isn't he the big Wall Street financier? You said Daniel's worried about a business deal."

"It's too long a story. It's about some new hedge fund that Roth's going to start up on his own, and he wants Daniel to be his lawyer. But, please, Caleb, I don't want to talk about that now. I'm still glowing. Aren't you?"

"That is an understatement," he said, lifting her hand to his mouth and kissing the palm, and lightly sucking on her fingers.

"Oh, darling. Just that feels so good, like I haven't felt in a long time."

"I know."

"But there is one more thing," Rachel said. "Remember the conductor, the one who's been calling me? I think that asshole Roth stole his father's car and left him lying on the ground in the parking lot. And the poor man was dying!"

"What?" Caleb said, distracted by her soft, smooth skin.

"Think about it. Roth gets off the train, and two hours later he's in his office in Manhattan, holding a meeting with Daniel and his client to close a big deal. How did he get there so fast?"

Caleb paused for a moment. "Rachel, that's quite a leap."

"No, no, I'm serious, Caleb. When he recognized me, why didn't he just say, 'Hey, aren't you the woman from the train on 10/10? I was really sorry about what happened.' But no, he got all ashen and walked out like a man heading to the gallows. There's something else going on."

"Rachel, be careful. You have no proof. He could accuse me of attacking him."

"Oh, dear. I hadn't thought of that," Rachel said, stopping to run her hands over her head. "This talk is just getting me angry all over again. I don't want to be angry any more tonight. I want, I want to feel you again."

Caleb had his hand behind her neck, and said, "I was just about to say the same thing. Like can we talk about you and me? Like what's next?"

Rachel smiled, "Like to get in the back seat again?"

Caleb starting laughing. "That would be a nice place to start! No, no. I'm kidding. I mean let's go ahead with our plan to have dinner this next week."

"I'm feeling the same way," Rachel said. "From what we are both saying, dinner will be the start of something wonderful."

"I agree."

Rachel was rubbing her thighs and letting out a little moan. "Thank god, I was beginning to worry you might never let go of whatever was stopping you."

"I was crazy to hesitate. My god, Rachel, you are such a dangerous woman: sexy, intelligent, always straight upfront—everything I've been missing. I can't believe I waited so long."

"You keep saying the exact same things I've been thinking about you," Rachel purred, leaning into his chest. "I guess I've just been thinking about all this for a lot longer."

"Okay, okay. We agree. But…" Then Caleb glanced at the clock on his dashboard. "Whoa! It's 1 o'clock. We've been here two hours. We'd better get home. I'll let you know where we are having dinner, and I'll see you Tuesday."

"I can't wait. It's so wonderful to know you feel the same way I do," Rachel said.

"And I do!"

"I know. Damn, I don't want to leave."

"You've got to. Before I hurt myself getting into the back seat again," Caleb laughed.

Rachel pulled her coat out of the back seat and put it on. She leaned across the console again and gave Caleb a hard, deep kiss.

"You made me feel alive again tonight, Mr. Drake."

Then she opened the door and was gone.

CHAPTER 23

A HALF HOUR AFTER RACHEL HUNG up on him, Charlie pushed open the door into Noel's Bar. Freshly spilled beer mingled with last night's stale odors. The TVs were blaring the first quarter of the Knicks game; they were out on the coast playing the Clippers so there wasn't a big crowd to watch two down-on-their-luck franchises battling in late February for the best lottery picks.

Billy, the bartender, who had attended Peekskill High School with Charlie, gave him a small nod and a short, "Hi, Chuck, how ya' doin' tonight?" No one called him Chuck except for a few kids who remembered him from Little League games where his dad, the coach, insisted everyone call him Chuck, not Charlie.

"Fine, doin' fine, Billy," Charlie said jovially, "just real fine tonight. Fine." Then he told himself to shut up. He was in a bar, and it would be nice to sound like an adult. But he was agitated after that woman hung up on him.

"What can I get you?"

"Just a beer."

"Did you get your job back yet?"

"Yeah. But I'm still tryin' to get my back pay, too. Not fair, not fair, what they did to me."

The door swung open again, and Charlie saw Arnette Williams coming in. He couldn't remember the guy's name.

"Charlie, Charlie Murray. Arnette. We spoke last weekend."

"Yeah, I recognized you. Sorry, just couldn't remember your name."

"Your mom said you were coming down here. Your dad's license plates did turn up; a cop in Queens stopped a car in December after the plates didn't match the registration. He was in a rush or something, so he just gave the guy a ticket for driving an unregistered vehicle. The cop saw your story last weekend. He happens to live up in White Plains. He said it was just a hunch, but he ran the plates again Thursday. And he found the notation about those plates coming from a stolen car. He tracked me down today."

"Give me a Miller Lite, please," Arnette said to the bartender. "Now, there's something else we can do, Charlie. There are surveillance tapes for all the bridges and tunnels around Manhattan. And I know for days like last October, they are archived forever."

"Really? Really?" Charlie stuttered. "I never knew that."

"Yes. It will be like looking for a needle in a haystack but we should be able to spot your dad's car, if it went into the city."

"Wow, you're doin' some work, some real detective work, aren't you? Aren't you?" Charlie said. "How can I thank you enough? By the time Mom and I were over the shock, we just didn't think about a stolen car report. I'm kinda dumb about that kind of stuff sometimes."

"You got any days off?" Arnette asked, sipping his beer. "I could set up an appointment at the video archive. I could use your help there."

"Sure, sure. I got all the time in the world. They haven't put me back on a full schedule yet. But at least I'm not suspended anymore. And I'm still trying to get that woman from the train to help me out. She's such a bitch. I tried to call her tonight and she hung up on me.

I could really use her help. Bitch. I think I'm going to go see her. Like I said, maybe she saw something."

"You know where she lives?"

"Yeah, I've been by a couple of times, but she's never home."

"Okay, but be careful. People get spooked if they've already said no before," Arnette said, draining the last of his beer. "I'll be in touch about the videos. I'd like to stick around but the wife knows when my shift ended."

+++

DANIEL SILVER GRIPPED the glass tumbler of Scotch. Rachel had been gone for over an hour, and he was puzzled; what was she doing out there? On one level, he understood why she was angry with him. But if he had seemed unsympathetic, or somehow taking Roth's side, well, that was just his way, always the lawyer.

Yet he had to admit that Rachel had raised some serious questions about his potential new client, James Roth. Yes, Roth was a legend in financial circles, and he had lived up to the hyperbole with the two energy companies where Daniel had represented Brightline, the solar panel firm from California. But Daniel had not noticed anything out of line. Roth had been in total control that morning. It had never occurred to Daniel then that the sharp-edged façade could have been hiding some darker, more sinister secret.

But on top of his incredulity about Roth, Rachel's story didn't add up either. Before tonight, she had never told him anything about the morning of the attack, and he had always assumed that was because nothing had happened, or at least that there was nothing to talk about. Tonight, out of the blue, and in a fit of rage towards him, she was talking about Roth stealing a car to get to the big deal closing, about a guy on the train who had valiantly protected her from Roth and her desire to have an affair with this mysterious protector. Had he missed some signals from her? He realized that Rachel had seemed distracted recently, but until tonight, he couldn't have put his feelings into words.

Daniel didn't think he was the jealous type, but he could feel it welling up inside. What if she was screwing around with this guy she had met on the train? If so, he would never forgive her. And now he guessed that she had purposely avoided telling him about something, and not just about her encounter with Roth, but something about that morning that she wanted to keep to herself.

Of course, there were things he didn't want her to know about either. Not many. But the long hours, the nights at the Harvard Club during his big deals, well, he hadn't always been a saint. No affairs certainly. Those required regular attention, or so his colleagues told him. But there had been the occasional trysts with strangers. He stayed away from massage parlors or call girls; he could lose his law license, or at least be reprimanded, if he got caught in a raid. Still, if Rachel had acted on her own illicit desires, he would be pissed. He loved the scintillation of his own fantasies, but he almost never followed through on them. How could she? What was she doing?

The Silvers' golden retriever, apparently hearing something or sensing Daniel's discomfort, raised his head, saw his master sitting in the high-backed wingchair and walked over, head down, tail wagging timidly. Daniel reached down to scratch the dog's ear, and thought quietly to himself, "What's next? How am I going to deal with Rachel's unusual behavior?"

The dog started pressing against his knee, the old hound's signal that he needed to go out. Daniel opened the door and let him out into the front driveway. He knew the dog wouldn't stray far. As he stood on the front stoop watching his dog pee, Daniel noticed a car drive by. "Strange," he thought. Cars were rarely out that late in the neighborhood. Still, Daniel didn't recognize the car and he didn't give it a second thought.

He went back into the den, and sat for a second, but then jumped up and went over to Rachel's desk. He stood over it, staring down at her papers: a stack of real estate listings for Manhattan apartments, a to-do list for the dinner with the Roths and her day planner, which he had always treated like her diary. He picked it up, opened it, and flipped to the past week, including today. There was a notation about the Roth dinner, but he noticed on Monday, a small note with capital letters: CD. He then turned the page to next week, and on Tuesday night, there were three stars with DINNER in caps written next to the stars and then, the initials CD again. What was going on with her? She hadn't mentioned anything about a dinner in Manhattan.

## CHAPTER 24

**A**FTER CALEB STORMED OUT OF the house, an uncomfortable silence settled over the Drake house. Over the next hour, Brenda managed to clear the table and get the dinner dishes in the dishwasher. The argument she and Caleb had more or less avoided, or he had cut short when he walked out, was already fading.

Brenda wondered where Caleb had gone; it had been more than an hour and he hadn't called. And he had not sheepishly walked back through the door, as she had hoped. She didn't know why she thought he would come home; he had never walked out before, so she wasn't sure what to expect. In truth, she was scared. Every fight they ever had, she won, or at least he had eventually acquiesced, even though she knew deep down that he was just placating her without giving up anything he wanted. But he had always stayed, always been willing to listen, even if she suspected sometimes he hadn't heard a word she said.

Brenda had been relieved right after the fight. She had blown off a lot of steam by yelling and shouting and letting Caleb know she was fed up. But now the worm of doubt told her that she had gone too far. Maybe she shouldn't have accused him so harshly of not having been a presence in her life for years. That was an exaggeration, and she knew it, just as he did. But she couldn't gloss over the growing helplessness she felt as she had watched him become quieter and quieter over the last months. She knew he was keeping something from her.

She believed there weren't many secrets between them, but then she had never told Caleb about an affair she had with her health club trainer, a muscular young guy just out of college. She had ended the relationship abruptly after leaving her daughter waiting outside school for an hour while she had a post-workout tryst. After having to make excuses to Abby, she quickly convinced herself that the infatuation was turning into an obsession, and the young stud wasn't worth destroying her marriage over. And jeopardizing her marriage was one thing, but hurting her kids fell into an entirely different category. She also was clear that Caleb would not forgive her. Once she realized the situation could cause a serious rupture and personal nightmare, it frightened her into ending the fling.

The affair may have ended, but the memories remained, like scars with phantom pains. She had thought about seeking professional help, just to talk her way through her feelings, but that might have raised questions from Caleb. She loved her kids, she loved her house, she even loved her husband, which in her view added up to mostly loving her life. Given a hard choice, she would choose where she was at that moment.

But now Caleb was gone, and his abrupt exit had an air of finality to it. She argued with herself that it was paranoia talking. She believed he could never leave Caleb Jr. and Abby. Yet she couldn't stop the panic rising in her throat, that kind of "oh, my god, what have I done" panic which leaves one with a slightly sick feeling. Every thought, every imagined outcome drove her pulse rate just a bit higher. Now Brenda found herself pacing around the kitchen, looking out the back door to see if maybe Caleb was just sitting in one of their deck chairs, and going to the front window to check and see if he was just parked out front.

With each passing minute, Brenda also couldn't help but feel that all her intuitions over the past four months had been right. Something was seriously wrong with Caleb, and wrong, too, in their life together.

+++

AROUND THE CORNER from her house, Rachel watched Caleb's car drive away. She smiled with contentment, the flush from Caleb's caresses still warming her. She began walking around the neighborhood, in no particular direction; she knew she couldn't go back home until she had gathered herself a little and come to grips with what had just happened.

As she walked, Rachel could see that the lights were off in most of the houses in her neighborhood, an affluent area with spacious lots and big homes set back from the street, most of them now hidden in dark shadows. There were no sidewalks here, and the street lamps cast eerie halos onto the empty street. Rachel's footsteps echoed softly in the night. She was glad she had her coat; the air was crisp, almost cold, and her breath left small white clouds hanging in the air.

As she walked, an old memory suddenly flashed into her mind. She couldn't remember the boy's name, but she was at a fraternity party at a neighboring college in Boston, and he was attractive but shy, and after a few hours of drinking and dancing, she had gone upstairs with him; actually she had led him upstairs and they barely got their clothes off before they were screwing madly on the floor. Later, even though she had been very drunk, she remembered in horror how he finally came: to a round of applause from some of his fraternity brothers watching through the door they had forgotten to close. Rachel never went back there. Never. But her memory of that moment of unbridled desire, of the wild abandon she had felt that night, well, it all came rushing back now, rekindled by Caleb and how she had felt writhing beneath him. And there was no denying it: her years of motherhood and a rather disinterested husband had buried those earth-shaking feelings deep inside her.

How real were her feelings for Caleb? Was she really ready to leave behind all the comforts and certainties of her life to venture out on her own, to throw her lot in with a man she barely knew? Was there reason enough in her disaffection with Daniel to leave behind all the good that was also part of her daily existence? How fair would it be to just announce that the life she had carefully constructed with him was now history, shattered by a chance encounter on a train in the midst of an attempted terror attack? How could she ever explain it to Hayleigh and Ethan? Two hours ago, no such questions had ever entered her head; now they were at the very front of her mind.

Rachel was starting to get cold, so she retraced her steps past the place where she and Caleb had parked. She stopped briefly there, feeling again the lust that had seized hold of both of them. Now she knew. She absolutely knew that she couldn't simply ignore the importance of what had happened in Caleb's car. That said, she still had no clue where her passion for Caleb might lead next. What she did know was this: that she hungered to see him again, to hold him again, to feel again and again what she had felt in his arms. And feel it again soon.

As she walked, she heard a car door click shut, but looking around Rachel saw no sign of a car nearby. Had she passed one in a darkened driveway when she turned down the street leading back toward her house? Again she turned around to look, but she couldn't see any sign of a car. Still, she quickened her pace and ducked through a row of bushes leading into the vacant lot just adjacent to her house. Through a far row of bushes she could see a light coming from her kitchen window.

Then Rachel heard a branch snap, and then another, and when she turned around, she saw someone approaching in the shadows.

"Who's that?" she said, her fear rising in her throat. Then she said, "You! What are YOU doing here? Why aren't you…"

Her question was never answered. Rachel never saw the big eight-inch knife as it drove into her mid-section and came thrusting up into her chest. A hand covered her mouth to stifle her scream, and then the knife plunged in again, crashing between two ribs on the left side of her chest and straight up into her heart. Rachel's eyes widened in horror as the knife came down one last time, across her throat to sever the jugular. Her body now limp, the attacker pulled down Rachel's pants and carefully ripped her panties.

As a final touch, her attacker dragged Rachel's body under the bushes, a spot not visible from the road, and covered her with leaves. There was only a light breeze now and then to ruffle the trees.

## CHAPTER 25

CALEB FELT INVIGORATED STANDING UNDER the stream of hot water in the shower stall. He had slept better than he ever thought he would given last night's drama with Brenda and Rachel, but now all he could think about was Rachel and their passionate lovemaking in the back seat of his car. It dawned on him that washing off the sex was a good idea; he hadn't bothered the night before, maybe wishing Brenda would have noticed if she'd come to bed. But she hadn't.

As he stepped out of the shower, he was wondering what he was going to say to his wife of more than 25 years. The truth? He hardly knew what that was, and he was certain he didn't know what he wanted to happen next. He had refused to talk with Brenda when he had walked in the door around 1:30 a.m., brushing off her suggestion that they not go to bed angry. Now, with her not coming to bed, he couldn't just ignore what had gone down between them last night. He wouldn't be able to avoid the conversation any longer.

Once dressed, Caleb went downstairs to the kitchen. The bare, now slightly outdated kitchen with its wooden cherry cabinets and tile floor, seemed like a safe haven this morning, a place with memories of a happier, less complicated time. He figured a cup of coffee would do him good, so he put on a pot to brew and then started looking for Brenda. She was in none of her usual places, not in the kitchen, nor the breakfast room or the den.

He finally found Brenda curled up on the big sofa in the living room. She didn't move but he thought her eyes flickered shut when he entered the room. Instead of turning around and walking out, he sat down in an armchair in front of the sofa and waited for her eyes to open again. It took nearly five minutes but finally her curiosity got the better of her and she looked at him.

"Why are you staring at me? How long have you been there?"

"Don't be coy. You know how long. I saw your eyes when I came in."

"I'm sorry. I didn't feel like coming to bed last night."

"I understand," he said, realizing that she was giving him an opening to move on, to not discuss what happened last night.

Still, as Caleb sat there watching her, the knot in Brenda's stomach tightened. Now she knew for sure it was not going to be a normal morning.

"Go ahead, Caleb, I'm not afraid," she said. "I'm ready to listen to what you have to say."

"Okay," Caleb said. "First off, I have not been having an affair. Let's get that out of the way right up front. You asked that last night, and I wanted to be sure you heard the answer."

Caleb stood up and moved over to the couch where she was sitting. "But you were right about one thing last night," he said. "The last few months have been different. Every second of every day since 10/10 has been a struggle for me. A struggle to get up in the morning. A struggle to get through the day. A struggle to be civil to people around me, including you, and especially the kids. It wasn't the same old Vietnam stuff. Oh, those nightmares will always be there. But I know where they hide; I know how they make me feel. This is different…"

He didn't take his eyes off Brenda, trying to sense her reaction. But inside he was struggling: how much should he reveal about what was really going on inside him? Just a few hours before, it had been so easy to talk with Rachel, but now, with his wife, he was holding back, resisting revelations about what he was really thinking and feeling. Still, he kept on talking, choosing his words carefully, realizing he wanted to spin a story that would be believable without revealing the intimacies, both emotional and physical, he had shared with Rachel.

"Brenda, since the attack on Indian Point, I keep remembering what I had vowed after 9/11: that I was going to change my life, that I was going to do something I truly cared about. After 9/11, I was filled—we all were filled—with determination, insistent that 'things will never be the same.' You remember. But guess what? For me, they were the same. Oh, it took a while for that 9/11 determination to wear off, a few months, maybe even a couple of years for some people, but in the end most people never changed. They stayed in their same old ruts. That was me. I was just like everyone else, falling back into the same routine, the same, the same, the same…everything."

Brenda shifted sideways on the sofa, swinging her legs down to the floor, and adjusting her robe a bit tighter around her neck. But she didn't take her eyes off of Caleb, listening to his every syllable, watching every movement of his hands and eyes.

Caleb paused, looking down and away from her, avoiding her eyes for a second while he gathered his emotions, wondering if she could sense his discomfort. "That morning four months ago didn't start a slide into the same old depression. It was a reminder that I hadn't done what I said I was going to do the last time and the time before that. I had another chance and, I did not, in fact, do anything. Again. I don't have a clue why."

"There has been another woman," he admitted finally, not really meaning to say it that bluntly, and not even realizing that he was going to say it before he did. But he did. He saw Brenda's eyes widen, but before she could say anything, he cut her off.

"Brenda, it's not what you think or what it sounds like. Let me explain.That morning, she and I were caught on the train together. She had the only working phone, but some guy tried to grab it, and she started screaming and I tackled him," Caleb started.

"Wait a minute," Brenda interrupted. "You're telling me this now, for the first time? How many times did you tell me nothing happened that morning? So, you've been practically lying to me the whole time? And, now, you tell me there's a woman involved in the story."

Brenda stood up abruptly. "Jesus, Caleb. I swore I wasn't going to get mad again. But this? What am I supposed to think? I don't care if you've been fighting your demons. You've been hiding something this whole time. Something important."

She stormed out of the room, and Caleb could hear her stomping up the stairs to their bedroom. Damn, he thought, this is not going the way I wanted. And smoothing this over wasn't going to be easy.

Caleb got up and walked back into the kitchen. He poured himself a cup of coffee and sat down at the island to figure out his next step. He couldn't just let this talk end now. But he also knew, after seeing the look in Brenda's eyes at the mention of another woman, that he couldn't tell her the truth. So, time to take the bull by the horns. He poured another cup of coffee, put in Brenda's favorite almond milk, and headed upstairs.

Brenda was sitting in their bed, two big pillows propped up

behind her back and her arms crossed.

"I'm not ready to talk," she said.

"Well, I am. This can't fester anymore. Besides, the story isn't over."

"No, I don't want to know your story. I want to know who the woman is," Brenda said.

"Rachel, Rachel Silver," Caleb said.

"Oh, the real estate agent from the city who lives in the big French Normandy? She's married, isn't she? So what else?"

Caleb now measured his words as carefully as he could. "Well, I would be lying if I said there wasn't a spark between us that morning on the train and afterwards. Who knows what it was? Attraction? Shared trauma? I figured the latter. But moments of danger, especially when lives are on the line, draw people together, to feel there's some humanity left in the world. We all felt it that morning on the train. And she…"

"She what, Caleb?"

"Well, she kissed me that morning. On the spur of the moment. And I thought that was it. But then she started calling. I never returned her calls. I didn't want to. I avoided her. I stopped going to the Ossining station. Then, a week ago, she appeared next to my car in the Croton parking lot when I was on my way to work."

"What? She's stalking you?"

"Well, I wouldn't go that far. But I stopped going to Ossining. She saw my car one morning and she followed me to the Croton station. She just wanted to see me again and I wasn't returning her calls."

"Then what?" Brenda asked, with a distinct chill in her voice.

"We talked. What can I say? For whatever reason, there was, there was, oh hell, another spark or something. I agreed to have drinks or dinner or something in the city. Later this week…Tuesday. I did it because I wanted to. I'm not sure I'll go through with it. But," Caleb paused, "I just wanted to. If it hadn't been for last night, I probably would have gone, and that would have been the end of it."

"Oh, without telling me."

"Do you tell me everything you do every day?"

"Don't change the subject, Caleb Drake."

"Okay, okay. Well, then last night, after our fight, I was driving around and she called me. She'd had a fight with her husband and needed to talk. We met, and we talked."

"Where?"

"In our car. Near her house. She told me that James Roth, the guy from the train who attacked her, had just shown up for dinner at her house, and she was terrified."

"So are you going to tell me what happened, or is this just another lie you are about to tell me?" Brenda asked.

"I'm not lying," Caleb said. But he sensed this was the moment of truth. Brenda's eyes were filled with fear and sadness, her mask breaking down right before his eyes. Revealing how attracted he was to Rachel, maybe even telling Brenda that he had sex with her would shatter their world and probably destroy their marriage. Right now. Right here. He wasn't ready for that.

"I left and I came home. I made that choice last night. But the things I'm feeling… well, I'm not sure what I'm feeling. Yes, she's exotic. Aggressive. Passionate. And I know she's unhappy, too. But I don't know what I feel right now."

"Caleb," Brenda said, drawing out his name in a way that splashed doubt all over his story. "Why don't I believe you? I want to. Believe me, I want to. But it doesn't sound like you. Any of it."

"Goddamn it," Caleb said, "I'm trying here. I'm trying to be honest, and all you can do is call me a liar. Fuck it."

This time he stormed out of the room, and headed back downstairs. He poured himself another cup of coffee and waited. He didn't have a roadmap on how to deal with this situation; Brenda and he almost never fought, and when they did, someone always gave in, sometimes with the pretense of solving the problem, but often just glossing over the real issues. This felt different. After about five minutes, Brenda came into the kitchen.

"You can't just walk out on me now. I want to know the truth," she said, taking a seat across from him at the island.

"What is it you want to know? I'm unhappy. I'm attracted to another woman," he said. "But nothing is happening. Do I want to know more about her? Well, yeah, I do. And I'm going to. Apart from everything else, we are going to go to the police together to report our suspicions about something that happened after we got off the train."

Brenda winced, as if he had slapped her across the face. "Caleb, what are you talking about? I don't ever want you to see that woman again."

"You can't stop me. You remember that newspaper story about the conductor's father and his missing car?" he said.

"Yes, we talked about it. But what does that have to do with what we're talking about?" Brenda asked.

"Well, Rachel has a theory that Roth is the guy who stole the man's car, and we're going to report it together, since we were both on the train and saw the old man collapse in the parking lot."

"No, no, no," Brenda interrupted. "Whatever it is, Caleb, stay out of it. I don't want you seeing that woman again! Something is not right. Do you hear me?"

They sat facing each other, now silent. But it didn't take long for Brenda's frustration and anger, and fear that her marriage was falling apart before her eyes, to boil over again.

"You want me to believe that you spent nearly three hours away from home last night, talking in your car with a woman you barely know, and now you want me to say, 'Oh, Caleb, what a good idea, go to the police with this woman' to tell a story I'm not sure I believe. What's going on with you? It's like I don't even know you."

"Bren, I don't know what you're implying. But a crime may have been committed, and I was part of what happened that morning on the train."

"No, no. You need to start facing the facts here, Caleb. Talk to me. Not her. I don't want you getting involved in something that has nothing, or at best, very little to do with you. Stay out of it."

"Brenda, I'm not sure."

"No, Caleb. Let it go. I'm serious. You're already walking on pretty damn thin ice. So we'd better stop right here. I might, we might, start saying stuff we regret forever," she said. Then she turned and left the room.

## CHAPTER 26

J AMES STUMBLED INTO THE KITCHEN. It was 5 a.m., and the stark white and stainless steel kitchen was dark. He turned on the under-cabinet lights, which lit the room just enough so he could see what he was doing. He remembered exactly why he had this hangover, this depressing, fuzzy-headed dislocation from too much alcohol and the shock of going to a dinner party and coming face-to-face with the woman he had assaulted on the train on 10/10. After the party, the car ride home with Sheri had been an excruciating 20 minutes of panic as he recounted for the first time out loud the details of that morning. Yet the relief of telling someone—after four months of silent anxiety—had not helped, and now he felt painfully deflated.

Since 10/10, James had tried to put that morning behind him, or at least to permanently bury it so deeply that it would never ambush him. In fact, he had so convinced himself that he was in the clear that he hadn't even done his usual "what-ifs," walking through every possible scenario and coming up with simple direct responses. That was his favorite tactic in his business dealings, like the morning of the mega-deal on 10/10 when he had strategized what it would be like if New York had been hit again by terrorists during his window of opportunity to close the deal.

That stunning success, however, was being obliterated by the cold reality of what had happened earlier that morning, of what he had done. He couldn't escape the fact that he had been foolishly arrogant to ignore the possibility of getting caught and having to face the consequences. When he finally recognized that woman from the train in his host's home last night, the memories came back with a vengeance. He had felt like a drowning man. No matter how he tried to spin the story in his head, there was no justifiable explanation for attacking that woman and then stealing a car from that old man who later died. Damn!

James found the coffee makings, ground the beans, and filled the drip machine with water. It wasn't long before the lush aromas of brewing coffee filled the kitchen, and although it would be more than an hour before the first wisps of dawn would light the backyard, he could make out the trees at the edge of the yard. His coffee finally in hand, he sat down at the island, searching for the best way to cope.

In his Wall Street milieu, he was still basking in the afterglow of the Brightline-Secor merger, but now he could see his carefully polished image suddenly vanishing before his eyes. He felt terribly alone, cut off from his inner strength and separated from his lifelong drive to always be in command, to be out in front of every problem. Now he had to go back to the beginning and try to carefully reconstruct that morning's events; he had to sort through all those what-ifs that he had been actively ignoring for the past four months.

What to do? Running away was out of the question, despite his strong instinct to do just that—to transfer funds to an offshore shell company, then move them again within hours, and then just disappear into the ex-pat diaspora that found refuge in out-of-the-way places like Phuket, or Goa, or Guanacaste. Romantic?

Sure. But he knew there was no way he could spend the rest of his life floating aimlessly around the Third World.

Confess? That presented another avenue of escape. It would be a way to control the message. And it would be his word against the old man's—a dead man who couldn't defend himself or contradict James' version of events. James could construct a panic scenario whereby when he discovered the old man had died, he just panicked, afraid he'd be charged with some crime or other when, in fact, the old man was just trying to help him by loaning him his car. But James knew that story had a major flaw: why had he never reached out to the man's family? And why did he do so only after the newspaper story about old man Murray's death?

No, neither option made sense to him now, in the cold light of his kitchen. The first one, running, just wasn't him, not in any shape or form. And the second, confessing, would pit him against the wide public sentiment that ran against Wall Street executives. In the ranks of public trust, Wall Street bankers rated on a par with used car salesmen, and for any prosecutor or jury, the chance to bring down a Wall Street titan would be pursued with gusto. He'd be fatally cooked.

Other options? What about paying the old man's family a boatload of money and sincerely apologizing, while insisting the old guy had let him have the car? There was, after all, no one to dispute that claim, and he could stick to it no matter what. But then again, James saw the flaw in this approach: who'd take the word of a Wall Street biggie over that of a hard-working blue-collar pensioner? In such a contest of credibility, James knew he was sure to lose.

So, as James sipped his coffee in that lonely kitchen, none of those options offered any escape—or any hope. And then there was that nasty wild card in the middle of this whole shitty situation: the woman from the train, the woman from last night, Rachel Silver. Keeping her quiet was key.

At this point, James considered waking up Sheri, so they could talk this through and map strategy together. Sheri was shrewd and tough—hardened by her years on Wall Street—and James knew she would have a clearer head. But he could not imagine her seeing any better paths to follow. There were simply no good choices out there. So he just sat there feeling paralyzed, and in the dark recesses of his mind he imagined a cop car pulling into his driveway, lights flashing.

Sheri walked into the kitchen, her face darkened by the shadows under her eyes and the sour, despondent look on her face. He smiled at her, weakly. "Good morning, honey. Everything okay?"

"You stupid son of a bitch."

The venom in her voice caused James' head to jerk back, and though he had stood up to kiss her good morning, he now quickly backpedaled, eager to keep a distance between them. He wasn't quite quick enough, though, and Sheri was on him in a flash, her fists pounding his chest. He grabbed her arms, and then wrapped his own big arms around her tightly, but still she kept flailing.

"Whoa, whoa, whoa. Sheri, what the heck is going on?"

She started sobbing, a deep wracking wail that made her entire torso shudder. "You idiot!" she said. "What have you done to us? What have you done to us?"

James had hoped, the way men do, that their nasty argument on the way home last night had subsided, but all of it was still roiling inside Sheri, all the shock about what had really happened on the train that morning, and all the danger she had seen in Rachel.

Still, James tried to tamp it all down. "What are you talking about, honey? No one knows anything about what really happened. There's no way to connect me to that now. It will go away."

"No it won't, you fool! I could see the way that woman looked at you. She's not going to let it go. Ever! A little poking here, a little poking there, and your life will be ruined! Our life will be ruined! And at the first hint of scandal, my dad will fire your sorry ass!"

"So what, honey? I've told you, I've got more than enough money for us to live on forever. Forever, Sheri."

She stepped back and took a deep breath, composing herself.

"It wouldn't be enough." She stared at her husband, a penetrating, scornful stare, like he was someone else, a stranger in her own kitchen, not someone whom she had married more than a decade earlier.

"Come on, what are you talking about?" James said, startled by the fierce, almost malevolent look on her face.

Sheri just sneered at him. "You'll figure it out soon enough. But let me tell you what we are going to do," she said, every inch the trading floor doyenne again, back in control. "Today I'm calling a moving company. We're moving back into the city. As soon as we can. I don't want anything to do with the suburbs again. Ever. I'll find us an apartment. You must have enough cash to buy something outright."

James took this like a sock in the jaw. "Come on, Sher. You're overreacting. Calm down. We can figure this out."

"I have figured it out. And here's the plan: You are going to keep your damned mouth shut, period! If you so much as utter a syllable, I will tell the police everything about your little escapade stealing that poor man's car!"

James' shoulders slumped and he began shaking his head. "What's wrong with you? How did it come to this? I should have…"

"Don't start that whining now. Buck up! It's over! There's only one way out of this. For both of us: You have my back, I have yours. There's no other way. And don't you ever forget it."

For a long time, they stood facing each other. With blank, cold stares. Then the kids came tumbling down the stairs.

"Mommy, Dad, can we have pancakes?"

## CHAPTER 27

THE DULL ACHE IN HIS back woke Daniel. For a second, he couldn't remember where he was, or what day it was. But as he twisted to try to relieve the pain, he knew that he was in his recliner in the den, and it had to be Sunday because there had been a dinner party at the house the night before. The digital clock next to the television read 6:45 a.m. He was surprised he had fallen asleep because he had been so agitated, but then he saw the half-empty bottle of Scotch and the empty glass next to the chair.

He climbed the stairs to the master bedroom. No Rachel. The bedclothes had not been disturbed. As a last measure, he looked in Hayleigh's room and then Ethan's; he knew they both were away at a soccer tournament, so maybe she just slept in one of their rooms. Nothing.

Now what? He didn't want to call the police. Bad enough that she was out running around in the middle of the night, so why get it broadcast through every bar in northern Westchester where cops hang out? "Hey, you know these rich lawyers; can't keep their wives happy."

But Daniel was still confused. Rachel's revelation about her run-in with Roth on 10/10, and her story about a stranger who defended her, was completely out of any context of their lives. And now, he couldn't even be sure Rachel was telling him her whole story.

Finally, Daniel made up his mind. He would wait until 8 a.m., and if she wasn't home, he was going to call the cops.

Each minute passed slowly—7:27, 7:45, then every minute counting down to 8 o'clock ticking off. He punched in 911 within seconds of his self-imposed deadline. He didn't wait for the operator to speak: "My wife's missing."

"Sir, where are you located?"

"I'm home."

"No, sir, what town are you calling from?"

"Croton."

"I'll transfer you now. Please stay on the line."

There was a five-second pause, then a single ring, then a voice: "Captain Blake here. How can I help you?"

"Yes, this is Daniel Silver. My wife is missing."

"Why do you say that, Mr. Silver?"

"She left the house last night around 10:30, 11 o'clock , and she hasn't come home. It's not like her."

"Does she have a car? Is it there? Maybe she just spent the night somewhere else."

"Her car is in the driveway. Her purse is on the counter. She left dressed in a jogging outfit, black, I think."

"Why did she leave in the middle of the night, Mr. Silver?"

"We had a…" Daniel started to say the truth, but then his lawyer's brain kicked in. "Officer, I don't know why she left. All I know is she said she was going out for a walk. That she needed some fresh air, and she walked out and hasn't come home."

"Have you checked the entire house, Mr. Silver? Sometimes people come back in and spend the night somewhere else in the house, or maybe she spent the night with friends."

"I did, and no, she didn't spend the night anywhere else. Well, she could have, I guess, but she would have called by now. She's been gone nearly 10 hours. I know this woman. It is not like her."

"You've already said that, sir. I will put an alert on our patrol manifest, and ask our officers to keep an eye out. Is there any place you can think of where we should check? A neighbor…"

"No, you don't understand," Daniel said, his voice rising.

"Sir, calm down! Let me get some information from you and, like I said, I'll have our patrol cars keep an eye out for anything suspicious. What's your address?"

"I'm at 354 Ridge Road, in the big French Normandy."

"Right. Know right where it is. Nice neighborhood. And what did you say she was wearing?"

"A black sweat suit. I don't know what kind of shoes. She's got blond hair…"

"Sir, I really don't think we are going to need a description. I'm sure she'll turn up soon," the policeman said.

This saccharine response pushed Daniel over the edge. "Goddamn it, Captain. Don't you get it? My wife is missing! I know it. Something's wrong! Why the fuck won't you listen to me and get off your ass and do something?"

"Sir, don't use language like that with me. You want me to take you seriously. I will then. Why are you so sure that something is wrong with your wife?"

"I didn't mean it that way, Officer," Daniel said.

"Mr. Silver. Officer Brown radioed in about 10 minutes ago, and reported that he was headed up into your neighborhood. Let me call him, and ask him to keep an eye out for anything unusual," Captain Blake said.

Daniel heard the radio crackle to life in the background.

"Just a minute Mr. Silver. I'm putting you on hold."

There was no Muzak, nothing but a soft buzz on the line. Daniel waited. In about a minute, the officer came back on the phone.

"Mr. Silver, you need to go outside, and I believe it's about a block down the street to your right. Officer Brown will be waiting for you there."

Daniel walked over to the dining room window and looked down the street. There was a police car parked at the corner, and he could see an officer standing at the far edge of the vacant lot.

"What's happening, Captain?"

"The officer on the scene needs you. He's found something."

Daniel walked out the front door, and took a right toward the corner, staying on the roadway while keeping an eye on the officer through the bushes. He turned down the street, walking past the police car, and approached the officer who was standing at the edge of the lot.

"Are you Daniel Silver?" Officer Brown said as he approached.

"Yes, I am. What's wrong, officer?" Daniel said.

"Sir, Captain Blake has told me you reported your wife missing. There is a body in what looks like a black sweat suit just on the other side here. We need you to take a look at it. So, please, follow me, and try not to disturb anything around the body."

Daniel didn't reply. He couldn't even begin to consider the worst possibility.

He and the policemen carefully pulled back the branches of the bushes and stepped into the vacant lot. Under the line of bushes, there was a pile of leaves, with an arm with a black sleeve sticking out. Daniel could see where a few leaves had been moved, and a head with blond hair sticking out. He knew immediately.

The officer, wearing white evidence gloves, leaned over and gently lifted up the head that had twisted sideways on the ground.

"Is this your wife?"

Rachel's eyes were wide open and blank, staring at nothing. There was a small dribble of blood down the side of her chin.

"Yes," he said quietly, and then turned away. "Oh my god. Oh my god." What happened here? He felt numb.

"Sir, let's get back out of here. The Westchester County Crime Lab technicians will be on their way. They need to have the area as clean as possible. It's been windy all night, so I haven't seen any trace of footsteps, but sometimes the crime lab boys can find stuff we can't see."

Daniel and the officer walked back to his car on the street. The officer climbed in and Daniel could hear the radio as he reported in.

"Yeah, it's a positive ID. Guy says it's his wife."

Daniel was stunned, unable to react. He barely managed to get out, "Officer, may I go back to my house?"

"Yes, Mr. Silver. You will be getting a call from county detectives. We haven't had a murder here in, well, not as long as I've been on the force. So the county always handles these cases."

"I understand," Daniel said, his feet shuffling as he slowly walked back toward his house, fighting back his tears.

## CHAPTER 28

THE PHONE RANG, JARRING CALEB and Brenda from their quiet retreats in adjacent rooms. They had avoided each other since their morning argument, and the peace and solitude were at least keeping the demons at bay.

"Yes, Mom. Everything is fine," Brenda's voice echoed into the den where Caleb was sitting. Brenda's mom must have sensed something was going on. From there, all Caleb could hear was a series of shorter and shorter, almost monosyllabic, replies: "I'm just tired. A long weekend. I'll talk to you tomorrow. Yes, I'll be home in the morning. Yes, Mom, no Mom. No, absolutely not."

Caleb had been soaking up the winter sun through one of the den windows, with the TV tuned to the NBA game of the week, something he rarely did. But he did not want to engage in small talk, which Brenda might interpret as letting bygones be bygones. He was almost certain she would seize on anything to return to their status quo. But he had no desire to go back to the way things were. He was still deeply confused about his desires, his needs, what he really wanted to do going forward, and seeing Rachel again was the only way for him to begin working out the answer. That was his next step.

Caleb could hear a soft, distant murmur coming from Brenda's desk at the end of the kitchen; it was the local soft rock station she liked to listen to when paying bills and updating the family accounts. He could hear enough to identify each song, Van Morrison's "Brown Eyed Girl," an Eagles song, Sheryl Crow, and the modern intruder into the soft rock, pop music mix, John Mayer. Then he heard the announcer come on, and whatever he had said initially, Brenda turned up the sound in time for him to hear "…Silver. Her body was found, according to Westchester County detectives, within a couple hundred yards of her house. She had been stabbed repeatedly. She was pronounced dead at the scene."

"CALEB?"

Caleb heard Brenda's scream from the kitchen, as if filtering to him across an abyss. His heart was racing, and the gasps he heard were his own. The radio announcer kept on, "…police are combing the area," but the words triggered his memory. He flashed back to a twisting jungle trail, the sweat and dirt of a one-day patrol that had turned into a three-day running gun battle caked on every inch of his body, and then he was face-to-face with a young Vietnamese soldier with raised rifle that jammed as he pulled the trigger. It had seemed a lifetime before Caleb got his M-16 to his shoulder and fired a burst that killed the young enemy fighter. That had been simple, reflexive. Life or death. Him or me. But this? Rachel dead? Now he simply had no clue what to do.

How could she be dead? He had watched her leave the car, with a bounce in her step, and in the rear view mirror he could see her stepping lightly over the curb and onto the sidewalk, then she had stood there watching as he drove away. Had he missed something? Now he wracked his brain for any revealing image; had there been a car pass by them or behind them? Had there been a car parked on the street in front of Rachel's? Nothing clear, or memorable, came to him. Shee-it. This can't be happening.

Caleb forced himself up out of the chair, using both forearms to lift the dead weight of his body, and managed to steady himself on his feet. When he entered the kitchen, Brenda, terrified, was holding the phone in her hand.

"Don't come near me! I'm calling the police. You, Caleb, you must have been the last person with her last night," she said, her voice rising as he came closer. "Don't come near me! Don't come one step…"

"Brenda, please. Stop. You have got to listen to me. I can, no, I will explain everything. But don't call the police. Not yet, anyway. You need to hear the whole story. And I will tell you everything. I promise."

"Promise! You promise? What the hell are you thinking? Why should I believe a single word you say? Less than 12 hours ago you said there was nothing to tell. Should I believe that, too?"

"Bren, I just didn't want to hurt you. Everything, well, almost everything I said, was true. But I did not kill that woman. I swear on our kids. I did not kill her."

"You killed before. You told me about it, remember? I've read the literature. Once a killer, it's easier the second time, and the third and…"

"Bren, that was different. And it was a long, long time ago."

"You never forgot. You've been telling me that for years. All your dark stories, the depressions, the distance, the emotional barriers you throw up. So don't argue now that it was a long time ago. As far as I'm concerned, it could have been yesterday. And now this!"

"You're right. You're right. But that was different. That was war. This is a woman I barely knew, who posed no threat to me, or to you. Why would I kill her? Why?"

"I don't know, Caleb. A weird moment of distorted passion? Maybe you've been having an affair for months, and she threatened to tell me, or her husband, or… Shit, Caleb, I don't know. I just know she's dead. Did you hear? She's dead," Brenda said, her voice now a shrill, slashing cadence. "And you were the last person with her."

"You don't know that."

"Oh, I don't, don't I? The news report said she'd been dead about eight hours when they found her this morning around 9 o'clock. You got home around 1:30. You'd better have a good fucking lawyer, mister; that's all I can say. And I want you out of this house. NOW," she started screaming, "NOW, NOW! NOW!"

Caleb moved quickly across the kitchen and grabbed Brenda, wrapping her up in his arms. She thrashed against him, slugging him with her fists, but she was unable to land any serious blows as he had her clamped in his arms. She collapsed, her body convulsing with sobs, the phone hit the floor, and then she went limp.

"Why, Caleb? Why? Why? I don't understand."

Caleb could find no words. Then Brenda started talking again.

"You have to go to the police. Tell them what happened. If you wait and they somehow find you, you will be the prime suspect. Oh, my god, what are we going to do? No, you have to go. You have to go." Brenda's voice was frantic now, and she'd barely gotten the words out when she started crying again. "How could you do this to me? To us? How could you…"

Caleb started hugging her again. He quieted her, and then he sat down and began telling her the story again, some of it for the second time that day—and most of the retelling didn't vary more than a word or two: The morning of 10/10. The fight on the train. The dead man in the parking lot, their frantic drive home, their evident attraction, the truncated kiss in her kitchen, the long hiatus when he had ignored her calls, Rachel's surprise appearance last week at his car window in the station parking lot, and then the call last night while he was driving aimlessly around, asking to see him. And how she got in the car, how she reached for him, and then, yes, he admitted, they made love in the back seat.

"Brenda, when I got home last night I wasn't sure what I wanted to happen next," he said. "And I'm still not…" He couldn't go on. "Oh my god, who could do that to her?"

Brenda sat there mute. Her expression had never changed, her gaze never wavered. More than once, he thought about reaching out to touch her to see if she was actually listening. But suddenly she started sputtering again, and telling him to go to the police.

"Caleb, Caleb. Stop trying to explain this situation away. She's dead! And you are implicated!"

"And what am I going to say to them, Bren? That I had sex with this woman in the back seat of my car and I watched her walk away? And she was alive when I left her there on the street? You do know how lame that sounds, right? This is not CSI or Law & Order. This is real. They will have me in jail before I can call my lawyer."

"Caleb, what else can you do? They will find you, you know."

"I doubt it."

"Really?" Now Brenda turned ice cold and put her finger right on the reality of the situation.

"Caleb, if what you say is true, suppose after dinner, after their guests left, when she told her husband what Roth had done to her, she told him about you as well. So you're part of the story. Her husband can nail you. And you said she called you last night, too. Well, the cops will find the record of that call. And how will you explain a phone call at 10:30 p.m. on the very night she was murdered? Have you thought about that?"

Caleb's shoulders slumped, stunned at her sudden insights

into the guilty circumstances of the situation. He knew Brenda was right as she uttered over and over again, "You have to go to the police."

## CHAPTER 29

J AMES WAS STRETCHED OUT ON the black leather couch in his den, barely watching the NBA game he had up on his big-screen TV with the sound off. He was cruising the Internet on his laptop, but his mind was elsewhere. On the fight he and Sheri had that morning. On Sheri's stunning announcement they were moving back to the city and her demand he drop his plans to leave Goldfarb & Case. And on the equally stunning dinner the night before, with Rachel Silver, the woman from the train.

How could life change so abruptly? James had no answers. Yesterday, he was a King of Wall Street, the architect of that brilliant Secor deal, and now, a breath later, his life was coming apart at the seams. What had triggered it all? James' mind kept returning to that awful day: 10/10. The terrorists. The train. The old man whose car he had stolen.

The NBA game of the week vanished from the screen, replaced by a flashing Breaking News Alert and suddenly staring right at him was a photo of Rachel Silver. He grabbed the remote and turned up the sound: "...was found in a vacant lot in the Ridge Road neighborhood of Croton-on-Hudson. Police say she had been stabbed multiple times. The local police are refusing to release further details, and they are asking anyone who saw anything unusual in the neighborhood to please call this number: 914-575-2000."

James jumped up and walked over to the big screen to get a

closer look at the picture of Rachel Silver, which had been put up again while the reporter kept talking about police activity in the area. Jesus, he thought. It's her. And I was in her house last night and if Sheri was right, the woman had recognized him from the train incident on 10/10. If today hadn't already been bad enough with the tongue-lashing he took from Sheri, he quickly focused on a simple fact: he and Sheri had not only been in the woman's house last night, the entire evening had been a little strange, even awkward. If Rachel had talked to her husband about her suspicions, then it wouldn't take long for the cops to be coming after him. Could today get any worse?

"The body was found behind us, in a clump of bushes," the local TV news reporter told his viewers. "And detectives are now trying to retrace the final hours of Rachel Silver…" As he spoke, the camera panned across the cordoned-off crime scene. Behind the yellow tape there was a frozen empty lot, surrounded by luxurious suburban homes. Fallen leaves and tree limbs covered the ground, detritus from the winter's many storms.

"Sheri," James shouted, "You've got to come here!"

He was startled. Sheri was standing right behind him, wide-eyed, like a frightened gazelle, saying, "Oh, my god, that poor lady!"

"What do you mean? She's dead. What about us? We were the last ones to see her last night. Now what? The cops will be coming to ask…"

"Shut up. Listen," Sheri said.

"…we're told that Westchester County detectives will be here soon. A Croton policeman also told us this is the first murder in over a decade here, so the entire community is stunned that a crime like this could happen here."

"Shit, shit, shit," James said, standing up and starting to pace around the room. "What are we going to do? We have got to get ahead of this! What are we going to do?"

"James, get a grip," Sheri said, suddenly switching off her apparent empathy for Rachel. "And what will they get out of us? Nothing. Consider yourself lucky. She could have destroyed us."

"Jesus, Sheri. What the fuck is wrong with you? The woman is dead. You had dinner with her last night. You don't think we are going to be suspects? You know how these things work. Cops go after people because they want to make the public believe they are safe. We could be easy targets. And I have a history with her. Remember? I attacked..."

"What are you talking about? We went to the Silvers, had dinner and came home," Sheri said. "What else is there? You went to bed. I went to bed. And since we're going into the city for a late lunch with Dad, we'll just say we didn't hear about it until later. Calm down. Think straight."

"Sheri, I can't believe you. First you slam the door shut on the suburbs, and my plan to start my fund, and now you are basically saying we should avoid the cops as long as possible. What's wrong with you?"

"I'm doing what you should be doing. Thinking about what's best for us. She's dead. Nothing will bring her back. So act like nothing has happened. And we'll call the police when we get home. Now, like I said: Calm down."

Sheri took a deep breath. She whirled around, walked over to the dishwasher and began putting away the dishes and glasses and the kitchen knives.

"Maybe I should call the police. Not wait," James said.

"NO!" Sheri yelled from the kitchen. "They'll be calling us soon enough anyway. Remember? We were there for dinner last night.

We are due at Irv's house in the city for lunch. We have to leave soon. I don't want anything delaying our get-together with him today. Like I said, we can call when we get back. We'll just say we heard it on the radio on our way home."

James and Sheri's one-hour drive into Manhattan seemed to take longer than usual. Traffic was backed up at the toll booth on the Henry Hudson Parkway, the usual Sunday afternoon crunch of people heading to Broadway matinees or family dinners. As they were crawling along in traffic, James had a brainstorm.

"Hey, love, if we're going to do this move…"

"We are doing it," Sheri said. "Get anything else out of your mind."

"I know. That wasn't what I was going to say. What would you think about coming back to work? Your dad would love it, I'm sure, and I think it might be good for you."

Sheri didn't respond immediately. "Let me think about it," she said, looking out at the Hudson River.

That was the last thing they said until they reached the Goldfarb building on Park Avenue.

"Welcome, Mister and Missus Roth," the building's parking attendant greeted them.

"Hi, Miguel," Sheri said.

"Yes, ma'am. Good afternoon."

When they walked into his spacious apartment, Irv greeted them in a slightly cool manner, but James pretended not to notice. He could sense Sheri was going ahead with her plan, and he wasn't sure how to handle the chagrin—and maybe a touch of fear—that Sheri's barbs had left him feeling. The conversation was banal, and James hardly joined in the chatter about the kids and some family friend that Irv had seen the night before. But as soon as they sat down to lunch, Irv cut to the chase.

"You two seem particularly quiet today, or at least you are James," Irv said, his mane of white hair flowing back off his forehead in waves that touched his collar. They were seated at a long dining room table, which was big enough for 20 people, but the three of them sat at one end, Irv at the head.

Sheri couldn't wait any longer: "Dad, we've decided to move back into the city."

The older Goldfarb smiled, and said, "Well, I was wondering how long it would take. A lot longer than I would have guessed at the beginning of your little suburban escapade." Then he went on:

"You know a few years ago, I was trying to diversify my portfolio and, well, we were recommending REITS to a lot of people as a safe real estate play, and I met some top guys in that area, and one of them told me about some apartments that were being dumped by a hedge fund guy who was in trouble. I bought five of them and sold off all but one of them over the last couple of years and," he added with a chortle, "made a hefty profit on them, too. But I kept one of the grandest. It's all free and clear. A five-bedroom overlooking the park in the Dakota. Must be 5,000 square feet at least. Got a maid's room, too. You want it?"

Sheri turned to James, who at one point would have done anything in his power to keep from getting more entangled with her father. She couldn't believe the words he said next: "You want us to buy it from you, Irv, or rent it? Either way is fine with me."

There was a long silence with old man Goldfarb staring at James. Finally, he spoke: "Let's clear the air here. I've been hearing rumors for months now that you are going to leave the firm, and start your own. Is that true?"

James paused for a long moment. So the old man knows, he

thought. One of the investors he'd been talking to must have broken his confidentiality agreement and spoken with the elder Goldfarb. James knew he could lie or obfuscate, but that seemed like just the wrong thing to do today.

"Yes, Irv, it was true. I was seriously considering that. But I've dropped those plans. Sheri and I have talked about a move like that for me, and it just doesn't make sense. As of today, I'm committed to Goldfarb & Case, and I'm putting my entire personal portfolio back into the firm this week. And we have some other big news, too. Sheri's also thinking about coming back to work."

"Really, Sheri. Is that true?"

"Yes, Papa," she said. "I've spent enough time on the sidelines, and the kids are almost grown up. They don't really need me anymore, especially if we move back into the city. So I'm ready. James and I haven't talked about it in depth yet, but the more I think about it, the better it seems."

Irv was all smiles now. "You have no idea how happy that makes me. James, will you put your decision in writing? A multi-year commitment?"

"Irv, I'll go further than that. I'll put in writing that I will never go into competition with you. I'm in for the long haul now."

"That won't be necessary. But let's be sure there's no confusion here. I would still like something in writing from you."

"Whatever you want. I'll sign it."

Sheri could hear the resignation in her husband's voice. She wondered what had happened to his steely resolve, and whether or not he had it in him to set this mess right.

"Okay, here's the deal," Irv said. "I'm just going to transfer ownership of the apartment to you all. Let's just call it a late wedding present. We'll figure out the tax implications later. It's clean and ready for occupancy. It's all yours. Let's have a toast."

They stood up and lifted their glasses of wine. "Here's to Gold-farb…," the old man paused. "Case is long gone. I think it is time: here's to Goldfarb & Roth."

In one swift move, he was announcing that James and Sheri were full partners. "Yes, that has a nice ring to it."

James was pleased. Maybe it wouldn't be so bad throwing in permanently with the old man. His name was now on the door, even though he knew that if Sheri weren't in on the move, the firm's name would never have been changed.

Later, as they drove back north over the Henry Hudson Bridge, Sheri took his hand. "You surprised me, James," she said. "Your asking buy or rent? And putting me on the spot about coming back to work, that was sheer genius. You caught Irv off guard. And me, too. That doesn't happen very often."

"I'm just trying to move forward, Sheri," James said. "I thought about it all morning after our fight, or whatever you want to call it. That's why I brought it up in the car coming down. But I know you're right. Maybe a change of scenery will help me forget that morning. Now I have something to focus on."

Then Sheri said: "I'm sorry about your plans for going out on your own. Well, not too sorry. Your move was going to be a problem for me, and even if you don't realize it now, for you, too. This way, you've got the firm behind you and you can go after anything you want. You are a full partner."

"I know, well, I guess, you're right," James replied. "But I have to get my arms around this. And let's not get ahead of ourselves. We still have the cops to deal with."

"Don't worry about that. You, we'll, be fine. Just tell the truth."

"Yeah, right. We should probably get a lawyer lined up. You

never know what these country cops are going to come up with. And a big fish like me, plus the story about the fight on the train. That is sure to come out."

"Like I said, honey," Sheri said, "don't worry about it. A month from now it will all be in the past."

## CHAPTER 30

THE PHONE IN ARNETTE'S HALLWAY rang just as he was putting on his leather coat at the front door. He had been watching a New York Islanders hockey game with three buddies when the news alert about Rachel Silver's murder flashed across the screen. He called in to the Westchester County detectives' headquarters and was told to get up to Croton as soon as possible.

"Hello," Arnette said, picking up the phone.

"Hey, it's Charlie. You know, the conductor."

"Oh, yeah. Charlie. What's up?"

"You remember that woman on the train I told you about who was part of that fight with the big guy? The one who I said was really pretty, and who I liked a lot."

"Yes, Charlie. I know all about it. I'm on my way up there now."

"She's dead, detective. Now she can't ever help me now."

"Yes, Charlie. That's true. But I really can't talk about it."

"Detective, I did call her last night."

"Okay, but you also told me at the bar you were thinking about going to visit her. Did you?"

"Yeah, I drove by and stopped down the street. I could see inside the kitchen window on the side of the house, and she was talking to her husband there so I got scared and didn't go up to the door."

"You were outside their house?" Arnette asked.

"Yeah, I figured if she changed her mind when she heard about my dad's car, I could get her to help me."

"Charlie. Why did you call me?"

"Cuz I heard about her gettin', being dead. And I wanted to tell you. I told you, she got in…"

"Charlie, look. I'm making a professional suggestion here: you should stop talking. And go down to the police station in Croton. Tell them what you know. I'll be there soon."

"Why?"

"Charlie. I'm trying to help you here, so let me explain. You just told a Westchester County detective a story that puts you in the vicinity of a murder."

There was silence on the other end of the line, then Charlie started speaking rapidly. "I just wanted her to help me out. Help me out a little, you know."

"Like I said, Charlie, you'd better go to the cops. Sooner rather than later. Trust me."

"Okay, okay. I don't. I don't…I will, okay, okay. I gotta go," he said and hung up.

Moments later, Arnette double-clicked his iPhone and asked Siri to call the Croton police HQ number as he drove up the Taconic State Parkway.

"Captain Blake, please," he said when the desk answered.

"Hold, please. Who's calling?"

"Detective Williams, from the Westchester County office."

In a few seconds, Captain Blake's voice was booming on the other end of the line. "Arnette, how are you, my boy?" the captain said. "I'm a little busy right now; you may have heard we got ourselves a murder. I was trying to keep the Westchester boys out of this, but hey, you got the crime lab, so that's not working. I was told you'd be on your way."

"You at the station? I thought I would stop by before going to the scene. And I wanted to let you know a potential witness may show up. Guy named Charlie Murray. I'm not sure what to make of it, but don't start questioning him until I get there."

"Sure, come on by. I'm going to be here all day and night the way things are going."

+++

CALEB HAD GONE upstairs to change into some tan slacks and a pull-over sweater. He could hear Brenda rattling around in the kitchen, and the TV kept droning on in the background about Rachel Silver's murder. He slowly went down the stairs, feeling the shame of having hurt Brenda, but also still believing there had been something between him and Rachel that went beyond just having sex in the back seat of his car.

Caleb stood in the door of the kitchen for a minute watching Brenda from behind. She saw his reflection in the kitchen window, and turned to him and said, "Are you ready?"

"Brenda, I feel like we need to talk first, before I have to open myself up to the cops. I know there's no excuse for what I did but you know I have been unhappy," he said, taking a step inside the kitchen.

"About what? Our marriage? Our life?" she said. "Look, do you think I haven't felt the distance between us getting wider? Hell, it's almost a damn canyon. But if you think I've just been sitting around on my ass waiting for you to find your way back to this life…"

"What are you talking about?" Caleb said.

"Oh, why not," Brenda said, throwing down the dish towel and taking a step toward him. "You've had your little fling. Poor Caleb. I can hear the story inside your head before you even lay it out for me. You were lonely. Your wife didn't give you what you needed at home. Rachel Silver made you feel like a man. Well, let me tell you something, Caleb Drake, I've had an affair, too."

"Jesus, Brenda, now is probably not the time to let it all hang out. I'm going to be a prime suspect in this murder, and, fuck, what are you talking about? Are we going to have true confessions, right here, right now?"

"Yeah, why not. It was last year. He was my trainer. And I ended it. Because I didn't want to destroy our marriage. But I had been watching our life slowly disintegrate. Remember, I told you that last night. That you had become absent. But no, you couldn't imagine your little Brenda doing anything about it. Well, I did. And it felt good. But in the end, I still wanted you, Caleb Drake. I still do. Goddamn, I can't believe I'm saying that after all that's happening right now." After a moment, she went on:

"So now, right here on this planet, we are no different. We both tried to find something that was missing in our marriage. Right? We have something that we both regret, or at least I do. Maybe, from here, from this starting point, maybe we can save that marriage."

"Brenda, Brenda, you think that having a tit for tat is going to…, " Caleb paused and looked her in the eye. "Maybe you're right. And what am I supposed to do now? Get mad at you? You had every right to go off and screw some guy. And I did the same thing. But we both did it without even taking a chance to talk to each other. Why? Why is that? What does that say about us, about each of us?"

"I don't know," Brenda said. "You tell me, Caleb. You said you wanted to talk before going to the police. I agree about the conversation. But it can come later. At least now there aren't going to be any illusions, or deceptions. You want me? Well, you have to meet me halfway."

Caleb nodded. "Okay, maybe we should just step back and take some time, right now. Let me settle down a bit before I…"

"Caleb, that's not the deal. You have to go to the police—now. I'm ready. Let's go."

At that moment, Charlie Murray was fidgeting by the back door of the Croton police station, waiting for Arnette Williams. The detective's interest in his case had given Charlie some hope that he could finally find out what had happened to his father on 10/10. The memories of that horrible morning still brought tears to Charlie's eyes, but the months of hearings and his suspension for abandoning his post had made his life a living hell over the past four months. Throughout it all, Charlie was trying to comfort his distraught mother, and hoping that Rachel Silver would come help him out. But she never did.

Charlie saw Arnette's car pull into the police station parking lot. The detective smiled as he walked toward Charlie on the door-step.

"Thanks for coming, Charlie. Come on inside; Captain Blake is in charge of the investigation here in Croton."

They walked into the station, which was abuzz with half a dozen people standing over desks, making phone calls, talking to people.

Arnette approached the front desk and said, "I'm looking for Captain Blake. I'm Detective Williams from the Westchester County station. This is Charles Murray. He may have information relevant to last night's murder."

The desk officer said, "Okay, let me see if he's free." He turned and shouted, "Hey, Cap, I got a Detective Williams here. Says he can solve your case."

Arnette started to protest, but then he saw the smile on the officer's face. "Just pulling the captain's leg a bit. You know him? He's so fucking wound up, he needs to lighten up a bit…"

Before the desk sergeant could finish the thought, Captain Walter Blake was standing behind him with a frown. "You know, you are a pain in the ass, Warner. Show these men in."

"So, Arnette, what have you got for me?"

Charlie couldn't hold back any longer. "That lady, we saw her on TV, and she got attacked on Metro-North by a big guy and then she and another guy left together. And around that same time my dad died in the parking lot…."

"Whoa, whoa, whoa. Slow down. Who are you?"

Arnette gently grabbed Charlie's arm and said, "It's okay, Charlie. Take it easy. I'll explain it for you. You go sit over there in those chairs."

Arnette and the captain walked back into his office, a glass-walled area at the rear of the police station, where there was some privacy but with a view of the entire anteroom in the police station.

Fifteen minutes later, Captain Blake, the chief of police in Croton, had heard the details of Charlie's tale, the whole story of 10/10, his dad's heart attack, and the disappearance of his dad's car. And Arnette had finished up by sharing Charlie's admission that he had been calling the woman repeatedly since 10/10, and that he had been cruising her neighborhood just last night.

"We have got to treat him as a suspect," Arnette said, "because of his own admission. But frankly, I can't see him as a killer. He's not that smart, and only a serial killer, or some really smooth operator, would be here talking to us if he had actually murdered her."

"Look, captain," Arnette went on, "he's just been trying to figure out what happened to his dad. We just found his dad's license plates on another car. And for him it's the first break he's had in months. That's why I think he started calling Rachel Silver again. He figured he would take one last shot at getting his back pay reinstated."

"So, Arnette," Captain Blake said, "you really think there might be a connection between what happened almost five months ago and last night's murder?"

"I have no idea. Maybe I'm just grasping at straws. But I've got a feeling. I'm heading over to the Silvers' house for a little while. I'll be back."

## CHAPTER 31

ARNETTE WILLIAMS MOVED SLOWLY AND methodically through each room of the Silvers' house. He had come directly from the Croton police station Sunday afternoon, and wanted to check the house before anything was disturbed. Daniel Silver followed him quietly, not saying anything but just keeping an eye on the detective. When they got to the kitchen, Williams opened a few cabinets, the refrigerator, and the dishwasher.

"Mr. Silver, did you have a dinner party recently?" the detective asked. He had been looking for anything that might be unusual, and the full dishwasher with four sets of plates and wine and water glasses seemed out of place in a house where everything else was where it should be.

"Yes, last night. I did a big deal with a guy, James Roth, back in October. Right on 10/10, in fact. This was a follow-up thank-you dinner for him and his wife," Daniel explained.

"Anything unusual about the dinner?" the detective asked.

"Well…" Daniel paused. The image of Rachel abruptly leaving the living room and then their fight about James Roth flashed into his mind. For a second, he didn't know what to do, but then his lawyer's brain kicked in: Don't ever give a cop more information than he has asked for. "No, no, there was nothing unusual about it. And they didn't stay very late."

Detective Williams took a long, hard look at this wiry, slightly nerdy lawyer standing there in a cardigan and corduroys, and wondered what he was hiding.

"Mr. Silver, may I call you Daniel?" Detective Williams started.

"No, you may not." Daniel said, immediately regretting that he didn't just lighten up, but he was on the edge of losing control of his emotions.

"Okay, Mr. Silver, I know I don't need to remind you that your cooperation will go a long way toward helping us solve this case. So, if there's anything you want to tell me, now would be a good time."

"Like I said, detective, if I do remember something relevant, anything, you'll be the first to know," Daniel said.

"One more question. I noticed a nearly empty bottle of Scotch by the armchair in the den, and a single glass. Were you drinking last night, Mr. Silver?" the detective asked.

"Yes, Rachel had gone out for a walk, and I just poured myself a drink, or two," Daniel said. "I fell asleep in the chair. That's why I didn't realize that Rachel hadn't come back until this morning."

"Did she often walk at night?"

"Often? No. But it wasn't unusual."

"Okay, I will have to ask you to stay in the area until we advise you otherwise."

"Does that mean I can't go to work?"

"Just be sure you let us know when you are leaving your house. And that we have your number at your law firm. I assume it is in the city."

"Yes, sir."

"Okay, the crime lab is waiting outside, and they'll be here for the next few hours. And I'm going to be looking around, too. Please don't disturb anything. I'll be back in later to finish up my look-around."

Arnette walked out the front door and tried to decide if the lawyer was hiding something, or if he was so distraught and trying to hide his emotions that it was skewing his reaction to every question. Probably the latter, the detective thought.

The February sun had begun to sink below the trees, and Daniel realized the kids would be returning from their weekend indoor soccer tournament in Connecticut; they were both members of the same club and this was their one mid-winter travel event. Their absence left the house morbidly quiet once the detective was gone. He went from sitting in the living room, almost catatonic with his muscles clenched, to pacing to the back window to watch the cops moving in a tight line, one step at a time, across the vacant lot. He finally went upstairs to see if Rachel had left a note or anything that might explain what she had been up to.

He wracked his brains for any clue, any hint over the last four or five months that she might have given him that something was amiss. Before the fight last night, he couldn't remember a single event or word or conversation that gave him any insight into what was going on in her life. That fact alone made him feel even worse, that he was so removed from his wife's day-to-day existence that he couldn't come up with an explanation for her outburst last night. But he knew he would have to have something to say to the kids.

If he had any doubts about whether or not the kids had heard the news, he knew immediately when they walked through the door. Ethan was stone-faced and sullen, and tears streamed down Hayleigh's face.

"Come here," Daniel said. He grabbed both of them in his arms. He couldn't separate his own sobs from theirs. Ethan's chest kept heaving and Hayleigh just kept crying and sobbing. "I'm so sorry. I'm so sorry," Daniel kept repeating.

While they embraced, the doorbell suddenly rang. Daniel left his kids standing in the foyer and answered the door. It was Detective Williams.

"I'm sorry to bother you again, Mr. Silver. Oh, I see your kids are home. I'm so sorry. But I need to finish up."

"Can't it wait?" Daniel said. "Please."

"No, I'm sorry, Mr. Silver. And I'll be out of here soon, but doing this today is vital. Otherwise, I'll have to ask you all to leave. Once I'm done, it's all yours again."

"Okay, okay. Go ahead. Whatever you want. Maybe you'll find something I couldn't."

Ethan finally composed himself enough to ask, "Dad, what's a detective doing inside the house? Wasn't Mom," he paused, "killed outside?"

"They are just looking for anything in your mom's things, or records, that might give them a clue about who might have done this to her. And they've been questioning me, too."

"Why?"

"That's their job. They have to eliminate anyone who might have seen her last night. Remember, we told you we were having a dinner party so we were at home together. But then we had a disagreement about something that happened with our guests. She got upset and went for a walk. I was in the den and I fell asleep and when I woke up in the middle of the night, she hadn't come back."

The detective came back in. "Sorry, Mr. Silver, I couldn't help but overhear. You said you had a disagreement about something that happened at dinner. You didn't mention that to me earlier."

"I'm sorry, officer. It didn't seem relevant."

"Mr. Silver, at this point, everything is relevant. Let me decide what is or isn't. You being a lawyer and all, you should know that."

Daniel stared at the detective; his suspicion of cops almost shut him up again. "It was nothing, officer. And, excuse me, can we go in the den? The kids don't need to hear all this."

"Sure," the detective said, following Daniel into the den.

"It turned out she had met the man who came to dinner before," Daniel said as he closed the glass doors to the den. "Actually, she may not have known his name before last night so maybe better to say their paths had crossed. On 10/10. But I knew him. I'd done business with him. He's a big Wall Street type."

"After they left," he said, "she told me about an incident on the train that morning of 10/10. Seems he and another guy got into a fight when Roth tried to take Rachel's phone away. I guess I would have been fine up to then. But then she started saying that she suspected that our guest had stolen the car of that conductor's dad who died at Phelps Hospital on 10/10. I told her everything she had described was, at best, circumstantial. That upset her. A lot. But that's all there was to it."

"So, your guest last night got in a fight with your wife on 10/10, Mr. Silver?"

"Yeah. That's what she said."

"Thanks. I'll check it out. And what was circumstantial?"

"She suggested that Roth had been in the hospital parking lot just minutes before the man was found. And then we read this week that his car had disappeared, and she thought Roth took it, or stole it, or whatever. But that's just speculation. As a lawyer, I thought it was way off-base. She had nothing to go on."

"I'll be back to you on that, and I'll be sure to ask Mr. Roth about that incident. I'm puzzled why you wouldn't have shared any of this earlier. Anything might provide a motive that could lead us to the killer," the detective said.

"I know. I'm sorry. I'm not thinking very straight, but I hope you can understand that. My wife was …" Daniel started to say.

"I do understand, Mr. Silver. But you have to know or understand where I'm coming from. Any bit of information. Any missing piece, might lead me to the person who killed your wife. You never know. Is there anything you want to add about her going out for a walk?"

"I have wracked my brains all day. She was upstairs alone after we argued and she suddenly appeared in the kitchen in her jogging outfit and announced she was going for a walk. I didn't have a chance to say a word before she was out the door."

"So you'd have to say it wasn't totally normal?"

"Like I said, she walked at night often enough that I didn't get alarmed. It is a really safe neighborhood, detective."

"I'm aware of that. One more thing. What was the name of the other gentleman in the fight on the train?"

Daniel paused again, thinking. "You know, officer, she never told me his full name, I think it was Caleb, and that he had intervened with Roth to stop him. She did say she had never seen him again after that morning of 10/10, but I wasn't sure that was the whole story."

"Why do you say that, Mr. Silver?"

"I don't know. A feeling. And she told me she had wanted to see him."

"Do you think they did see each other?"

"Like I said, detective. She told me she hadn't, but I wasn't sure I believed her."

"Okay, I think that's it for now. Remember, Mr. Silver, let us know where you are going to be."

"Sure, sure," Daniel said.

Detective Williams resumed his search, but he couldn't stop thinking that it was the second time today that he had heard about this fight on a Metro-North train the morning of 10/10. He was in the house for another hour. He kept overhearing Daniel trying to explain to his kids what had happened and trying to figure out when the funeral should be and what they were going to do. So when he decided to leave, he simply stuck his head into the living room where the Silver family was sitting, and quickly said goodbye.

## CHAPTER 32

**B**RENDA REACHED OUT TO STROKE Caleb's hand. She hadn't touched him since they had faced each other in the kitchen, not even a half hour earlier, when she had demanded they go to the police. They were sitting in the Croton police parking lot, and Caleb seemed paralyzed.

"Darling, it will be okay. Just tell the truth. Are you sure you want to do this without a lawyer?"

"I don't know. Why should I even be doing this? There's no way for them ever to connect me with her. How could they? I don't think she ever told her husband about us, or at least any details."

"What if she told a friend? What if there's a diary?" Brenda said, her voice turning edgy again. "I shouldn't even have to be saying these things. And remember, there are phone records, too. But this, you going to the police, is the right thing to do. If you ever became a suspect, there would be no defense as to why you hadn't gone to them in the first place."

"I know. I know. I know," Caleb said, each "I know" getting more clipped. "Don't you understand? Throughout my entire life, I have stayed out of trouble by stopping myself, by being in control of my emotions and my desires. Now I feel like in two spans of 45 minutes, I forgot all my own rules, and I've risked everything. For what?"

He looked at Brenda in agony.

"What? What do you want to say, Caleb? I'm not sure anything could surprise me tonight."

"Let's just say that I've said 'no' lots of times, maybe too many times."

"Great, Caleb," Brenda said. "Now you're telling me that women just threw themselves at you, and you turned them down but you would have been better off fucking around all these years."

She stopped and just shook her head. "Caleb, whatever you did or didn't do in the past, there is no avoiding this. There's only one thing to do.

"You have to believe in your innocence, Caleb. I do. You coming here has convinced me of that, at least."

Caleb sat there, as if in a trance, staring off through the windshield at the police station door. People were coming and leaving, some in pairs, some alone, each opening of the door suggesting another crisis or another sad story to be told. A uniformed cop ran out of the door as Caleb watched, jumped in his car, switched on the lights and siren, and then zoomed out of the parking lot. The sound jarred Caleb.

"You okay, Caleb?" he heard Brenda say.

"Yeah," he said. "Yes, I will be okay." With an air of resignation, he shook his head back and forth, and added, "I guess I'd better get this over with."

Caleb slid out of the car and turned to close the door slowly, trying to latch it without making any noise, as if he wanted to slip inside the station without being noticed. Then he straightened up and stood next to the car, staring at the city building with two small white globes on its façade with the word "Police" on them, their glare almost making him squint. He began walking deliberately toward the steps up to the door, thinking that this moment was unlike any he had ever experienced before. He suddenly wondered if he was on a fool's errand and if he might not end up in a jail cell tonight as a prime suspect in Rachel's murder.

Unlike his "white light" moment heading off as a raw grunt to Vietnam, he could feel the torment of knowing that he had made a huge mistake last night. Simultaneously, though, he remembered the rightness of what had happened between him and Rachel and how alive he had felt this morning, coupled with his wish to see her again. In these last few hours, his desire had bled into guilt, and he might as well be a walking morality tale about what happens to people who let their emotions and their lust get out of control.

"Caleb? What's wrong?" Brenda said.

He heard her voice as if it were coming from a long hallway, the words muffled and echoing.

"What? Why?"

"You stopped."

He looked up and realized he was standing in front of the door, within reach of the handle but not opening it. His resolve of just 15 seconds ago had evaporated. Oh god, he thought, how am I going through with this? He had an impulse to turn around and run back to the car, to get away from what was happening.

He felt Brenda's hand on his shoulder, and she reached around him and opened the door. "Go ahead, Caleb. Everything will be okay," she whispered in his ear.

He glanced at her, and thought "She's right. I can handle this. I have the truth on my side, and I, more than anyone, can make people believe me."

He stepped into the hallway lit with bright fluorescents. Down the hallway, there was a sign for the police offices. He walked through the door into a room bustling with activity, and saw a uniformed policeman standing behind a wide wooden counter.

"May I help you, sir?" the officer said.

"Yes. My name is Caleb Drake. I have some information about Rachel Silver."

Behind the desk, he saw another cop sitting talking quietly outside an office to a familiar looking man in jeans and a polo shirt. He couldn't recall where he had seen the man.

The desk sergeant looked skeptical. "Sir, we have a lot of people offering help with Mrs. Silver's murder. We're kind of busy."

"I've known Rachel Silver for about four months, since 10/10," he said matter-of-factly, then abruptly stopped. "Officer, I know that man speaking to that other policemen. He's a Metro-North conductor, right? He can confirm what I'm about to tell you."

"Okay," the desk sergeant said. Then he turned to his boss: "Captain Blake, you might want to come over here. This gentleman says he has some info about the murder."

Captain Blake got up and approached the desk. "Yes, sir. What can you tell me?"

Caleb repeated his name. "I told your officer that I've known Rachel Silver since 10/10, and that conductor over there, his name is Charlie Murray, right? He can corroborate my story."

"That's right. That's right. I remember, I remember you, too," Charlie said, from where he was seated. He started to say something else, but Captain Blake interrupted.

"We can talk about this later, Mr. Murray. Mr. Drake, why don't you come back here with me. We can go in my office. Is this your wife?" Captain Blake said.

"Yes. May she come with me?"

"Sure," the captain said, and led the couple back to his office. One whole wall was covered with pictures of Little League teams and plaques honoring his long years of service in the department.

He closed the door and said, "So, what's on your mind, Mr. Drake?"

"It goes back to 10/10. We were on Metro-North, the 7:38 out of Ossining, my usual train into the city," Caleb began, then he recounted every detail from that morning, from the train stopping, Rachel's cell phone, the fight, and then getting off the train.

"Excuse me, Mr. Drake," Captain Blake said, "that's a good story but I haven't got all day. Is it leading somewhere?"

It was the second time that day Caleb had told the story so he realized it sounded a little flat and scripted and, maybe, insincere.

"Please, let me finish. It's all relevant. Or at least I think it is."

"Okay, but get to the point."

"As soon as we got off the train, despite having said he'd help everybody, her attacker just ran off, going up the hill toward the hospital. It took us about 10, maybe 15 minutes to get up there and when we did, I found a man slumped against a car in the parking lot, clutching his chest. I didn't know this at the time, but it was Charlie Murray's dad."

For Caleb, it all came out in a rush now: "We found out this week that the old man had died, and I've tried to remember if he said anything to me when I propped him up against the car. If it was anything important, I can't remember it; he was mumbling and almost unconscious. I borrowed a car from a nurse, and got Mrs. Silver home in the Ridge Road area. We live about a mile apart. We went inside together, and we had a brief intimate moment, a kiss, it was like we were relieved to be safe and needed to feel each other. We didn't see each other again until about a week ago. I was sitting in my car at Croton station—I had gotten there a few minutes early—and suddenly there was a tap on my window. It was Rachel."

Caleb noticed that Captain Blake suddenly stopped fidgeting and was now concentrating on him. "I, I," he stammered for a second. "We talked for about five minutes, and she kissed me again. We agreed to have dinner in the city this next week. I said I would call her to set up a time and place. But as of last night, I hadn't done that yet."

"Saturday night?" the captain asked. "Last night? The night of the murder."

"That's right. Well, my wife and I had a fight last night. It was a big one, one of those things that happens in a marriage, and in our case it's an old story; I can shut down when I get depressed. Since 10/10, I wondered what the hell I was doing with my life, and then Rachel showing up set me off again." He paused and looked at Brenda for reassurance. She nodded.

"Keep going, Mr. Drake," Captain Blake said.

There was a knock on the door. It was Detective Williams.

"Captain, the desk sergeant told me you were interviewing someone about Rachel Silver. Mind if I join in?"

"Not at all. Mr. Drake has been telling me quite a story, and he's right up to last night," Captain Blake said. "Mr. Drake, this is Detective Williams from the Westchester County police. He is investigating the case."

"Okay. Should I go on, detective?"

"Sure, the captain will fill me in later."

"Well, it must have been about 10 p.m., maybe a little earlier, and I started driving around. I was near Rachel's house when my cell phone rang. It was her. She said she needed to see me. And I said, 'Well, I'm just down the street.' It was where I had ended up. Within a few minutes, she was in my car, in the back seat. This time when she kissed me, we just kept going. When we were done, she said, 'I want to do this again, soon, in a bed.' We agreed to go ahead with our plan to see each other in Manhattan."

Williams had taken his eyes off Caleb to watch Brenda's reaction to her husband's admission of having sex with another woman. Her face remained stoic, but the small shake of her head back and forth said more than anything else; was it sadness, anger, or just resignation to her husband's infidelity? But her reaction also told Williams she had already heard the story, maybe in more detail, so it was unlikely Caleb was hiding something.

"Afterwards, Rachel and I talked," Caleb went on. "I honestly can't tell you for how long, but it was more than a few minutes, and then she got out of the car, and was gone. I drove away. That was it. But the next thing I knew, I saw the news about her murder."

Captain Blake and Detective Williams exchanged glances, then the detective spoke up: "And you've told your wife all this?"

Caleb paused, but only for a second. "Yes, this morning. At first, I lied to her. I had to say something because I'd been gone for at least two hours last night, maybe longer. I told her about Rachel, but said that nothing had happened. But when the news came on, Brenda freaked out and accused me of killing Rachel. So then I told her everything. All of it. I'm pretty sure she believes me now when I say I didn't do it," he said, looking again at Brenda. "But I knew I had to come to see you in any case."

"Do you want a lawyer, Mr. Drake?"

"Why would I?" Caleb said flatly. "I didn't kill her. I'll help you in any way possible."

The captain and the detective exchanged a glance.

"Then, would you be willing to give us a DNA swab? That will help confirm your story," Williams said.

"Ok. Sure," Caleb said.

"Anything, else, Mr. Drake?" Detective Williams asked.

"You know, there is one more thing. After the sex, Rachel told me about the dinner party that she and her husband had hosted last night. It turned out that the guy her husband had invited was the same one who attacked her on the train on 10/10. And it totally unnerved her. Made her furious, too."

Detective Williams asked, "Tell me, Mr. Drake, what do you know about this man who attacked Mrs. Silver on the train?"

"Not much," Caleb said. "Big guy. Pushy. Rachel told me his name was James something, let me see, oh yes, Roth. James Roth. A Wall Street guy. Rachel said she and her husband had a big fight about him. Seems her husband was keen to do business with him, even wanted to excuse this guy's behavior on the train. That's why she called me. She was livid. And she had other suspicions, too."

Captain Blake zeroed in. "What kind of suspicions?"

"She suspected that Roth was the guy who stole Charlie's dad's car and maybe caused his heart attack, too."

"So," Detective Williams said, "you're the guy who fought with this guy Roth on the train, when he attacked Mrs. Silver."

"That's right. Why?"

"Well, Mr. Drake, this is the third time today I've heard about that fight on the train on the morning of 10/10. And it would seem that all of you, including Mr. Roth, are somehow connected to the events of last night."

"Captain Blake," Williams said, standing up. "I think we need to find this guy Roth."

## CHAPTER 33

SHERI ADMIRED HER OUTFIT IN the front hall mirror: Chanel jacket, gray silk blouse, black Manolos, and tight leather pants. The inspection trip later today to the apartment in the Dakota, now hers, felt like a coming out performance in New York City after a long absence. She wanted to look perfect. And she did. She could have been 10 years younger than her late 40s. The doorbell rang, startling her before she could get her coat on to walk out the door and hop in the car for the drive into the city.

Through the door's security eye, she could see Detective Williams, an imposing six-foot-four former linebacker, dressed in a blazer, tie, and a long woolen duster. She cautiously opened the door, peeked around its edge and said, "Yes, may I help you?"

The detective quickly produced his badge, almost a reflex because he knew his physical presence and his blackness often frightened people, especially women home alone in the suburbs. "Yes, ma'am, I'm Detective Arnette Williams of the Westchester County Police Department. I have a few questions for you. Do you mind if I come in?"

"Officer, I was about to leave for the city. Can we do this another time?"

"I only have a few questions. It's about the dinner party you attended on Saturday night. I came by in the evening yesterday, but I guess you were away. No one answered. I thought I'd wait until today."

"Yes, we were in the city. For a late lunch with my father. Is this about the dinner we went to at the Silvers' on Saturday night? We heard about the awful news on the radio driving back from the city."

"Yes, that's exactly why I'm here," Detective Williams said. "May I come in for a moment?"

"Yes, yes. Please come inside. I was only thinking about leaving. I'm so sorry. She was such a nice lady. Her husband invited us to the dinner. My husband and he were in a business deal together last fall. And it seems he was looking to do some more work with my husband."

"Tell me, did you feel any tension, or did anything seem wrong between Mrs. Silver and her husband, or between her and your husband? I've been told that they had met before."

"My husband told me on the way home that he had only recognized her as we were saying our goodbyes. Detective, maybe I shouldn't say this, but my husband had a little too much to drink or something, so he probably shouldn't have been driving. But we stopped by the side of the road awhile. And that's when he told me they had been on the same train together on 10/10. He had not realized that at first."

Sheri continued, "But I didn't notice anything unusual between them. I mean, not really. She left the room abruptly but then came back. She was quiet after that. I spoke with her just before dinner in the kitchen and she seemed fine. There was some…" she stopped.

"What were you going to say, Mrs. Roth?"

"Well, maybe that's why she got upset, or ill, whatever. But she didn't say anything. I couldn't put my finger on what was going on with her. Tension, I guess. I mean, we had just been talking out in the kitchen, and then suddenly, she was leaving the room. God, I feel terrible, but you know what my first thought was?"

"No, ma'am, I don't."

"I mean I was wondering at first if this wasn't some woman my husband had had a fling with."

"Is that possible?"

"No, no, I don't think so. As I said, James, my husband, had a business deal with her husband. A big one. At first, I had my suspicions, but my husband swore I was wrong."

"But you asked him?"

"Not exactly. On the way home, we talked about how the evening seemed a little strange, and I told him exactly what I just told you about my initial reaction. Then he told me all about that morning on the train on 10/10, and I knew he was telling me the truth. You know, Detective, you can tell when people are lying or telling the truth. Can't you?"

"No, ma'am, actually I can't. I learned a long time ago that you can't always tell. In fact, I've been surprised more times than I can count. So I never take anything at face value. Did your husband mention the fight he had with Rachel, and another man, on the train?"

"Yes, he told me everything."

"Does he know who that other man is?"

"No, I mean, all he said was that he had the fight, and then it was over. He said he was apologetic, but he never got either Mrs. Silver's name, or that of the other guy."

"From what I've been told, your husband made it into the city that morning for a meeting. Did he tell you how he got there?"

"No, he didn't. Well, that's not true. He told me he got a ride with a stranger into the city."

Williams paused for minute, gathering his thoughts. Her answers weren't giving him any openings.

"Where are you going this morning?" Williams asked.

"Oh, my husband and I have decided to move back into the city, and I'm going to look at an apartment."

"I see. Why the move?"

"Gee, is that any of your business?"

"No, of course not. But I'm just asking. You have a nice house here, and it looks like you still have kids at home," he said with a little wave of his hand at the breakfast table. "Usually people don't make the move until their kids have left home."

"Well, we just decided the time was right. My husband's job is getting more intense, and I've decided to go back to work with him. We're both investment bankers, and I've been out of it for a while, but my father is happy I'm coming back to work with him. It's his firm, and now my husband and I are partners in it, too. That's why. We've been thinking about it for a while and it only works if we are living in the city."

"I see. Well, you'll have to give us your contact info. This investigation is going to take awhile. Since you were at the Silvers' house that night, you are apparently among the last people to see her alive. I'll want to talk with your husband."

"Okay. I'll let him know."

"I may call this evening. What time does he get home?"

"Hah, who knows?" she laughed. "Sometimes it is after 9 o'clock. But he usually lets me know."

"Okay. I will call if I can come by. Oh, when is this move going to happen?"

"Soon. I'm going to look at an apartment this morning. If I like it, we'll move as soon as it can be arranged."

"You won't be selling this first?"

"No, we'll just put it on the market. Who knows, we might even keep it. You know, a weekend place in the 'burbs."

"Must be nice," he said. "But please, keep me informed about your plans."

"Thank you, officer."

He couldn't help looking over his shoulder as he walked away from the house. He guessed it was at least 7,000 square feet with lots of bedrooms, and Lord knows how many bathrooms. Even in the dog days of winter, the place had an air of being well kept. He couldn't help but feel a pang of attraction for the beautiful, tall blonde. She was put together like those rich women he had seen around, but almost never came in contact with: confident, every detail in place, and seemingly unperturbed by anything, let alone the details of what had happened to her dinner hostess. Almost too perfect.

Her poise should be setting off my alarms, he thought, but she had acted just matter-of-fact all the way through. She had to fumble for some of the details of that night, questioning her own memory, all things he had learned to look for when trying to get information out of people. He definitely would be questioning the husband, but now there would be no way of surprising him. Of course he knew that was a risk when he first went to the house.

Sheri watched the detective leave, peering out the window in the darkened foyer. She could feel her heart pounding, the residual adrenaline coursing through her veins.

Her racing heart reminded her of how vital it was to be at the top of her game now. There was too much that could go wrong if she and James didn't play this situation exactly right. She didn't want to be surprised again like she had been just now. She had been a little flustered at first, but she thought she had pulled it off.

Still, the detective was right: she and James were certainly among the last people to see the dead woman alive. She had seen too many TV shows where bystanders got sucked up by overzealous detectives and prosecutors not to be a little bit worried. And it was exactly what James had been worried about yesterday. She needed to talk to him and make sure they had their stories straight.

With that in mind, instead of leaving as she had intended, she went back to the kitchen to be sure the dishwasher was empty, and that everything was put back in its right place. She went upstairs to do a quick check of her bedroom closet, a big walk-in with well-organized racks of fancy dresses, her workout clothes and dozens of dress shoes and sneakers. There too, everything was in its place, looking neat and clean, just the way she liked it.

When she was satisfied that everything was in place, Sheri Roth went back downstairs, grabbed her long mink coat and hopped in her Mercedes AMG E63 for the drive into the city. As the engine rumbled to life, she remembered how she had insisted on a car that equaled James' big BMW but with a bit more pizzazz. That felt right today, too.

## CHAPTER 34

JAMES NURSED THE DOUBLE BOURBON he had poured the minute after he walked in the house. Sheri had greeted him at the door, and said she was going upstairs to change her clothes, insisting that he come with her. He was sitting on the side of the bed watching her shed the sleek designer dress, and search for a sweatsuit and slippers.

"I just wanted to fill in the details of my chat with the detective today," Sheri said. She quickly ran down the timeline she had talked about: the dinner, the strange atmosphere before they sat down to the dinner, the early departure and then the drive home.

"I told him that you had revealed everything to me. The fight. That you had apologized to them on the train. That you had not recognized her at first, but only as you were getting ready to leave," she said.

"But I'm worried, James. He asked me how you got into the city on 10/10. I said you told me you had gotten a ride from a stranger," Sheri said. "But you know what that means. Someone is pointing the finger at you about what happened in that parking lot. He wouldn't be asking otherwise."

"Fuck," James said. "Do you think they've found the guy I had the fight with? Or I suppose Rachel could…"

"Wait," Sheri said. "Don't ever call her Rachel. Always call her Mrs. Silver. You have to make our ties to them seem very superficial and impersonal."

"Okay, okay. But maybe she told her husband about some suspicion she had, and he related it to the police."

"Maybe, but it doesn't matter who told them. You just have to stick to the story that I told them you told me," Sheri said. "And, you had better get it fixed in your mind. The detective said he might come by late tonight."

"Really? God I'm exhausted," James said. "I hope he doesn't. Is that it? I need another Bourbon."

"Yes, we're done for now. Just be cool. Think before you speak."

James got up and went downstairs and poured himself another double Bourbon. He sat in the kitchen, pondering what was going on in his life. At least the Bourbon was a salve to another unsatisfying day at work: no deals, just a lot of sitting in his office, trying to decide whether to make some calls or just wait to see if the phone was going to ring. Work was supposed to offer him an escape. But it had been hard to put out of his mind what Sheri had warned him about over the phone. Now he knew in detail what she had meant.

Sheri walked into the kitchen, went to the refrigerator, and poured herself a glass of wine. Then, she turned to him: "Are you okay?"

"Yeah, yeah. I'll be fine. But I think I know what I'll do. I'll apologize to the detective for not calling immediately yesterday afternoon," James said.

"No," Sheri said, "Remember: we didn't hear about it until we were driving home late yesterday."

"Okay, okay. But what's the big deal? We're totally innocent," James said. "But I can't help but think there's some reason the detective didn't call us in, instead of just showing up on the doorstep. But you know how these investigations go. We were there. We were among the last people to see her alive. And there's the whole incident on the train; from what you said, the police seem to know all about that. They could drag us into the list of suspects, leak a story to the papers, and suddenly we're convicted in the media before we can even blink. I don't want that, so our stories have to be straight."

"Good point," Sheri said. "But go slowly. Like I said, think carefully. This cop is pretty good. He clearly has more details than he's letting on, even if what he knows isn't confirmed."

"What about the kids?"

"Remember: they were gone. Jimmy was skiing. And Ellie had a sleepover. They weren't here. By the way, they weren't very happy about the move into the city. Worried about their friends, their soccer, etc. I was kind of surprised."

"They'll get over it. The apartment is going to be fabulous."

"It is. I went by today," Sheri said. "More than fabulous. By the way, I told the kids they could keep going to Hackley."

"You did?"

"Sure, why not? We can afford it."

"Right. Right. But you know what? I bet they won't last six months there. Wait and see."

They both heard the doorbell. James glanced at his watch.

"Who could that be? It's after 9:30."

"I bet it's that detective."

"At this time of night?"

"He said he wanted to speak with you today. He said he would call, but I bet he's trying to surprise you."

James walked slowly to the door, slowly enough so that the doorbell rang again. But he wanted to be sure he opened the door without any sign of anxiety or having rushed there. As he stood behind the closed door, he said loudly, "Who is it?"

"Caleb Drake."

James opened the door and peered out. The man standing there appeared vaguely familiar but he couldn't immediately place him.

"You don't know me," Caleb began. "Well, that's not entirely true. We met once. On 10/10. You were on the train that was stalled, and you and I had a brief fight over Rachel Silver's phone."

James tightened his grip on the door handle and inhaled sharply. Seeing the man from the train standing in front of him, one of the connections between him and Rachel Silver, was a blow to the gut. He had been ready for the detective, and determined to present a calm and collected face in that circumstance. But this was different. He knew he was turning pale right in front of this guy.

"Well, what a surprise, Mr. Drake," James said. "I had put you out of my mind months ago. What can I do for you?"

"May I come in?"

"Frankly, no. The last time we met, you were violent. You're lucky I didn't press charges."

"And why didn't you? There were plenty of witnesses. Even the conductor saw us fight."

"I closed a big deal that day, and I just wanted the train episode to be water under the bridge. What do you want?"

"Rachel Silver. That's who I'd like to talk to you about. That's why I'm here. The police most likely think I killed her because I was with her on Saturday night. But I told them all about you, and that morning on the train. Frankly, I think you killed her. I figure it's only a matter of time after they talk to you that they come up with the evidence to nail you."

"Mr. Drake, get off my property before I call the police. You are delusional. And don't go around making accusations you can't back up. Or I'll have your ass in court before you can say good morning. Now, good night. And don't ever come back here."

Caleb turned and walked slowly down to the driveway. He looked over his shoulder, and imagined that he could see Roth peeking out from behind the curtains. He could only hope they would do something stupid now.

"How did he take it?" Brenda asked.

"Like someone electro-shocked him," Caleb said. "God, if he isn't guilty of Rachel's murder, then he does have something to hide from that morning."

James closed the door, and watched through the curtains until the car pulled down the driveway and drove away. He nearly slumped to the floor, the two glasses of Bourbon on an empty stomach, plus his pounding heart, making him feel faint.

He turned away from the door, stepped into the hallway, and almost ran into Sheri.

"James, what's wrong?" Sheri asked. "Who was that? I couldn't get close enough to hear everything you were saying. It didn't sound like the detective."

"The guy from the train who tackled me when I tried to take that phone away from Rachel."

"Oh my god! What did he want?"

"He thinks I killed her. He says the cops think he did."

"Oh my god. Who is he?"

+++

CALEB DROVE AROUND aimlessly, staying off the main highways of Westchester County heading north away from New York City. He and Brenda hadn't said much since leaving Roth's house, but Brenda said she wasn't ready to go home yet, so he kept driving.

The drive seemed to be a fitting end to a day spent waiting for the next bomb to drop. Caleb had stayed away from work, not his usual pattern on a Monday. He was still distraught and just needed a day to gather his thoughts, talk with Brenda, and wait for another call from the police. But when Caleb suggested dropping by the Roth house, mostly to satisfy his own curiosity if it was really the same guy from the train on 10/10, Brenda agreed.

As he drove along the dark, tree-lined country roads, Caleb couldn't help but see the irony: 48 hours earlier he had been driving alone when he got that fateful phone call from Rachel. Tonight, he was driving again, this time with his wife, trying to escape the day's dramas that the call had somehow set in motion.

Along Route 9W, he pulled into a small turnout above West Point, one with a vista looking all the way back down the Hudson Valley. He turned off the engine and just sat there, looking at the faraway twinkling lights of the towns along the river.

"What are you thinking, Caleb?" Brenda finally asked.

"I'm just thinking about my life," he said.

"That I figured. Be a little more specific, why don't you? And I'll say it again, I thought you were magnificent yesterday with the police back in Croton."

"Thanks, but it won't matter. They are going to do what they do: follow the evidence. If they always bought what everyone in a murder case told them, no one would ever get convicted. So this is far from over."

"Well, I think they believed you. But what were you thinking just now?" she asked.

"Funny, I was wondering if I'm just fooling myself, trying to play out some fantasy about what my life should be, or could have been. And I was wondering if I had forgotten all the good things that I have right now," he said, turning to Brenda. "I do love you, you know."

"I'm sure you do, Caleb. And I love you, too."

Caleb leaned back and laid his head on the headrest. "Look at all those lights down there, all those nice homes close to the river, all those people safe and comfortable in their safe little suburban lives," Caleb said. "Can I tell you a secret?"

"Sure, honey. What is it?"

"Well, the other day I was standing in a Starbucks on Park Avenue, and outside there was a parade of young men, and women too, all very well dressed, all marching up the avenue with their leather briefcases. Do you know what I wanted to do, Brenda?"

"No, what?"

"I wanted to go stand in the middle of the avenue and shout: 'Stop! You have no idea where you're headed! One day—either tomorrow or 20 years from now—you are going to wake up and say, Shit, where did the time go? Where did my life go? All those years chasing money. Chasing security. Staying cozy in your rut. And for what? Stop! Think! Feel!' Yes, that's how I feel right now. Where did it all go? What happened to the life I dreamed of living?"

Brenda studied her husband's face and suddenly felt very detached—and angry. "Well, it seems to me you've done pretty well for yourself, Caleb Drake," she finally said. "You built the most respected PR firm in New York City. What, 150 people working for you? More Fortune 500 clients than you can handle. A fine family. The same wife for over 25 years—a wife who loves you. And now you're pissing on all of that. How do you think that makes me feel?"

"You're right, Brenda: I should be content. Totally content. And I don't mean to take anything away from you. But you know what?

I can still see those two strange jets flying low over the Hudson River on that beautiful autumn morning and, well, they missed their targets at Indian Point, but they smashed open the shell I've been living in. Suddenly I realized that nothing in my life was really done by design. It was one small decision after another, just putting one foot down after the other, and then one small mistake—Rachel—and it all might come tumbling down, like some worthless house of cards. One damn mistake!"

Brenda was having a hard time leaving her anger behind, but she felt a surge of empathy, reaching out to touch the man she had loved for what seemed like her entire life. What Caleb was saying went far beyond words, and it was exactly what she craved, what she had craved for ages: something real, something authentic, something naked and pure. And, she could feel it; he was saying he needed her.

"You know, Caleb, we all were terrified that morning. We all had visions of nuclear clouds, of waves of radiation coming our way and destroying everything in their path. When I got in the car that morning and started driving, I was sure I'd never see you again, that I would never hug our kids again. It was the loneliest feeling in the world. And I bet Rachel Silver felt the exact same way. Sitting there on that train, feeling totally helpless—until you stepped in to help. You say now that it was a mistake. Well, I say it was an honorable thing to do. And I'm very proud of you for doing it."

"Proud? That's the last word I'd use to describe myself right now. I guess I should be glad you feel that way, but I can't help but wondering how you're going to feel in a week, or a month, or when I end up being charged with her murder."

"Caleb, come on. You don't need to go there. You've done the right thing. You're innocent. And someday everyone is going to realize you tried to help that woman, and then things spun out of control."

"But look where it led. And in the meantime, that day, 10/10, ended up making me feel like I was stuck in the same old trap."

"Oh, honey," Brenda said, finally reaching up to touch his face. "I get it. But let's keep talking. Just like this. I'm ready to go home now."

"Me, too," Caleb said, turning on the car and heading back down the highway toward home.

## CHAPTER 35

**D**ANIEL WAS STILL SITTING IN the dark den where he had been since he and the kids had returned from Rachel's funeral. The ceremony had been small and solemn, a gathering of a few close friends and her colleagues from the city. But the sadness of the funeral had faded into the background as day had turned into night.

The kids had gone upstairs almost as soon as they got back to the house. He had tried to reach out to them and comfort them as best he knew how, but the lack of emotional foundation with them had made his gestures feel awkward and, in the end, they didn't really seem interested in sharing their feelings or thoughts with him. He was having a hard enough time dealing with his own distress.

The phone rang.

"I know you've had a hard day, Mr. Silver," the voice on the phone said. "But I really need to speak with you. May I come over?"

Daniel finally recognized the voice as Detective Williams.

"I thought you might give me a few days before harassing me," Daniel said. "We had her funeral service today, and thanks to you I couldn't even bury her. But at least the rabbi gave us dispensation for that injustice."

"Mr. Silver, I'm not trying to harass you. You know the rules in a murder investigation; we still need the body. And you're a lawyer, you know the drill. After the first 72 hours, it gets harder and harder to solve a crime. And we're still in that window. I doubt you forgot that. So, please. It's only a couple of questions."

"Why don't you ask me on the phone?"

"Well, I'm in the neighborhood. I wanted to look at it in the dark. Get a sense of what your wife might have been doing, or who might have had a chance to see her out a window, maybe even without recognizing what was happening."

Reluctantly, Daniel said, "Okay."

The doorbell rang, almost immediately.

When Daniel answered the door, he couldn't even muster the courtesy to ask the detective inside, making him stand in the foyer while they talked.

"You were closer than I realized," Daniel said.

"I was right outside. This neighborhood sure is quiet at night."

"It is. I hear the same car almost every night of the week. It must be someone who works a night shift because it's the same loud muffler, probably has a hole in it, going by every night between 10 and 10:30… almost like clockwork. "

"On weekends, too?"

"No, I never hear it on weekends."

"I'll make this quick. Did you ever hear your wife talk about the man from the train?"

"Which one, Roth?"

"No, I can't give you his name right now. He's become a suspect. He was the one who apparently tackled Roth when he was trying to get her phone."

"Other than telling me that a nice man had helped her that day, she never mentioned his last name. I told you that yesterday."

"Would you be surprised if you found out she was having an affair?" It was a calculated question, and Williams watched every muscle in Daniel's face.

"Excuse me? An affair? Are you kidding me? Don't you think I would have known?"

"Usually, Mr. Silver, the spouse is the last one to know."

At that, Daniel erupted. "Who the fuck are you anyway? Coming here late at night. On the day of my wife's funeral! And laying that kind of story on me. No, I tell you, no, she wasn't having an affair. She told me all the time about people hitting on her when she was showing them apartments, and she never, never—I tell you never—did anything about it. She always insisted."

Detective Williams waited a few heartbeats, then he went in for the final shock. "Did you have sex with her that night?"

Daniel started sputtering, spewing a string of profanities that caused Williams to take a step backward, in case he needed to protect himself. The foyer closed in around both of them. But his close proximity gave him the chance to see the wave of doubt sweep over Silver's face.

"No, I told you we had a fight, but…" Silver started and stopped almost immediately, and instead of fidgeting and letting his eyes dart nervously around the room, he caught himself: "Is there something, is there something else you want to tell me now?"

"Mr. Silver, the preliminary crime lab report has come back. Your wife had intercourse shortly before she died, and there was semen in her vagina." He watched Silver's shoulders slump and his hand reach out for the door frame.

"Oh my god, Rachel. Oh my god. I knew…" he said, talking to himself and then stopped. After he took a couple of deep breaths, he looked up at the detective with an anguished scowl on his face. "Leave me alone. Please. Just leave me alone."

"You were about to…"

"Get out, get out now," the lawyer said.

Williams opened the door, turned one last time to look at Silver, whose eyes flashed with anger and pain.

Once back in his car, the detective paused for a minute. He was almost ashamed of himself, putting Daniel Silver through that ordeal on the same day as his wife's funeral. But the rawness of the moment had accomplished what he wanted; he had surprised Mr. Silver and gotten what he thought was an honest, unfiltered reaction. In the end he knew that solving the case carried more weight for him than the sensibilities of one potential suspect.

Williams headed south toward Briarcliff, pondering his next move. He was trying to get a sense of the landscape around Rachel's murder, and lay out a blueprint for what did or did not happen that night. He knew he had alerted Sheri Roth that he would be contacting her husband today, and that was the final "to do" on his list for the evening. It was a fairly quick drive; he timed it and noted the distance of about five and a half miles and calculated how long it would have taken them to get there. In his mind, he wasn't really thinking about either of the Roths as possible suspects, but they had to be in the mix; they were with Rachel on Saturday night, and if there was truth to what happened on 10/10 between Rachel and Roth and Caleb Drake, then it wasn't too far-fetched to develop a motive for them being involved in Rachel's murder.

As he approached the house, he was about to pull the same trick he had used with Silver: Call, say he'd like to come over, and then be there inside of a minute or two. But when he stopped the car, he saw Caleb Drake on the porch of Roth's house talking with someone he presumed to be James Roth. He watched for a minute as Drake whirled around, walked down the driveway and drove away in his Audi. As they passed, he saw Drake's wife was in the car, too. He couldn't believe that man was at the Roth's house. He had to be acting on his own. But why?

Either way, Roth couldn't be anything but upset. He dialed the Roth's number.

A clearly agitated male voice answered. "Who is it?"

"Mr. Roth, this is Detective Williams. Is now a convenient time?"

"Damn, what the fu…" Roth stopped.

"Is something wrong?"

"Well, it is late, and yeah, I'm …" Roth stopped again

"Have anything to do with Caleb Drake?"

There was silence on the line.

"I happened to drive up as he was walking away. I think we need to talk, Mr. Roth. Now."

"Jesus Christ. I'm not really ready or in the mood right now."

"Mr. Roth, if we don't do it now, I'll have to ask you to come into the Croton police station tomorrow. It won't take long. I just have a few questions."

"Dammit. I can't tomorrow. A big meeting, so, shit, I'm here."

"I'll be there in 30 seconds."

When he rang the doorbell, Sheri Roth opened the door. She looked as ravishing as she had that morning, but she was now dressed in just a navy blue t-shirt and a pair of white warm-up pants.

"Good evening, Detective. We were expecting you. Although we were a little surprised to see this guy, Caleb, what's his name, Drake?"

"Frankly, I'm surprised, too. What did he want? Do you know him?"

James appeared from around the corner of the foyer. "I hadn't seen him in over four months, and I barely remembered his face. We had, uh, an altercation on the morning of 10/10. I was a bit out of control, and wanted to talk to whoever Rachel Silver—I now know who she is—was talking to on her phone."

"And what happened?"

"He tackled me. Blindsided me, knocked the wind out of me. Little bastard."

"But he told me that afterwards you asked him and Rachel to help you get off the train. Is that true?"

"Oh, so you've heard the story. Well, yeah, I knew I'd been a bit of an asshole, and I needed their help. And they did help."

"But then you left them on the train?"

"Yes, I was in a hurry."

"What did you do then?"

"Excuse me, but what does that have to do with Rachel Silver? I thought you were investigating her murder."

"I'll get to that. I'm just trying to figure out what happened. You got into the city that morning, didn't you?"

"Geez, I got a ride with a stranger from the parking lot. He dropped me off in upper Manhattan, and I got a taxi downtown."

"Did you see anyone else in the parking lot?"

"No, I got in the car with this guy and we drove off."

"So, there's no one who can confirm your story? Do you remember the driver's name?"

"No, for god's sake. We listened to the radio the entire time. You know there was a lot of shit happening that morning. We got to the city, I thanked him and got out. I couldn't even tell you what kind of car it was."

Williams switched quickly to the dinner party. "So, you left the dinner party at what time?"

"It was early. We barely finished dinner. Dessert was served, and then it was like, dinner was over."

"Did she recognize you?"

"I don't know. I was talking to Daniel. Sheri thinks she did, but who knows."

"And then?"

Roth repeated almost verbatim the same story as Sheri had told him that morning. The drive home. The talk about 10/10. Going to bed. Getting up in the morning, and then later hearing the news on the radio, heading home from the city after a late lunch with her father.

"Moving into the city, I hear," he said, turning to Sheri. "How was the new apartment?"

"It was beautiful," she said, "And yes, we will be moving soon. It's ready to move in."

"We've been talking about it for a while," James added.

Williams paused. "Okay, I guess that's it for now. I apologize for bothering you so late."

"Sure, sure, detective. I get it. And I apologize for my harsh language a few minutes ago. I was just taken aback by that man knocking on my door and accusing me of murdering Rachel Silver."

"Is that what he said?"

"Yeah, you asked earlier, but I wanted you to hear my side of the 10/10 story. So yes, he said the police had him as the prime suspect. But he said he thought I had done it. What a crock of shit."

"Well, Mr. Roth, I'm sorry. He shouldn't have been here, and certainly not suggesting that the police have a suspect. Let me be clear: I am the lead investigator, and we have narrowed the list of people we want to talk to because they saw her Saturday night, but we certainly are not ready to start naming suspects."

"I told him that if he repeated that charge in public, I'd haul his ass into court."

"Don't worry, I will be speaking to him."

"Thank you, officer. Is that all?"

"Yes, it is. I'll be in touch, and you may still be asked to come into the station in the next few days and make a formal statement."

"I understand. Should I bring a lawyer, too?"

"Oh, that's entirely up to you. Statements really aren't inter-rogations. But if you are more comfortable, no one will hold it against you."

"Thanks."

"Good night, and good night, Mrs. Roth."

"Good night, detective."

Arnette Williams walked to his car. He actually was glad he had found Roth in such an agitated state. The man probably revealed more than he would have otherwise. But on the other hand, it was hard to get a read on what was going on in his head. He was defi-nitely defensive about the morning of 10/10, but less conflicted, it seemed, over the night of Rachel's murder. And his story of that night matched his wife's perfectly, so their alibis seemed solid. Ei-ther that, or they were very carefully covering for each other.

Roth stood semi-frozen in the doorway as he watched the de-tective's car drive away.

"You okay, honey?" Sheri asked, stroking his shoulder, trying to soothe his agitation.

"Damn, that was hard." He couldn't focus, his thoughts were in a jumble as he tried to remember exactly what he had said to the detective, and wondering if, in fact, he had said the same words to Caleb Drake. He had repressed the events of four months ago so successfully that he had almost forgotten exactly what had happened. Now, under pressure, he was having to draw on those foggy memories of that morning, and he was confused, unable to conjure up the scene.

"Don't worry. You did great, James. And thank god we had a chance to talk beforehand. There won't be anything for them to pin on us," Sheri said, still stroking him.

"Well, this sure doesn't feel like it's over," James said. Then he walked past Sheri and headed back into the kitchen for another glass of Bourbon.

## CHAPTER 36

T HE CROTON POLICE STATION HAD emptied, and its fluorescent lights brightened the rows of wooden desks, the linoleum floors, and the small waiting room with worn wooden benches. Arnette Williams and Captain Blake were alone, with the chatter of the police radio loud enough to hear in the background. A fender bender out on Route 9 had taken the one patrolman on duty out on the road.

"I thought you might need a cup of coffee," Blake said. "It's getting up on midnight, and you've been listening to those tapes for two hours now. Any better idea about what's going on here?"

Williams nodded his head, preferring to stay buried in the tape of Caleb Drake's interview and figuring the town cop would go away. But the captain wasn't moving.

"No, I've been listening to the section about Drake's meeting Rachel Silver," Williams finally said. "I've been doing this a long time. And nothing triggers for me. No hesitations. No repeats. No past tense. Maybe that's the clue. It's too neat. Too rehearsed. Not the first time I felt that today."

"Well, the poor guy had his wife right there. I can't imagine what that was like. Didn't he say that he had admitted to her he had just 'seen' her," Blake said, holding up his hands in the universal quotation sign, "the night before? Must not have been a pretty scene when she popped up dead on News 12."

"True. You can tell he's a guy who keeps it under control. The

V-neck. The chinos. The loafers. Expensive haircut, too, and damn, he doesn't look like he is in his 60s, does he? Very buttoned-up guy who watches after himself. You have to believe this whole thing makes him feel totally out of control. One minute everything is fine, he resists the temptation of this beautiful lady, and four months later, everything gets fucked up when he finally gives in to her. At least that's how he tells it." Williams paused, but only for a moment.

"You got to figure he knew we'd get to him. That's the only reason he came in—the phone records, the forensics, his absence from his house, his wife. A smart perp takes the bull by the horns and gets ahead of the investigation. But he admitted to stuff he didn't have to. And he really didn't act guilty, other than towards his wife, which he'll have to deal with on his own. I don't think he did it, and there certainly isn't enough to indict him, but he can't be ruled out either."

"But if you don't mind me asking," Blake said, "who else is on the radar?"

Williams hesitated for a second. He didn't like sharing any info, even with a fellow cop. But then usually by this point, 48 hours into an investigation, he already had a pretty good idea of who should be the prime suspect.

In quick order, he ran through his list of other possible suspects: Daniel Silver; maybe a jealous husband striking in a fit of rage—couldn't dismiss that out of hand. Charlie Murray; he had admitted being in the victim's neighborhood and having a grudge against her. James Roth; he was in the Silvers' house that night and there was the whole 10/10 connection that cast a shadow on him. Each had possible motive and maybe opportunity, but to the detective, none leapt forward as the most likely suspect. That left Caleb Drake, but Williams was pretty sure he hadn't done it.

"In other words, captain, I got nothing right now," Williams concluded.

"Well, I got news for you, detective. Sorry I didn't tell you this before you started your detailing of your investigation. But I wanted to hear what you had to say. I'm pretty much in agreement with you. But our Westchester D.A. isn't buying it."

"Rasmussen? That hack?"

"You guessed it."

"Don't tell me."

"Yup, there's a grand jury sitting in White Plains. He's going to seek an indictment of Caleb Drake on Friday."

"That's only four days away! What does he want? How did he know so quickly, and without talking to me?"

"He wants all our files and your presence Wednesday morning to discuss it. Called as soon as the M.E. report came in, and I let them know—guess that was a mistake—about Drake's admission of having sex with her. They called this afternoon."

"What a prick. Looking for a front-page story."

"I'm sorry I didn't let you know sooner, but, to be honest, I wanted to see if we were on the same page. I'd looked at everything and couldn't pin it on anybody. But I hadn't interviewed everybody, so I figured you might have a better idea."

"The only one who I didn't get a clear read on was Roth. His encounter with Drake clearly shook him up. But he was so agitated, I couldn't really tell where he was coming from. But if Roth isn't hiding something, I'm giving up my badge. That's totally a gut feel. If that shit Rasmussen goes after Drake, everything gets buried. I'll never get anything out of the Roths."

"Now what?

"I'm going to have to try to talk Rasmussen out of the grand jury hearing. All he is doing is making sure I'm not going to find the real killer. What time Wednesday?"

"10, at the courthouse in White Plains."

"See you there."

Two mornings later, Williams drove up the Bronx River Parkway from Mount Vernon, carefully navigating the narrow, winding "parkway," a throwback to when cars couldn't go much faster than 40 miles an hour. Even though the speed limit remained the same, cars zipped by him at the tail end of rush hour, probably people late to work as usual.

He exited toward the tall apartments and the glass and concrete office buildings of downtown White Plains, a transformed urban zone that had benefited from the rise of commercial real estate prices in Manhattan. More and more businesses were setting up shop there, and it still was the seat of government for Westchester County, one of the wealthiest suburbs of a mega-metropolis in America. Between The Westchester and the Galleria malls—two gigantic economic engines—the movie theaters and restaurants, and the ever-expanding roster of hotels and high-rise condominiums, White Plains was now the center of life north of New York City.

That fact alone made the district attorney's job there one of the highest profile positions in New York State, and the lawyers sitting in that chair had for years used it as a stepping stone to higher political office. But they were saddled with one of those unavoidable social realities: the disparity between the largely white social and economic elite and the vast warren of lower income blacks and Hispanics who worked in the homes and on the lawns of the suburban lords, and who committed, or were at least perceived to commit, a disproportionate percentage of the crimes in the area. D.A. Stephen Rasmussen, who had already announced a run for governor in the fall, had been accused of racism more than once for his aggressive prosecution of minority offenders; he hadn't had a successful prosecution of an upper middle class white man for a violent crime in a long time. Caleb Drake was the perfect instrument for his political ambitions, and it was obvious to Williams, and maybe to a lot of observers in Westchester County, that the ambitious D.A. wasn't going to let anything get in his way.

As he neared the courthouse, Williams ran through the list of arguments he was going to give Rasmussen. But he knew how hard it was to derail a zealous prosecutor, especially an ambitious one who had been accused of being soft on white men who broke the law.

The underground parking garage was a maze of pillars and sharp turns, and Williams had to find spaces that weren't reserved for the dozens of prospective jurors who arrived at the courthouse every morning to sit through hour after hour of jury selection in both county and state courts. He drove past the small area reserved for grand jurors, who were often seated for three to four months at a time, if only for a couple of days a week.

Walter Blake, in his dark blue police uniform, sat in the starkly furnished waiting room of the district attorney's office. Why was it that modern government offices were so depressing, devoid of humanity? At least the grand old government offices had dark woods and ornate ceilings and marble floors. The plasterboard, linoleum and fluorescent lights made this one feel more like a morgue than an official government hall of justice.

"Hey, captain. Did you get any sleep?"

"Not much, you?"

"Hardly any."

"Gentlemen," the receptionist said. "The district attorney is ready for you."

It was 10:03, which surprised Detective Williams. He figured Rasmussen would make them wait as a power-trip maneuver.

The captain led the way through the door. Williams scanned the walls: the diploma from SUNY-Purchase, the law degree from NYU and the New York State Bar document lined up in prominent, can't-miss-them positions.

"Good morning, gentlemen," District Attorney Rasmussen said, not rising from behind his desk. "Thank you both for coming. I just want to be sure we are all on the same page here. Murder isn't taken lightly by this office. Please sit down."

Williams and Blake looked at each other, realizing they hadn't decided who would go first.

Detective Williams jumped in. "Mr. Rasmussen, we both feel that it is premature to seek an indictment against anyone. There are too many loose ends, too many unanswered questions to let any information go public."

"Well, too late; I have filed the request for the indictment after a preliminary hearing of evidence yesterday afternoon. The grand jury hearing to issue those indictments is on Friday. And have you forgotten that grand jury hearings are closed?"

"With all due respect, sir, the grand jury in White Plains has been a straight conduit to the Journal News for a long time now."

Williams knew this would piss off the District Attorney because, at least among local law enforcement, everyone suspected Rasmussen was the source of the leaks.

"Be careful, detective," Rasmussen said. "Any accusation of leaking confidential information, which is a felony, might be construed as slander, an equally serious charge, at least among people supposedly on the same side."

"Yes, sir, I know that. I'm just telling you that in my best professional judgment, there is no—or very little—justification for taking this case to the grand jury this week. It's not even four days since the murder."

"Well, we got the DNA match. We have motive. We have physical presence. What more do you want, detective?" Rasmussen said.

"DNA? It takes a couple of weeks…"

"Detective, I put a rush order on that analysis and it's already back. We have a match with Mr. Drake, who I presume is your prime suspect. If he isn't, he should be. I mean he screws this woman and who knows what really went on between them. It's a perfect set-up for some conflict between them. He's married. She might have been putting pressure on him. He might just have lost it thinking she was going to out him. I think that's enough for a jury to decide."

Captain Blake started to intervene, but Arnette put his hand on the captain's arm. Might as well protect him now.

"Steve," the detective said. "You are going to make this hard. My intuition tells me they were just acting on something that been brewing for a long time, and it was the first time. Not exactly a scenario that jibes with your story. And what if the grand jury doesn't agree with you? "

"Oh, geez, detective. They will. It's a slam dunk case. And spare me your doubts, detective. I know you don't like me much. That's been clear before. Too bad. But if you're not on board for this case with me, that's too bad. You could have a nice moment in the limelight, too."

"I'm sure you'll take up most of the spotlight anyway," the detective said.

'We're done here, gentlemen. Have a nice day."

Outside the D.A.'s office, Blake grabbed hold of Williams' arm. "What are you going to do now?"

"I'm going to continue my investigation. But I guess for now I'm not going to interview Roth again. Trust me, by the evening news, there will be a leak that the Westchester County's D.A.'s office has enough evidence for the grand jury to get an indictment in this case. The stories won't mention any names. But with the hearing coming up, Roth is going to be more cautious. Who knows, Rasmussen is probably talking to Roth's lawyer right now, telling him not to worry about the subpoena he is getting but to be sure he shows up. If I let Roth be for a few weeks, I might be able to catch him off guard the next time."

"I don't know. He'll get his story straight and lock it in, if there's anything to hide," Blake said.

"That may be true. But face it: his wife has given him an airtight alibi, and I would wager my month's salary that his account won't vary one word from hers. So there's nowhere to go right now. With time, even if they are involved in any way, they will stop rehearsing the story and inconsistencies might creep in. I'll just have to keep digging and digging. Maybe we'll get lucky. But for now, I have to wait for the grand jury hearing."

"Looks like you don't have to worry about being around the courthouse on Friday. There's not a chance in hell he will call you to present your suspicions to the grand jury."

"Hah, you got that right! Thanks, captain. I'll be back up in Croton tomorrow."

## CHAPTER 37

CALEB WAS STILL AWAKE, SITTING in his den and waiting for Brenda to fall asleep before he went up to bed. They hadn't fought, but the uncertainty over what was going on with the Croton police and the Westchester County detective bureau had left them exhausted. And he didn't want to re-start the conversation in the bedroom because he knew it would keep them both awake. They had discussed his conversation with his new lawyer, an expert in criminal law, all day. And enough was enough. He had taken the brunt of the lawyer's criticism for having gone to the police without him present, but Brenda kept insisting it was the right thing to do.

The phone rang.

Caleb picked up and said, "Hello."

"Hello. You don't know me. But consider me a friend."

Caleb thought he recognized the voice, but he couldn't place it and he knew he had probably never heard the voice over the phone before.

"I'm going to hang up," Caleb said. "We've been getting crank calls. I'm tired…"

"Don't hang up. You need to hear what I'm going to say. If you hang up, it may be the end of you."

Caleb hesitated, then waited on the line.

"Okay, this will be short. You are under investigation by the district attorney for the murder of Rachel Silver, and he is presenting his case to a grand jury that is sitting in White Plains. The preliminary hearing has already happened, and now it's up to the grand jury whether or not there are grounds for an indictment. The hearing is at 10 o'clock on Friday morning. He hasn't called you to be a witness, nor will he. But you have the right to ask to be heard. If you are as innocent as you claim to be, you need to talk to your lawyer about submitting your petition to be heard. That's all. That's my advice. From my vantage point, it's your only hope of avoiding a public trial."

The phone clicked off before Caleb could say a word. He knew the case had been advancing rapidly, but there had been no indication that the D.A. was going to seek an indictment. Now there were no doubts. He was facing the most critical moment in his life.

+++

THE CLOUDS WERE hanging low on the late winter day as James and Sheri drove down to the courthouse in White Plains from their home in Briarcliff Manor. The last snowfall had melted about 10 days ago, but the tan concrete, bunker-like buildings stood out starkly amid the few spindly trees with their bare branches. The street ended at a large municipal parking garage and the concrete facades of the government buildings on either side left the impression that they were in a concrete gully, with no windows looking onto the thoroughfare.

Inside the building, the Roths navigated the wide hallways and fluorescent lighting that cast no shadows as they found their way to the hearing room. Some people, usually carrying briefcases, walked briskly as if they knew where they were headed. But just as many were holding small pieces of official looking papers in their hands, trying to figure out if they were in the right place. The Roths tried to follow the signs, but didn't really know where they were going.

The plain wooden door into the grand jury room did not really hint at the magnitude of what would be decided inside today, or for that matter, on any given day. Their lawyer was waiting for them in the hall, and told them to take a seat in an adjacent waiting room. He told them that the D.A. had confirmed they would be among the first witnesses called. It wasn't more than 10 minutes after they had taken a seat that a bailiff stuck his head in the door and called James Roth's name. Sheri was left behind, waiting her turn.

The proceeding began with the grand jury foreman swearing in James Roth. Then District Attorney Stephen Rasmussen took over.

"Thank you for being here today, Mr. Roth. You have been sworn in. I want to remind you that this is a criminal hearing that will hear the evidence and facts presented to determine if there are sufficient grounds to issue indictments that will then allow me to proceed to a trial," Rasmussen said.

"This panel is aware of the standards necessary to reach that outcome. You are under oath and any subsequent discovery of untruthful testimony will be prosecuted to the full extent of the law. Do you understand?

"Yes, sir."

Rasmussen ceremoniously walked up to a podium in the center of the room and opened his file folder. He carried himself with an air of such utter confidence that everyone in the room couldn't help but feel the morning's proceedings were nothing more than a perfunctory hearing.

"When did you first meet Rachel Silver?" Rasmussen started.

The district attorney's first question nearly floored James, not because he wasn't expecting it but because he had hoped it wouldn't be the first question asked; he had wanted to get into a rhythm answering questions. He silently blessed Bennett Wilkins, his lawyer, for preparing him that Rasmussen probably wasn't going to waste any time. They had time for only one prep session, but it had been enough. Now he answered, quite smoothly:

"Well, I met her on 10/10. I didn't know it at the time."

"Can you please explain that, Mr. Roth?"

He quickly described the events of that morning and how he had aggressively grabbed at Rachel's phone and had been knocked to the ground by a man he didn't know and then how he'd been given a ride into the city to close a major energy deal. He then recounted the dinner four months later at the Silvers' house, which he characterized as a business/social dinner. He told the court how Rachel had left the room, and when she came back, his wife Sheri later said that she wasn't the same. He wasn't sure if Rachel had recognized him immediately. And at first he did not realize she was the woman from the train, but by the time they left, shortly after dessert was finished, he was pretty sure that she was the woman from the train. He went on to say that he hadn't discovered the name of the man he had fought with on the train until earlier this week.

"Who was that man, Mr. Roth?"

"I believe his name is Caleb Drake."

"Have you ever spoken with Mr. Drake?"

James paused for effect. "Well, not exactly. But a couple of nights ago he came to our house and knocked on the door—and he threatened me, too. That's when he told me he was Caleb Drake."

"When you say threatened you, what do you mean?"

"He accused me of... he accused me of killing Rachel Silver.

And he said he would make sure the police get me for it, no matter what it took."

"Have you seen him since that encounter?"

"No."

"Thank you, Mr. Roth. That will be all."

Roth knew he shouldn't exhale as loudly as he wanted to, but the relief he felt as he stepped off the stand was all-encompassing, as if a bungee cord inside him had suddenly gone slack. As he stepped down and started toward the door, he barely heard his wife's name called to testify.

Sheri Roth strode by him on her way to the stand and was sworn in as he left the room. Her back was slightly arched like a ballerina and her shoulders squared. She was calm and confident, as always, her make-up perfect. She looked like a conservative, well-to-do suburban housewife in a white blouse, demurely buttoned up to her neck, and a form-fitting knee-length navy blue skirt.

Sheri's performance on the stand was as convincing as her appearance: her answers were precise when needed and vague about her recollections when they shouldn't have been anything else. The D.A. was leading her through a scenario that eliminated any suggestion of undue tension or hostility in the Silvers' living room that night, at least not between the Roths and the Silvers, and how unexpected it was when the evening wrapped up so early. It went just like Bennett Wilkins, their lawyer, said it would, but then he had been in touch with the D.A. during the week.

Rasmussen dismissed her and called the coroner, followed by the head of the county's forensic department, Vernon O'Malley.

"Mr. O'Malley, thank you for rushing the DNA sample I sent you earlier this week. Can you confirm that it belongs to the subject of this hearing, Caleb Drake?"

"Yes, sir, I can. There was a 100 percent match with the other sample that the Croton police department sent to us," the forensics chief confirmed.

"Did they tell you how they got that sample?" Rasmussen asked.

"Yes. A Captain Blake in Croton told me that Mr. Drake had provided that sample voluntarily."

"Thank you, Mr. O'Malley. That will be all."

Rasmussen then called to the stand the first cop to arrive on the scene, to confirm that it had been cordoned off immediately, and the crime scene preserved, other than the entry of Rachel Silver's husband to confirm her identity. When their testimonies were complete, the D.A. asked the jury panel to accept at face value the murder scene evidence as sufficient justification to indict. That would seal it: Caleb Drake would be tried for murder.

Addressing the jurors, Rasmussen said, "I normally would close this hearing right now. I believe there is sufficient evidence to confirm an indictment. But my duty as an officer of the court requires me to honor a request from the subject of the indictment to testify in his own behalf. He has waived his immunity. His attorney will be present, but he is not allowed to ask any questions or engage with his client in any way."

Rasmussen called the bailiff over and whispered to him. The bailiff then walked to the door of the hearing room, opened it, and called out, loudly enough for everyone to hear: "Caleb Drake."

Caleb barely heard. By this time, waiting in the hall, his world and his future were unfolding at an eerie frame-by-frame speed— and he felt there wasn't a damn thing he could do about it. "Caleb Drake, you are being called!" Finally, the bailiff's voice penetrated

Caleb's consciousness and he looked up, with a deepening feeling of dread.

All he could do was sit there paralyzed. And with good reason: what would happen over the next few minutes could well lead to the end of his life as he knew it. He had survived the jungles and the traumas of Vietnam. He had survived the jungles and the brutal back-biting of doing business in Manhattan. But now, thanks to the strange events of 10/10 and a quick dalliance in the back seat of his car, he might well be going to jail for the rest of his life.

His lawyer, Bob Day, was sitting next to him, shaking his head back and forth. Caleb didn't turn to him; he knew that he was doing this against his lawyer's advice. They had argued angrily about it for more than an hour yesterday in the wake of the anonymous phone call, and again this morning, the lawyer saying it was crazy to put himself at the mercy of the district attorney. But Caleb was adamant. He was going to testify. He was innocent.

"Caleb!" It was Brenda, shaking him by the arm. "Caleb, they're calling you. This is it!"

"I know. I heard him. I'm just preparing myself."

Every feature of his surroundings now snapped into absolute clarity: the clerk, the wooden door, the jurors, the light pine hue of the jury box, the D.A.'s navy blue pinstripe suit, his red and navy striped rep tie. Each detail was sharpened by the same sterile fluorescent, shadowless light inside the courtroom as out in the hallways. Caleb stepped through a small gate and stopped in front of the jurors. The foreman stood and read him the oath. Caleb remembered his lawyer's instructions, and loudly and firmly replied, "Yes, sir, I do."

"For the record, please identify yourself and where you live," Rasmussen said.

"I am Caleb Drake. I live at 87 Hillside Drive in Ossining, New York."

"Thank you, Mr. Drake," Rasmussen said. "You asked to testify this morning, Mr. Drake. Before you begin, I would like to know how you discovered this hearing was taking place this morning. And I remind you that you are under oath."

"Uhh," Caleb paused, but knew he had to answer truthfully. "I received a phone call Wednesday night at my home, telling me that the hearing was scheduled, and that it would be in my best interest to testify."

"Who called?"

"I have no idea. The caller ID was blocked, and all they said was that they were a friend."

"Mr. Drake?" Rasmussen asked.

"I swear, Mr. Rasmussen, that's all the person said. I didn't recognize the voice, and then he hung up. That's all I can tell you. It was a man."

"So then, why are you here? I'm sure your lawyer told you not to testify."

Caleb was momentarily stunned. His prep session with his lawyer had dismissed the possibility that the district attorney would make any fundamental mistakes, such as essentially opening the door for Caleb to tell his side of the story. The best they could hope for, his lawyer had said, was that a juror or the foreman would step in and ask questions, which he warned almost never happens in New York State, or in Westchester County. But if that happened, then Caleb could go down paths that the D.A. would normally never allow in any proceeding before the trial.

The only positive note that Caleb's lawyer had sounded was that he had heard rumors that Rasmussen, because of his blatant politicking in recent weeks as he neared his final announcement to run for governor, had alienated the unusually strong jury foreman. The foreman was an African-American high school administrator, and he and Rasmussen had already clashed more than once on several high-profile cases that had come before the grand jury. Such hostility and confrontations were almost unheard of in grand jury settings, so it had become a subject of gossip in White Plains legal circles.

Still, Rasmussen seemed to ignore the possibility of any tension with the jury and continued to bulldoze ahead, convinced he had a slam dunk case.

"Well," Caleb said, "I am here to tell the court that I had absolutely nothing to do with Rachel Silver's death. I am 100 percent innocent, and even the investigating detective knows it. You are the only…"

"Excuse me, Mr. Drake, please be careful what you say about me and the court. Or I will insist that you end your testimony now," Rasmussen said.

"Mr. Rasmussen?" the foreman interrupted, breaking with almost all the usual norms of a grand jury hearing. "But I and my fellow jurors would like to hear what Mr. Drake has to say. After all, it's unusual that he's here in the first place."

"I was just letting him know that his testimony should stick to the case, not his opinions about the court," the district attorney said. "But proceed, Mr. Drake."

Caleb had watched with surprise the interaction between the D.A. and the grand jury. So his lawyer was right. The rumors were true. This foreman and district attorney were at odds. And the foreman was now taking over the proceedings with little regard for how things usually work.

"Mr. Drake, please proceed," Rasmussen said, checking the papers on his podium instead of looking at Drake directly.

"I met Rachel Silver the morning of 10/10. We had stood on the same train platform for—I don't how many years, four, five, maybe more—and we had never exchanged a word. But that morning when our train stalled on the tracks and everybody was starting to panic, she was on her phone when a man tried to grab it. That man, I now know, was James Roth. And he just kept at it, trying to grab her phone. And, well, I don't know what got into me, but I jumped in to help. The guy took a swing at me, and missed, and then I pinned him to the floor. It was over before anything really got out of control…"

Caleb paused here to collect himself. "After that, Rachel and I helped get passengers off the train, and when we got to the parking lot at Phelps Memorial, we found a man lying on the ground. I tried to give him CPR, and Rachel ran inside to get a nurse. Then we wheeled him inside. From there, a very kind nurse loaned us her car and we made our way home, to what we hoped would be safety for us and our kids and our spouses."

Was Caleb getting his message across? He had no idea. But it did feel good to get it all out. Just as it had happened. After a moment, he looked up and made eye contact with everyone on the panel, just as his lawyer had coached him to do. And then he added, with emotion in his voice, "All this took only 45 minutes, but my life has not been the same since."

For the next 10 minutes, Caleb recounted the rest of the day and the following months: his decision to not return Rachel's call, or try to see her even though he was attracted to her. He described the morning at the Croton-Harmon station, the first encounter they had in nearly four months, and then the subsequent fight with his wife and driving off into the night. He told the jurors about getting Rachel's late-night phone call and about her having had a fight with her husband and their decision to meet.

"In my car, all the pent-up feelings, about 10/10, about our separate lives, just started pouring out. So, yes, it is true: Rachel and I ended up having sex that night in my car. It was impulsive. It was heat of the moment. But at the time, it felt right. Then we sat and talked, it must have been for a couple of hours. At least. The next day, when I heard the news about her death, I was shocked. And I knew I had to go to the police. Believe me, I figured there was almost no way that I could be connected to her. But I knew it was the right thing to do. If I had been guilty, why would I willingly give a DNA sample to prove it? But I swear on everything that I hold dear, that afterwards I watched her walk away from the car, headed for home, and then I drove away. I did not kill Rachel Silver. Nor would I even think of doing so. Ever."

Caleb tailed off, now totally spent. He feared that the D.A. had made his case, and that the jurors were now inclined to support the indictment, meaning he would soon be standing trial—for a murder he did not commit. But at least he had been able to tell his story.

"I have another question, Mr. Drake. You say that there was no way to connect you and Rachel Silver. Isn't it true that she called you that evening?"

"Yes," Caleb replied.

"So, you knew when you walked into that police station that eventually the investigators would get to you. After all, that call to you came at what time was it, 10:30, 11:30?"

"Yes, sir. That is true. But it could have been…"

"That's all, Mr. Drake," the D.A. said, with an air of finality as if he had proven Caleb's guilt.

"I have no further questions," the D.A. said.

"Well, I have a few," the foreman said, again breaking precedent. "Mr. Drake, we've heard testimony that there was an encounter earlier in the evening between Mrs. Silver and Mr. Roth. Did you discuss that with her?"

"Yes, she was agitated. She thought Roth had something to do with the death of Sean Murray, the man we found in the parking lot of Phelps Hospital. But she was mostly upset that her husband, instead of supporting her suspicions, had defended Mr. Roth."

"How upset was she?" the foreman asked.

"I couldn't tell you that. We talked about it for a while, but our conversation turned back around to, well, to us."

"And how would you describe 'us,' Mr. Drake?"

"Well, she wanted to see me again. She made that very clear."

"Would you have?"

Caleb hesitated. "Probably not. Oh, I don't know. Yes. I told my wife that I needed to see her again, to work out my feelings. I was feeling ambivalent. Rachel and I connected. We really talked. So who knows what might have happened."

"So she wasn't threatening to go to your wife, pressuring you?"

"Not at all. She wasn't like that."

"Anyone else have a question?" the foreman asked.

One woman raised her hand. "Mr. Drake, do you have any idea who might have killed her?"

"No, I don't. I wish I did. I'd like to help the investigation. But we weren't together long enough for me to get any inklings."

"Thank you, Mr. Drake. We appreciate you coming to testify today."

But Caleb refused to step down. He just sat there for a long moment, totally silent, seeing his life and his marriage and his relationship with his children dissolve before his very eyes.

"That will be all, Mr. Drake," the D.A. said.

But Caleb had one more card to play. "Actually," he said, "I have one request, which I understand is my right in a case like this."

"That will be all, Mr. Drake," Rasmussen said.

"Wait," the foreman interjected. "What is your request?"

"I request that the jury hear from Arnette Williams, the lead detective in this case."

"No, absolutely not!" Rasmussen said.

"Well, Mr. Rasmussen," the foreman said, "as we understand it, according to the New York State grand jury handbook, it is the defendant's right to call for a witness to give testimony. And why wouldn't you let us hear from the detective?"

"It is not necessary," Rasmussen said. "I told you. There is enough evidence in front of you already."

"Well," said the foreman, "this is a murder case, and you're asking us to make a decision without all the available evidence. So I'm inclined to hear out the defendant's request." At this, several members of the grand jury murmured their agreement. But Rasmussen was having none of it.

"Excuse me, Mr. Foreman. The judge should decide this witness's request. I'm calling him now. Bailiff, can you please find Judge Saltieri and ask him to join us?"

In a few minutes, Judge Raymond Saltieri strode into the courtroom and quickly took charge. He was a salty, old-school taskmaster, and he had a reassuring presence. At the judge's request, the foreman provided a quick summary of where things stood: the defendant wanted the lead detective in the case to testify and the D.A. was opposing that. Then the foreman added that he and the other members of the grand jury were inclined to hear the detective's testimony.

"Sounds reasonable to me, Mr. Rasmussen," the judge said. "In fact, my question to you would be this: Why didn't you put the lead detective on the stand in the first place? What's the rush?"

"Your Honor, I believe that the evidence I presented here was more than sufficient to support the indictment," the D.A. said.

The judge just chuckled. "You mean sufficient, in addition to what was leaked to the Journal News earlier this week."

"Your Honor!" Rasmussen said.

"Fine, members of the jury will ignore my remark. But I hereby grant the request of the defendant. Bailiff, please ask Detective Williams to come in, assuming he is in the building. I'm headed back to my chambers, although I wish I could stay to hear this one!"

"And Mr. Drake, I'm sure you would like to hear this too, but court rules don't permit you to stay. Please wait outside. We'll both hear about it soon enough."

"Thank you, your honor."

Caleb stood up and walked slowly to the door, sensing the tension in the room and figuring that he was being watched. He turned around at the door to take in the jurors, all of whom were still looking at him. He left silently.

Detective Williams came into the courtroom in less than a minute. As he did, the D.A. sat stoically in his chair. Before the grand jury convened, he had considered gambling and calling in Detective Williams himself. But he didn't trust him after their testy meeting earlier in the week. In fact, he knew the cop was not a friend of the D.A.'s office, and he hadn't wanted to take the chance. But with Drake's testimony, Rasmussen could feel his case crumbling and knew he had to try to regain control.

The foreman swore the detective in. Then Rasmussen said, "Detective Williams, would you please identify yourself for the court."

"My name is Arnette Williams. I'm a detective, lieutenant grade, with the Homicide Division of the Westchester County Police."

"Do you know why you're here today?" Rasmussen said.

"Actually, no, although I was told outside that the target of this indictment, Caleb Drake, requested that I testify. I know that's highly unusual."

"Have you been in touch with Mr. Drake, or more to the point, are you the person who called him earlier this week to inform him about this hearing?"

"No, I am not. And frankly I was here this morning in the hope that you might call me yourself."

"So, Detective Williams, in your best judgment, could anyone other than Mr. Drake have been Rachel Silver's killer?"

"I don't know. As I told you earlier this week, I think it is premature to say for certain. There are too many unanswered…"

"That wasn't my question, detective. I asked you if you had any other suspects."

"And I told you: it is too early to say."

"Detective, please answer my question."

"Mr. Rasmussen, excuse me, but I'm curious," the foreman interrupted. "Usually, the lead detective is one of the first witnesses in a felony murder indictment, but you left him out completely. And now he's pushing back on your line of questioning. Do you have any idea why he didn't call you, Detective Williams?"

"Not really. And, yes, I am the lead investigator on this case. I have investigated more than 300 murders during my career as a police officer, first in New York City, and for the last 10 years here in Westchester County. I expressed my concerns to the District Attorney earlier this week, but he ignored me. I told him that any hearing would effectively end any chance of finding the real killer of Rachel Silver."

"Why has the district attorney ignored your advice?" the foreman asked.

"You'll have to ask Mr. Rasmussen that question."

The foreman edged in toward the detective. "Do you have any proof that Mr. Drake should *not* be indicted today, detective?"

"There's nothing that absolutely eliminates the possibility that he was at the crime scene in the vacant lot. But without revealing too many details about the attack, nothing adds up to him being the killer."

"Any other questions?" the foreman asked, turning to the jurors.

One juror spoke up. "Is this just a gut feeling, detective?"

"When I listened to the transcript of his first interview with the Croton police, and then I interrogated him myself, I thought he was innocent. As I have studied the medical examiner's report, and talked to everyone involved, I became convinced that he was not the killer. Everything about the killing points to a cold-blooded, almost dispassionate attack. I could not piece together how someone could go from making love..."

Rasmussen jumped up. "Jurors, I have to object to this testimony! It's prejudicial and unrelated to what we are here to establish. The detective should not be on the stand!"

The foreman glanced up and down the row of jurors. "Mr. Rasmussen, I know that we are not lawyers, or judges, but if I've learned one thing this past month, it is that you are an officer of the court, and you are required to allow this testimony. Judge Saltieri has ordered it, and I think we all feel you should not be trying to prejudice us about the detective's testimony. The other thing we have learned is there is a wide leeway in what can be said in these hearings. So, Detective Williams, please proceed."

"Thank you, Mr. Foreman. I want to be clear about several things. One, there were no signs of force in regard to the sex. So we have a scenario where two people made love to each other, and then, according to the D.A., one of them almost immediately sticks a knife into that person, having followed her out of the car into the lot. It just doesn't happen that way. Not even in the movies."

"But isn't this unusual? For a detective to confront a district attorney?"

"I'm not sure what else I can do. This man is being railroaded for some reason—most of us here in the room know what it is— and I cannot be a party to it. And I feel like the sooner we stop this, the better chance Mr. Drake has of getting his life back. I'm sure it's already been like a wrecking ball into his life. Maybe it's already too late, but I had to try to stop it now. And I believe keeping this case out of court for now gives me the best chance of finding the real killer. Even if in the future I recommend an indictment against Mr. Drake, which is still possible."

District Attorney Rasmussen couldn't sit still. He stood up, red-faced and clearly agitated.

"Are you telling the court, Detective Williams, that in your what, 20 years plus, your hunches have never been wrong?"

"No, sir, I didn't say that. I have thought many times that someone committed a crime, but they turned out to be innocent. And I've been wrong about someone's innocence, when it turned out they were the guilty party. But I've also seen lives ruined because a zealous prosecutor overstepped his bounds and tried to force a trial when the evidence didn't warrant it."

"Zealous? Mr. Foreman, I ask that you ignore the detective's last remark. It is prejudicial," District Attorney Rasmussen said.

"Agreed. We will disregard the detective's last comment," the foreman said, but with such a pro forma, matter-of-fact tone that no one in the courtroom doubted that he agreed with the detective.

"I have no further questions," Rasmussen said quickly, realizing he had better cut his losses.

The foreman said, "Thank you, Detective Williams. The jury appreciates you having been here today. You are excused."

+++

CALEB AND BRENDA were sitting outside the courtroom. They hadn't known whether to leave or stay. But they figured they might get a chance to see Detective Williams. And when he walked out the door of the court, he approached them immediately.

He shook Caleb's hand. "I'm not sure why you called me, but I'm glad you did. I'm not saying you are off my suspect list, but I think there is a miscarriage of justice under way, and I didn't want to be party to it." Then he added, "Be sure your lawyer reaches out to me if the indictment is handed down by the grand jury. And be prepared: Rasmussen isn't going to let this go."

With that, Williams turned and walked away.

"A miscarriage of justice"—Caleb let those words sink in. For the first time in four days, he had a glimmer of hope. He took Brenda's hand and they left the courthouse.

## CHAPTER 38

THE CALL FROM CALEB'S LAWYERS came at the end of the week after the grand jury hearing. Caleb had stayed home from work again, as he had nearly every day since Rachel's body had been discovered. The kids were at school and he was alone in the house with Brenda, filled with dread every time the phone rang.

"Caleb, it's Bob Day. I hope you're sitting down," the lawyer teased, then he plunged right in: "No indictment. You're a free man."

"No! You're kidding! I can't, I can't... "

"Believe me, Caleb. There won't be anyone coming to arrest you and take you down to the station to book you. Turn on the TV. News 12 TV trucks are outside the courthouse in White Plains, and they are going live with the D.A.'s comments."

Caleb jumped up, ran into the den, and turned on the TV. Stephen Rasmussen had just started speaking.

"...a sad day for justice in Westchester County. I don't know whether to be angry or scared. Because some questioned my motives, the grand jury in this case has dismissed my request for an indictment."

"We know who the killer is. And he's not going to trial. But I can tell you this: my office won't stop investigating. We will bring the killer of Rachel Silver to justice. You know who you are. Don't stop looking over your shoulder. We will find enough new evidence to bring this case to the grand jury again. I will leave no stone un-turned. Thank you."

The reporters started shouting at him. But the D.A. walked away from the microphone.

Caleb sank to his knees and put his arms around his chest. He had been resigned to a trial, to total humiliation for himself and his family, and now it was over. At least for now.

Brenda touched his shoulder.

"Caleb, it's okay. You are okay now," she said, getting down on her knees too and putting her arms around him.

He was crying.

"Why don't I feel relieved, Brenda? This isn't going to go away. You heard him. He accused the grand jury of politics, of not exe-cuting their duty properly. He might as well put my name up on a neon billboard. Wait. Just wait. If you think it's been hard, it's only going to get worse."

"Jesus, Caleb, give yourself a break. You should enjoy this mo-ment. You are free. You're not going to jail. Can't you appreciate your good fortune?"

Caleb stopped crying. He wiped his eyes and pulled himself up to the couch. There was real truth in what Brenda was saying. He shouldn't beat himself up about his mistakes, but instead just revel in the fact that justice had been done; he wasn't going to be tried for a crime he didn't commit.

"You're right, Bren," Caleb said. "You know how I am. I don't cut myself a lot of slack when it comes to my personal conduct. I know, everyone says we all make mistakes. But I always held my-self to a higher standard. So that's why I am not jumping up and down right now. We shouldn't even be here like this. None of this should have happened. It's all my fault."

"Honey, I'm here with you. We'll get through it."

"Brenda, I have caused you so much pain. I don't understand how you can feel that way."

"Caleb, I believe you. I believe in you. What's happened to us isn't normal. We can go back now and start working on us. We need to talk to the kids, too, let them know that everything is going to be okay. That's what I want. Get back to the way we were."

"Brenda, I hope you're right. I hope you mean it. Because we are going to be tested like never before."

"Stop it, Caleb. You're doing it again. Please, for once, look at the bright side, at least for a moment. You've been cleared. There's no evidence against you. That's what the detective told you. Start acting like it's true. Or I'll start thinking the D.A. is right. Start acting innocent, damn it!"

"I'm not innocent, Brenda," he said. "No, no, I'm sorry. I don't mean it that way. I didn't kill her. I am innocent of that. What I am guilty of is exposing me, of exposing us. And I'm guilty of hurting you. Even if you forgive me, I still have to forgive myself. Don't you understand? I hate, hate that this happened to me. To us."

"Caleb, we can work through it. Together. And I know you didn't kill her. Let's start there. The rest of our stuff will take care of itself."

"You think? Really? You were the one who just a couple of months ago was screaming at me to open up, to let you inside my head because it had been years since you felt connected to me. Do you still feel that way?"

"Oh, I feel connected to you now, Caleb Drake. I've listened to you talk about yourself in ways that I haven't heard from you in a long time. Maybe never, in fact. It's like you've gotten in touch with that side of you that always hid from me, probably from everybody. What I want more than anything right now is for you to get back to being yourself, your old self, the young man I fell in love with."

"I'm not sure I know where he is, or who he is."

Brenda pulled Caleb up to his feet, and hugged him. Long and hard. "Sure you do, Caleb. You just have to look for him."

They embraced for what seemed like a long time. Caleb felt some of the tension of the last week slowly releasing. Brenda broke the embrace, and stepped back from him.

"Don't you think we should have a glass of Champagne?" she said.

"Hah, don't tell me you were so optimistic that you had one chilled?"

"I did, and it's ready to go. Come on, let yourself enjoy this moment. We can worry about the other stuff later."

"You know, I've been thinking about something. Maybe it's too early to be thinking about the next step, or what my strategy should be. And I didn't want to talk about it until I knew the grand jury verdict. But in all my years in P.R., my advice to my clients has been that the best defense is a good offense. I need to get my story out there to the public. I'm going to tap into my contacts, and ask New York magazine to do a story on me, you know, the guy who was wrongfully accused."

"Do you think that's a good idea?" Brenda asked.

"Sure, I've dealt with the editor a number of times for my clients. He'll assign someone good to do the piece."

"I don't know. Seems risky."

"Honey, I know what I'm doing. If I do nothing, the world will only remember that I was the prime suspect, and the subject of a grand jury hearing. This way, my side gets told. I know it seems out of character that suddenly I'm willing to put myself out there in a public forum. But I think I'm right."

"I guess. Let me get the Champagne."

"Good idea. No matter what else, I'm going to sleep better tonight than I have in two weeks."

+++

"JAMES, YOUR WIFE is on the phone," his secretary said through the intercom. "She said it's urgent."

James laughed. Once again, he had been sitting there all morning, not really doing much of anything or even trying to do anything. He would have taken her call whether it was urgent or not.

"Hey, Sher, what's up?" James said.

"You haven't heard? The grand jury didn't indict that guy Caleb Drake. He's still out there."

"Wow, really? Our lawyer made it sound like this was a slam dunk. Now what?"

"You should call the lawyer. Ask him exactly that question. That means the cop is probably going to come snooping around to us again. Remember we heard he was the one who testified that he didn't think Drake did it, so he's going to keep investigating."

James had hoped to put the whole murder issue and 10/10 behind him, but now he might have to worry again about a cop digging through his life. "Sheri, when can we move into the city? I want to get out of the suburbs, get the hell away from there."

"James, you know the list. Thoroughly clean. Repaint. Put in the new appliances. They are doing all that this week. That's about as quick as I can get it done. And I want it done, too. I'm so ready to come back to work."

"Yeah, I need you here. Maybe it will get my mind off this whole shit show. Damn, I really thought the D.A. was going to nail that guy Drake. After what the detective did, showing up at our house, do you think we need to hire security for a while?"

"Don't be crazy, James. Forget that. It would make us look afraid, or even guilty. If they knew who to look for, or where to look, someone other than Caleb Drake would be under arrest. The D.A. and everyone else will forget about the murder. It will just be one of those unsolved murders. So stop worrying."

"I guess you're right. But Sheri, you know what else I'm worried about? The old man…" James started to bring up the incident with the car in the hospital parking lot on 10/10.

"Stop it! Don't bring it up! Ever again. It's over. And that day, 10/10, is behind you. Focus on the great stuff you did—and will do."

James let her words sink in, trying to let her advice take hold. "I wish it was that simple. But yeah, you're right. I've got to get focused again. Start doing something around here. That day has become a worm inside my head, eating away at, well, at me. It has been really hard to concentrate."

"James, you have got to snap out of this! It's been two weeks since that woman was murdered. It has nothing to do with us! And nothing is going to connect you to what happened on 10/10. So get over it. That's my advice."

"Okay, I'm trying. I'll see you tonight. When did you say we could move?"

"In about a week, honey. Why don't you come home now?"

"Good idea. I'll call the car. Be home in an hour."

James hung up, dialed his car service on his cell, and ordered the car for 15 minutes. He looked at his desk. Instead of stacks of papers with the various deals that he usually had in motion, there was nothing; it was clean. He wondered what it was going to take to snap him out of his funk.

+++

ARNETTE WILLIAMS SAT at the desk in the Croton police station where he'd been working for the past three weeks. There were tapes of his and Captain Blake's interview with Caleb Drake, his notebooks of what had transpired with the Roths, a folder with Daniel Silver's name on it, and another folder labeled simply "Deceased."

Strange, Arnette thought, how murder victims fade into anonymity: a number, a date, an address, or just "deceased." A generic designation made it easier for him to stay dispassionate. But Rachel Silver's case was different; it had him by the throat. Was it his hostility toward the damned D.A.? Or his sympathy for Caleb Drake? Or his empathy for Daniel Silver? He wasn't sure why, but day and night Rachel was front and center in his mind, the beautiful blonde who ended up stabbed to death less than a block from her home.

"Hey, detective, what's up? You still here?" It was Captain Blake, interrupting his thoughts.

"Yes, I just came to pack up my stuff. I'm going to be working out of the White Plains department offices from now on. My captain ordered me back there," Williams said. "Says there are some other cases that need my attention."

"Well, you're always welcome here, you know. I'll keep my guys alert too for anything they might hear out on the street. You never know. Oh, by the way, that guy, Charlie Murray, the conductor from the train, he called me yesterday after the announcement about the grand jury decision. Hey, that was something, wasn't it? Wish I could have seen the D.A.'s face when Drake asked for you to testify. Woooeee, that was big!"

"I wasn't inside when Drake asked for me, but I could tell the D.A. wasn't happy to have me called to the stand. And he was right to be upset. The jury believed me, not him. So what about Murray?"

"Oh, he was telling me the story about his dad's car again, how it never showed up and what should he do about it. I asked him if he'd filed a stolen car report, but he said that you had done it for him. Then he started rambling on about his suspension and his hearings," Captain Blake said. "I finally just told him to go to the Peekskill police—that's where he lives—and follow up with them."

"Oh yeah, I had forgotten about that. I'll have to look into it again once I get some of these other cases off my desk," Williams said. "Thanks again, captain. You were a big help. I'll let you know if I need anything else."

"Any time, detective. And good luck! The Silver case doesn't look like it's going to be solved any time soon."

"I hope you're wrong. I hope you're wrong."

+++

DANIEL SILVER WAS wrapping up another week at work. His law firm had given him a lot of leeway about showing up; after all, he was a senior partner. But after the grand jury's verdict came in, he decided the best thing for him, and for Ethan and Hayleigh, was to get back to the office and start rebuilding his future—and theirs.

The phone rang, and through his glass door he saw his secretary pick up the line. Normally, she would have just called out to him but he had been keeping his door closed to keep his partners from stopping in and sympathizing. There was nothing they could say that was going to make him feel any better.

The phone on his desk buzzed, and he could see it was the line to his secretary. "Mr. Silver, it's a James Roth. Do you want to talk to him?"

"Uhhh, I guess so. Put him through."

He heard the line go live and said, "Hello?"

"Hello, Daniel. This is James Roth. I wanted to reach out to you finally and let you know how sorry Sheri and I are about your wife. I should have called sooner, but, frankly, I just didn't know what to say, and after the police questioned us, I don't know, I felt like it wasn't the right thing to do."

"I understand, James. There was, and is, nothing really to say. I'm still in shock, and a part of me can't believe what happened."

"I understand," Roth said. "I thought it was going to be wrapped up by now. Or at the least, a jury would be hearing the evidence of who killed Rachel."

"So did I," Daniel said. "So did I. Let's just say what happened with the grand jury was one in a thousand. District attorneys almost always get their way. But not this time."

"Sheri and I were shocked, too. But really, that's not why I'm calling. Remember our conversation regarding my plans for starting a new business?" James said.

"Sure, I remember."

"Well, I've had a change of heart. I'm staying here at Goldfarb & Roth," James said.

"I thought it was Goldfarb & Case?"

"It was. No longer. Sheri is coming back to join me here, and her father made us both partners in the firm. So I'm looking for new counsel for my future deals, not that I have any irons in the fire right now. But I'm wondering if you'd like to meet and discuss terms for a retainer relationship?"

"Well, sure. Why not? When?"

"Well, it's Thursday. How about next Wednesday?"

"Fine. I'll see you at your offices then," Daniel said.

Daniel hung up and stared at the phone. What was going on? He knew Roth had never been a prime suspect. The newspaper reports, which he assumed were leaks from the district attorney's office, didn't mention anyone other than Caleb Drake. But with Caleb off the hook for now, Daniel had assumed that everyone was a potential suspect again, including Roth.

But Daniel knew he needed some new business quickly to make himself feel like he was still in the game, and Goldfarb & Roth would be a real prize for the firm. He packed up his briefcase and headed home, to another night in front of the TV with his bottle of Scotch. Or, maybe he should take a break and take the kids out to dinner at their favorite hamburger joint in Briarcliff.

Daniel hadn't been out of the house much, except to go to work, since Rachel's death. And he needed to connect better with the kids. Since the house was still filled with the sights and smells of Rachel, getting away from it for a couple of hours with the kids would be good for everyone. He needed to bring some life back into the house. And he hoped he could find the strength to make it happen.

## CHAPTER 39

**F**OR CALEB, THE WEEKS HAD been rushing by since the grand jury verdict. Winter was slowly blending into an early spring, and he was trying to keep his focus on his company and his clients. But the hearing and the murder kept popping up, distracting and worrying him. The Journal News ran a series of stories about Rachel Silver's murder, most of them with anonymous quotes attributed to law enforcement sources that continued to cast suspicion on him. The stories convinced him to go ahead with his plan to sit for a New York magazine article, and after a call to the editor, a writer came to see him the following week.

The writer, a young rising star at the magazine named Heather Jones, spent an entire day with him at Drake & Associates to kick off her interviews, and then interviewed him three other times, once surprising him at the train station in Ossining to commute with him into the city. Each time, he grew more uncomfortable with her questions, which focused more and more on his relationships with Brenda and Rachel Silver—and less about his acquittal. He tired of repeating how he and Rachel had connected with each other but there really hadn't been an affair underway because she was murdered before they had a chance to pursue it. A photographer followed him for a day and did a simple set-up in the foyer of his offices, saying he needed a formal portrait for the cover. He knew calling up the editor to see how the story was developing would backfire, as would pressing the writer too hard about her approach or overall theme. But as each week passed, his impatience and his anxiety grew about whether trying to control the narrative and get his story out there had been the right move.

He wasn't prepared, however, to walk up the ramp after getting off his Monday morning train at Grand Central Station to see his face staring back at him from the Hudson News magazine rack with the headline, "Guilty or Not Guilty?" He felt a wave of nausea, and the knot in his stomach tightened as he fumbled for change and paid for a copy. He walked quickly out the Vanderbilt exit toward his office on Madison Avenue, darting through the crowd of commuters while imagining people recognized him.

His receptionist was a little wide-eyed upon seeing him, and as he strode past, she said, "Mr. Drake, Mr. Drake…" He didn't want to stop, but he had to after the second time she called his name.

"Yes, what is it?"

"I'm sorry, but a messenger delivered a stack of these a few minutes ago," she said, putting on the counter the copies of New York magazine with his face on the cover.

"I already have a copy. Get rid of those, please, or, I don't know… Hand them out to people in the office. They are going to have to get up to speed on this… this disaster."

He shut the door and threw the magazine at his desk. And after taking off his coat, he sat down, clenching his jaw. He found the cover story on page 42, and opened the magazine to a two-page telephoto shot of him on the train platform in Ossining. The cover headline was repeated, and the subhead read, "A grand jury refused to indict Caleb Drake of murder. Not everyone believes he is innocent."

"Fuck. Fuck. Fuck," Caleb shouted out loud. "How could I be

so stupid? Fuck!"

He read the first paragraph:

"Rachel Silver got into Caleb Drake's Audi on a cold February night. They talked. They had sex. She never made it home to her husband that night. The next morning her corpse was found in a vacant lot within sight of her house, stabbed a dozen times. The police said she died without a fight."

The article repeated the district attorney's case almost verbatim, with the report about his semen in Rachel and the lack of any other credible suspect. But then the story went on to discuss Caleb's military record in Vietnam, as a lieutenant who led patrols deep into Viet Cong territory and who was known for reporting high body counts, a killer by the Army's own standards. Not only had the writer dug up his military records but she interviewed acquaintances from his old high school, fellow graduates of Cornell, and competitors in the public relations world in New York City. What she painted was a portrait of a man without a lot of close friends, an aloof businessman who rarely took part in the industry's social events. He almost never talked, even with this closest friends, about Vietnam. In short, someone who had a dark side that very few people knew or could even imagine.

The writer did give him space to tell his story, but in retrospect he probably was a little too open, admitting that he and Brenda had been working on some problems, and that he had been struggling with another bout of mild PTSD after the 10/10 attack. But he thought if anyone bothered to read as far as his account of what happened that fateful night, they couldn't help but believe him. The problem was that not many people would read that far, and the writer's account left little doubt that she was skeptical of his story.

"Damn," Caleb said out loud again. "I should have known better." There was a knock at his door.

"Come in."

Oscar, one of his best and most gregarious employees, opened the door and came in, shutting it behind him. "Boss, Jesus, you really got burned," he said, holding up the magazine. "I hardly know what to say. Uhhh, don't you think you should have spoken to a lawyer, or maybe to one of us before going forward with this?"

"Oscar, just like my grand jury hearing, I simply could not imagine that an innocent man had to be so worried. I guess I underestimated the D.A. I mean, he's clearly the source for a lot of the crap in the story. But now I wonder what people really think about me. All those old acquaintances dredged up from 40 years ago, or more. Hell, some of them I haven't seen since high school or college. She paints a pretty dark picture of me."

"We are already getting a few calls from your long-time clients. They think the piece is a hatchet job, so I wouldn't worry about it. But be ready to be asked some tough questions."

"When I cool off. Listen, Oscar, I better call my wife. Let me know if you hear anything else."

Caleb dialed the home number. It was busy. He dialed again a few minutes later and it rang. Brenda picked up and said without pausing, "No, I'm not answering any questions."

"Whoa Bren, it's me, Caleb."

"Oh Jesus, Caleb, the phone started ringing off the hook about 15 minutes ago. What's going on?"

"The New York magazine article is out," he said. "And you'd better get ready. It's going to be a bad few days."

"Oh no, Caleb. I'm so sorry. What happened?"

He gave her a quick overview, and a description of the cover.

"I should have been more careful. But I never imagined this would happen. Just tell reporters to call the office. I'll handle it."

"Caleb, they weren't all reporters. Some were hostile crank calls, asking me what it's like to know I have a murderer in my…"

"Stop, Brenda. Don't listen to them. Let it go to voice mail. Just tell your friends to use your cell phone. I'll try to get home early tonight and we'll talk about it."

With great care, Caleb laid the phone softly in its cradle, afraid he might slam it down and break it. He could feel an anger well up, and it was threatening to spill out in ways he wasn't sure he could control. Simultaneously, his old PTSD demons were jabbering in his head, ready to take him down again.

For the last month, he had harbored hopes that his nightmare was over. With the grand jury weighing in his favor, he figured he could begin to put the horror of Rachel's murder behind him. But he still had not been able to shake his fear that he would succumb to the depression that had haunted him off and on for years.

And now this, this damned hatchet job in New York magazine. Instead of feeling that the world had finally heard his side of the story, he was facing more doubts about his innocence. The threat was real, and he wasn't sure he could handle the stress. How in the hell was he going to cope now?

## CHAPTER 40

*Three Months Later*

CALEB'S EYES WANDERED OVER THE black walnut boardroom table and his collection of black and white photographs of New York City scenes on the walls. It wasn't really a boardroom but a fancy meeting room for clients. He never had been particularly fond of large staff meetings, preferring to call his direct reports into his corner office, with its views up and down Madison Avenue.

Today, however, there were 15 people around the table, including him. He could hear their breathing, and when he looked up, some stared at him, some looked down at the table, and some gazed blankly out the windows.

He hadn't slept well last night, not just because of this crucial meeting—after all, he hadn't been sleeping well since 10/10. But he knew what he wanted to do: close the firm. Closing the doors would free him. He figured he could then convince Brenda and the kids to head to a place where the label "killer" wouldn't follow him around like it did in his own neighborhood. After the New York magazine story, three months of whispers, catcalls, and harassing phone calls finally had forced him to move out and into the city. He left Brenda and his family behind.

Caleb glanced at his watch. It was 9:05; two people were still missing, but he decided to go ahead. He cleared his throat.

"You probably all suspect why I've called this meeting. I'm going to start, even though Richard and Hannah aren't here yet. As I recall, they had events last night."

He paused as the door opened, and Richard, his account person for pharmaceutical companies, briskly walked in, and before he could close the door, Hannah, their rep to the fashion industry, pushed it open behind him.

"Sorry, I'm late," Hannah said.

"Me, too," Richard added quickly.

"That's okay. I know you both were working late. But you haven't missed anything, except the funeral dirge that's been playing on the music system." His attempt at humor hit the table with a dull thud.

But he laughed. And, impulsively, he threw out every prepared word he had spent the night memorizing. It had been a simple, very formal speech about what a good run the firm had had and that it was time to move on. Instead, he decided to speak from his heart.

"Look, you all know I have had a hell of a time. I've discovered firsthand what it's like to be on the other side of a media mugging. I probably should have hired all of you right off the bat to handle my case. I just never thought… I just never thought that an innocent man needed to be so… so goddamn worried about the out-of-control lies and stories. I was wrong."

"Last night, as I sat in what remains of my life, I decided to close this place down. Not today, but within the next few months. That will give you all a chance to go out to find work somewhere without a dark cloud hanging over your head. It'll take the rest of the summer, but by the fall I want to shut down."

There was an audible murmur through the room, and it seemed

everyone was going to start talking at once. But the word that rose above the others was clearly distinguishable: "No!" He also heard, "You can't be serious," "He's got to be kidding, right," "We're all in this together, he's got to hang in there with us."

No? He was shocked. The weeks of despondency, his lack of focus, the short shrift he had given to some of the firm's major clients had added up, in his mind, to a perfect storm that everyone around the table should have wanted to get away from. He sure did. But now, hearing that emphatic "No!," he began to get emotional, a reaction that had become almost normal for him. He tried to gather himself, trying to understand why these people might want to support him or stick with him.

"I'm not sure any of you understand," he said, and then he paused.

"Hell doesn't begin to describe what I've been through since that night in late February four and a half months ago. Maybe you all followed the stories. Maybe you haven't. Despite the public lynching, the reports have missed some of the things that have been going on. There's no reason you should have known. I've... I've kept most of the worst stuff to myself. But I guess you all are about the only friends I have left, so to be fair to you, to let you understand why I'm ready to do this, let me give you some of the details about my life over these past few months. Maybe then you'll understand..."

Once again, Caleb had to stop, trying to find the right words to relay what was happening to him.

"I can't walk down the street in my home town, where I've lived for more than 20 years, without people turning and staring, sometimes even saying outrageous things to me. Even here in Manhattan, after that New York magazine piece about a month after the grand jury refused to indict me—oh boy, did that come out wrong!—I'd walk into a restaurant, and at least one person would recognize me, sometimes more, and then I could see the whispered conversations, and well, it's New York, so sometimes I could hear them, too.

"My kids, too, were so quiet and depressed that I was worried sick about them. They finally confessed to me that kids at school were shunning them, and sometimes being cruel in ways that only teenagers seem capable of. They kept it from me for a long time because they didn't want to worry me.

"My wife supported me, at first, especially after the grand jury cleared me of wrongdoing, but it got to her, too. Her friends stopped calling. She got jeers from passing cars when she walked down the street in Croton or Briarcliff where she usually does her shopping. We haven't been able to talk about anything but the grand jury hearing, and then there was the detective who kept coming by, the calls from the district attorney's office, which finally stopped, by the way, after my lawyer stepped in and was ready to charge them with harassment. The assault on our lives has been incessant.

"I tried to help her through it. I reported the harassment to the police. I even confronted one guy in a grocery store parking lot when we were out shopping. But that upset her even more.

"I finally decided the best way to defuse the situation was to get out of there. So, I left home more than a month ago. Moved out. I couldn't bear to see my family's pain. You'd think after the grand jury refused to indict me that the onslaught would have ended. But no, it got worse: crank calls, my front lawn spray-painted with the word 'killer.' It was the threats that finally pushed my wife beyond her limit. She didn't ask me to leave. I just knew it was the right thing to do. I took an apartment here in the city. I'm hoping that will quiet things down. If I'm out of the picture, maybe they'll leave her alone. But the move won't repair my marriage. I'm hoping I can convince Brenda to stick with me, by moving to another place, to another part of the country. But first, I need to free up all of you."

The room was eerily silent: there was not a single sound, no paper shuffling, no shoe scraping on the floor, no sound of anyone shifting in their seat. Nothing. Caleb couldn't help but feel that time had stopped. He waited for a few seconds, but the silence was almost intolerable.

"I don't know what else to say, guys; I'm not sure the firm can go on like this. I thought we'd lose more clients by now and I'm sure we will over time as contracts come up and our customers who've been loyal up to now feel enough time has passed to gracefully exit. I don't want to be here while the company withers away. I'd rather…"

Oscar Ballard, his most valued employee, stood up, cleared his throat and started in: "Mr. Drake. With all due respect, I'd like to say something. It's not just me talking. We all suspected something like this might be happening today. I mean, none of us could ever remember you asking for a meeting of everyone at 9 o'clock in the morning. So we had our own meeting yesterday. Everyone has asked me to speak on their behalf."

Everyone nodded in unison.

"Oscar, I haven't really finished what I was going to say…"

But Oscar barely paused. "Well, it's pretty clear where you are heading, and we'd like you to hear our side of it before you dig yourself too deep a hole… We're sorry for what you've gone through. And you're right: we didn't know about all the stuff out in Westchester. Or for that matter, what had happened with your home life. But I'm sure no one here is surprised. We've been through the questions about you with our friends and family. We have all been asked what it's like to work with a murderer or some equally silly crap I won't even dignify by repeating. But to us, that's beside the point. Not that we don't feel for you, but there's more at stake here.

"First of all, we all want to be clear: we want to be here. We had a show of hands last night, partly because we wanted to be sure everyone was on the same page. It was unanimous."

Oscar had walked around to one side of the boardroom table to get closer to Caleb. Caleb kept looking directly at him.

"Let me share some of the things we discussed last night. We were all surprised, because for the most part, since February, we've been sticking to ourselves, trying not to let your drama intrude on our jobs.

"Everyone has had the 'talk' with a client. It's not complicated or long. Most smart people think you're innocent. Maybe not too smart, but not guilty. Their reaction was the same, or at least there was a common theme: If a PR company can survive a crisis like this, and keep going strong, then they must know how to take care of other companies' problems, too."

Oscar stepped back to his place, and took a sip of water from a bottle he had brought with him. During the brief break, his co-workers were nodding their heads up and down and sharing glances of agreement.

"Oh," Oscar continued, "there were some curious questions: what's Caleb Drake like? Do you think he's guilty, etc., etc. But not one client has admitted to wanting to leave for that reason. Yes, we have lost some, but they always seemed to have a solid explanation: a change of business fortunes or a failure on our part. Not one client has said, 'I don't want to be associated with Drake & Associates.' For that matter, you wouldn't believe the number of cold calls we've gotten for new business from companies in a crisis mode. There's nothing else for me to say. If you want to quit or resign, that's your call, but we won't be closing the front door…we'll change the name if you want, buy you out, whatever. We hope if that's your final decision, you'll give us good terms. But we will stay in business."

There still wasn't a sound in the room.

Caleb raised his head. He had been looking down at the table for about half the time while Oscar spoke. His gaze moved around the room, catching people's eyes, seeing the bowed heads of others. No one avoided his eyes. He fought back tears.

He realized he needed to compose himself. Then he started: "I really don't know what to say. This is not what I expected. I guess that's clear. And, frankly, I'm not sure what I want to do now."

Oscar answered. "We would all like you not to think too long or hard about anything but staying here and helping us continue to build this company. I didn't mention it, but several of the new clients, the ones who cold-called after the New York magazine article, said they would really appreciate your input, to know what you think they should do with their own companies."

"You never said anything," Caleb replied.

"No, you yourself have said you were not really paying attention, that your focus was elsewhere. I assured them I was talking to you and getting your input," Oscar said. The other people in the room laughed, a bit nervously, like they had all done the same thing.

"Ahh, I see. Well, it is probably true that you knew what I would have said anyway. But, seriously, let me think about it. I can't imagine the bad things that have been happening to me will ever cease. But on the other hand, I know how the world works: people will forget my face, they'll forget what happened, and I will just be another anonymous white guy in the crowds of Manhattan.

"In some ways, I am right where I wanted to be. I have wanted a change in my life for a long time. Obviously, my life is a lot different today. I know myself well enough to know I probably should stick around for a while. Maybe being here will help me get my feet back on the ground. With your help."

With that, Oscar walked over to Caleb at the head of the table. Caleb stood up as Oscar reached out to shake his hand. Everyone in the room followed suit, some of the men and women giving him hugs and thanking him. They all then slowly filed out, finally leaving Caleb alone in the boardroom. He knew immediately what he wanted to do. Talk to Brenda.

The phone at his house rang about six times before going to voice mail. It was only 10 o'clock in the morning, so Caleb wasn't sure why she wasn't home, but then he hadn't lived there for a month, so who knows. He had been talking to Brenda at least every other day, but they hadn't seen each other. She had no idea he had been considering shutting down his firm.

The day he moved out, their conversation had been tense, with Brenda almost silent as Caleb again asked her to forgive him. But he guessed it was too late. Their hope for a new beginning had been stymied, and with the lingering problems in their relationship, they had nothing to fall back on.

That's why Caleb had left. He hoped his absence would give Brenda a respite. Yes, that was his hope. And now, if his staff really wanted him to stay, if the business world was ready to not just forgive him but actually value his insights, maybe the rest of the world would begin to forget and forgive, too. Yes, there was hope there as well. And maybe that would open the door for him and Brenda to get back together and work on repairing their marriage and building a different life together.

He tried her cell phone.

"Oh, Caleb. What do you want?"

The tone in her voice was startling, the curtness unlike anything he had heard from her before.

"Uhh, I want to talk with you. To let you know what an extraordinary thing just happened here at work." He started to tell her what had gone on in the meeting.

"You know what, Caleb?" Brenda interrupted. "I don't really want to know. Your work has nothing to do with us anymore. You know I've had enough. I've been telling you that for a couple of weeks now. I'm at a divorce lawyer's office right now. I want out. You'll be hearing from him in a few days. Goodbye, Caleb. I hope you find a way to put this whole disaster behind you. But it will have to be without me."

She hung up. Caleb sat unmoving at his desk, the phone handset still in his hand. He had known that Brenda's patience had run out, but she at least had agreed the separation would just be temporary until things settled down. What had happened? He was having a hard enough time reconciling what his staff had just told him. But now this. Brenda divorcing him?

What now?

## CHAPTER 41

**D**ETECTIVE WILLIAMS GRABBED THE GLASS of Jack Daniels, rattled the ice cubes a couple of times, and headed for the basement.

"Hon, you didn't finish your dinner," his wife said.

"Not real hungry tonight, darling. Got some work to do."

"You know the chief told you to stop working all the time on that case. The grand jury's ruling is weeks, wow, even months old. Time to let it go, don't you think?"

"What makes you think that's what I'm doing?" he said, but he saw the skeptical look on her face. "Okay, okay. But that's why I brought everything home. The chief doesn't have to know. This one just keeps eating at me. I can't let it go."

"Okay, but don't stay up too late. And please be quiet when you come up. You woke me up last night."

"Sure. Okay, darling."

Arnette went down to the basement, turned on the overhead fluorescents and flipped the floor switch for the two flood lamps to come on. Then it was all shining brightly: an entire wall of pictures, newspaper clippings, and his own notes, showing people and places connected by different colors of string. This was his way of trying to piece together a coherent story about what had happened on 10/10, plus the crimes he now believed were somehow connected.

There was no link to the terror act itself, which held its own fascination for him: two black Americans, both converted Muslims, one a college grad, one a street hood from Detroit. Together they had put together what they hoped would be a deadly attack, using hundreds of pounds of Semtex, all of it loaded onto two private jets in Allentown, Pennsylvania. So armed, they had come damn close to turning Westchester County into a Chernobyl-like wasteland. Arnette had heard all the claims about how the domes could never be breached, but he also knew from secret reports—shown to him by a friend in the Department of Homeland Security's New York office—that one of the domes had in fact been breached. The official report noted, correctly, that at the time of the attack the reactor had been shut down for inspection and upgrades, but it glossed over what would have happened if the reactor had been near full power on that fateful day. Still, as a detective, what intrigued Arnette the most were the two terrorists themselves. What drove them to become jihadists? Why do such a thing? Arnette really had no clue. He had read several in-depth magazine articles about them, but the two men and their motives remained for him beyond comprehension.

Still, this much was clear, and the evidence was now pinned up on Arnette's wall: those two black Muslims had triggered a strange chain of events, a chain that somehow had led to the murder of Rachel Silver, just a few steps from her own backyard. And in Arnette's mind, all the trails that might lead to her killer were just as dead as she was. All the colored strings on his wall led absolutely nowhere. He wasn't even sure whom he should focus on further.

Still, Arnette knew he was missing something. But what? One lead he had finally pursued related to Sean Murray's car, the one that had gone missing from the hospital parking lot the morning of the attack. Sean's son Charlie, the train conductor with the almost childlike IQ, had pestered Arnette for months to track down his dad's car and they finally found it impounded by cops in Manhattan. The car had been found abandoned in the city in December. Because it had not yet been listed as stolen, it had been dumped in a police lot in Queens, nearly lost amid the hundreds of other things going on in New York. Arnette pulled some strings and had the NYPD crime lab go over the car with a fine-tooth comb, but they came up with nothing. No prints, no hair. Nothing. No surprise: it had been more than eight months since the old man's car had disappeared.

Arnette had gone further: several times he interviewed the nurse who had been on duty that morning at the hospital. She remembered Caleb Drake. She remembered helping him wheel the old man into the ER. And she remembered, of course, how Caleb had pleaded with her to loan him her car, so he could get home to help get his wife and kids to safety. According to Caleb, when they found the old man on the ground in the parking lot, Rachel had said he kept mumbling, "he took it, he took it." But the nurse told Arnette she never heard that; by the time they got Sean Murray onto the gurney he was unconscious, and he never said another word. So for Arnette, there seemed nowhere else to turn. He had hit a dead end. Still, giving up was not an option.

+++

CHARLIE MURRAY'S FOREARMS were flat on the long, wooden bar that stretched nearly all the way to the door of Noel's, one of his big nighttime hangouts in the small Hudson River community. Charlie was down to the dregs of his fourth Budweiser but he wanted another one. Thursday was his day off so he wasn't quite ready to head home to face the depressing situation there or think about his problems at work.

Charlie knew his Mom had gone to bed hours ago, more despondent than ever over her dead husband, and that made him sad. And the crap at work just kept getting worse. After the grand jury hearing, the newspaper stories about Rachel Silver's murder trickled out for a few weeks. The reports always mentioned him as a "person of interest" in the ongoing investigation. While his work suspension for leaving his post during an emergency was long over, his Metro-North supervisors were still trying to figure out what to do with him. Charlie had been told that every time the railroad put him back on a train to collect tickets, someone would recognize him and complain.

"Hey, Billy. Can I have one more?"

"Getting late, Charlie. You sure? You've had plenty."

"Aww, come on, the game's not over yet. It's only the 6th. Hate it when the Yankees play out on the coast. Maybe I'll stay up to watch the whole thing."

"Not here you won't. Not tonight. Got the go-ahead to close at midnight. So this is last call anyway."

"Okay, one more, please."

"Sure, Charlie, whatever. This one's on me."

He sipped his beer, keeping an eye on the game. As the 7th inning stretch came, the broadcast switched to the local news channel, Channel 12, and an anchor came on to tout the top stories for the news show after the game.

"Indian Point I went back on-line today. The Power Corporation spokesperson praised the hard work that had repaired the main reactor and the electrical substation in record time, just eight months after the terror attack on 10/10. In other news…" the anchor continued but Charlie had stopped listening.

Charlie teared up. He couldn't help himself. Every time there was news or a report related to 10/10, he would get emotional, remembering his dad, the sadness in his mother, his own dismay over never finding out who took his dad's car. What happened?

Charlie stood up abruptly.

"Gotta go, Billy. See you later."

"Take care, Charlie. Drive safe."

He had barely gotten to his car door when the lights inside the tavern went out, and the parking lot's floodlights went dark.

Charlie had parked around back of the bar in a small adjacent lot, dark but for one faint light from a side street. He fumbled for his keys, then had trouble finding the lock on his car door.

A quick-moving shadow moved toward him with a soft shuffling sound on the gravely pavement. As he turned toward the sound, Charlie saw a long, thick pipe coming at his head. He started to duck, but the pipe struck him square on the side of his skull. He tumbled to the ground, rolling to avoid the next blow. He never saw it coming. The second blow left him on the edge of consciousness, just enough so that he could feel the knife plunge into his ribs.

## CHAPTER 42

Detective Williams lifted the yellow crime scene tape and ducked into the parking lot behind Noel's. Williams could hear the traffic driving by on Main Street, which ran past the bar's front door as well as a bunch of storefronts and struggling businesses that managed to stay alive in the rundown neighborhood.

A couple of Peekskill policemen stood guard around the perimeter, where a small crowd of 10 or 20 people watched the county's forensic team fan out across the small lot behind the bar. They were picking up and examining pieces of debris and bagging anything that looked unusual.

Williams approached a small group of young men, lounging against a wall with their jeans pulled down low, the tops of their underwear exposed, and the baggy legs obscuring their Nike shoes.

"You a cop?" one of them said as Williams approached.

"Yeah. Any of you out last night?"

"No, bro, we all home in bed by 9 o'clock, just like always. We ain't seen nothin'."

"I didn't ask you if you saw anything, wise guy. I want to know if you were out here."

That shut them up. He scanned their faces, getting nothing. But he kept probing: "Any of you know the white guy that got killed?"

"No, he white? Didn't even know that." The small group laughed in unison.

An older man standing at the back of the group said quietly, "Yeah, I'd seen him before. I had a beer or two with him from time to time. Saw him last night. He was kinda out of it. I went home early. He was still there. But I didn't see nothing outside."

The young boys scowled at the older man.

"He say anything to you?" Williams asked.

"No, I barely knew him. I heard the bartender call him Charlie, but that's about it. Pretty sure he worked for the train company, you know, Metro-North."

"Thanks, my friend. If you think of anything, here's my card," Williams said. "And the rest of you, stay out of trouble."

"Yeah, man, whatever."

Williams turned back to the lot and walked over to the body, covered up by a white sheet. The medical examiner was writing notes and motioned to the gurney guys to come on over.

"Wait a minute," Detective Williams said. "Let me have a look at him. You find anything unusual about the wounds?"

"Not much. Multiple stab wounds, mostly frontal. Took a blow to the head. Surprised, maybe, from behind or the side."

Williams pulled back the sheet. There were black and blue marks on Charlie's face, and it looked like his skull had been partly crushed, and he could see the jagged tears in the shirt and the blood that had saturated the cloth.

"Damn, I know this guy. I was working with him on a stolen car case," Williams said to the medical examiner.

The medical examiner continued, "Cops here said the bartender told them the guy had five or six beers, at least. Got up sudden like and walked out about midnight. Bartender had parked out front last night, so he never came to the back after he closed up. Said he left about five minutes after the vic."

"The wounds look angry?"

"Nope. First thrust probably killed him so the rest may just be for show. Not sure though. The head blow didn't kill him, I don't think. Face bruises probably came when he fell from the blow. Pipe's over there. Wiped clean, as far as I can tell. Probably got clubbed from the side. Then he tried to roll away, stunned, and that's when he got stabbed. Bartender said he had a pretty good-sized roll last night; it's gone, and no wallet either. Could be a robbery gone bad?"

"Maybe. Thanks. Let me know if anything else turns up. Hey, do me a favor. Check the stab wounds against the Silver murder from last February, please."

"You kidding me, right?"

"No, I'm not kidding."


A short time later, Williams stood in front of Charlie Murray's house, one of those two-story, clapboard houses on a street where every house pretty much looked the same, except for the paint. He walked up the steps to the front porch. He had been a couple of times before to talk with Charlie, but this was a really sad moment. What was he going to say? He knocked. Horrible business.

The door opened. "Rose?" he said, holding up his badge.

"Yes, are you here about Charlie? He didn't come home last night, and I finally called the station to ask about him."

"I am, ma'am. May I come in?"

"Sure. You've been here before, haven't you? I've seen you."

"Yes, ma'am. I was working with your son to help find your husband's car."

"Oh, that's right. That's right. So, any news about my Charlie?"

"Ma'am, you should sit down," Williams said, motioning to the sofa in the living room. Just then, another woman walked out of the kitchen, dressed in a nurse's uniform. She nodded at the detective and said, "I come in to help Rose a few times a week."

"Okay, thanks. Rose, I have bad news: Charlie's dead."

The color immediately drained from her face, and Williams thought she was going to faint.

"No, no. That's not possible. He was fine when he went out last night."

"Ma'am, I have to ask you a couple of questions, because it appears he was murdered."

"Murdered?"

"Yes, ma'am. Out in the parking lot by Noel's. Guess he'd been drinking inside. His wallet and his money were gone. Did you ever hear Charlie mention anyone who might be angry with him? Or who wanted something from him?"

"No, no! Everyone loved Charlie." She started crying. "Oh, they made fun of him sometimes. But no one didn't like him."

"Ma'am, I'd really appreciate it if you would let me look in his room."

"Please, please go ahead. It's on the right at the top of the stairs. Joanne, would you get me a glass of water? What am I going to do now? What am I going to do? Charlie always took good care of me."

Williams climbed the steep wooden staircase, with its plain tan runner up the middle. There were a few landscape paintings on the wall, and a plain faux brass chandelier lighting the area. He opened the door to Charlie's room and felt like he was entering a time warp. There were posters of the Knicks and the Yankees, most of them pretty faded, plus a few pieces of sports memorabilia on the shelves of a bookcase: a Yankee hat, a signed baseball with an illegible signature, and a few knick-knacks. The impression was of being in the room of a 16-year-old, not a 50-year-old man. On the right side of the room, there were two closet doors. The closest one contained Charlie's clothes and uniforms. The other was locked. Williams went over to the desk and opened the main drawer, and there in a corner was an old brass key with a cloverleaf top.

He inserted the key into the lock and opened the door. An automatic light immediately went on, and the detective instinctively slipped on his gloves for handling evidence. The wall in front of him was covered with pictures of women, most of them appearing to be passengers on a Metro-North train. But one side of the wall was filled with pictures of Rachel Silver, some slashed with angry red lines.

Williams backed out of the closet, pulled out his cell phone and dialed Westchester Country forensics. "I need a murder team up here in Peekskill," he said, quickly rattling off the address.

A couple hours later, the detective was sitting in front of Captain Blake's desk, holding his head in his hands. He felt dazed.

"I can't believe it. I forgot the cardinal rule: if the most obvious thing is right in front of you, go for it, don't let your prejudice blind you to what's right in front of you. I just didn't think Charlie Murray was smart enough to pull the wool over my eyes."

"Don't beat yourself up," Captain Blake said. "You yourself have said you've been wrong about the guilty ones—and about the innocents. You still could be. You need to remember, you verified his alibi more than once. At the time Rachel Silver was murdered, he was at Noel's. Maybe he was just a pervert."

"But Jesus, captain, he sure looks like the killer. And I'm so glad now I did what I did with that prick D.A. He was all set to railroad that guy Drake, based on nothing. And now we have this."

"Yeah, Caleb Drake. I hear things haven't gone so well for him anyway. He moved into the city a month or so ago. That story in New York magazine just did him in. I bet we responded to half a dozen calls from the wife. Hate calls. Vandalism of their property. It drove her right over the edge. I hear she's going to divorce him."

"Well, I've got to talk to Mr. Drake. Maybe he knows something. Who knows, maybe he did in Murray. From pent-up rage at the guy who had harassed his dead lover. Who the hell knows anymore? I mean it makes no sense that anyone involved in that whole mess on 10/10 would kill Charlie, especially if he was Rachel's murderer. But who knows? He was still pressing the issue about his dad's car.

## CHAPTER 43

CALEB STARED AT THE RETURN address of Jameson Jones LLC in New York City on the manila folder on his desk at Drake & Associates. He had read the 15-page document, a formal petition for divorce by Brenda (Swanson) Drake. He had been married to her for 25 years and the end of their life together came down to this single pile of paper. On one hand, he just wanted to sign it, send it back and get it over with. But on the other hand, he wasn't quite ready to give up. He just didn't know where to begin. Brenda had been refusing to take his calls or to respond to his pleas to at least listen to him.

Still, he had turned a corner. The depression that had followed the harsh, often virulent backlash from the New York magazine article about him and Rachel's murder was finally beginning to fade. He still regretted agreeing to that article, his own naiveté leading him to believe he could control the narrative, just as he had done so many times as a publicist guiding writers on behalf of his clients. But getting screwed by the story ended up working in his favor. Most people felt he had been unfairly treated.

His employees' expression of faith and confidence in him also had shaken him out of his post-Rachel depression. Now it was up to him to live up to their belief in him.

How different this reaction was from all those frequent dark periods that had shadowed his life since Vietnam. His PTSD had always lurked close to the surface of his psyche. The trigger could be something mundane: a car collision, a friend's accidental death (there had been several of those in his life, especially as he got older), or even stumbling upon an EMT tending to a heart attack victim on Madison Avenue. For years, he refused to watch any of the Vietnam-inspired movies, not after he had sat through the first 40 minutes of "Apocalypse Now"—and then bolted out of the theater. He had had nightmares for a month after that. He then knew instinctively to avoid any images, even ones conjured up by Hollywood, of those days in the jungle. But like his father's generation, which never talked about their World War II experiences, Caleb never talked about his in Southeast Asia, so the memories just tormented him, waiting for their moment to surge up and tear apart his psyche, again and again and again.

Caleb knew now that 10/10 and Rachel Silver's murder had changed him profoundly, their intertwined tragedy conspiring to push his old demons far behind him. The ancient past seemed less important in the wake of these new tragedies in his life. So now, instead of being paralyzed by these fresh traumas, Caleb had admitted that he couldn't handle his debilitating condition alone. He had resolved to seek help and deal with his PTSD once and for all. For the very first time, he was allowing himself to hope there could be a new beginning. He was ready to face life head on, come what may.

The truth was clear now: prior to Rachel's murder he had been despondent about failing to take the opportunity to change, to overturn the numbing inevitability of his life, a life that had fallen into place without being purposely chosen. Now, he was determined to make the changes that he had always dreamed about—but had never seized. He wanted to start writing again. He wanted to travel to places that he dreamed about visiting. He wanted to play his guitar again. And he really yearned for the stimulation of new friends, artists, musicians, writers, creative types who could inspire him. Or just spend more quality time with his kids.

That said, he still had hoped that his future would include Brenda. But when she rejected his request to come away with him, to start over fresh, he realized that he had to go forward alone and restore the foundations of everything he had built all those years. And his employees were giving him the vehicle to do it.

There was a knock on the door. His secretary Ellen stuck her head in the door. "Mr. Drake. There's a gentlemen here to see you. Says he's from the White Plains police. Says you'll know. Do you want me to tell him to come back?"

"No, I can see him. Where is he? In the lobby?"

Detective Arnette Williams was waiting in the foyer of Caleb's office, admiring the rows of trophies and awards from the world of public relations that were lined up on a shelf. Before this year, Williams had never heard of Drake & Associates Public Relations, but all those awards told him it was a successful firm. Nice offices on Madison Avenue on a high floor looking out towards Bryant Park, with Rockefeller Center to the north and the Empire State building to the south. At the window, Williams looked all the way down to Battery City, and he wished, oh how he wished, he could still see those Twin Towers rising majestically into the sky.

Caleb Drake walked into the foyer. "Detective Williams? What are you doing here?"

"Can we talk, Mr. Drake? Somewhere private?"

"Sure, come on back."

Caleb led him down the hallway, a row of glass-walled offices on one side, and on the other side, the modern office version of a monk's library in a medieval monastery: rows of open cubicles, the only sign of individuality a small potted plant, or a tiny stuffed bear, or a Yankee or Met hat stuck in a visible position.

Once in his office, Caleb motioned Williams to a chair in front of his desk. "So, what can I do for you, detective?"

"I take it you haven't heard?"

"No. What?" Caleb said, suppressing a worried groan.

"Charlie Murray. You remember him?"

"Of course. The train conductor on 10/10. He saw the whole incident between me and James Roth."

"That's right. Well, he was found stabbed to death early this morning. Brutally. In a parking lot outside a bar in Peekskill."

"What?"

Williams didn't say a word, watching Drake like any trained investigator would, looking for the slightest flinch, or shielding of his eyes, or the involuntary twitching of a neck muscle. But the detective saw nothing of the sort. And Drake seemed as shocked as anyone could be.

"Oh shit," Caleb said. "That's terrible. He didn't deserve anything like that." Caleb's thoughts flashed immediately to what Murray's death meant for him, and it was clear. He said out loud what had popped into his head:

"So that means Roth and I are the only living witnesses, at least who came forward, to what happened with me and Rachel and Roth that day on the train."

"That's right."

Caleb paused. "So, have you spoken with Roth yet?"

"No, I thought I would talk to you first. I called your home, but your wife said you had moved out and that your office was the likeliest place to find you. You know I have to ask: Where were you last night, Mr. Drake?"

"I was in my apartment. Reading." Caleb paused. "Oh, hell, I was reading over these divorce papers that my wife just sent me. I keep carrying them back and forth between the office and my apartment, not knowing what I want to do with them."

"I'm sorry to hear that, Mr. Drake. I thought you two were pretty tight after the grand jury hearing."

"We were, but you wouldn't believe the shit that happened after that damned magazine article came out a few months back."

"You mean the one about you being a philanderer and a bad husband and probably a murderer?" Williams said.

"Yeah, that one. How could I have been so stupid?"

"Yes, what a world we live in these days. The grand jury clears you, but the press smears you anyway. And the smear will last far longer than the truth."

"I'm afraid you're right, detective."

"And I guess you also underestimated the venality of our good friend, the D.A. To me, that story in New York magazine looked like it was right out of his personal campaign playbook."

"Yup. And I underestimated the ambition of an unscrupulous young writer. Long story short, it was all too much for Brenda. She filed for divorce."

"I am sorry," the detective said again. "So you were home alone last night? Where, here in the city?"

"Yes. I ordered in. I can tell you from where. They delivered pizza about 10 p.m. or so. I had been to a charity reception earlier in the evening. I can give you names of people who saw me there."

"Okay. And I'll need the name of the pizza parlor, too."

"No problem."

"Mr. Drake, had you spoken with Charlie Murray recently?"

"Not since right before the grand jury hearing. Oh, I take that back. He called me a couple of weeks ago. I had nothing to say to him. He was complaining, as usual. And I had nothing to tell him."

"Did he sound distraught?" Williams said.

"Yeah, or drunk, or both. I wasn't sure. He wasn't making sense. But this can't have anything to do with Rachel, can it? She said he seemed creepy but harmless. And he was always looking for some-one to vouch for him with Metro-North."

"I doubt his killing is connected. But I still have to look into any possible link to Rachel's murder. Look, he was in a pretty dicey area of Peekskill. It may be nothing more than a botched robbery."

"Still, what a shame. He really seemed so harmless. Didn't he live with his mother? What does she say?"

Williams paused. "She's pretty upset, as you might expect. She's got no one left at home. But we're taking it slow, checking into Murray's life. I guess there's really nothing else to do right now. But I will stay in touch. Don't forget to send me the name of that pizza parlor."

"Don't worry. First thing when I get home."

"By the way, when I was waiting outside, I overheard a cou-ple of your employees getting off the elevator. They said they were glad you're still here. What's that all about?"

"I was planning to close this firm. Try to get on with my life. But the staff wouldn't let me. Believe it or not, detective, they say my problems have been good for business."

"You're surprised?" Williams said. "I'm not. We seem to be liv-ing in an upside-down world, where rumors are more powerful than truth, and where shabby misdeeds get spun into virtues."

## CHAPTER 44

EVERY DAY WAS STILL A struggle for James. For months, he had arrived at work, walked into his office, with its views out toward the Statue of Liberty, and sat down at his desk without a plan for the day. Through the open door, all day long he could see Sheri, who came to work with him now, standing over the trading desks and leading her team with the same self-assured prowess that had always been her trademark. Her return to the trading world hadn't gone unnoticed; he often heard the verb that someone had been "Golded," a begrudging label of respect for having been on the wrong side of one of her trades on behalf of Goldfarb & Roth.

Still, James was feeling increasingly better, getting back his old drive. For the first time in eight months, he had three deals in the works, all of them multi-billion dollar projects that when signed and delivered would re-establish him as one of the premier dealmakers on Wall Street. As those pieces fell into place, he had begun to wonder what had taken so long for him to get his focus back.

In truth, Irv Goldfarb deserved the credit for getting him back on track. His father-in-law had sat him down and read him the riot act. In one of his more memorable, blunt-force verbal attacks, Irv had compared him and Sheri with a simple vulgarity: "You became the pussy and now she has the balls." But the words that most stuck in his mind came when he had tried to explain to Irv that he was tired of being viewed as a bad guy, with a reputation as a cutthroat competitor, or more bluntly, an arrogant asshole. To that, Irv had laid it out plainly: "James, it's only business. It's only business. What they think about you personally doesn't matter. They'll hate you one minute, and invite you to their daughter's wedding the next."

Still, putting his struggle behind him had not been easy. The memories of 10/10, and the old man dying in the parking lot as he drove away in the man's car, still surfaced from time to time, often at the most unexpected moments. But he wasn't debilitated by the memories anymore, and his immersion back into work energized him again, submerging the psychological dramas of the year under layers of work and activity. At the very least, James felt alive again, ready to push on and not freeze in the face of unknown and unpredictable consequences. He knew he would never be free of what he had done to the lives of others, but maybe he could live without the burden weighing him down every day.

This morning James was flipping through the stack of newspapers on his desk. He finished the sports section of the New York Post, then he glanced over at the Journal News, which he still got delivered to his office, even though he and Sheri had moved into the city. And there it was: the picture of a grisly crime scene under the headline: "Metro-North Conductor Stabbed to Death." As he read the sparse details of what had happened to Charlie Murray, he remembered the man's name, his face, and how he had been fighting the impulse to send the poor man some money.

Instinctively, James turned around to the lower drawer of his credenza and opened a safe. Inside were stacks of neatly packaged $100 bills, in bundles of $10,000 each. He reached to pick one up, but then stopped. No fingerprints. You never know, he thought. He got up, walked past his secretary's desk, and then headed down the hall to the supply room. There he found a stack of mailers, with the U.S. Postal Service logo on them. Without putting his fingertips on the flat surfaces, he picked one up by the edge, then pressed it tightly under his arm.

James returned to his office with the envelope stuck under his arm. Once inside, he closed the door and eased the envelope onto his desk. Then, with a letter opener, he took three stacks of bills out of the safe, using the letter opener to slip under the paper band. Then he carefully pushed each stack into the mailer. Using a small folded note card, he picked up the envelope and put it in a briefcase.

"I've got to run a quick errand," he said, walking past his secretary with the briefcase in hand. James had Charlie's address memorized; he had been thinking about sending him money for a long time; maybe it could help him buy a new car. But now he figured he could at least help out Charlie's mother, the woman he had widowed.

After stopping in a Duane Reade pharmacy for a cheap, throwaway ballpoint pen—he paid with cash—James entered the post office. There, with methodical care, he got the envelope out of the briefcase, holding it again with the note card. He addressed it slowly, using his left hand, and then he went to a stamp machine, paying with bills and putting too much postage on the envelope. Then he slipped the package into the nearby mail slot.

Done. Now, maybe he could sleep better, knowing he had helped the poor widow. After all, she had lost her husband, maybe because of his own indifference, and now she had lost her son, too. Money couldn't fix anything, but maybe it could help ease her pain. And his conscience.

Or so James hoped.

+++

DETECTIVE ARNETTE WILLIAMS WAS waiting in the spacious foyer of Goldfarb & Roth when James Roth came hurrying back from the post office, striding purposely with his empty briefcase in hand.

"Mr. Roth," the detective said as he stood up.

"I'm sorry, Mr. Roth," the receptionist said, "this man has been waiting for you. He says he needs to see you."

James recognized the detective and approached him like someone waiting for him on the first tee: hand outstretched, a smile on his face, and a confident, relaxed demeanor.

"How are you, detective? What brings you to my part of the world?"

"You don't know?"

"Uh, sorry. I'm not sure. Oh wait, I read the Journal News today. Is it about that train conductor?"

"Yes. I just wanted… actually could we go into your office, or someplace private?"

"Sure, follow me," James said, quickly wondering if he had left behind any evidence of taking the cash from his safe.

As they walked across the trading floor, Detective Williams heard a sharp female voice barking out orders in rapid-fire succession. It was Sheri Roth, hovering over the traders, clearly in command.

"That's your wife, right?" Detective Williams asked over James' shoulder.

"Yup, hard to miss, isn't she?"

"That's always been true. I'll need to talk to her next."

"Sheri!" James shouted.

She glanced up, but Williams added, "But first you. Alone."

"Okay, come on in. You want coffee, detective? Water?" he asked, waving Sheri off for the moment.

"I'm fine, thanks."

They entered Roth's office, with its bank of windows framing the Hudson. But Detective Williams wasn't interested in the view.

"I'll get right to it, Mr. Roth. Where were you the night before last?"

"Sheri and I had a fundraiser. You know, one of those New York charity deals. They usually end early, so we were home by, I don't know, 10 o'clock. No later. I went right to bed. Sheri came to bed a little later. I was asleep, but it wasn't long after."

Then Sheri barged in. "Hello, Detective Williams. I thought we were done with you."

"I was just talking to your husband, Mrs. Roth. Asking him a few questions… privately."

"Whatever you have to ask him, you can ask me too."

"All right then. What time did you come to bed the night before last?"

"Detective," James said, "I was about to tell you I wasn't sure, but she was next to me in the morning. We came home together. We went up to the apartment together."

"What is this all about, detective?" Sheri asked.

Williams repeated the news about the conductor and then asked, "I take it you haven't heard? So what were you doing while your husband was asleep?"

"As I'm sure James told you, we went to a fundraiser, a charity for autism. We came home early. He went to bed right away. I did some work and came to bed later. I can't tell you the exact time."

"Working on your computer?"

"No, I was writing notes to some of the people we met that night."

"That was long enough for your husband to go to sleep?"

"Well, you know, he often takes sleeping pills. So it doesn't take long for him to doze off."

"I have to ask you both again: Why did you move back into the city?"

Williams kept his face totally blank, giving no hint of what was going through his head. He had nothing substantive on these people; this visit was a pure fishing expedition. But the detective was hoping to throw them off-balance, maybe catch them in some inconsistencies. He had a vague feeling in his gut that James had killed Rachel, and if he had, then why not kill Charlie Murray, too? Hence his probing.

"Detective, why did we move back into the city?" Sheri said. "We told you the reasons months ago. Our kids were getting older. I was itching to go back to work. We were bored in the suburbs. And my father had a great apartment in the city that was just sitting idle. The time seemed right. Now, what more do you want to know?"

"I'm just asking," Williams said.

"Wow, but what does any of this have to do with his murder? It's sad. I always felt bad for the conductor. What was his name? Murray, right?"

"Yes, ma'am. He also had an axe to grind about what happened that morning. He was still trying to find out what happened to his father's car."

"What does this have to do with us?"

"Did he ever call you, Mrs. Roth?"

That startled her. Slowly she said, "Why, yes. About two weeks ago. Here at work. I don't know how he found my number, but he was rambling, talking rapidly, wanting to know, let's see, just like you said, mumbling about what had happened to his father's car."

"Why didn't you report it? Sounds like a harassing call."

"Because it happened only once, and I felt sorry for the poor man. No need to overreact to a single phone call," she said. "Detective, is there anything else we can do for you? I'm running a position in oil futures today that is pretty volatile. I need to get back to the floor."

"Okay. But I may be back in touch. Soon."

She whirled on him, a glare now in her eye. "I suggest you contact my office, detective, and my secretary will put you in touch with our lawyer. This is a waste of our time—and yours. Please leave us alone."

With that, she turned and walked away.

James shrugged and then said, "You heard her. I think it's time for you to go. I don't have anything else to add, or say. My secretary will show you out."

Williams left the office, a step in front of Roth. Call it instinct, but Williams couldn't help but feel the same thing he always felt after talking to those two: what were they hiding?

+++

"Hello, detective," Daniel Silver said as he opened the door to his house. "Please come in."

With one quick glance, Detective Williams could see the house hadn't been touched since Rachel Silver's death back in February. And this was June.

"You know why I'm here, Mr. Silver," Williams said. It had taken him a couple of days to wrap up another case, so it was now four days since Charlie Murray's death.

"No, I don't know, detective. But I've been thinking about calling you for the last day or so. I was reading a story about 10/10 and I couldn't help but think about Rachel and how she was convinced there were untold stories about that day."

"What prompted that, Mr. Silver? Was it the newspaper stories about Charlie Murray, the conductor on the train?"

"Oh, right," Daniel Silver said. "The conductor. That's where I was reading about 10/10. You don't think that's connected to Rachel, do you?"

"I don't know," the detective said. "Murray seemed to have called everyone under the sun. Did he ever call here?"

"As a matter of fact he did, detective. He called here a couple of weeks ago. He was pretty distraught. Didn't say why. Just kept mumbling something about why she didn't help me. I told him it was late, and he should go to bed and sober up."

"Really?" Williams asked. "He apparently called Drake and the Roths, too. Well, his murder has gotten me some time to look into this case again. He was one of the witnesses to the fight on the train over Rachel's phone, too."

"What do you mean, 'time to look into it?' Do you mean you had stopped?"

"I was pretty obsessed with your wife's murder, Mr. Silver. My superior in the detective bureau finally told me to drop it. But I can't. It's like those cases you read about, where a cop just can't let it go. Rachel's murder is like that for me."

"But how could you cops let it go?" Silver said. "This was a big case. And the D.A. said he wasn't going to let it go."

Williams sighed. "Yeah, he kept looking into it for about 15 minutes after the grand jury wouldn't indict. Then the press dropped the story. America's Most Wanted did their show, then they dropped it. After that, the D.A. started looking for another high-profile case that would put him in front of the cameras in the heat of his run for governor. You know how it works, Mr. Silver."

"Yes, sadly I do," Daniel said. "Still, has there been anything new? You, we really need to find Rachel's killer."

"Well, there was nothing new—until Charlie Murray's murder. Is that connected to Rachel's death? I have no idea... yet. But they were both on the same Metro-North train—in the very same car—on 10/10, and now they're both dead. Mr. Silver, I have to ask: where were you the night before last?"

"I was here. My kids were here. I went to bed before my son. Many nights I just take an Ambien and I'm out. I'm sure my son can tell you what time that was because I said goodnight to him beforehand. Tell me, detective: It's getting less and less likely that you'll find out who killed Rachel, isn't that true?"

"I'm not giving up, Mr. Silver. I promise you that. I've interviewed every possible suspect and every one of them—except Caleb Drake—had an airtight alibi. And you and I both know he didn't do it. So I'm stumped."

"Shit, I keep hoping something will turn up. Do you think that's possible?"

"Your guess is as good as mine, Mr. Silver. But I keep coming back to what happened to those people on the train that awful morning. There are five who stand out: Your wife. Caleb Drake. James Roth. Charlie Murray. And, up the hill, Charlie's dad and his missing car. And look what happened to them."

"What do you mean, detective?"

"Well, think about it. Rachel's dead. Sean Murray's dead.

Charlie Murray's dead. And Caleb Drake has been cleared by a grand jury. That leaves the Roths, or James Roth anyway."

"Does that mean you've ruled out me?"

Williams laughed. "Always the lawyer, eh, Mr. Silver? Yes, I ruled you out on Day One. Maybe I shouldn't have? But anyway, you weren't on the train."

"No, I wasn't on the train. And I couldn't have killed my wife. Not in a million years."

"So who does that leave. I spoke to the Roths this morning. Tough nuts. They have never changed their stories, not one iota."

"James Roth? Are you kidding me? I'm his corporate attorney now. I talk to him two or three times a week, and we have lunch at least once a month. I've been on a squash court with him. Damn, I'd be flabbergasted if he were involved."

"Hmm, I didn't know you had a connection to him."

"Yes, it started about a month after our dinner. He called to commiserate about the grand jury hearing. Then he asked if I would consider taking on Goldfarb & Roth as a client. You know, that's why I invited him over in the first place. At the time there were rumors he was starting his own firm. He never did that, and now he's a partner at Goldfarb, with his wife. But you probably knew that already…"

"Yeah, I did know that. It was hard to miss this morning, seeing Mr. and Mrs. Roth in their luxurious offices. But I didn't know you were his lawyer. I find it intriguing that he would want you working closely with him, or for that matter, you with him."

"What do you mean?"

"Oh, nothing. Nothing."

## CHAPTER 45

C ALEB SAT BACK IN HIS high-backed leather office chair, survey-
ing the room, the three television screens on the far wall flick-
ering with the start of the local news on his three favorite chan-
nels: two network affiliates and the Westchester cable station. Less
than a month had passed since his employees had talked him into
staying on the job, and to keep open his public relations and image consultancy business. He still couldn't quite believe how much
their expression of faith in him had affected his outlook, and it felt
like more than just a momentary change of attitude. He was feeling more alive and more unburdened than he had in decades.

Why should that be happening now?

The devastation of his former life was virtually complete. His
marriage was dissolving. He could feel Brenda turning the kids
against him, although he hoped they were old enough that whatever estrangement she was trying to engineer would not last for
long. But he no longer had a home, a wife, or a family. He had been
through months of vicious attacks and fabrications about his behavior, and all of this had eroded, slowly but steadily, the life he
had built over the past 40 years.

But instead of feeling crushed and depressed, Caleb was actually where he had wanted to be for years: free of the constraints
imposed by a lifetime's worth of obligations and commitments. Although he once wished to leave behind his job too, keeping Drake

& Associates alive was offering something new, something exciting: he was becoming the go-to guy for crisis management. He had seen the financials this week and the company was doing better than ever, enough so that there was no question he could afford the kind of apartment, on a high floor on the Upper West Side, with a terrace overlooking the Hudson, that he had dreamed about for years.

A news alert appeared on the Westchester channel's 6 p.m. broadcast, so he flicked on the sound: "Peekskill police have arrested an unemployed day laborer in the murder of Charles Murray, a long-time village resident and a Metro-North conductor. They discovered the suspect with Murray's credit cards and a large quantity of cash. Police say it appears the murder occurred during a simple robbery gone wrong. Our reporter also learned through his sources in White Plains that police now believe that Charles Murray may have been responsible for the death of Rachel Silver in February. More on that coming up…"

He turned off the sound. Charlie Murray? Rachel's killer? Really? He thought Detective Williams had dismissed that possibility months ago. He wanted to call Williams right away, but he figured the detective would call him.

Hearing Rachel's name again gave him a shudder. He still wished he had not gotten involved with her, but at least now, maybe he could begin to put the whole episode in its proper place, put it somewhere that didn't haunt him every single day.

Could this really be true; the cloud of suspicion hanging over him for so many months might soon be gone? Wow! If that threat of a murder indictment did disappear, Caleb could see a whole new future opening in front him. Indeed, he had already felt the weight lifting, but now there was almost nothing to stop his excitement about what could come next.

+++

DETECTIVE WILLIAMS WAITED under a tree on Central Park West, his eyes focused on the front door of the apartment building across the street, while black town cars and stretch limos zipped by in both directions, interspersed with bright yellow New York City taxi cabs. It was nearly 7 o'clock at night and he had been staking out the Roth's posh apartment building for more than an hour. He was glad he had cleared the stake-out with NYPD's Midtown North; several times he had had to flash his badge when patrol cars had pulled over to question him.

His intent was to surprise the Roths. He figured they'd soon be returning from the office, and when their limo pulled up to the front door of their stately building at 72th and Central Park West, he'd be ready to pounce. Another 15 minutes passed, and then he saw the limo do a U-turn across the lanes of traffic and pull up in front of their building. Before it had stopped, Williams was dashing across the street. He saw James Roth get out of the car, followed quickly by his beautiful wife.

"Mr. Roth! Mrs. Roth! May I have a minute?"

The driver—Williams realized he was not just a limo driver but also a security guard hired by the Roths—jumped out of the car with a hand reaching under his coat.

"Whoa, buddy," Williams said, flashing his badge. "I know these people. Stay cool."

"It's okay, Raymond. The detective here is just leaving."

"Didn't I tell you, detective? Call our lawyer," Sheri Roth said, hurrying toward the door.

"Please, I just want to ask you something. Do either of you know anything about the $30,000—in cash—that Rose Murray got in the mail this week?"

"What?" Sheri Roth said. "Who's that?"

"You remember: the widow of the man who died in the hospital parking lot. The man whose car disappeared. The woman whose son was murdered in Peekskill. Ma'am, I told you about her just a few days ago. Someone sent her that money. And I want to know who and I want to know why." As Williams could see, this was all news to Sheri Roth.

And she was irate now: "Detective, I have no idea who you are talking about. You came to see us, you harassed me and my husband at work. And now, in the middle of the sidewalk, you're suggesting we sent some woman $30,000? Are you crazy? I'm calling our lawyer right now. You can expect a restraining order by morning. And if I ever see you again, detective, it will be in court. Mark my words!"

"Okay," Detective Williams said, "if that's where it has to be."

"Wait a minute, detective. Maybe we can talk..."

"James, come! Do not talk to this man! Come inside."

James shrugged at the detective. He wanted to respond further to him, but he was not about to ignore his wife and her command.

As Williams watched them walk into their building, his cell phone buzzed. He knew the number: it was his office in White Plains.

"Williams. What's up?"

"Did you hear? They found the guy who killed Charlie Murray."

"Really? Who was it?"

"Some low-life up in Peekskill. A long criminal record. Even one count of attempted murder. He had Murray's credit cards and cash on him, and they found a knife on him, too. There's little doubt he did it."

Williams whistled to himself. "Well, I'll be. I thought it would be… Well, I guess that's not what I was expecting." He clicked off and shook his head. This put him right back at square one in the Rachel Silver case. Now what?

## CHAPTER 46

JAMES AND SHERI DRESSED IN silence. James Jr. and Elizabeth had been eating dinner, but they came into the dressing room and started asking about plans for the next afternoon.

"Dad, are you going to be able to make it to my soccer game tomorrow?" Elizabeth said.

"Hey, and what about my basketball game?" James Jr. said almost simultaneously.

Neither of them asked Sheri. It had been months since she had left the trading desk during the day, and James had been taking the chance to spend more time with the kids. Given her mood right now, James knew there wasn't a chance in hell she would go to their games anyway.

"I'll try. Let me take a look at my schedule," James said. "Now, scram, we have to get dressed."

James knew Sheri was seething. He didn't know why, but her silence and her body language were clues enough that something wasn't right. He paused for a minute in his dressing room, and gazed down at the streetlights on Central Park Drive. It was a view that had calmed him many times over the previous months, usually at 3 a.m. after waking up in a cold sweat from another nightmare. But tonight he felt truly calm for the first time in months.

"Let's go," Sheri said, her brittle voice betraying her mood.

He started to ask her what was going on, but she cut him off.

"Not here."

His resentment flared at the rebuke. What the hell was eating at this woman? He plodded after her as they headed out of the house. They said goodbye to the nanny and told her they wouldn't be too late, 11:30 at the latest. James stopped at the dining room table and gave James Jr. a jostle on his shoulder, and waved good-bye to Elizabeth.

"I'll try to make it tomorrow, sweetie. Be sure to leave me a note about the times."

Their stretch limo was waiting. They were on their way to the annual American Financial Association dinner, a command per-formance demanded by Irv Goldfarb. Irv had told Sheri that he had pushed the AFA to give James its Financier of the Year award, but swore her to secrecy. She ended up having to cajole James into attending. Now she wished she hadn't.

As soon as they got into the car, Sheri asked Sam, their driver tonight, for privacy. "Complete privacy. Windows, too. Radio on, loud."

"Yes, ma'am."

The partition rose silently between the driver's compartment and the hi-tech window shading that faded the panes to black. In the back seat, Sheri and James could no longer hear the announc-ers from the Yankees game on the car's radio, tuned to 1010 WINS.

As soon as they were sealed in, Sheri turned and started slug-ging James, "What the hell are you doing? I've been telling you for months the whole 10/10 incident is over! We are free and clear of everything! How could you send that woman the money? And $30,000? For what, god damn it?"

"Who said it was me?" he said, pushing her away.

"Come on, Roth. Don't be an asshole. Who else has $30,000 in random bills just lying around? I know about your safe. Your secret stash. And who was moping around like a man consumed by guilt for months? This is so typical of what you've become!"

He stiffened, struggling not to explode. "What the fuck do you know about what I've become?"

"Look at yourself!" Sheri barked. "You have let yourself go! Let me tell you: People are talking. They say you've gotten soft. Not on your game. They say you're pussy-whipped. They say that having me back in the office has cut your balls off. And I know, damn it, what my father said to you. He told me he gave you a little ass-ripping. Now he thinks you're back on your game. But this? Sending money to that Murray woman? It's insane."

James almost smiled. This was how Sheri used to talk when they first started dating: the locker room cadence, the quick ego-deflating jabs, that caustic sneer in her voice. She was tough, and even sexy. But it had been years since James had heard her talk like that, and her hostility towards him made her seem crass and out of control, and the insults were just making him more and more angry.

"So, you're back in fighting form, eh, Mrs. Roth?"

"Damn right! Someone has to be in the saddle. You even stopped fucking me like you used to, like you meant it, so I might as well start acting like the man around here!"

He raised his hand and came within a breath of smacking her. Sheri flinched. But instead of apologizing, she slid to the other side of the seat, and kept firing insults at him.

"Come on, I thought I had you going there! Where's the old James Roth? The bully. The guy who always refused to finish second. He never…"

James raised his hand and said quietly, "You need to shut up. Now."

"Why should I...?"

"I said, Shut up! And if you don't shut up, Sheri, I'll throw your ass right out of this limo!"

Sheri paused. And something inside her told her she now faced a crucial crossroads. She could push their marriage over the cliff, right here in the car. And as she well knew, life has a way of serving up key moments that can change personal history, some-times dramatically. Choices made in a split-second can be just as life changing as those made after considering every conceivable twist and turn. Sometimes even our mundane, seemingly innoc-uous choices can become monumental: take the kids to school or not, say hello to the neighbor or not, cancel a breakfast date with a business associate or not, get to work 15 minutes late. On 9/11 and 10/10, those seemingly minor decisions had changed peo-ple's lives forever. And now, in a burst of clarity, she saw the danger ahead: pushing her husband into a corner where he had no way out could be fatal. And she knew she still needed him. Desperately.

A long silence hung awkwardly inside the limo. Then James dug his fists into the leather seat and raised himself up. He, too, knew this was a crucial moment.

"Sheri, you need to listen to me. After what happened to the old man when I stole his car on 10/10, I couldn't figure out for the longest time what was wrong. For one thing, I looked at myself in the mirror differently." Then James stopped.

"That's not exactly what I mean to say. It was just that after 10/10 I saw myself differently. I used to love just looking at my face. That probably doesn't sound that weird to you. I mean, the fact I used to love doing that. But I stopped. I didn't like it anymore."

James shifted on the seat, turning toward Sheri. "For those first few months after 10/10, I was ecstatic. I had the world at my feet. I was in control. The hottest ticket on the street. I was the guy who had closed the landmark deal on the very day Indian Point was attacked. I could do anything. James Roth, Master of the Universe. I was ready for more. Ready to go out and start my own firm. Leave Goldfarb, even though I was married to the founder's daughter. I wanted more. Who wouldn't?"

He pointed his finger at her. "You remember, Sheri. I was driven. Charging ahead like there was no tomorrow. Then. Then..." his voice trailed off. "Then we had dinner that night at the Silvers and there she was. It was like seeing a ghost, an apparition. Up to that moment, I had put that morning on the train out of my mind. It had simply ceased to exist. And then seeing that woman from the train, after all those months of denial, everything I had buried came rushing to the surface. I'm still not sure exactly what happened at the Silvers. But from that night on, I began to see everything that was wrong with my life."

He stopped and looked Sheri right in the eye. "I haven't been the same since, I know. Oh, I have deals in the works for the first time in months, and I admit that feels good. But here's the truth: giving money to that poor woman, the old man's widow, was the first thing that I've done in months that raised my spirits. She's lost her husband—thanks to me!—and now she's lost her son, too. She's got nothing left. I had to do something..."

"James, you have GOT to get a grip!"

"Oh, I have a grip. More than ever before. Don't you get it? I murdered that old man. I didn't shoot him, or strangle him, or stick a knife in him, but I might as well have. And I can't live with that thought. Sheri, I'm thinking about turning myself in."

"What? Have you gone crazy, Roth?"

He recoiled at the look of horror on Sheri's face. "Go to the police?" She was screaming at him now. "Over my dead body! Over my dead body, you asshole! You have no fucking idea what I've done for you, what I've sacrificed, or the risks I've taken to save what we've got! Believe me, you have no idea!"

She was within an inch or two of James' face, shouting, and punching him in his chest with her fists. All sense of restraint was now gone; Sheri Roth was out of control. James grabbed her forearms and wrapped his arms around her, pulling her as close as he could. But that just made things worse. She struggled against him, finally trying to smash her elbow into his groin. He pushed her away violently and she rolled onto her back on the floor of the limo, almost hitting her head on the far seat. Her legs were splayed apart, and her eyes ablaze with anger. But James saw something new in her: Fear.

"Listen to me, Sheri. Please. Just listen to me."

"I will not! All this self-pity of yours makes me sick! That old man was on his deathbed anyway. He might have dropped dead of that heart attack just by walking across the parking lot that morning. You did what you had to do."

"Exactly. I did what I had to do," James said. "Listen to that. I didn't do the right thing. I did what I had to do. Well, I'm tired of living that way. I'm not going to retire or anything; I'm just going to do everything differently."

"Forget it, shmuck! You are going to keep on doing exactly what you've been doing for your whole life!" Sheri re-arranged her dress, patted down the wrinkles, and pulled herself back onto the seat. "And I'm going to tell you why: because you are as trapped as I am."

James had no idea what she was about to say.

"Listen, carefully, James: on the way home from dinner at that woman's house, that Rachel Silver, you told me about 10/10 and what had happened that morning. Your whole sordid little tale about being a callous murderer, how you pushed that man down and stole his car. And you were right: no matter how you spun it, that's how it was going to play out: James Roth, murderer!"

Sheri was ice cold calm now. "And when we were in that living room and she walked in, I saw that look on Rachel Silver's face. Shock. And pure hatred. And then and there I knew we were in trouble. James, it wasn't just your reputation on the line. It was the reputation of Goldfarb, of everything my father had worked for. The Street is all about relationships, and if my father's firm was labeled as a place harboring a murderer, our firm would be dead. Finished."

Sheri looked him straight in the eye. "So, my dear husband, when you fell into bed that night, I was tired, too. But I was too upset to sleep. And I knew something had to be done. I knew I had to confront that woman, that Rachel Silver. Maybe even threaten her. And guess what?" she laughed. "That's exactly what I set out to do! I even grabbed a knife from the kitchen on my way out."

"Oh, my god, Sheri, don't tell me!"

Sheri was silent for only a moment. "Yes, I did it. I killed Rachel Silver. And you know what? It turned out to be easy. I didn't plan it that way, but when I got near her house and parked, and I saw her walking alone down the street, well, I followed her into that vacant lot. And it was all over before I knew it. Back home, I washed the knife in the dishwasher and threw away my running shoes the next day when we went into the city. Done! And then, when we heard about the indictment of Caleb Drake, I was elated. Over the moon. I figured we were home free."

"Sheri, what the hell have you done?"

"I saved us. Yes, that's what I did. We had a problem, and I erased it. Then I put it out of my mind. Then this week, when news of the conductor's murder came out, I thought again: we're home free. One less person to worry about. No more Charlie Murray."

James was aghast. His wife was a murderer.

"Listen, Roth: one day Murray called me out of the blue. Bizarre. And I knew he would never let the matter drop. Hell, I was ready to kill him, too. But we got lucky. Whoever killed Charlie Murray did us a favor."

Sheri now sat back against the leather seat, and she looked damn near triumphant. "You see, James, thanks to me it's now just your word against Caleb Drake. And that poor sucker will always be tainted by his little back seat fling with that Silver woman. And that taint will never go away. So here is what you are going to do: You are going to shut the fuck up! And never say another word about this to anybody. Got it? Forget 10/10. Erase it from your brain. And as for that $30,000, if they ever trace it back to you, you better have a damn good explanation."

"Oh my god," James said, trembling. "Oh my god."

A moment later, the limo pulled up in front of the Hilton. And there was Irv Goldfarb waiting for them on the sidewalk, smiling with pride at his arriving golden couple.

## CHAPTER 47

NYPD OFFICERS DIRECTED THE LINE of limos toward a drop-off lane in front of the Hilton hotel. The sidewalks along Broadway teemed with tourists in short-sleeves and shorts on this mild early summer evening, the steel barricades squeezing them into a narrow path carved out on the street side of the sidewalk.

Sheri and James got out of the car, after telling the driver they would call around 10:30 to advise him where to pick them up. Sheri waved at Irv, but he was in conversation with another white-haired gentleman at the edge of the crowd, and he gestured to her to give him a minute. Sheri guided James away from her father to the other side of the entrance. She was completely poised and composed, as if nothing had happened on the ride over, and she took James' hand, stopping him at the bottom of the steps leading into the hotel.

"You know, you are the one being honored tonight," Sheri said quietly.

"What are you talking about? Have you forgotten what just happened in the car? I feel like throwing up. I'm ready to get back in the car and go home. Me? Being honored? Are you kidding? Why?"

"No, James, I'm serious. You better have something to say."

"Jesus, Sheri, you really are something. You just told me..."

Sheri put her finger to his mouth, "Shhh, not here. All that's over. Just think about tonight."

James stared at her incredulously, his eyes wide and shaking his head. "I can't believe you. Okay, okay. But what am I going to say? That I'm grateful for being acknowledged as The Best? That's what people will expect. Even if they've heard rumors about my demise."

"How about surprising them? Be gracious. Show them the new James Roth."

"Damn it, you didn't hear a goddamn thing I said, did you? Well, at least now I know why."

She cut him off abruptly: "Not here, James," nodding towards the bankers heading into the hotel behind them. "James, the past is past. What's done is done. What more do you want me to say? I did the right thing. You did the right thing. We have got to move on. If I can live with what I did, you can, too."

"Oh, I get it. I don't have a choice. But all this time, I was worried about them coming for me. Now I have to be worried about them coming…"

"Enough." Sheri's eyes were blazing as she pulled them a little further away from the hotel entrance. "James, if you don't let this be, someone, probably that black detective, will start digging around again. And, sooner or later, they will come for us. We will be toast. Don't ever forget that."

She was speaking so fast that she was tripping over words, and since she was talking in a whisper it was hard to hear her. Standing on a sidewalk in front of the big hotel, they appeared to be a couple in the middle of an argument, not a bad one, just a little dust-up.

Then Irv walked up to them with a big smile. "Hey, kids, come on! Don't hang out here on the street," he said. "Let's go inside. You're in for a great night. Trust me."

Sheri turned, the anger gone from her face and a big smile in its place. She winked at James. "I told you so," she whispered. "And don't ever forget what I said."

Irv stopped them. "Hey, do you know what I just heard on the radio? They think they found the killer of that woman up in Westchester, the one Sheri says you knew. Remember?"

Both Sheri and James froze.

"Yeah, it was that conductor on Metro-North," Irv said. "He was murdered earlier this week. And when the cops searched his house, they found evidence tying him to that woman's murder. Can you believe it? A pervert apparently. Had pictures of the dead woman all over a wall in his bedroom."

Sheri grabbed James hand and squeezed it. She leaned in close and said, "Nothing. Not a word. And now we really are home free." She almost laughed out loud.

They paraded into the lobby, the tall, handsome, square-jawed James Roth and his statuesque blond stunner wife, Sheri Goldfarb. They were the kind of couple that turned heads, of both men and women, when they walked into a room. In an instant, they were laughing and shaking hands with what seemed like everyone in the room. They were in the midst of a self-congratulatory crowd of financial viceroys who believed they hadn't won a lottery but were actually deserving of their wealth and status. The news cameras zoomed in on the Goldfarbs as the crowd parted to greet them.

The cocktail hour had ended about the time Irv Goldfarb and the Roths arrived, and the lights already had dimmed a couple of times, so they glided directly into the main dining room. The room, with its 20-foot high ceilings, was decorated with an Arabian Nights fantasy theme. In look and feel, the association dinner was more like a convivial society wedding than a business gathering of New York's financial upper crust.

The Hilton ballroom was jammed. The American Financial Association gala was a big deal every year, and this year was no exception. The speaker was Bill Gates. The wines were all top-flight white Burgundies and California Cabs, and the lobster salad followed by filet mignon was by no means your typical rubber chicken fare. Michael Bloomberg, no financial slouch in his own right, welcomed the crowd, and then took a seat on the dais beside Bill Gates—and just a few seats away from another celebrated guest, Irv Goldfarb.

James felt better now, and as he guided Sheri through the maze of tables, he couldn't help but swagger a little as he basked in the hearty hellos and backslaps. It felt like forever since he had reveled in this kind of approval. Nearing the front of the room and Table 1, he could see the CEOs of Citigroup, JPMorgan Chase, and a couple of the latest hedge fund darlings and their wives. Their combined net worth, James knew, was well into the billions of dollars.

"James, welcome!" Robert Wallace greeted him. "My wife, Candice. Hello, Sheri, so nice to have you back on the playing field!"

"Yes, it has been rather thrilling, Robert. Hello, Candice," Sheri said, sitting down next to her. By the time James had taken his seat next to Wallace, the two women were busy talking about their Christmas plans in St. Barts and discussing who among their friends were purchasing apartments in the new Carnegie Hall tower.

"So, James, someone told me Goldfarb & Roth was in the market for a new corporate jet," Wallace said. "Guess those rumors about you quitting a few months ago were all fabricated, huh?"

"Well, Bobby," James replied, using the man's golf course moniker. "Sometimes you just have to take a break."

"Oh god no," Wallace said, "we thought you had retired or something unimaginable like that. Why I even heard you were going to be a player in my world, and then you just vanished. Poof!"

"Hah, I guess a lot of rumors got repeated. None of them true, by the way. I'm all in with Goldfarb & Roth," he said, with a little emphasis on his name. "But I guess I'm just more relaxed than you are, Bobby. When was the last time you took a day off to work on that sand game?"

"Buddy, I'm ready for you. I've been taking the chopper during my lunch hour to work with my pro at Baltusrol. You heard of that place?" he teased.

"Yeah, Bobby, I cleaned your clock there a few years ago."

Laughter tittered around the table. There was no need for any tension. Everyone knew it was all in good fun, boy banter that even the women around the table tolerated, if not fully appreciated.

They all fell silent while Bill Gates got up and spoke briefly about innovation and market domination. Mercifully, it was a 20-minute boilerplate talk about how not only was the world changing, it had already been forever altered by technology, and then he went on to his pet projects focusing on healthcare in the developing world. Most of the people in the room had heard it all before, and they would have been more impressed if Steve Jobs were still alive and making the same points.

Then Michael Bloomberg took the podium:

"Folks, I've known Irv Goldfarb for 35 years, at least. He helped me out when I was getting started in my media company, and we've been friends ever since. You all know him from Goldfarb & Case, one of the early giants on Wall Street, and it's now Goldfarb & Roth, a firm we all wish we owned. Me included! Irv, it's all yours…"

The aging lion of Wall Street stood up, hugged his friend Michael Bloomberg, and then walked to the microphone, his bearing proud, his back ramrod straight. The audience began applauding, and soon everyone in the room was on their feet, paying homage to the man who had pioneered the whole concept of an independent M&A firm. Then Irv cleared his throat and took command.

"Thank you! Most of you know me, apparently. Or maybe you don't and that's why you're clapping. My friends know better!"

The crowd laughed.

"I'm up here tonight not to get an award, or to be reminded of how old I am by receiving some Lifetime Achievement award… again. No, tonight I have the honor of giving out one of the biggest recognitions this group bestows on professionals in the financial industry. Many previous winners are here tonight, including me. And mine was before most of you were born!"

Again the crowd laughed.

"The man we are here to honor tonight has been around our business now for 15 years. He started out in a small firm and quickly got the reputation of being a cutthroat, no-holds-barred dealmaker—the kind you don't want going after the same company you are trying to buy. I figured that out a long time ago, and I tried to hire him myself, but he landed at J.P. Morgan, making them more money than he did for himself. Little did I know that this same man would soon be sitting at my Passover table every year, with my daughter at his side, or that he'd end up with his name on my door."

A murmur went through the crowd and some applause, too.

"Let me put on the record what you've all heard about the Secor deal. You remember: that was on 10/10, the day terrorists attacked the Indian Point reactor up north. All the principals of the Secor deal were in town when the news hit. And most of them were ready to run for safety. But James Roth stayed cool and saw opportunity in disaster. James got the principals around the table and argued that the worth of the deal was actually bigger and better because of the attack, and that both sides indeed now had more to gain—if they acted with courage and resolve. And they did. James won the day. And the result was one of the most successful energy sector deals in recent memory."

The crowd broke into applause and some happy whistles, too.

"You all know he's been quiet for awhile, but let me tell you, he's back, and he's on fire. And that is why he's the honoree tonight... James Roth, Financier of the Year. Come on up here, son."

James rose slowly as the crowd began a slow clapping that soon ballooned into a raucous round of hoorays and cheers. His tablemates stood and clasped his hands. He was about to walk away from the table when he turned and took Sheri's arm: "Come. Come with me."

At first, Sheri fussed and declined. But James pressed and she stood up, gracious as always. The applause now became thunderous.

When they got to the dais, Irv Goldfarb planted a kiss on the cheek of his daughter and gave James a huge paternal hug. It was a very public seal of approval. When the applause finally quieted, James stepped to the microphone and drew Sheri to his side.

"Thank you, Irv. Thank you, everyone. But if anyone deserves this award, she's standing right next to me. She keeps me honest..."

For a second, he stumbled for words, because way in the back of the room, standing next to one of the columns, James spotted a black man in a leather jacket. He was no Wall Street titan. It was Detective Arnette Williams! Or so James thought—and it sent a jolt of fear and adrenaline coursing through his system.

"She keeps me honest," he began again, his words coming out

more slowly now, "and she keeps me charging forward. Pushing me to do this deal or that, to take care of our children's college educations, and to pay for our new house in the Hamptons. And it's not just about us. In this family that I feel so privileged to be a part of, we keep driving, we keep pushing, but at heart it's not about the money. It's about helping our clients. It's about providing them with capital and the kind of top-quality advice that all companies need to get ahead in this competitive world. At every step, it's about adding value. Yes, adding value. That's what we do."

While everyone again applauded, James scanned the rear of the hall for any sign of the investigating detective. But no one was there.

"I am deeply honored tonight," he said, his voice far stronger than before. "And frankly, I'm very surprised, too. And grateful. We work in the greatest industry in the world, and we serve the greatest wealth-generating mechanism ever created by mankind. We should all feel lucky. I know I do. Thank you all again."

James stepped back from the microphone, and Irv presented him with the shining plaque, the association's highest honor. With Sheri on his arm, he moved to the far end of the dais, smiling and waving to the crowd. Bill Gates and Michael Bloomberg greeted them there, and the photographers and TV cameras eagerly snapped them together, five smiling titans of the financial industry. The footage would end up on the 11 o'clock news. By the time he got back to the table, James was shaking inside and he wanted nothing more than to bolt straight out of the room. Sheri grabbed his hand and leaned in close: "Are you okay? You look like death."

"Yeah, I'm just excited," he lied. Excited, hell. He was scared out of his wits. Here he was on top of the world—and all he could think about was Detective Williams watching his every move, still waiting for him to make a fatal mistake. Or was that just an illusion? Maybe. But the flood of panic he had felt up on the dais was all too real. And now James knew the agonizing truth: it would be like this for the rest of his life. No matter how much success and happiness he and Sheri would garner, fear would always be right on his shoulder, fear for himself and for Sheri, too.

## CHAPTER 48

*Four Months Later*

THE RISING SUN REFLECTED OFF the buildings in Jersey City, and the bright oranges and reds shimmered across the wakes of the boats heading up and down the river. It was October 10th, a year to the fateful day that had turned Caleb Drake's life upside down and brought him to this moment, alone in his penthouse apartment on Riverside Drive.

Caleb was ready for an early morning run, dressed in tight black leggings and a gray Nike t-shirt. He went through his leg stretches while looking out over the river from his bedroom, a simple Zen design with muted earth colors and bamboo floors; his down comforter embroidered with Chinese symbols lay smoothed out on the bed.

This early morning workout and his apartment symbolized what was happening in Caleb's life—a new attitude in a new refuge in a new personal landscape. He had a renewed sense of purpose and energy. His staff had instigated it, but now he had made it his own. Caleb truly felt like he was starting over, at nearly 63 years old, struggling to get his middle-aged body back in shape, and struggling to get his life back on track, or at least headed in a direction that he wanted.

For the first time since he first recognized his Vietnam-induced

PTSD, he was putting those war traumas, and his demons, in a box tucked deep away. He knew they were there, and that they would never fully disappear, but their existence didn't threaten him every day with the possibility of shattering his peace of mind. He also was coming to grips with the lingering trauma of Rachel's murder eight months ago and the dissolution of his 25-year marriage just a few months ago. Even those dark moments were beginning to fade into the background.

Caleb put his earbuds in, tucked his iPhone into an an armband with a holder, and then turned on his favorite music track for running, a compilation of Tom Petty, Crosby Stills Nash & Young, and Jackson Browne. He headed for his private elevator, waiting for the doors to open onto the marble lobby and entrance, with its wrought iron and glass double doors.

"Good morning, Mr. Drake," Mario, the doorman, said as he walked by. "Up early today?" Caleb just nodded at him as he headed out the door toward Riverside Park, turning north in the direction of the Cathedral of St. John the Divine.

Caleb quickly fell into a steady pace, his rhythmic footfalls freeing his mind to roam without constriction. Although his daily run had become a meditation, today's anniversary of 10/10 drew him consciously to the events of the past 12 months.

Despite feeling calmer and more optimistic today, Caleb couldn't stop reliving that morning on the train. The question this morning was the same one as always: why did I ever step in to protect Rachel Silver? One split second and his life had been forever altered. Yes, it had been the right thing to do, but the unforeseen consequences of his actions almost ruined him.

He could feel his pace picking up, driven by the surge of anxiety that always accompanied his memories of Rachel and 10/10.

He also had to be honest; the full telling of that day's events and their aftermath couldn't be blamed on one moment, even if he liked to think he had made only one mistake. He didn't have to drive her home; he didn't have to go inside her house; he didn't have to avoid her for months, which probably allowed some fantasy to blossom for both of them; he didn't have to let her into his car in the parking lot that day; he didn't have to invite her to dinner; he didn't have to drive by her house that night; he didn't have to take her call; he didn't have to make love to her right there in his back seat. Each of those decisions had led to the next and then to the next. That chain of decisions was what still woke him up at night. But despite his latent fear that those memories could still derail his recovery, he always reminded himself, as he did right now, that those choices were all driven by a deep, burning desire to do something different with his life, to live a life filled with more excitement, one with more meaning and purpose.

Caleb crossed over to the bike and jogging path alongside the Hudson River. Even though it was Sunday morning, there was a steady stream of bikers and runners going both ways on the path, plus a stream of cars heading down the highway toward midtown Manhattan. His lungs began to burn as he kept up his quicker pace, but the stepped-up effort didn't slow or stop the cascade of thoughts pouring through his mind.

A picture of Charlie Murray, that poor twisted man who got caught up in something he couldn't control, popped into his mind. At least Charlie's torment was over. The reports of his obsession with Rachel had been a surprise. Caleb still didn't believe the press speculation that he had killed Rachel, but he knew it didn't always take facts to convict someone. Detective Williams had assured him that he was almost certain that poor Charlie wasn't Rachel's killer.

But Caleb also figured that with an easy scapegoat like Murray, the real killer would never be found now. For one obvious reason: the D.A., the aspiring governor, and his cohorts would stop looking and search for fresher headlines.

Caleb couldn't keep the Roths out of his mind either. They seemed untouched by the whole ordeal; he kept seeing Page Six reports of their society escapades. (Like every self-respecting PR man, Caleb followed the latest gossip.) And if the Roths had any worries, or, in fact, any connection to the older Murray's death, Caleb saw no sign of it. If they were guilty, or even if James Roth were somehow responsible for Sean Murray's death—as Caleb fiercely suspected—they were going to get off scot-free.

That left Brenda. The thought of her now as he ran brought him up short, and he stepped off the trail where there was a small metal bench facing the river. Breathing hard, Caleb put his hands on his knees and bent over to catch his breath.

The fact was he still hadn't fully severed ties with Brenda; the divorce papers were still unsigned on his desk back home. He just wasn't ready to take that final step of signing. In some fundamental way, too, his emotional life was stalemated by his inaction. Sure, he had been out on a couple of dates, including one last night with a beautiful art gallery owner, but he couldn't bring himself to take the next step, asking her to bed. So how free was he really?

On impulse, he pulled his iPhone out of its holder and dialed Brenda's number.

"Hey, it's Caleb," he said when Brenda picked up.

"You sound out of breath. What do you want?" she said.

"I'm out on a morning run. And I just wanted to hear your voice."

"How many times have I told you: call my lawyer. This is getting ridiculous. I've told you over and over that I don't want to talk to you. And, dammit, Caleb, when are you going to sign those papers?"

"You know what I want."

"Do I? Do I really? Do you really know? You know what I am absolutely convinced of now? I'm convinced you always wanted to be on your own, to be alone. You were always acting like it anyway. Getting anything intimate out of you was always a struggle. Then I pulled back and became like you, because there was no reason to be any other way. Now, Caleb, you can be who you really, down deep, want to be. You need to just accept that and move on. I have."

Caleb gazed across the river as he let her words sink in. In his heart, he knew she was right.

"Caleb, you still there?"

"Yeah, I was just thinking," he said. "Here's my... well, you know I've said it before: It began with one mistake. And I'm being punished for it."

"One mistake is all it takes, Caleb," Brenda said. "But think about it. That mistake has given you the chance you've always wanted. If it hadn't been for that 'mistake'—your word—you would have just found some other excuse. I believe that. It's time to accept that."

"But..." Caleb started to say.

"No, no buts, Caleb," Brenda said. "It's over. Run home and sign those damn papers. Now. Goodbye."

For a long time, Caleb sat immobile, listening to the pulse of his breathing. Through the muffled sound of people running behind him and the cars whizzing by on the highway, he could hear and feel his own thoughts coalesce: Yes, she's right.

His promise to himself after 9/11 and now 10/10 had been

identical: Change your life. Stop wallowing in the morass. Step out. Be different. Don't be trapped inside a haphazardly built life, a mind-numbing routine scraped together with bits and pieces of detritus from other people's lives.

His first chance after 9/11 had slipped away in a dark collective depression; so many people stunned into mute inaction by the naked evil of the attack on the World Trade Center towers, so many people unable to find a reason for why one person died in that inferno and another had lived. He, too, had slipped into that collective inertia.

The second chance? Would he let that slip away too? Again Caleb clearly saw his choice: No! And he felt the rush: Time to stop dithering, Caleb told himself. Time to set those plans in motion to start writing, to travel to some of those places on his bucket list, and open himself to new experiences and new people. And most of all, to reach out to his kids and try to get back in their good graces. He had already taken the first steps to restore his equilibrium by starting with a psychologist friend a self-help group focused on PTSD and trauma, two debilitating phenomena that ate at him every day.

His phone vibrated in his sports armband. What? Could Brenda be calling back? He glanced at the number on the phone and didn't immediately recognize it.

"Hello," he answered.

"Hi, Caleb, thanks for picking up on a Sunday morning. It's Brad. Remember, I'm the guy who saw his buddy blown up by an IED."

"Sure, Brad. Absolutely. What's going on?"

"I just had the urge to tell you something, and you said to call whenever I needed to talk."

"And I meant it, Brad. Are you okay? I can come see you if you want," Caleb said, hearing a note of tension in the man's voice.

"No, no. It's not anything like that. God, no. In fact, I've stopped waking up in the middle of the night, terrified a bomb has gone off in the room. I've finally been sleeping through the night. I can look at pictures of my friend Steve without breaking down in tears. I actually went out on a date last night. I was able to talk about normal things."

"Wow, sounds like real progress, Brad. I know how it feels. It wasn't that long ago that I was still avoiding big crowds, and I still have to pause before I open up the New York Post, afraid that my picture is going to be on Page Six again. It's a good feeling, isn't it, to stop worrying about that kind of stuff."

"Oh, you have no idea, Caleb. Instead of shutting down, I'm finally opening up to my oldest friends, telling them about the horrors in Iraq. The terror. The blood. The dying. You helped me get there. I was so lucky to find your PTSD group."

"You took the words right out of my mouth. Not shut down anymore. That's where I am, too. Breaking free. Feeling free. But just hearing about your progress… Wow, you have no idea how much that means to me."

"Yeah, the group has been so much better than all those army shrinks I talked with after my deployment. I felt like you'd all been there, and you knew, you really knew, what I was going through. So, thanks. That's all. I'll see you Monday night. We're still on, right?"

"You bet, Brad. I'll be taking part in these sessions for a long, long time. There's a lot of work left to do. I know that's true for me. Probably for everybody there."

Brad's gratitude was just what Caleb had needed to hear. Sitting there, he had a little smile on his face. The idea to start the group had been the result of a conversation over drinks with his psychologist friend Joe, another Vietnam vet who had devoted his life to helping people cope, not just with the aftermath of war but with any kind of trauma. Caleb was amazed how a simple announcement pasted on the bulletin board of an Upper West Side community center about a support group for trauma victims had produced a dozen inquiries. After one session, plus a rising clamor from other interested people, Joe had to limit the group to 20, a size he felt was optimal. From that beginning, there was always a wait list and he was considering organizing a second group.

Caleb mused that the genesis of the group had started him on the path toward a real, lasting recovery. The meetings had helped him understand how those long years of trying to ignore his PTSD had only made it worse when another trauma, like 9/11 or 10/10 or Rachel's murder, triggered it. Now he also believed those powerful, usually suppressed emotions were nearly universal in people who suffered any kind of trauma. Indeed, he could see that the world around him was filled with people in pain from the daily onslaught of violence and terror. By recognizing his own demons and a desire to do something about them, Caleb had found the means to help others with similar struggles. The psychologist had told him that after 9/11 most of his new patients were suffering depression and paranoia because of the attack, even though they weren't anywhere near the Twin Towers when they fell. Sharing that experience with others was giving Caleb a profound sense of well-being and purpose. For the first time in a very long time.

He shouted, "Yes!" loud enough to startle another runner passing by.

He stood up, turned on his music again, and began running back toward his apartment, faster and faster to the point where he wondered if people watching him might think something was wrong. He felt like he was back in front of his building in no time, ready to go up and sign the divorce papers and get on with his life.

"Mr. Drake," he heard through the ear buds. "MISTER DRAKE!"

He turned around and there stood Detective Williams.

"Detective! What are you doing here?" Caleb said, pulling the ear buds out. "I swear I was just thinking about you."

"Funny, I was about to say the same thing," Williams said. "I don't know. I woke up this morning, early, earlier than usual, saw the calendar and I just decided to drive down and see you."

"Hard to miss the date, isn't it?"

"Yes indeed," Williams said. "And I keep asking myself if I will ever get rid of all my questions, and all my doubts, about what really happened that day."

"I'm working on that, too," Caleb said.

"Everything okay with you, Mr. Drake?"

"Yes. In fact, everything is pretty good. I was about to run upstairs and sign my divorce papers, and get that over with. I don't really know what I've been waiting for. Except, I guess, I was still wondering if I could somehow turn back the clock to a year ago. But I know now that's just not possible."

"I can only imagine, Mr. Drake. Well, I don't really have anything to say that might make things any different. You know, the case has officially been put in the unsolved category, a cold case. Who knows if anything will ever change."

"Did you convince them that Charlie Murray didn't do it?"

"Yes, more or less. That's why it's officially listed now as an unsolved murder. But I had to return all the files to the office, and they are locked away. So for me, it's officially over."

"Officially?"

"That's right. But you know me: I'll be keeping my eyes open."

"Well, I'm finished with it. Just trying to forget. You want to come upstairs? Have a cup of coffee?"

"No thanks, Mr. Drake. I just wanted to say goodbye. Maybe let you know that someone else is thinking about the anniversary, too," Detective Williams said. Then he reached out and shook Caleb's hand. "Stay strong, Mr. Drake."

"Thanks. Thanks, detective. I do appreciate that."

Caleb entered his apartment, still sweating from the run and knowing exactly what he wanted to do now—without delay. He found the divorce papers on his desk, went to the last page and signed the document with today's date, 10/10.

Caleb held up the page and inspected his signature. Doing so brought him a surge of emotion, a feeling of liberation, a feeling of freedom and relief. Even though he could feel his burdens lifting, he couldn't dismiss that he was still going to have to live with the tattoo of suspected murderer. He would always have to be ready to deal with someone recognizing him and saying, "Hey, aren't you the guy who was accused of murdering his lover?" That was never going to go away. And he would also know that he, and he alone, was responsible for the actions that had branded him.

This moment, this anniversary also wasn't going to magically transform his worldview, that split in his psyche that seemed forever in conflict. One side was the sunny, optimistic face he showed the world, a public, rose-colored vision of the present and the future. But underneath that sunny exterior and optimism lurked a viciously negative world-view, one that expected the worst, a fatalism that he doubted would ever go away. In truth, it was his last line of defense: expect the worst out of everything and everyone, and then you won't be disappointed if the results are just a little better than that worst case you had imagined.

Therapy had helped him understand the reasons for that black place inside him. It wasn't really a mystery. The war, his experience in Vietnam, had almost obliterated his youthful naiveté. Then, as he began his postwar life in Manhattan, his real world encounters—the back-stabbing, the relentless self-interest, the outright lies to his face—fueled the quiet despair that always burned underneath.

But the truth be told, right now, right at this second, Caleb was amazed at himself. Cooling off in his apartment after his run, one full year after the traumas of 10/10, he had not only survived, he was unbound and marching toward a new life. Unlike so many setbacks and previous periods of depression, this time he had not been immobilized into a simpering victim, cursing the gods and crippled by a sense of unfairness and rotten luck. This new beginning was making him more hopeful than at any point in his adult life. Now he could clearly see the promise of a better life in front of him.

Caleb chuckled out loud. How strange it all was! These recent traumas—Rachel's murder and the resulting public vendetta against him—had triggered events that might actually lead him to a saner, less troubled life. The older traumas now seemed manageable. By surviving the new ones without disintegrating, he could see there was only one path: Forward, not back.

Across the river, the morning sun was still reflecting off the high-rise apartments. To his right, the towers of the George Washington Bridge gleamed, and if he leaned forward just a little, he could make out the torch of the Statue of Liberty standing, majestic and unbowed, in New York Harbor.

Caleb felt the tightness in his chest ease as he forced himself to inhale deeply and then exhale slowly. Life would go on. The past was past. He would build a new future. With his memories. With his demons. With his dreams.

## ACKNOWLEDGMENTS

My deepest gratitude to Dr. Steve Fochios for his pointed question, "Do you have anything to say?" To my wife Donna, who kept me focused on the most important things in life, and guided us to the place where I had the time and creative energy to devote to my writing. To Marvin Shanken for giving me the opportunities that fulfilled many of my career goals, and freed me up to pursue a lifelong dream. And to Paul Chutkow, who cajoled and guided me through the task of putting the finishing touches on this novel; without him, 10/10 would not exist.